REPORTED MISSING

REPORTED MISSING

SARAH WRAY

bookouture

Published by Bookouture
An imprint of StoryFire Ltd.
23 Sussex Road, Ickenham, UB10 8PN
United Kingdom
www.bookouture.com

ISBN: 978-1-78681-197-4
eBook ISBN: 978-1-78681-196-7

PROLOGUE

'There are two ways to be fooled. One is to believe what isn't true; the other is to refuse to believe what is true.' I read that somewhere once, or a version of it anyway. Now, it keeps washing up into my mind.

Maybe I chose to ignore some of the signs with Chris, maybe they were never there. Everything is distorted through the prism of Kayleigh's disappearance. It's like reading a book backwards.

But now I have to decide how to think of us from here, which memories to keep and the ones to push aside.

CHAPTER ONE

Thursday, 5 November

I am suddenly awake and upright, groggy from the red wine and sleeping pill. It's nothing, I tell myself. Just the wind. I begin to relax, remembering that it's Bonfire Night. It's just fireworks in the distance. The banging and explosions must have woken me.

I start to relax again, then my whole body stiffens. There are voices outside, whispers, low murmurs – close to the caravan. I strain to hear. The dread in my chest is like setting concrete. A click against the window, then another... stones.

Not again, please not again.

A thud against the side of the caravan, followed by another. Everything shakes, glasses rattling. They're going to tip it over. I panic, run to the door and throw it open, a rush of cold air. It's pitch-dark but I sense people scattering in what seems like all directions.

How many are there?

A hissing, then something screams past my ear. A loud crack to my right and an explosion of light, a smell of burning. A firework. Panicked, I think of the gas bottles. But it whistles back into the sky and arcs away again. My eyes have adjusted to the dark, and I stamp out the embers on the damp grass, smoke catching in my throat. Something sharp whips across my cheek and stings. I raise my hand to my face and it's wet, blood.

'That's for your pervert husband and what he done to Kayleigh!' a girl's voice shouts. I can't tell where she is or how close.

I turn to go back into the caravan, and another pebble smacks against the side of it, bouncing off. Someone is flicking a lighter on and off but I still can't see who's there.

They came to the house before I moved out, but how did they find out I'm here?

'Where's your husband?'

A voice from the other side. 'Where's Kayleigh? Where's he taken her?'

Rhythmic clapping, a football chant. 'Where's your husband, where's your husband, where's your husband?'

'You must be too old for him, love. Heard he prefers them young!' Sniggers.

'Oi!' The girl's voice appears from around the side of the caravan. Something lit is hurtling towards me. It hits the step just in front of my feet, a sharp bang, a ball of blue light. Speeding streams of coloured light fly past my face, leaving a blurred trail behind them.

I just see limbs and bobbing heads, then dark shapes running away towards the park entrance.

I go back inside and lock the door. Knees pulled up to my chest, I sit in the caravan in the dark, shivering, my heart thumping, for what seems like hours. I can't calm down. Things have been quieter recently. Why again now, all of a sudden? I think back to earlier this evening; a phone call. Silence, breathing. Wrong number, I tried to tell myself. But it was like before, when it first happened.

I check the doors and windows one last time. I keep the lights out to hide any silhouette and push a chair in front of the door with cups and saucers crowded on the seat. Above each window, I carefully balance knives and spoons. Should anyone come back, I need to know straight away. I am ready.

Finally, after this procedure is complete, I can rest a little easier, at least enough to just lie here in some sort of peace. The world always feels like it's swimming slightly these days, my eyes are gritty and hot at the rims. Despite its dingy furnishings – the faded, garish cushion coverings and the stark little gas fire, there's something about life in the caravan that is soothing; it's like playing shops or post office as a child. The compact space and the dual-purpose furniture are comforting, the smaller versions of chairs and appliances.

I had felt safer here. And it is too painful to be at the house, the credit-card promotions and pizza offers still arriving with his name on, his acoustic guitar propped against the wall.

When I block out for the briefest moments why I ended up here, I have a fleeting feeling of serenity. Then it slams back in, I'm falling asleep, then I'm tripping over and falling off the cliffs, awake.

He is still gone. Chris, my husband. Almost four months now. 112 days.

I rearrange the crockery on the chair once more, making sure it clatters if I nudge the chair even slightly. I pour myself half a mug of vodka, pull on my woolly hat and crawl under the covers, shivering. I have to remove a glove; the phone requires a human touch. Then there he is, warm and alive, lying out on a picnic rug, squinting from the sun, pushing the camera away with mock coyness. I play the video again.

CHAPTER TWO

Friday, 6 November

After what feels like just a few short hours' fitful sleep, I wake and push the curtain back, wiping condensation away with the bottom of my fist. My mouth is dry and foisty. I didn't mean to drink so much again last night.

It's a blustery, wet day, the windows lashed with rain as I look across the deserted caravan park, the pavements darkened and the grass sodden. A figure in a raincoat dashes past, holding their hood up.

I am glad I don't have to go into work anymore, but especially on days like this. In recent weeks I have barely left the cocoon of the caravan, living on toast and powdered soup. Until the booze runs out. Then I am lured out again.

As I make coffee, I flick on the TV to break the silence. The weather report, an advert for a kitchen chopping-and-blending device, trying to be too American, breakfast TV. A flicky-haired woman, blank-faced and waxy with foundation, stares, forced sincerity, into the camera. She'll be back after the break to talk about the rise in testicular cancer and to meet Tim, diagnosed with an aggressive strain of the disease. She'll also be looking at a preview of spring fashion.

The TV clock says it's 8 a.m. and the familiar lilting newsreader announces, even-voiced, there's been another suicide bombing at a market in Iraq. There could be snow this week, probably in Scotland. The pound has fallen against the dollar. What does that even mean anyway?

I used to find daytime TV depressing – all the payday loan adverts and property shows. How many people who are at home all day are in a position to be inspired by a property development programme? Unemployed people, new mums, elderly people like Mum? I used to moan to Chris about the staff at the home putting Mum and the other residents in front of the TV all day. 'Corrosive,' I think I called it. So self-righteous.

But now I find it kind of soothing myself, the blandness. I avoid music these days; I just search for voices on the radio, background noise, like I used to hate Dad doing when I was young. I don't focus on anything – films, TV, books. I used to love all that stuff: murdered women, missing kids, mysteries. But now I'm living it, I'm like the thinnest glass. The panic is never far from the surface.

When the newsreader says the name, I stop still, my chest freezes. I should have expected this. Deep down, I did. Images cascade in all at once. *Close your eyes, breathe in through the nose, out through the mouth*, like the therapist said. I'm still loath to admit that this does actually work sometimes. I gulp the lukewarm instant coffee, feeling queasy, and force my attention to the TV.

Seeing Shawmouth on the national news is still a strange kind of novelty. The reporter stands on the seafront, umbrella straining in the wind, with the beach and a row of shops in the background: a grotty café, a closed newsagent, a fake shop made to look like a homely, welcoming bakery, but it's just a sticker – a council initiative aimed at getting investors to see the potential in abandoned buildings. It's a gift to the news lot; they'll love this gloomy setting. They always tried to make it look like hell on earth here; the kind of place teenage girls disappear.

The kind of place grown men flee from the first chance they get?

But the truth is, we aren't used to national attention here. People keel over with strokes and heart attacks. They die peacefully at a grand old age in their favourite chair. Occasionally there's a stabbing or a domestic murder – but reporters don't travel north for those people. I wonder why my thoughts have automatically turned to the way people die? Would Chris being dead be better than him and Kayleigh being alive together somewhere?

They probably wouldn't have filmed if it had been a bright, beautiful day – people, especially when they've moved away to live in some overpriced beige box in the suburbs down south, love to be smug about what a shithole it is round here, but it can really have the charm of an old Technicolor photo on sunny days.

'Kayleigh Jackson is still missing,' the newsreader announces. Kayleigh's young face is up on the screen, a photo she took herself with her phone from a high angle to flatter, pouty. But you can see she's pretty anyway. Badly back-combed hair with dark roots, floury foundation and too much mascara making spidery lashes that spike out, but the fresh-facedness shines through. The school uniform gets me all over again, my stomach twisting.

'The family of missing schoolgirl Kayleigh Jackson will hold a candlelight vigil next Sunday, on what will be Kayleigh's fifteenth birthday. The St Augustine's pupil vanished after 17 July and has not been seen since. Kayleigh's family has repeatedly appealed to their daughter or anyone who might know anything about her disappearance to get in touch.'

They're going to play the video again, I know they are. Shot around a week after Kayleigh went missing. I grip the worktop. I can't bear to watch it again but it feels cruel to look away.

Kayleigh's mum, Janice. I think about her a lot. I've never actually met her. Not really. I saw her through the glass once. In the early days, I didn't know what I was doing, nothing had sunk in. Strung out, I found myself outside Kayleigh's house, standing at the fence, looking in through the window. I think I wanted to tell her that I was sorry but that it wasn't true about Chris. It couldn't be true. Selfish, really. When she saw me, she banged on the window. She burst out of the front door. She was shouting something at me, her face red and twisted like a wrecked car, but all I could hear was white noise. Someone restrained her, an officer came out and shooed me along, shaking his head.

We don't know each other, but our lives – mine and Janice's, mine and Kayleigh's – have become so intertwined somehow.

Janice looks tired and drawn, grey-faced. The ends of her sleeves are twisted into the palms of her hands, along with a screwed-up tissue. She shakes with grief, barely able to get her words out and look into the camera. A police officer places a useless, non-committal hand on her forearm as she sobs, the press cameras clicking and flashing.

'We're not angry,' she pleads into the camera. 'Just come home, Kayleigh. We just want you home with us again where you belong,' she says, before collapsing into sobs again.

It didn't take long, a couple of weeks after Kayleigh went missing, for the papers to stick the boot in with Janice too, perhaps growing bored of trying to wring column inches based on nothing out of Chris. All they have is that Chris and Kayleigh both disappeared on the same day. Just that one day, this invisible line linking them together.

They mentioned Kayleigh's 'absent father', her home in 'one of Shawmouth's toughest estates', and described Janice, completely irrelevantly, as 'unemployed'. I was ashamed to feel gratitude creeping in, that the heat was off me for a bit.

The newsreader's voice pulls me back. 'Police say they are pursuing multiple lines of enquiry and they're calling for members of the public with any information about the teen to come forward,' she says before moving on to the next news item. A row over fracking.

Multiple lines of enquiry. I roll the term around in my head. It doesn't give you much hope, does it? That was the term they used then, too, just before Detective Fisher took Chris's laptop away, and his toothbrush.

'It's routine for a missing person,' Fisher had said. They had to investigate all possibilities to find Kayleigh. 'And your husband, of course,' she added, as an afterthought.

Someone must have seen the visit to the house; them taking the items away in sealed, clear bags. Because things got much worse after that – the word was out, the mood had shifted.

CHAPTER THREE

Friday, 6 November

As I walk along the seafront, the neon of the arcades is inviting against the grey sky – the childhood excitement of seeing the coloured lights and the cartoonish primary shades of the seaside has never left me. The green fields of Yorkshire, the slick glass city buildings of London don't make my heart swell in the same way. The slot machines bleep and shimmer as I pass the open fronts of the arcades. I always look in to check, just in case. It's habit.

I see Chris everywhere – at night when I sleep, although increasingly the details of his face are slipping away from me. When I quickly dig out a photograph to refresh the image, it feels distant; the features have somehow changed, yet I can't put my finger on what is different. I see him in the street, lost in a crowd; in the back of a taxi whizzing by; at the supermarket, disappearing around the corner of the next aisle. It's the shade of his hair, a similar balance of height and weight, a fur-hooded parka coat that he used to wear. Each time, there's an involuntary surge in me – *it's him, he's back*. Decisions I've been unsure I could ever face are resolved in a second: it was all a mistake, there's an explanation, we can work something out. I still love him and I want to reach out and touch him. But the person always morphs back into themselves and I am left bereft all over again, kicking myself for getting swept up once more in what couldn't be real.

At first I would often retrace my steps around the town, the same route I took when he first went missing. It's been a while, though, and now it feels familiar yet strange at the same time, a half-remembered dream. After last night's firework attack, now the vigil, I almost got back into bed. I'd have stayed there all day again, like before. But something propelled me to get up. Who's going to stand up for Chris if I don't?

This time, though, I no longer have the expectation that I'll run into him, see him coming towards me from a distance, sheepish, loving, sorry. I clung on to that hope at first, but it started to fade then evaporated altogether. I couldn't hold on to it. The shock of his absence, the gaping hole; it doesn't subside.

17 July – the last time Chris was seen, the last time Kayleigh was seen. Once a completely meaningless day. Now forever marked on the mental calendar. Will the people of Shawmouth always remember the date, or will it fade and disappear for everyone but Janice and me?

I drift into the first arcade and look for the attendant. It's still early, not even 9 a.m., so it's fairly quiet, although some people are already here playing the machines. Two boys, their school ties taken off, jab and wrench at a blaring game.

An old woman perches on a stool in front of one of the fruit machines, slurping out of a polystyrene cup and grabbing coins from an old margarine tub without averting her eyes from the rolling fruit. The lights cast coloured shadows across her face. There's a man in a striped jumper, cheering his horse on in the Grand National game, tiny plastic horses racing against each other in the encased glass, the winner fixed, pre-programmed. There's a plastic badge on his jacket; his name is Matty, it tells me. I wait near the machine but he doesn't look away from the latest race. He shouts and jeers the horses on as if at a real race, but it doesn't look like his has won, as he kicks the side of the machine and punches his fist against the glass.

He's about to put more coins in when he notices me standing there. He looks me up and down, one eyebrow raised. 'There's a change machine over there, love.' His hair is greasy, white flecks of dandruff at the temples.

'I don't need change. I—'

'Has that new machine swallowed the money again? I'm sorry, love, but it's not my—'

'It's not that.'

'Well, I hope you're not looking for a job as you are seriously out of luck!' He gives a small laugh to himself.

I rummage in my bag. 'I… I… Have you seen this man?' It always sounds ridiculous when I say that, like something from a cheesy TV show.

He looks at me strangely. 'What man?'

I finally retrieve the leaflets from my bag.

'He's my husband,' I say, pointing to the picture. 'We live round here. He's missing.'

'Missing? Really? Not another one. That's three people in a year! Fuck me, that's awful.'

I have his full attention now.

'How long's this one been gone? Sorry, love, how long has your husband been missing?' He puts a protective hand on my arm but I wriggle away. His nails are dirty.

I hear the boys celebrating again behind me and the machine plays a louder jingle. 'Get in, you little bastard! *Yessss!*'

'He's been missing since July. The last day of the school term?' I think this detail might help since so many kids come in here. 'You, er, you might remember? I… I was hoping I could leave some of these leaflets in here. I think he might have been in here, that's all.'

I tried to keep the leaflet simple, to the point. It reads: *Missing. Have you seen this man?* There's a picture of Chris, wearing his jogging gear and grinning. There are strips with my mobile number at the bottom to tear off. Jeannie – my best friend – said

I should change it, that I shouldn't give it out. But I have to keep it the same, in case he tries to call.

I see the recognition fall across his face. 'Oh. So it's not *another* missing person, is it? It's *him*.' A grimace of anger is spreading now. 'Listen, love, don't come in here and try and pull the wool over my eyes. Are you taking the piss?'

The old woman is staring, listening in, one hand in the box of coins but gawping over, the lights dancing on her face.

'I'm not trying to trick you.' I try to sound assertive and direct.

He's edging closer to me, invading my personal space.

'I told you he's my husband!'

'Look.' There's a sneer across his face.

'Hey!' the woman shouts over. 'I'm watching you, matey.'

It's hard to tell but I assume she is addressing him. He steps back a little.

'And what makes you think he's been in here? We don't allow nonces in here, love. I am personally very careful about that.' He jabs at his chest, puffing it out slightly.

'I'm not just asking in here, I'm asking everywhere in town,' I say, as if it will make any difference.

'Alright then. Give me some of your leaflets.' He is already yanking them from my hand.

I try to hold on and a few tear.

'Sure, I'll put these out for you, my love.' He makes a theatrical show of walking to a nearby bin and dropping the leaflets in before pouring his cup of coffee in on top of them, holding his arm higher than he needs to for dramatic effect, not looking away from me the whole time.

I see the old woman shake her head. At me or him? But she is already putting coins into the slot again.

Matty is teeing up his money for the next race. I think about appealing to him, tearing a strip off him, using his name, but I know it would be pointless. I give up and leave.

The wind is getting up outside, a freezing gale pushing my breath back into my mouth. The waves are crashing high, close to the railings above the beach, sometimes sloshing across the road. It's dangerous but people still walk close by. The boys from the arcade are over there now, standing near the edge, leaning over then running away when a wave comes. One of them gets drenched and screeches, the sound mingling in with the cries of the seagulls. People have been pulled in this way before, dragged into the sea, drowned. I worried that the sea had taken Chris, but the helicopters, the lifeboat searches brought up nothing. Not Chris and not Kayleigh either.

I carry on up one of The Parades, stopping every now and then to attach a leaflet to a lamp post. It will get damaged in the wind and rain but not immediately. You never know when the right person will walk past.

From a certain vantage point in Shawmouth, at the top of The Parades, by the train station, there's an angle from which you can't see the road or the promenade. It looks like the whole town, all these houses and people, shops and cars, just float on the sea. That's why in the neighbouring towns they call people from Shawmouth 'floaters'. The name has always given me the creeps. Shadowy shapes in the eye. Dead bodies, drifters, people who can't commit or decide. Pennywise the Clown: 'They all float down here.'

The Parades are a set of parallel streets between the top of town and the sea. Mostly streets of houses, giving way to a street full of bars, and on the next one a couple of restaurants and B&Bs. Close together, these streets, but occupying different worlds.

As you get nearer the sea, down the sweeping avenues, the houses get more expensive.

Old, three-storey, candy-coloured terraces, faded yellows, pinks and blues, with white detailing like the icing on Christmas gingerbread houses. I used to imagine we'd live in one of these one day. We'd be tidy then, when we had one of these houses. We'd have solid wood floors, classy chandeliers, fancy serving bowls. We'd lounge around barefoot – a carefree, magazine life. God knows how we'd ever have the money, though. What do you need to do to own one? Be a doctor, an old-school academic, the lucky recipient of an inheritance, the beneficiary of someone's death? I like to study the families as they come and go from these houses. The fragrant wives gleam: lean, healthy, 'lit from within', as they say in the magazines; dressed in expensive casuals. Slim thighs in well-cut jeans, a tasteful white shirt that doesn't crease or pull. They walk pedigree dogs, bundle babies into 4x4s. The men are clean-shaven, tight-torsoed, like catalogue models; the catalogues I spent hours poring over as a kid – I was thinking ahead to my life about now with someone like Chris, what it was going to be like.

I try to look into the houses as I pass, imagining my alternate life, being careful to make it look like a casual glance in case anyone should notice me. The houses all look pristine; have cleaners, no doubt. Wood floors, high ceilings, white paintwork. They look welcoming, calming.

I'm out of breath and too hot in my coat now, after walking up the hill. I used to go swimming, jogged sometimes with Jeannie. I barely do any exercise now.

Up near the river and the train station, they call this area 'The Fields', the wild area surrounding the river and a few playing fields. Chris used to play football there sometimes on Sundays.

Chris was last seen on CCTV on the wide road that runs along the top of The Parades, separating the town from the river and the fields: 9.37 a.m. Shirt on, loosened at the neck, work rucksack on his back. He wasn't picked up anywhere else on camera. An article in the paper said the surveillance cameras in the town had been 'prioritised' due to budget cuts. Up to a third of them shut off to save money, they said.

On the film, he just crosses the street and then vanishes. I found myself craning my head, trying to catch the last glimpse, to see round the corner, beyond the screen. Did he meet someone? Kayleigh? Jump on a train to start a new life somewhere else? He always talked about going to America, said they needed teachers there. But his passport is still at home.

Detective Fisher had me watch the video to confirm it was Chris, and I made her play it over and over. It was him. And at the same time, it wasn't. I don't want that to be the latest memory I have of him, a grey figure drifting past. Glowing white eyes, supernatural.

There were a couple of other reported sightings too, but Detective Fisher was cagey; she shared what she wanted to. Probably only what she was allowed to.

The CCTV is why I often come here, though this is the first time in a while. Chris and I used to come here too, when we first moved back. I run the tape again in my mind. Stand on the same spot, the last place I know he was. Was it here? Or here? I close my eyes, but I can't feel anything.

I go further along, towards the water. People sometimes sit here by the river in summer, walk their dogs. Mum and Dad sometimes brought me for picnics when I was little. Chris and I would walk here on Sundays or after tea on summer evenings, watching the last sun of the day fade. He's into nature, the beach, bike rides – more so than me. That's why I thought he'd like it in Shawmouth after the shock of leaving London subsided.

I've always been fascinated by this place. It's quite deserted now. The weather, the time of day. I get closer; the ground is already sodden and slippery underfoot.

'DANGER,' the red sign blares. 'The Cut is DANGEROUS and has claimed lives in the past. Please stand back and beware all slippery rocks.'

They call this section of the river 'The Cut'. Chris liked it here too. It has a certain beauty, something ethereal and fairytaley, I've always thought. The water is higher than usual at the moment, fast-flowing and playful, skittering over rocks, but not violent like it can be. The narrow gap and stepping stones inviting you to stride across. But it's a cruel mirage. The water here runs faster and deeper than the rest of the river. No one knows how deep it goes. There's a network of caverns and tunnels underneath – they hold all the unseen water.

Dogs, a young couple, even a child – they've all been sucked in over the decades, gone for good. As a child, this place was a bogeyman drummed into us.

I stand at the edge now, letting the rushing water hypnotise me, like watching road markings whizz by on a car journey. I am woozy, as if my head is rolling back and forth. I'd have kept back before, obeyed the sign and my mother; I wouldn't have dared get this close or let Chris either. The muddied edge is ragged and uncertain. It could collapse; I could slip.

I notice the cold after a while, feel like I am breaking out of a trance. I check around, shake myself out of it and head back into town. I am tired. But I have to complete the circuit or I feel superstitious.

Roaming the glut of bars and pubs near The Parades, I peer through windows, occasionally stopping and watching to see who's entering and leaving. By day, the bars and pubs look stark and grubby, unrecognisable from the dark, thronging evenings.

There's a cleaner in one of them, wiping down the bar and putting upturned stools onto the tables.

'We're closed,' she says when I go in, without looking towards the door.

'I don't want a drink. I was wondering if…'

She looks up now and I can see she recognises me, she knows who I am. It's often women who do.

'Something of a local celebrity,' Jeannie said once, a misplaced tentative joke.

From the picture they kept using in the paper, I assume. Taken on our wedding day, swiped off my Facebook before I changed the settings.

I consider just leaving, especially after the incident at the arcade, but my feet are rooted to the spot. If people are going to start pushing again, I have to push too. Jeannie always said I'm like a Weeble; I bounce back up.

'I was wondering if I could leave some leaflets. I'm... erm... looking for my husband. He's missing.'

The woman doesn't look surprised or ask for any more details, but she glances behind, seemingly checking if anyone else is there. She bites her lip.

'So can I? Leave a few leaflets here?'

She twists her wedding ring, eyes darting.

'Let me see,' she says, holding her hand out for a flyer. She looks round again before examining the leaflet and takes a few moments to read it – her eyes move from top to bottom, not the cursory glance people usually give.

Her posture is hunched, like she's trying to make herself smaller somehow, to take up less space. 'It's not really for me to decide...' She meets my eye. 'I'm sorry. Really I am. I'll ask the fella who owns this place when he gets back though.'

There's a pile of flyers behind her, for takeaways and taxis, a 99p drinks night at one of the clubs on the same strip. I look at the pile and back to her.

She just shrugs, apologetic. 'Sorry, if it were up to me, but it's not my place, you know? It's more than my job's worth. I'll ask him, I promise.'

I can tell that she is sincere.

'OK, thanks, I appreciate it. Maybe I can come back later in the week?'

She doesn't answer. She has already returned to the cleaning, rubbing hard at an imaginary stain on a table already shiny with polish.

After they showed me the footage of him on the CCTV close by, I wondered if around here, the bars, is where he might have been that weekend, when he didn't come home. But no one had seen him, he wasn't there. It's not like we ever really came to these pubs. He's more of a real ale type. But he came sometimes with the football lads. 'Just for a laugh,' he had said. I thought maybe he just needed to let off some steam, drink a bit too much; blow the cobwebs off.

He'd been going to the pub after work for 'a quick one' more often, or so he said, and so I stupidly believed. He'd been playing with his phone more, always fiddling with it. Before, I used to answer his mobile for him sometimes, if he was driving or in the shower. But suddenly he was taking it everywhere with him and leaving the room when it rang. I didn't think much of it at the time. He was always glued to it for the internet anyway.

'You can talk,' he'd say, if I challenged him. 'You're just the same.' He had a point.

But looking back now, wasn't this different? Was he talking to *her*? Did he have two phones? Could he really be that cunning? Maybe it was just nothing. Maybe the accusations about Kayleigh are just contaminating everything, the whole life we had before this.

CHAPTER FOUR

Saturday, 7 November

I wake at 6 p.m. in the caravan. I slept most of the afternoon. I sleep better when it's light outside; it passes the time. People are busy with their lives during the day – work, children, shopping. Sometimes, when I am wretched with tiredness, I turn off the fire in the caravan and snuggle under the covers, letting sleep take me.

I wasn't going to drink tonight; I want to get things under control. But I need to take the edge off.

I pull on jeans, boots and a thick jumper and Puffa coat, which makes a swooshing sound each time I move. This is all I ever wear now, my hair scraped back, no make-up. I don't want to look like my old self, prefer people not to take any notice of me. My wardrobe back at the house is full of bright dresses, flowers, dots, vintage. Career Becky, sporty Becky, Saturday pub-lunch Becky. 'A real clothes horse,' my mum used to say. Back then, we used to go shopping together at least once a month on a Saturday, cakes and coffee in Marsh's department store. I'd feel warm and content, looking forward to spending the evening with Chris or maybe going out with the girls, the Sunday stretching ahead – a lie-in, no plans.

There's no one around at the caravan park, only a few caravans with their lights on. It's mostly deserted for the winter, no holidaymakers, just the odd person. I imagine men eating from tins, trying to get out of the way of rows at home, or perhaps they're in work boots, labouring in the area on one of the new housing developments.

I leave the caravan park, walking underneath the arches of the rusting blue 'Welcome to Sandy Nook' sign. My hands and lower legs are freezing from the dampness of the grass, breath blooming in a cloud in front of me, the smell of burning on the air. In the distance I can hear fireworks again, coloured glitter erupting in the sky, who knows how far away. For a moment, I wonder if the attack the other night really happened, but the drying scab close to my eye reassures me I didn't dream it.

I tighten as I approach it, turning onto the seafront. The concrete bus shelter, an ugly textured concrete shell – if you scraped against it, it would graze the skin right off. No buses stop here anymore, but kids like to hang out here sometimes. Have they always done this? Is it because I'm here? There's been a campaign by locals to get it knocked down. Antisocial behaviour, they argue.

Whooping and low chatter: they are here tonight. I can smell marijuana. But as much as I want to, I can't hide away in the caravan forever. And if I do, it will be on my terms, when I choose. I have these flashes of defiance, moments of relative strength, and then they're quickly gone.

A boy appears from inside the shelter, staggering out into the road as if pushed. 'You wanker!' he shouts, laughing and circling his arms to try and steady himself. He doesn't seem concerned about the threat of a car slamming into him. But there's very little traffic tonight – just the odd car every now and then, the whooshing as they pass merging into the sound of the waves across the road. When he sees me, he rights himself and his eyes narrow. He's excited about giving the group something to do, and he disappears back into the bunker. It all goes quiet and I try to speed up, but they start to appear, file out one by one, some with their hands in pockets. I try not to make eye contact.

'Alright, love?' one of the boys shouts, voice surprisingly deep. 'How much you charging? Oi, love – answer me, you ignorant cow.'

I rush on so they're behind me now. Not daring to look back.

'Fuck off then, you pikey bitch. Get back to your scratty caravan.' A girl this time. They all laugh, but the sounds are more muffled, as they're back in the bus shelter again. There isn't any other way back to the caravan park than past the shelter.

Reaching the cash machine outside the shop, I chance a look back but there's no one. A man walking his dog on the other side of the road, but no sign of the kids from the bus shelter. I am almost out of money. Earlier this week I cashed in some coppers I had been saving, an ongoing game with myself that I've played since I was young. Chris and I used to cash in a carrier bag-full once every few months and use the money for a day out in town. A film, out for tea and a few drinks.

I try the first card. 'Sorry, your request cannot be processed at this time.' I snatch it out. Shit, I need to keep better track of which ones are working, which are maxed out. My hands are shaking as I rifle through my purse for another card. It's in the machine and I have to close my eyes and picture the blue plastic, the raised numbers, to conjure up the PIN . So many numbers. Again, insufficient funds. A third one. The screen freezes then blinks before spitting out £20. Since it's working, and it could stop doing so at any time, I repeat the process and take out another £10. I don't want to push it; alarm the algorithm about erratic activity.

Bright white strip lights shock my eyes coming in from the darkness. The bell above the door rattles as I enter the shop, and two women standing close to the counter stop talking as I enter. One, wearing slippers with a loaf of bread tucked under her arm, is slowly looking me up and down, holding eye contact. My face burns, the blood pumping in my ears. I look to the owner. Don't know why. What do I expect him to do, chuck her out for looking at me? I see him a few times a week, mostly when I buy vodka and bread or milk, but he's one of the few people who are quite pleasant to me. Perhaps he hasn't heard the stories. He let me put a 'missing' picture of Chris in the shop window at first, and he said he'd take some leaflets a while back. But I don't see them anywhere now on a glance across the counter, and there's nothing on the noticeboard.

He refuses to look at me, checking off a list in his notepad, purposefully counting nothing. One of the two women stares, hard-faced. I flee into an aisle, my heart thumping in my chest, and pretend to look at the papers and magazines. Newspapers: the last thing I want right now. Up to the magazines. Before me, the weeklies are a sneering wall of gaudy pink banners, tanned breasts – skin stretched taut, veins close to the surface, white teeth. Screeching headlines: a single mother who spent charity money on a boob job, a woman who had sex with a ghost.

'You want to be more careful who you serve in here,' the woman says to the shopkeeper, raising her voice to make sure I hear her. 'Really careful.'

'Please, madam. I don't want any trouble here.'

Fight or flight?

I run for the door, empty-handed, the stupid bell chiming again as I go. Outside, my chest is tight. Chris's 'missing' picture, from when he first disappeared, is gone from the window – you can still see the tacky marks where the tape was, replaced by fading neon stars, blaring out cheap deals on cans and frozen food in black marker pen.

I don't want to risk facing the women when they come out of the shop so I run most of the way back along the seafront to the caravan, slowing down as I get close to the bus shelter. But I don't hear anything and there's no sign of anyone now. They must have moved on somewhere else.

Without even thinking about it properly, I head straight for the social club, Barnacles, when I get back to the caravan park. I just need a drink to calm down, take the edge off the night. It's dead inside, a couple of blokes drinking frothy pints.

Barnacles is low-ceilinged, claustrophobic, with woodchip paper, a deserted pool table in one alcove corner and a television in the other corner of the room, attached to the wall. Not a flat screen, one of the old ones with the tubes in the back. There's a table with a corner sofa and seats underneath, torn maroon pleather, cheap yellow foam spewing out.

Julie is behind the bar. She runs the caravan park. 'She probably runs the whole town. I wouldn't mess with her,' Jeannie said about her when I moved here.

'Hiya, love, what're you having?' Julie greets me. 'We've not seen you in here for a while.'

Her voice is gravelly, like that of a heavy smoker, and her skin looks matt and tanned, leathery. Even though it's winter she wears her usual uniform behind the bar – a short denim skirt with flip-flops and a vest. Julie knows who I am, what's happened – a lot of people around here know. 'It's none of my business, as long as you pay your way and don't bring trouble to my door,' she'd said when I moved in, shouting back over her shoulder as she showed me to the caravan, walking ahead, dangling the keys off one finger.

'Innocent until proven guilty in this country, and as far as I'm concerned we ain't none of us responsible for other people's actions.' I was touched at the time; no one else had really shown me any kindness. Since then she's always been friendly but kept her distance. She takes the caravan rent in cash and she doesn't pry, and that suits me.

'Double vodka and a pint, please, Julie,' I say, putting the money on the counter: £2.30 for a Fosters and £1.50 for a vodka. An extra shot for £1. I know the prices in here off by heart.

Julie's eyebrows rise slightly at my drink request but she just jokes, 'Not in a cocktail, the lager and vodka, I presume?' A few seconds later, 'Fosters is off, love, I'll need to change it. Sit down and I'll bring it over.' She gestures her head towards the seats. I feel self-conscious sitting here alone, not knowing what to do with my hands, instinctively touching my hair over and over.

A while later, Julie brings over a circular tin tray with the lager and vodka, along with a jacket potato with baked beans poured over it and a limp, browning side salad drizzled with thin bean juice. 'It needed using up, so you're doing me a favour. I hate waste,' she tells me. 'Saves you cooking back at the van, eh?'

Her rings chink against the side of the plate when she puts it down. I have never seen anyone wear as much gold as Julie. You wouldn't think that running a caravan park would be that lucrative. Each finger has at least four gold rings stacked up close to the knuckle. Many are plain like wedding bands, others are studded with diamonds. I notice one tarnished ring is a heart wearing a crown clutched by two hands. I think of all the dirt and moisture that must fester underneath the rings.

'How you doing, love? Good to see you up and about.'

'I'm alright, thanks, Julie.'

'What have I told you, kid? Think on: don't let the bastards grind you down.'

She picks up some glasses and goes back to the bar.

I probably wouldn't have eaten anything at the van; sometimes I like feeling empty and hungry, floating. But I appreciate the gesture from Julie after what just happened at the bus stop and the shop, so I thank her for the food.

The potato has been microwaved and the middle is still hard, the skin gritty and earthy, but I eat it anyway, realising I am actually quite shaky, that I haven't eaten yet today. When Julie comes back over, the plate is clean and my glasses are empty. I notice her checking. 'Another round, love? I've got some sticky toffee pudding on the go if you want some?'

I order just the lager.

'Hey, it's karaoke in a sec. You getting up?' Julie smirks and nudges me, her laugh chesty.

The next lager starts to make me feel warm and fuzzy. I can't afford to be going out drinking like this but I need it right now, and at least it's cheap. That's why people come here.

'It's what keeps me going in the winter, this place,' Julie often says when it's busy.

Chris and I didn't used to think anything of blowing £100 on a night out just after payday. We'd go out straight from work on the Friday, have a few drinks and a pizza then stay out in the pub until closing, knowing we had nothing to do the next day but laze around at home.

It dawns on me slowly that 'Delilah' is being belted out by a drinker from the club. I've seen him before, white-haired with dark eyebrows, big lamb chop sideburns, cowboy-style shirt, strained by his solid-looking beer belly. He has a deep, booming voice that could pass for a good one if you don't pay attention too closely. He doesn't sound much like Tom Jones, though. I feel a little dizzy, and the disco ball lights bouncing around the room are not helping.

From the dance floor, the man throws one arm out in front of him dramatically as he belts out the lyrics. I've always liked karaoke – watching it, not performing. I like to see people show-ing off and really giving it some. It strikes me as something that people with the right attitude and a zest for life do; the sort of people you want to be around. Perhaps that's why I like coming in here, to Barnacles. Sometimes, not very often, I want to be alone but around people, and this is the ideal place for that. Usu-ally I just want to be alone.

The bar is filling up and getting warm under the low ceiling. Most of the tables are crowded with glasses and people on stools, clustered together. Thankfully, no one bothers me and I keep my table to myself. If anyone sits down, I will need to leave, but I realise I am feeling OK, to my surprise – as OK as I can, anyway. Not raging or hysterical, not cramped up from the inside out with anxiety. It's just the drink, I know that, but I'll take it for a short respite.

I put my coat on the table to hold my spot and order a treble gin and tonic. It's served in a fingerprint-marked half-pint glass, the tonic warm and flat. I gulp it down and order another one before returning to my seat.

Someone drops a drink. Shattering glass pierces the air and people cheer like in school dinner halls. I jump; an image breaks into my brain. The brick through the window, the red spray paint across the front of the house and on the pavement outside. 'Nonce.' It was Jeannie who saw that, who had to break it to me that someone had written it. I cowered in the bathroom after the brick. Had to call her and Dan to come round and help clean up.

The day after the brick, I saw an advert in the classifieds in the paper; it was non-descript, but the words jumped out at me. 'Escape' the heading beckoned. The small print said that as well as for holidays, static caravans were also available for short-term rents 'very cheap rates'. That's when I decided to move here to the caravan park.

Jeannie says I should go and stay with her at her house; she always has. She hates me being in the caravan. She seems to take it as a personal failing. But I think she wants a pet version of me to move in, to eat my vegetable-packed dinners and take my baths and say yes, it's all helping, that I'm coming back to life, that I can see a way ahead. She wouldn't want me staying for long if she saw what I'm really like.

Next up on the karaoke is a woman with dyed black hair styled in a wet-look spiral perm. She has tight leather trousers on and a thin T-shirt with a bejewelled tiger on the front, a tanned shoulder poking out on one side. When she turns with the mic I see she has heavily fake-tanned skin, and a gold tooth glints. Her voice is growly with an affected American twang and another accent I can't quite place. She winks at people in the crowd from time to time as she walks across the stage area, singing 'Still the One' by Shania Twain.

There's a spirited atmosphere in the bar. Some people get up to dance, mock slow-style, old-school spins. Glasses clatter from people bringing the next round back from the bar. As I look round it feels like everyone is smiling or laughing, holding shouted conversations over tables. The room gently swims and I feel a certain sense of contentment, alone in this crowded place, no one bothering me. I watch the glitter-ball sequins glide round on the roof, feeling like they are sweeping me along with them.

An older woman in a lilac skirt suit and floral blouse gets up to sing Cilla Black's 'You're My World'. She's small with short, severe hair, hot-brushed into submission. There's something about the words, the song, and the tears threaten to swell up. I fill my mouth with the remains of my drink and hold it in there, focusing on the burning numbness, on breathing through my nose, to quell the crying. She gets a whoop from the crowd and is followed by a local Michael Bublé, a male Patsy Cline and an unlistenable Kylie, who gets good-naturedly booed off.

When the karaoke is finished, I start to feel awkward and fidgety again. I don't know where to look; should have brought my phone. The club is starting to empty out in some areas. Julie is wiping down the bar, probably getting as much done in advance as she can for closing. Or maybe she will have a lock-in like she sometimes does.

'Hey, did you hear on the news they're having a vigil for that wee lassy?'

At first I wonder if the Scottish accent is addressing me, and I panic. Should I turn around? But someone answers.

'Aye, terrible business. Terrible. Are you gonna go over to the vigil, like?'

'Aye, I expect I will. Pay my respects. Show some support to the family. It doesn'ae look good for the wee lassy, being gone all this time, does it? Imagine being the mother, poor woman. I'd be gone mad.'

It's dangerous, but I allow myself a sneaky look round. The woman speaking, the Scottish one, is the Shania wannabe. The tiger on her T-shirt looks like it's leaping out of her, teeth bared. She's sitting at the table behind me, bronze-painted talons draped around a half pint of lager. I quickly look back round to my table, but I am straining my ears to catch the rest of the conversation. Morbid compulsion.

The man's voice again. Easier to hear now it's less busy, and he's booming, self-important. 'She's no angel in this either, mind. She should know where a fourteen-year-old is.'

'Well, it doesn'ae look good, and she's going to have to live with that.'

'I don't know what to make of it all, me. It's a weird old do, that is for sure.'

'You not having an opinion, Jimmy? That's gotta be a first!' The table laughs.

A new voice. 'What do you think about this fella they're all saying it was?'

My stomach twists.

'God knows,' says another. 'Ah don't know enough of the facts of it all, and neither do you.'

'You don't usually let that stop you. But it's odd, isn't it? You cannit deny that it's weird, them both going missing on the same day. I mean, come on. There's a rabbit off somewhere.'

'True enough, Pat, it's true enough. I heard he was a teacher down London. Not up here though.'

'Really? Is that right?'

'Aye, that's what I heard, aye.'

'*Eurgh!* Dirty bastard! I wonder why he went into that profession then... Not.'

My hand goes to my forehead. I get these mental spasms; cramps, like small electric shocks. They're coming back. Images that flash into my head. They're all flesh-coloured, it's blood, open wounds. I squeeze my eyes together as hard as I can to squash the thought, imagining them like tiny pin dots.

I have to press myself down into my seat to stop from turning around and shouting. That they don't know anything. Chris left teaching because he was tired, because he wanted a life outside work, because he wanted to spend more time with me. That's all.

'Well, there's plenty at it these days. All these bloody celebrities and that.'

'They'll string him up round 'ere if they ever get 'old of him.'

'And the rest.'

Someone loudly slurps the remainder of their drink through a straw, and the table murmurs their agreement.

A different voice this time. 'But you see these young lasses running about town in next to nothing, don't you? They're tarted up to the eyeballs like they're in their twenties. I've seen 'em myself down the Butcher's Arms on a Friday. And they're still in bloody school. I've told the landlord in there he shouldn't be serving them, but they just want the money. Then, later on they're off up The Parades getting legless and getting up to Christ knows what.'

'Aye, we wouldn't have got away with it. My mother would have had me back upstairs to get changed, sharpish!'

'Right, guys,' says Julie. 'Time to drink up. I need my beauty sleep – and so do you, by the looks of it, Jimmy.'

I wonder if she is moving them along for my sake.

As she comes past, she taps her long nails a couple of times on my table, but she doesn't say anything or look at me.

CHAPTER FIVE

Sunday, 8 November

When I open my eyes it's early morning and I am back at the caravan, asleep on the couch, fully clothed under a sheet but not the duvet, shivering. It's even colder in the bedroom so I use it for storage and sleep in the main room.

I know immediately that I am going to vomit. My stomach is awash with liquid, my mouth dry, head thick and clogged. I know I won't make it to the bathroom so I make a leap for the kitchen sink, sheet still tangled around my legs. My stomach contracts multiple times but nothing comes up, my mouth is paralysed open in a dry heave. After a few retches, acidic yellow water shoots out. I hang over the sink, recovering before the next wave comes. My head is pounding. I've been here enough times to know that bland water will only make the situation worse, so I open a cold can of Coke from the fridge and the fresh fizz burns my throat.

There is semi-dried mud on my jeans, on the knees. Dirt under my nails. I must have fallen on the way back to the caravan.

Lying on the sofa, I fumble in my mind's blackness to recall what happened last night. I remember the shop, the bus shelter, being at Barnacles.

I look around to check no one else is in the van, suddenly afraid I had brought someone back with me. Surely I wouldn't do that? So why does it enter my head?

I remember the karaoke. My memory is like a TV that won't tune in, the evening replayed in flashes. Did I get up and sing? I didn't talk to them about Chris, did I, at Barnacles last night? I wouldn't talk about it, surely. I instinctively check my phone. At least I didn't send any texts or try to call anyone. I turn to lie down, to sleep off the sickness.

I lie most of the day in the caravan, listening to the rain, under the covers in an attempt to stay warm and rest, dwelling on everything: the fireworks, the vigil. It feels like the resurgence of it all. It was bound to happen; it's never gone away. I've been living in a suspended state – I convinced myself that Chris would be back. It's unfathomable that he wouldn't be. I tried to make everything around me stop until he returned.

I have no place to be most days, which I am thankful for. No one expects me or needs me to be anywhere. Except when I visit my mum, and it's debatable whether she is even aware most of the time.

Because it's so cold in the caravan, everything feels wet. My clothes, the covers, even my hair has a mist of moisture. My teeth chatter, nose numb. My head feels like I have brain freeze. But I don't dare to keep the gas fire on overnight, for fear of carbon monoxide poisoning – I read about it happening to someone at a caravan park. Perhaps a heavy headache and that's it; you just don't wake up. Maybe if it gets too much, that's how I'll go. It would make it easier for people like Jeannie to bear, if it looked like an accident.

'And you say that you knew, is that right? You could just "feel" that she was dead?' a posh-voiced woman asks on the radio.

'Yes.' A crackly phone line.

I catch the conversation halfway through. I am trying to find a spot to grip on, understand the context of what they're talking about. Just something to distract me; take my mind off things.

'I just had this sensation, you know? It was really weird. I got this massive pain in my stomach. They say that's where she was fatally injured. Maybe the point of impact. The crash.' The voice on the phone line wavers. 'I just hope she didn't feel any pain.'

I can picture her hunched over the phone, an embroidered, cotton hanky up to her mouth. *Bastards for getting her live on the air like this*, I think. But I know myself what vultures these people can be. And I could always switch it off, couldn't I?

'Thanks for that, Ruth. Thanks for calling in. It must be really painful for you.' The woman's snivel is cut off part-way through. 'And, Professor Benson, it's not just a twin thing, is it? They say it's possible with any people who are very close.'

'That's right. It's not even always relatives, you know, that's just it. We can't underestimate the strength of emotional connections, human connections. As this research shows – husbands and wives, even close friends.'

'This new research from a US university adds weight to the idea that people might be able to sense when a loved one is in pain or has died, even when they're miles away. We're taking a look at people who have experienced the phenomenon—'

I reach over and snap the radio off. Janice has said that she believes Kayleigh is still alive. That she'd know somehow if she wasn't. Would I feel something? Would I know if Chris was physically hurt? Could I feel if he was completely gone? I close my eyes, but it's just white space, silence. There's nothing coming through. Maybe we weren't close enough, but didn't we know each other inside out, tell each other everything? Evidently not.

A few times each week, often more these days, I allow myself a fixed time to pretend that everything's fine, that my life isn't shattered. Sometimes I lie with the lights out and picture putting all the bad stuff in a box for a while, closing the lid and locking it. This was advice I got from my short-lived stint with the therapist when I told her that I couldn't sleep. Surprise, surprise. This is what she suggested. I was hoping for some pills. I got them myself anyway from Boots. I just have to take double the amount these days to get any effect.

I was all geared up to presume anything she told me was mumbo jumbo. But it turned out in this case she was right. It worked for a while, helped me sleep, then it stopped. Maybe because I used it in the daytime so much my mind just got wise. You can only trick yourself for so long. The days and hours blur quite a lot, especially when I take the sleeping pills and drink. I could say the drinking and pills don't help. That's what Jeannie says, but she's wrong – because the truth is, they do.

So I block out the fact that Chris is gone, that half the town hates me because they think I lived with and protected 'a paedophile', and the fact that I don't know what to think about it all and can't keep a thought in my head for over three seconds.

I pretend that Chris is here with me, that none of this ever happened. Sometimes I imagine we're lying on the beach in Spain, the sun warming us both, or we're staying in a cosy log cabin somewhere remote in winter, with a fire roaring and enough supplies to last us weeks. When it does work, I can allow myself to picture the scene so vividly, to almost believe it. Sometimes I try to stay awake to enjoy the dream, but I usually drop off to sleep, and wake up again shivering in the caravan, plunged back into my real life. It's worth it for the short respite.

I try it now, slow breathing, imagining clean, cool, pale-blue air. But now I can't conjure the soothing images so easily. They get polluted. The thoughts about what's really happening are pushing their way in like smoke under the door, they're creeping in through the cracks around the window.

When I eventually get up, I busy myself, like most days, first of all with the Facebook page that I set up in the first week after he'd gone. I post a new update or picture at least once a week. Few people share them or comment anymore. They've either tuned it out of their lives, or they just don't want to be associated.

It's more habit now, superstition. There is still that tiny glimmer of hope that stops me closing it down.

Today there are two red notifications. Excess saliva seeps into my mouth. Activity has slowed down a lot since those first weeks. The kindness of the messages and support I received from a few strangers then kept me going for a while, before the word spread, before the perception of me as the simple grieving wife warped in people's minds. But I think it was the vitriol that really drove me on. With the vigil coming up, the increased attention – perhaps I'll need that resolve again now.

They posted defaced pictures of Chris, his eyes scratched out. 'You get what you deserve,' they said. I was a whore and a slut and worse besides, and they threatened that I was next.

Today, someone has posted to the page the news story about the vigil. There aren't any reactions yet, and I close my eyes and delete it, lying to myself that it was never there. I can't face the comments; I know what they will say.

The other alert is from an account called 'The Watchers'. A video. My blood feels like it's suddenly infused with icy water, speeding through my veins. They have posted before. Regularly when the news first broke. My hand hovers over the mouse pad, wobbling. I know I shouldn't watch it but the film is already playing.

A shaky handheld camera. An empty car park at night, a distorted voice.

'We're here to meet a creep we have been messaging on the internet,' a male voice whispers, breathless. 'He thinks he's here to meet a thirteen-year-old girl. He's travelled from Cheltenham to Newcastle. He's in for a surprise.' The sound of two men laughing, one shushing the other.

After a while, a car pulls up. The sound of tyres moving slowly across gravel, a car door closing. A man comes into view. Then I realise I can still hear the sound. Running, breathing. A shout. But my eyes are closed. Like another bad dream.

I force them open. Night-vision camera. The man is older, fifties, a denim jacket, the glare of a light bouncing off his glasses.

'This is a mistake,' he says, panic etched in his face. He tries to run, darting one way then back the other. He's cornered by the two men. One wears a plastic animal mask, too small for his face, the other a gaudy clown mask.

'You're right it's a mistake, mate,' one of the men says. 'You ain't been talking to "Annabelle". It's been us all along, fella.'

'I haven't done anything. Just let me go.' His voice is a whimper.

'We've got all the WhatsApps, mate. All the chat is logged, pal.'

The man's hand goes up to his face and he tries to block the camera. 'What are you going to do to me?'

The dread in me is physical, a dragging heaviness. But the men in the masks, their voices are calm. There is no violence. Only a lightness of foot, the shifting from one to the other, blocking the man's escape.

'Police are coming, pal.'

'Please, no. It's all just a misunderstanding. I can explain.'

'It's too late for that, mate. You can explain to the coppers. Just stay calm, yeah.'

The man begins to cry, and something shrinks and shrivels inside me.

Soon the police arrive and guide the man into a car, protecting his head as he gets in. The video ends. Green text and data superimposed on a black background, an increasing amount filling the screen.

'The Watchers. Protecting Britain's children,' a distorted voice says. 'We're always watching.' Then the film ends.

Twenty-one likes already.

I delete the post.

'Are you sure?' it asks.

Pressing my hands hard against my ears, I take deep breaths. I get up and close a crack in the curtains of the caravan.

I look through photos, searching for an unpublished one I can scan and upload, touching each photo one time to acknowledge it before I can turn the page, and starting again if I miss one. There's one of us on the beach, me scrunched under an umbrella, sweating in a bright, synthetic-fabric kaftan and wide-brimmed hat, terrified of getting tan lines for an upcoming wedding we were going to back at home; him stretched on the sand and bathed in sunlight. We'd booked a cheap, last-minute deal to Spain the spring just gone. The hotel was a bit grim really. Feral cats living round the pool, scrawny-looking things. A loud man from Essex got a nasty scratch right across his face when he tried to look into the bushes where the cats gathered. Chris and I had given each other a knowing look, stifled laughter.

But the holiday had been good for us. Really, I prefer the cool weather of England, but sunny days do change your world, even if only temporarily. I can't conjure that back now, if I ever felt it, but I remember distinctly that's what I came away thinking. We'd be more active when we got home – do up the house, finish work on time – we'd make the most of life. 'Won't we, won't we?' we said repeatedly, a mantra to ourselves.

We'd sat on the balcony drinking cheap Spanish wine, eaten outside, read books on the beach all day and taken afternoon naps. It was a relaxing week, my first beach holiday, but by the last day I'd been feeling twitchy and started making my to-do lists and plans, much to Chris's amusement, or perhaps irritation, I couldn't quite tell. Maybe I am never in the moment, I don't make the most of things when they're there and then they are gone. Maybe I didn't make the most of Chris while I had him.

I'd felt like an uptight spoilsport when he went to swim in the sea. The sea makes me anxious and I didn't want to have to dry my hair again that night. Sitting there on the sand, I couldn't even enjoy my book or the warm sun. I couldn't let Chris out of my sight. I watched him bobbing and floating on the turquoise glittering water the whole time, terrified he'd get sucked under the waves. I was looking for danger in all the wrong places.

I glance at the clock: 11.50 a.m. Half the day is already over. I received a message yesterday from a man named Gary in Leeds. He had seen the posters my cousin Emma distributed round the city centre there.

I am surprised that she bothered to do it – I hadn't really believed her when she said she had. I imagined she'd recycled the posters, or just dumped them over the wall.

Gary's message was brief. Text speak, badly spelled. He said he thinks he may have worked with Chris on a building site a few weeks ago, in Sheffield. I can't really picture this, Chris doing manual labour. He struggled to put up a shelf in the house. But in his message, Gary said to call him after midday – he'd be working in the morning, even on a Sunday.

I fidget as the minute hand on the clock crawls round, wash up some cups, pointless tidying – anything to keep my hands busy. I feel like minutes must have passed but each time I look up, the hand has moved around thirty seconds or less.

Every now and then the wind throws a spray of rain across the side of the caravan, startling me.

I wonder if Jeannie will lend me the money to get the train to Leeds. I'd prefer to ask someone else but I am at a loss as to who. Finally it hits 12.01 and I reach for my mobile and dial.

'Yes?' the unfamiliar voice says, gruff, distracted – still doing something else at the same time. You can just tell, can hear that his mouth is directed slightly away from the phone.

'Hi – Gary? It's Rebecca Pendle. I'm calling about the poster. About my husband.'

Silence.

'You sent me an email, a message on Facebook?'

'Oh right, yes.' He sounds unsure.

I push on.

'You said you may have worked with him on a building site? Do you—'

'Aw Christ, I meant to message you back. I wasn't sure what to do. It's probably best you rang us anyway like, best to speak in person, I suppose.'

My hope is already fading. 'So do you have some information, Gary? Did you speak to him? Do you have his number or something? I'm his wife. I'm just really worried about him. Just want to know where he is, that he's alright.'

'I think I got it wrong. I shouldn't have emailed you.' His voice has a slow Yorkshire drawl to it.

Speak faster, I think. I notice that I am wiggling my feet and toes, nervous energy.

'I checked with the fellas at work. They said it's been all over the news. I don't follow it, me. Wife says I should. But it's always just bad news, isn't it? Non-stop bad news.' He trails off again.

'So this man you met at work?'

'Yeah, right, sorry. He's not Irish is he, your husband?'

'No.'

'That's what the lads here said. The guy I meant. Who I thought I meant. He was Irish. I should have remembered he had an Irish accent.'

'You're sure it was Irish?'

'One of the other lads knew him from back home. Got him a job on the site. There's not much work over there at the minute. Sorry, the poster jogged my memory, but I should have checked first before contacting you.'

'No. You're sure it was work you recognised him from? Not somewhere else? You're not mixing things up?'

'I'm pretty sure. He just looked a bit like him, I guess.'

'Pretty sure?' My voice is rising. How can he be so casual?

'I'm sorry, I am sure. I shouldn't have got in touch.'

'Right,' I mumble, restraining tears. 'Thanks, anyway.' *For nothing*, I feel like adding but restrain myself.

I take the phone away from my ear and hear him say he's sorry, three times in the background, more distant each time.

It's not the first time. I should be prepared, shouldn't dare to hope. There've been sightings at reservoirs, on trains, conversations with confused homeless people, even cruel pranks, but all roads lead back to the same place. He's just vanished, gone. And so has Kayleigh.

I know it does me no good but I can't help looking at his Facebook page every time I check my 'Find Chris Harding' page. Most days, then: sometimes more than once. Usually ending up in a state, head thumping, eyes swollen. I used to nag at him for always being online, especially in those last few weeks, but now it's one of the closest connections I have to him.

Sometimes I write him private messages on there about my day, about how much I miss him. Sometimes I beg him to come back; other times I get angry and just demand answers. They never show as 'read'. Of course I know he won't update it or reply – but I can't give up on the idea. If he did, what would he say? Where would he be? London? Spain? Somewhere more far flung? Or perhaps not far away at all.

He is there as soon as I load the page, and a small electric current of pain runs through me. Sometimes I touch his face on the screen. Jeannie would hate it if she knew I was doing this. She thinks I'm doing OK now, that I'm a bit more stable than I was a few weeks ago when I was drinking more, when I could barely face getting out of bed at all. I let her and everyone else believe it because it makes *them* feel better. Now that the initial shock has died down – for other people, not for me, not for Kayleigh's family – there's nowhere to go with it, nothing much else to say on the subject.

It saddens me that I have learnt some things about Chris from this Facebook page, things that I didn't know before. What he thought about the local election in the spring ('absolute shambles'). I didn't even know he'd voted, or who for. Labour, I'd presumed, but I hadn't asked. When did we stop talking about that stuff?

I didn't know that he was currently reviving his teenage love for The Stone Roses, sharing 'She's a Waterfall' and 'Sally Cinnamon' videos on his page. He said that one reminded him of me and he used to sing it to me when we first met.

I didn't know he'd kept in touch with his ex-girlfriend, Jenny, from Peterborough. So long ago that he lived there with his parents. But there she is, liking and commenting on his posts. Asking him how it's going and whether it really is 'grim up north'. *Smug*, I think. Her teeth are very white. He changed his picture in May to one of him with his guitar. He used to have one of the two of us together, a blustery day on the beach when we first moved here. Before that, our wedding picture. I rolled my eyes then – I'd never have a coupley picture as my profile shot, I said. 'It's so naff.' But really I thought it was sweet that he'd do that. Now it hurts that he changed it and that he's trapped there behind the glass on his own, without me.

If I could get the password and get in – and believe me, I've tried – I'd change it to us again. Although I bet that would freak a few people out. But it would be a sign that I'm still here, that I still love him, that I haven't just presumed the worst like everybody else. That maybe after all this is cleared up, we could still be together. Even if I don't know whether that's really true.

Did I neglect him? Neglect us?

Not long before he went missing – three nights, maybe – I came in from work and he'd got in before me. He was under the duvet on the couch, even though it was summer, still light outside. I was annoyed at him lounging around, not being busy cutting the grass, making tea. 'Why don't you go for a run or something? It's a beautiful day!' I said, yanking the curtains open. I didn't know where the anger, the irritation had come from; I just wanted a reaction from him.

Was I even really annoyed or did I just think I should be? But he shrugged it off. 'Come and snuggle up with me,' he said, holding the duvet open, in just his boxer shorts. 'Let's watch *Lost Boys*.' One of his favourite films.

I told him, 'No. It's a waste of time.' I hadn't even taken my bag off but I was already tidying up around him, making my point, whatever it was. 'I've seen it before, Chris.'

I missed my chance.

Had we had drifted apart? Maybe it was too hard to see it at the time, when you're right up close. Like when you go for a meal or on holiday. You've put the time in, spent the money. 'How is it? Are you enjoying it?' In the moment, no one wants to say, 'It's cold,' or, 'It's not as nice as the last time. It isn't what I expected.' It's only later when someone will break the ice and admit, 'It wasn't that good, was it?' It's too risky at the time. When you're right there in it, you think you can still salvage something, things might get better.

There's Kayleigh's page too. I can rarely stop myself looking at that, either, scanning through as I have already done hundreds of times before, to see if there's any trace of him, a shared link, a like, a comment – God forbid, a photo that I might have missed before. No privacy settings enabled, access open.

'They haven't got a clue, these kids. They just don't care. Their lives just out there for everyone to see.' I heard someone say that on the bus. She told her companion that her granddaughter had been contacted 'over the internet' by 'some bloody fella three times her age'. 'We didn't have to worry about all this type of stuff,' she said. 'It's a bloody nightmare.'

I wondered if she had seen me, recognised me, and was making a point, but I think she was just talking to her friend.

I don't really expect to find photos of them right there on Facebook. Even if any of this were true, Chris surely wouldn't be so naive as to have photos on Facebook with a teenage girl, even if she might. But surely the real reason there's nothing there is because they had no contact at all. They went missing on the same day but they must be two strangers, parallel lines.

At first I was alarmed when Kayleigh started posting again, there was even a small well of hope. But her family obviously just gained access, and now they post to the account to keep Kayleigh's friends updated and to keep Kayleigh in their minds. The change in tone is stark, jarring. She grew up in an instant. From posts about tickets to see Nicki Minaj and showing off her latest bright blue nails and pouty photos, so many photos – the camera face perfected just so – to the latest posts since she went missing. One just after her disappearance reads:

Kayleigh Jackson: Still no news about Kayleigh. Please keep searching, everyone, and keep Kayleigh in your hearts and minds. Lifeboats and helicopters out to sea today. Thankfully, nothing was found. We have to believe Kayleigh is still out there somewhere. Someone must know where she is. If so, please speak up. We, her family, are going out of our minds. Kayleigh, if you see this, we love and miss you. Please come home. Janice Jackson (Kayleigh's mam).

Comments underneath addressed to Kayleigh: 'We miss you babe. Cum bk.' 'See you soon Kayleigh English lesson isn't the same without you!' 'Miss you bb.' 'We won't give up KJ.' Sixty-eight comments, rows on rows. I can't say the same about Chris's page.

I watch the video of Kayleigh again, the one I always watch. It's in the park, on a sunny day. It must be this summer because I remember the song was in the charts – Chris used to listen to Radio 1 in the car. He said it made him feel young; 'I like to be down with the kids,' he joked. I wince to remember stuff like that now. A throwaway comment now imbued with new meaning. They said this one was the 'soundtrack of the summer'. Chris and I laughed about the daft lyrics – something about being a wizard of love and having a magic wand.

In the video, Kayleigh's in the park with her friends, standing on the edge of the roundabout facing outwards. She's wearing cut-off denim shorts and a cropped vest.

When I first heard the song, I thought it was called 'Cherrypopper' not 'Cheerleader' – but I've looked up the lyrics online since finding this video. Now, I could recite the whole song. Kayleigh pushes the roundabout slowly with one leg then lets it glide for a while, the song playing out of someone's mobile phone close by, a tinny, hissing sound. Then she's dancing, arms in the air, whirling round on the spinning roundabout, her top riding up, slim white tummy on display, a green jewel sparkling in her belly button. Then there's a flash in my mind again, so sudden and violent it makes me jump, like a baseball bat full force into a mirror. Kayleigh's stomach, that glinting green jewel, Chris's hands. I have to shake my head to clear it.

Someone passes Kayleigh the phone and spins the roundabout faster, and she turns it around to film the park whizzing by, a series of coloured lines.

In another time, another circumstance, if it was Ellen, Jeannie's daughter, I'd be cheered by the film – a show of teenage jubilance – but now it just gnaws at me, twisting the knot in my stomach tighter. I see my own reflection in the computer screen, Kayleigh flying across it every now and then like a tiny cartoon Tinkerbell. My hair is lank, greasy, eyes circled with grey.

When the roundabout slows down, Kayleigh's friends are all laughing, bent over and pointing. When she steps off she can't walk straight, zigzagging all over until she falls, and the camera goes black to the sound of laughing.

CHAPTER SIX

Monday, 9 November

I try to avoid going back to the house as much as possible. But I have to go today because I am going to be out of money again soon. It's only a matter of time before the credit cards I have are maxed out or blocked. Borrowed money, borrowed time.

The fact he took the money still stings. It doesn't chime with the version of Chris – of me and Chris – that I know. It was partly his money, it's true. But it was *our* money; that's what hurts. Would he really take it and use it for something so hurtful? There's an explanation; there has to be.

After he'd gone, I went to take money from the joint account so I could move to the caravan: pay the first month's rent, get a few essentials. I just wanted to escape from the house, stay in the caravan where no one would come and find me.

It even occurred to me that Chris might be annoyed at me for using our joint money like this, without consultation. We were saving together bit by bit, £100 a month, for… we hadn't quite decided what for yet. A trip around the world one day maybe. More likely a new kitchen or a loft conversion, if I'm honest, but something for us. I was definitely angling more for the holiday-of-a-lifetime option, but having savings for the first time ever gave me some comfort. I didn't feel so trapped. If one of us lost our job, or if an opportunity for something came up… we had choices.

But the machine said: 'Sorry there are insufficient funds in your account to complete this transaction. Press OK to continue.'

What if it wasn't OK, though? No option for that.

I tried again – perhaps I had typed the pin in wrong, encountered a glitch, a ghost in the machine, but the same thing happened again. I marched into the bank straight away, full of indignation. It didn't even cross my mind that he had taken it, on top of everything else.

When I finally managed to get someone to see me, she explained calmly, matter-of-factly, that all the money from our savings was gone. All £6,000 of it.

'There's just sixty-seven pence, I'm afraid,' she told me. She couldn't meet my eye.

I couldn't focus on the information. I tried not to give too much away to her, to keep myself together. But she probably still thought that I was another daft woman who was too lazy to look after her own finances and had been left high and dry by her husband. And she might have been right.

Probably left her for someone younger, perkier, I bet she was thinking. Again, possibly true. Although most of them probably didn't have a missing fourteen-year-old girl factored into the equation; I had that on them.

I demanded a statement from her, just to get past standing there looking helpless more than anything, to look purposeful. The print-out she gave me showed that the money had been withdrawn gradually, in dribs and drabs over about three months before he went missing. The numbers and transactions jumbled before my eyes. Cash, no paper trail.

Had he spent it as he took it out, something impulsive? Presents and treats for someone. Perhaps it was a demand, I grasped, something beyond his control. Or was he squirreling it away, a longer-term plan?

* * *

It's eerily quiet on the housing estate, few lights on. Too cold to be outside, a night to huddle indoors with loved ones. Chris and I might have opened a bottle of red wine, watched a box set. I'll never finish *Breaking Bad* now, not without Chris. We'd be on the sofa. Heating on. My legs draped across his lap. I press my lips together and breathe through my nose slowly to kill the memory, quash the emotion.

The housing estate where we live – lived? – is deserted like always: beige identikit houses, still so new and pristine. We moved here from London last summer, when Chris finished teaching. I needed to be nearer to Mum and it was a chance to make a new start.

Chris loved London. So did I, but I needed to get out too. Friends were shocked that we'd move back here. 'You know what they say about those who tire of London, Becs…' Perhaps I *was* just a little bit tired of life by then, though. I was tired of the commute, the work-eat-sleep routine, the non-stop people, the tiny flat, the constant social whirl, the mice, the litter. I needed to get off the wheel for a while, rest and recuperate. *We* needed to.

I didn't think I could tolerate one more summer in London. Not the way I was feeling then. Once I had been excited when it was all new. But it had lost its shine for me, and deep down I really thought Chris was ready for something new too.

There were good things about living in London, of course. I miss the balmy evenings drinking in Soho and Covent Garden after work. Walking home late on warm summer nights, the streets still buzzing with activity. The exotic fruit and veg at corner shops, open all night – huge tomatoes, bright peppers, fruits I had never heard of. It's true that there's a thrill in the air in London that you don't get anywhere else in England – definitely not in Shawmouth. A sense that something exciting could happen. Maybe I talked myself out of London because I needed to be with Mum.

'We'll walk on the beach all the time, eat healthy, save up. We need to slow down a bit. It will be good for us, it's what we need,' I'd said, and I'd meant it.

Some weeks in London we barely saw each other, Chris and I, with early starts, meetings, drinks in the evening. We were so paranoid about not seeing friends, about drifting away from people in adult life, that we sometimes forgot each other, snatching a quick kiss before passing out asleep or rushing out of the door to work.

'We'll see friends all the time. You can pretty much walk anywhere,' I'd told him. And I know that is true now because I have done it so many times looking for Chris, rediscovering places I had long forgotten.

I'm standing outside the house now, our house. 12 Primrose Close. I used to think it was cute but now I hate the way all the streets here are named after flowers. It's twee and cloying. I just think of the flowers withering and dying, dried-out husks tied to lamp posts, like the ones that I saw outside Kayleigh's house, left by local people as a mark of support for her family.

I look up at the windows, almost expecting to see him appear. People say that, don't they? 'I just expected him to walk in one day.' It's a cliché but it's true. Except in my case, I don't know what I'd do if he walked back in. I think it's better than the alternatives but I can't be sure. Another reason I can't live here at the house. Everything; it's all Chris. The thoughts come even thicker and faster here.

We bought this house with what was left over after selling my parents' place when Mum went into the home, and some money from Chris's parents to make up the deposit. I knew it's what my parents would have wanted, for me to get my own place. Dad didn't agree with renting. He was keen that the money from him and Mum was put to good use. I never wanted to discuss it, because it was talking about when they were gone, but he'd plough on anyway, good-natured but serious. 'I'm telling you, Rebecca, don't squander it all on bloody clothes and shoes and daft holidays. You need to put down some roots, get a place of your own.'

'I prefer old houses, with a bit of character, you know?' Chris had said. We'd rowed a bit when I told him it was such an obvious thing to say. 'Oh, of course, shall we get one of the fancy three-storey Victorian ones on The Parades? Silly me. I hadn't thought about those.' I didn't need to be so sarcastic. Sometimes I just can't help myself.

Of course everyone prefers old houses with solid wooden floors, high ceilings, sash windows. 'But it just isn't practical, is it?' I'd said, internally rolling my eyes at myself as I heard the words come out of my mouth. But it was true. We didn't have the time or skills to do up an old place. And we certainly didn't have the money. I just wanted somewhere to live, somewhere that was ready to move into. With Mum and everything, I just didn't have the mental space to think.

Sandra and Geoff, Chris's parents, said if we must move up here – *were we really sure?* – that the house was a good investment, the right time to buy. The value would go up, it would be in a catchment area eventually. I winced at that. Chris listened to them, more than he listened to me on this particular issue, it has to be said. So he came around to the idea and then we just got swept up in the whole thing. Before I knew it, it was done. I was waking up in Primrose Close. Maybe it was a distraction, for us both – for me from Mum, for him from the massive change to his life this would be. The house, the planning, it was something to focus our energies on.

The plans for the estate looked cosy. It had a holiday village charm. 'Community focused,' they boasted. Everything was supposed to be developed with community in mind. There's a communal space, a little garden for each set of houses for the neighbours to sit and chat. Bins and parking spaces are designed to be set a little away from the houses, for the aesthetic appeal and also to give people the optimum chance of bumping into each other and interacting. This was all the spiel we got anyway. It probably did sound fake, but by a certain point we both blocked out any doubt. It was happening.

The one catch, though, which was mentioned less – but to be fair wasn't hidden from us – was that the development wasn't finished. They still hadn't built the school or the shops. The village pub was on its way and the rest of the houses would be finished soon, they said. Demand was strong for the properties, it wouldn't be like this for long. We got some money off for that, for the inconvenience of temporarily living on a building site.

But even after months, no one else came. The pub didn't materialise, neither did the school or the shops we'd been promised. It became harder to contact the company we bought from; they just fobbed us off. It was all still in the works, they promised; there had just been a slight delay. It was clear what the real story was. The economy suddenly tanked and the work just ground to a halt. They had our money, our signatures. We had the house. All the other stuff was hardly going to be a priority for them. Will it be even harder for them to sell the houses now that Chris's name is attached to the estate?

I try not to look at the house, keeping my eyes fixed on the keys and the lock, the task at hand. Despite this and the fact that I have no real affection for the house itself, the memories still flood in. Good memories, mostly. Chris and I, we were happy here. The day we moved in, Chris scooped me up and carried me through the front door, kissing me as we went in. I said he would hurt his back. We ordered pizza and slept on a mattress in the front room the first two nights, before we bought a bed. It's already too much.

Inside I slump down against the wall in the cramped little hallway. I have to pull my knees right up to my chin to be able to sit down in the narrow space. I press the heels of my hands into my eyes and breathe slowly. I am glad to be alone, cocooned for a moment, calm in the silence.

The door between the tiny entrance space – you can't really call it a hall – and the rest of the house taunts me. Part of me wants to go inside, perhaps lie on the bed or take a bath. I miss the full-size comfortable mattress and a hot bath when I'm at the caravan.

In through the nose, out through the mouth. Breathe. I put my hand on the handle but I can't do it. I can't go in. I am scared it will overwhelm me; that it will set me back. I'll be in bed again, like before.

I search the drift of post instead, adding most of it to the rest piled on the windowsill, starting to block out the light. Official letters for Chris. I open most of them now, just in case there's a clue, but there's nothing. Marketing sent in brown envelopes to scare you into opening it, fast food offers, bank statements, the emptiness of the account unchanging. My new credit card and the pin number have arrived – another temporary reprieve. Along with it, overdue bills that need to be paid, some with a reminder of what the consequences will be if I fail to send what I owe.

I stuff the most urgent ones in my bag and leave.

CHAPTER SEVEN

Monday, 9 November

This isn't my first experience with a missing person. The common denominator is me.

Mum went missing for a whole day before she moved into the nursing home. She was living in sheltered accommodation then. She wanted to live as independently as possible and in her own flat for as long as she could, and that made us feel better too. We went around to see her, Chris and I, the same as every other week, but she'd gone. We knew straight away something was wrong because the door to her little flat was open, not just unlocked but wide open, and banging against the wall as we approached. A boiled egg with toast sat uneaten on the table, just the top of the egg taken off, the gas ring was still burning, the TV blaring out. I was afraid there'd been a break-in, rushing into the bedroom, worried that Mum had been tied up and robbed. My racing mind even considered that she might have been kidnapped. Perhaps she'd be in the communal games room or someone else's flat, chatting. But she wasn't.

That was a sudden flash panic. With Chris's disappearance, it's something that has gradually morphed, more of a slow, nauseating churn. At first I made myself believe he'd be back, it was a blip, an anomaly. When the police took his things, something fell away. As I watched them walk away from the house and get into the car, I knew deep down then that this was something different, the doubt started to leak in. Then it poured.

We searched all day for Mum. The damp fog in the air didn't help. Chris and I looked in many of the places where I have since looked for Chris. The arcades, parks, the beach – although the idea of her in any of these places alone in her condition was surreal to me. In the end she was found walking near a busy dual carriageway in her nighty. A driver spotted her and phoned the police, thankfully. I think she may have been trying to get to our house but I didn't draw attention to it. Could she really have known how to get there? I felt guilty – guilty that she was desperate to come and see me, that she missed me so much. And guilty that I underestimated her, assumed she couldn't possibly understand where we lived or how to get there. But like the carers say, she has flashes of lucidity and then they're gone and sometimes she's almost like a little girl again.

We were told to wait at the police station while they went to collect her. When they brought her back, she looked bemused, shivering, her hair blown wild by the wind, her pink furry slippers matted and muddied.

After that and the panic about the times she had left the gas on, we knew she couldn't live on her own any longer. It wasn't safe anymore.

I've come to visit Mum today. I'm trying to gauge how she is.

'I've brought you some bonbons, Mum; the strawberry ones that you like.' I put the paper bag on the table, taking one of the pink, powdery sweets and popping it in my mouth.

'Where's your dad?' Mum asks, prompted by seemingly nothing. 'Where's your dad? I want your dad, not you!' She's lashing out as if to scratch me, her face twisted up. Sometimes she gets like this, other times she's perfectly polite, still others docile and dribbling as if drugged.

Not again, I think. I take a deep breath. Who knows what sparks these sudden thoughts and tangents in her mind now? He's died dozens of times this month already for Mum. But at least he comes back.

'He isn't here, Mum; we've been through this.' My voice sounds tighter, exasperated.

Her eyes well up and she throws the covers back, revealing hairy, varicose-veined legs poking out from the bottom of her nightgown. 'I want to see your dad!' She begins to wail, not angrily like sometimes, more a childlike whimper.

I try shushing her.

The staff here have told me that it's OK to fib. It's a white lie. 'Save her the heartbreak all over again,' they said. I didn't agree at first; it felt like tricking her, disrespectful, but I relent now.

'He's just gone to make some tea, Mum. He'll be back soon with a fresh pot and some biscuits for us all. Chocolate Hobnobs, you like those, don't you?' I feel uncomfortable with it, about to abandon the idea, but Mum turns her head and blinks the tears away, calm drifting into her face.

'He'll be here any minute.' I nod encouragingly.

The home, Sea View, is, unsurprisingly, on the seafront. It used to be the biggest hotel in Shawmouth, probably sold out most summers back in the day. Mum and Dad used to tell me how holidaymakers would travel from all over the UK to come here on holiday. 'The beach would be heaving. You've never seen anything like it. There was barely a patch of sand spare,' Dad would say. I probably wouldn't believe him if I hadn't seen the old photos myself. And from the pictures it looked to be true. Blankets and umbrellas as far as the eye could see. Women in swimwear. Who actually sits about in swimwear on Shawmouth sands these days?

A few years ago, Shawmouth was named 'One of Britain's worst beaches' by some travel website. I remember Jeannie emailed it to me. They said the sewage spewing into the sea was toxic, high levels of bacteria. 'Finally putting Shawmouth on the map,' everyone round here joked.

The nursing-home residents often sit in the window, blankets on their knees, looking out to the sea. Mum sometimes gets confused and thinks she's on holiday in Blackpool again. We used to go for the day when we were younger to see the illuminations. Then her and Dad would go for a few days on coach trips with friends from their social club.

It was only after Dad died that I realised how bad Mum had got. He had a massive heart attack in the garden and that was it; he just keeled over and died. People would say after, 'Bless him, he loved his cooked brekkies though, didn't he?' and, 'If only he'd given up smoking,' as if the idea that his death was perhaps preventable was some sort of consolation, when in fact it made it all the more upsetting. To think it was maybe partly his own fault, my fault, Mum's fault.

Before, Mum and Dad were always out and about – down the pub with friends on a Saturday; Zumba for Mum on a Wednesday; Dad would meet his mates on a Sunday afternoon. He had never mentioned she was having any issues. I didn't visit as much as I should have from London.

She went downhill pretty fast after he died. She started forgetting things, small things at first… where she'd put things. She'd struggle with people's names, repeat herself over and over. I'd notice it on the phone and when we got the train down every few weekends. Sometimes she seemed unable to comprehend even basic information. At first I thought it was just part of the grieving process; that her mind was on other things, like mine always seems to be: it won't focus.

So we moved here, to Shawmouth. Somehow, I thought everything would improve then. But Mum started getting confused about who I was. She wasn't washing, an unpleasant musky smell emanating from her that I tried to ignore. I couldn't look after her anymore. I couldn't keep dashing out of work in the middle of the day. I know she would understand. It wouldn't work, her living with me. But I still feel guilty about leaving her here, thinking of her alone at night, bewildered in the afternoons.

Mum shifts again, her eyes upturned. 'Is Chris with you?'

'Not today, Mum. I already told you. He has to work.'

She smiles but her eyes look panicky.

I try to visit Mum at the nursing home on weekdays now. Rarely on a weekend. There are always too many other people here then.

Some weeks, Mum's really the only person I see or speak to, if I don't see Jeannie or go to Barnacles. When I did go on a weekend at first, Mum would get anxious when everyone kept looking over, when it was all in the papers. I'm not sure if she fully understood why. Maybe it would be different now things have died down – well, had died down. But the staff here say that routine is good for her.

Some cookery show is starting on the TV in Mum's room and she claps in excitement. I smile to myself. Mum never could cook. Maybe that's why I can't either. We sit watching it in silence for a while.

I must have dropped off to sleep because I wake with a jump that makes my chest hurt. Mum has knocked a glass of water onto the floor from the bedside cabinet. The sleeping pills make me so groggy.

She is starting to get agitated again, the covers are lifted up and her head is under them as if searching for something.

I gently move the covers down. 'Mum, what are you doing?'

'My ring is gone.' She is rubbing frantically at her finger, scratching the skin red raw.

'We took it off, Mum, you remember. We took your ring off ages ago now, didn't we? Because your finger had got a little bit swollen.' This was months ago, maybe the start of the year. I remember the screams of pain as we wiggled the ring off with washing-up liquid. We almost had to have it cut off, Mum's sausagey finger pulsing inside it, squelching around the band.

'I want my ring!'

'Not now, Mum, please. I really… I just can't do this now. Why are you going on about this now?'

'I want my ring. My wedding ring is gone.'

'For God's sake. It isn't gone, Mum! It's right here!' My face feels hot and I am shouting. I know I shouldn't be. My fuse; it's so much shorter these days.

I storm over to the dresser, tipping out Mum's little trinket box. A porcelain, heart-shaped dish with a bird for the handle on the top. I slam the lid down, lucky it doesn't crack. Spreading out the beads and costume jewellery, my fingers search for the familiar shape of the ring. I hold up thin, fragile, gold chains and pearls to check whether it's become entangled.

Some clip-on earrings I doubt she will ever wear again – chunky pearl-and-gold flowers, a gold bangle and some green pearlescent rosary beads. I don't remember the last time Mum went to church. Not for years, though, I'm pretty sure. Dad's watch is there too – he wouldn't wear a wedding ring. 'People just didn't then,' they always said. So Mum bought him the watch instead. Somehow it's still working, and when I lift it to my ear, I can hear it, a dull ticking.

'It's a quality watch, that,' Dad would always say. 'You get what you pay for. They don't make them like this these days.'

All these things… just the touch of them sparks a vivid memory… a voice or a smell. I imagine that's what it's like for Mum too when for her those memories all get so jumbled up.

I look again. But the ring is not there. Mum's wedding ring. I instantly feel upset. I always loved it. She said she didn't like traditional rings. 'Boring, too plain.' So she had an engagement-style ring. As a child, I was transfixed by the large brown stone at the centre of the ring.

'Oh, Mum! What have you done with it?'

'I didn't!' wails Mum again. 'Wasn't me.'

I help her to look in the bedclothes and under the bed, although I know it won't be there. I scan the room slowly, waiting for a twinkle to catch my eye.

The small gold carriage clock ticks loudly.

'Why did you take it out, Mum? How can you have lost it?'

'Wasn't me! He took it!' Mum shouts. Spittle collects in the corner of her mouth.

'Who took it?'

'He did!' She points at the TV. 'Brian!'

'Brian? You mean Dad?'

'No, no, no. Him!' She shakes her head. Quieter. 'He took it.'

'Well, let me see about finding it today, OK? If you don't get upset now, I will find it for you today. I'll do some investigations.' I tap my nose.

'Simon,' she says.

I feel the blood in my ears. 'Simon?'

And Mum starts to laugh, covering her mouth with her hands. 'Simon,' she says again, more to herself this time. She lays her head back against her pillow and closes her eyes as if she's tired herself out. I kiss her head. She looks up at me, childlike again.

On the way out, I look in the TV room where Mum often sits, to see if Simon is around. Even though it's cold outside, it's too hot in the home. What felt like a cosy burst of warm air after the wind outside now feels stifling, and I rush to take my Puffa coat off again and carry it over my arm. I know it's a horrible coat but I don't care these days. It keeps me warm and I feel like I can hide away in it – I wouldn't have been caught dead wearing one before. I can feel sweat gathering under my arms and between my legs in my skinny jeans.

The residents – the staff call them clients but I can't get on board with that – sit in a semicircle in wooden-legged armchairs around a small TV; it must strain their eyes. A drab room – Anaglypta wallpaper, yellowing in places, and a maroon carpet with a clashing blue and yellow floral pattern. The pictures are all watercolours of children, boats or fruit. Nothing to get excited or startled about. Likewise, the residents are a sea of muted shades – bottle greens, maroons and fawns, some military blue. No shocking pinks or drop-dead reds here.

The air smells of sweet, powdery air freshener and cleaning products.

I try the dining room but it's empty, the places set for the next meal, in each a rectangular placemat and plastic-handled cutlery. As I start down the corridor to leave, I see Simon coming out of the staff kitchen. He's probably just starting work.

He beams at me, his black hair looking floppy and freshly washed, falling over his eyes. He's a carer here at the home, one of the few things that eases my guilt about Mum living here. He looks crumpled, like he's just woken up. I've often wondered if he lives here. Some of the staff are residential, at least part of the week. I am curious about Simon's real life. He still seems very youthful, but the few lines around his eyes and the grey flecks at his temples tell me he must be older. At least my age, thirty-five? Most likely a little older.

He's wearing similar clothes to usual: faded brown cords that kick out at the bottom, making his legs look cartoon-skinny, and a burgundy hoody, a band T-shirt I don't recognise. Soft features, long eyelashes.

'Hi, Rebecca. How goes it?'

'Oh, you know.' I force a smile.

He pauses to think and then gestures backwards towards the kitchen, inviting me for one of our regular cuppas. He makes a show of pulling out the chair for me to sit down, mock chivalry. I start to reply with a curtsy, then I stop halfway. I remember what Mum said, the beautiful brown stone in the ring.

'You going to see your mum?'

'Just been... How do you think she is?'

He considers before he answers me. To remember my mum's behaviour or to choose his words carefully? 'Not bad. A bit tired actually.' I notice he avoids my eye. 'She's been a bit agitated, you might have noticed?'

'Yeah, a little.'

'She's been awake in the night. You know how she is; she goes through phases where she's more confused than at other times. When I'm on night shift, I've been listening to the radio with her and sitting in there until she falls asleep. Don't worry about her, she's in good hands here. We're looking after her. You need to make sure you're looking after yourself, you know. She can sense it, don't underestimate that. Mums know, and all that.'

'Thanks. I am, I promise.'

He raises an eyebrow. Do I look that bad?

'You're going to get me shot,' Simon says, 'encouraging me to skive off like this.' He has his back to me in the staff kitchen and is pouring milk into sage-green cups.

He looks more serious when he turns round. 'Actually, to be honest... I mean she's fine, absolutely fine. But, like I say, she has been a little more agitated recently. You know, like before...'

The atmosphere becomes less chatty and jokey, the frost setting in after the word 'before'.

He keeps his back to me to say the next thing. 'I suppose it's with it cropping up on the news and everything.'

'She shouldn't watch it... I did tell you not to let her.'

'She is an adult, Rebecca. We can't police what she takes in all the time. You can talk to her about it a bit, you know. She might not remember or understand everything but sometimes it's best to carry on as normal.'

'Ha, normal.' I get like this, snipey. Simon has seen it before. But he doesn't deserve it. I scrutinise his face. There's a faint scar above his lip that I hadn't noticed before, lightly puckered. He stares back at me for a few seconds, then his face relaxes again and he glances away.

We've talked a lot at this table. When Mum first came in there were a lot of tears. He helped me manage things, find more information, navigate the official system. Who to contact, how to fill in forms. It's well beyond what he's expected to do as part of his job and I was touched at how far he went out of his way. He also helped me understand what to expect – about what Mum could and couldn't do, how she might decline. And he showed me how to interact with her again, in this new, unfamiliar way.

And after Chris left too, we talked a lot. Having Mum to talk about took the focus off me. The back of my neck prickles.

'Anyway' – he breaks the silence – 'it might not be that. It's common for people like your mum to go through mood swings, off periods. It's not always an external influence. Maybe I shouldn't have mentioned it, with everything that you're going through, but you're here now. And we agreed to be honest with each other, didn't we?'

'She's lost her wedding ring. Reckons someone's nicked it. Ugh. Have you seen it?'

'Me? Doesn't ring any bells from washing her. Could it have slipped off?' He seems breezy.

'No, she wasn't wearing it. It was in her jewellery box, remember? We had to take it off her. It was too tight.'

He scratches his head. 'Oh, yeah.'

'I'd hate for her not to have that ring.'

'OK. Leave it with me. I'll keep a close eye on her and keep you updated. OK?'

'Yeah, ta.'

He turns away and busies himself putting the milk back in the fridge.

'How come you're here, Simon, in Shawmouth?'

His head whips around.

'Me?'

'I don't remember you from school. Do I?'

A flush up his cheeks, his eyes fixed.

'No, I know I am pretty forgettable, but don't worry, we didn't go to school together.'

'It's fine, you don't have to tell me. I've just always wondered.'

'I just came for the job.'

I find this hard to believe.

'Really? You moved here, for this job?'

'Yep. I'll tell you what I reckon would be good. Bring some more of those old magazines and photos in.' He runs the sentences together seamlessly, so I don't have a chance to ask him more about it. The subject is obviously closed. 'She really responded well to those from when you were little and when she was younger. She was looking at the ones of her and your dad again, you know, when I popped in the other day. You know that one of them at the beach? She said that's Blackpool and that she and your dad had gone dancing there at the top of the tower. She said it was 1971 – their wedding anniversary.'

'Really?! Did she? That's actually right. It was their first anniversary. And Dad always joked that he gave her chip paper to celebrate – you know, the paper wedding thing. And she remembers all this, how? She didn't even know my name last week!'

He shrugs. 'It's just the way it is. You can't predict it. And anyway, I love old photos and I'm dying to see some more of you as a kid.'

'Oh God. How embarrassing. They're at the house, actually. I just had a few with me. So I'll have to – I need to see if I can get the rest. I'll do my best.'

A puzzled look flickers across his face but he doesn't ask any more.

'So how are you really, anyway?' he asks me, filling the silence that is settling on us. He reaches out to touch my arm but I slide it away.

Simon knows about Chris, about Kayleigh; of course he does. But usually we focus on Mum, the weather. We talk around it.

'Listen,' he says. He looks more hesitant now.

My stomach drops at the fear of more bad news.

'Do you fancy coming round to mine for tea one night? We can talk more if you like, or just hang out or whatever. I'm always in a rush here.'

I freeze. My lack of response hangs there, awkwardness growing.

After a while, which feels like minutes, he steps in. 'Anyway, just forget it. Don't worry about it. Maybe another time,' he mumbles, looking embarrassed.

Finally, I answer. 'Come round for tea? Chicken nuggets, chips and beans? What are we, ten?' I mean it as a joke but it comes across with more malice than I intended. He looks wounded and I feel bad.

'Well, the offer's there if you ever feel like it. Nothing fancy – just a catch-up, you know? As friends.'

I think of an early date with Chris, round at his flat. He threw his housemates out for the night and cooked heart-shaped pizza. 'Even the dough,' he told me, full of pride. He'd remembered I said pizza was my favourite food. He hadn't cooked for me in a long time when he left. I know that I won't go to Simon's. Somehow it would feel like a betrayal, some kind of acceptance.

There's a screeching of chairs and the saucers clatter; I realise I have jumped, spilt the tea, and it's burning through my jeans and into my thighs.

'What the hell is that?!'

'Oh, hello cutie.' Simon's bending now. 'This is Doodlebug, he's our new cat, for this place.' He pulls the cat in close to his face and makes kissing noises.

'A what now?'

'The residents love him. Your mum even had a little stroke of him the other day. Didn't she, Doodlebug?'

'Doodlebug?! Is that appropriate? Calling a little cat after a bomb?'

'Jim named him – you know Jim – a few doors down from your mum. I think it's cute. We mainly call him Doodles anyway.' He scratches the little black cat under its chin.

I shake my head and give it a little stroke. I am glad the conversation has been shifted on.

'Anyway, I best get off and… you know, do stuff.'

'Yeah, I better get back to work.' He pretends to be engrossed in the cat.

It's starting to get dark when I set off. I like this time of day – the air is fresh and biting and the sky is a navy-blue colour. I decide to walk; it gives me something to do, and I feel better about being out and about when it's dark. I am less likely to be recognised, and I feel a certain freedom in that. I walk along the seafront, the endless snake of cars moving slowly in both directions, people impatient to get home from offices and shops to cook family teas, watch TV, take children to evening tap classes and football clubs. In the distance, the traffic streams look like chains of lights.

CHAPTER EIGHT

Monday, 9 November

'So, how's it going? Caravan and stuff. Any news on the house? Or… work?'

I've come round to see Jeannie at her house. I think she was surprised when I accepted her invitation, used to me refusing. She is sitting sideways on the sofa facing me, one leg tucked underneath her. She tries to make the last question sound light-hearted, but I know it's the main thrust.

Jeannie is my closest friend. Friends since secondary school and one of the few people from round here I really kept in touch with when I was in London. When we were at uni – Jeannie in Edinburgh, me in London – we used to get the coach to see each other at least once a month. Get drunk on vodka and diet cherry-ade, go dancing on £10, share a single bed in the halls of residence.

'Yeah, I'll see. Maybe I'll go back soon,' I lie. I can't go back, not yet. Ever? I don't tell her that I've had letters from work. Voicemails. Asking me to come in for a meeting. Debbie from HR hoped I was fine. I should come in for a 'chat'. Delete. A letter came on headed notepaper. Sounded like more of a compulsory meeting than an informal chat this time.

I imagine they're looking to get more official now, patience wearing thin. Maybe they consulted a lawyer, were advised to terminate my contract, stop paying my sick pay – £88 a week. Covers some of the mortgage and bills, not all of it, but I still can't really care that much. The credit cards pay the rest. So many plates spinning.

'It's a decent job, Becs. They'll make allowances. They've been flexible with you so far. You need the money.'

It's true they have, so I feel guilty for hating it but I do. I work in a printing factory – supposedly as the marketing coordinator, managing the design of garish leaflets, sending pointless letters. It's more an office manager job, really. Re-ordering stationery and coffee, taking minutes. But they've paid me since Chris left, and before that they let me have time off to see Mum when I needed to. 'Not easy for a family business but we do our best,' my boss Mike would often remind me.

In London, I used to be on my phone as soon as I woke up when I was doing marketing at the university. I loved the job, thrived on the deadlines and problems, even the constant hum of anxiety about a mistake I had failed to spot; a message I hadn't passed on; a schedule not mapped out. It almost makes me laugh to think I thought I was stressed then, compared to this.

'You need structure,' Jeannie says, determined not to change the subject. 'I know you're not that keen on the job anyway. But you need something. Now you're up and about again, that's progress. But you need to keep busy; have something else to focus on. I know you think I am nagging you but it isn't good for you to sit about all day moping.'

She sees my hackles rise and holds her hands up to calm me.

'Sorry, mope is the wrong word. I take that back. I just don't think it's good for you to dwell too much. Being busier might be good for you.'

'Like I said, maybe. Soon.' I might as well go along with her. I know that Jeannie thinks I have to start thinking about moving on. 'I know it isn't easy but you can't stay stuck like this forever,' she says, when she's feeling brave. She doesn't think he's coming back, clearly.

She changes tack slightly. 'What about the house? You must be freezing in that caravan now it's winter. You need to look after your health. And it's a waste of money.'

'I can't think about this stuff right now, Jeannie,' I snap.

'Well, when then? You are still welcome to stay here as well, if you can't be at the house. You wouldn't have to pay.'

'If I'd known you were going to ambush me, I wouldn't have come round.'

I offer her a top-up of wine but she shakes her head. She's hardly touched hers.

We both stare at the TV for a while.

'Do you really believe it's unrelated? Chris and Kayleigh?' Jeannie asks me. I didn't notice before but she is quite drunk now, red dots on her cheeks, glassy eyes. We've only had two glasses of fizzy rosé and I feel pretty much nothing. I keep glugging it back.

'I can't drink like I used to now I've had kids,' she always says. 'Combination of surviving on two hours' sleep a night and living off half-eaten kids' food.'

Dan is clattering around upstairs.

'So, do you then?' she slurs again, emboldened, waiting for me to answer.

She's always been a drunk blurter. Any problems she's having, things she feels are festering between us will come out after a few wines. It's usually been good to clear the air, but this time I don't especially want to go there.

EastEnders is starting in the background, the theme tune grating and setting my teeth on edge.

'What do you want me to say, Jeannie?'

I think of telling her the story of a couple I read about once. They were both in New York, but not together. They were involved in a late-night, high-speed car crash – both drivers killed instantly. Investigations found that the drivers were married to each other, but they'd been separated for several months. Police initially suspected some kind of murder or suicide pact, but they said in the end neither could have known the other's whereabouts that night – it was just a terrible coincidence.

There is nothing to lead to Chris or Kayleigh. Not as far as I know anyway. The trails are cold – they're both simply gone.

'I have to believe that, don't I, Jeannie? I mean if I don't... then, what can I do?'

I had been hoping for a relaxing night to take my mind off things.

'Don't think you have to do anything.'

I don't like the arrogant tone just under the surface of her voice. I bite at my tongue to stop myself snapping at her. She doesn't deserve it. She's the closest thing I have to family besides Mum. And Chris.

'Becs? I am not trying to hurt you, you know. I'm just trying to talk to you. Apart from anything else, I mean, what about the gambling and the money? His job? He did lie to you, Becs. He cleaned you out.'

I feel like I have been slapped again.

Detective Fisher told me about Chris's job after he went missing, after they took his stuff away; that he'd been sacked two weeks earlier and hadn't told me. He'd been fired for gambling online at work. I don't think she believed me that I didn't know. But I had no idea. I was still making him sandwiches every morning. He was still leaving 'for work' every morning.

If it weren't for that, perhaps I'd never have any doubts about any of this; I'd never believe for a second that any of this could be true. But it's planted a seed of doubt, for other people – for Jeannie, for the police. And maybe for me too sometimes, although I push it out. He lied about this and I didn't have a clue. What else was he lying about? What else was I too stupid to see? I even considered lying myself; saying that I did know about his job, the gambling. Because it was, it is, skewing people's view of him.

I go to the fridge and get the second bottle of wine, the air hissing out when I twist the cap. I stand for a moment, enjoying the cool air on my face.

Jeannie makes her voice gentler now. 'I know you miss him and I know it's hard. But you can't abandon your life forever. Can you? You can't want that.'

Maybe that's it. The hardest thing. His disappearance would be easier to bear if it wasn't so open-ended. But I have nothing to hang it on: the screeching of car wheels, the torturous sound of a skull crack or a final death rattle. Would I really prefer that? Some kind of finality, however painful? But now, when I look back to make sense of what's happened, it's just still water, an empty street. No sign of a disturbance at all.

A creak from the staircase. Dan comes down the stairs holding the baby, ducking to avoid the slope of the roof. My eyes roll involuntarily. That's the end of that – mine and Jeannie's night in, having any kind of proper conversation.

The baby's face is purple, twisted into something goblin-like. Sam, I need to call him Sam, not 'the baby'. Dan jiggles him up and down half-heartedly, giving Jeannie a questioning 'I give up' gesture. He looks so tall. He is anyway, but my perspective looking up at him from the sofa, the chandelier-style light casting a wobbling starburst shadow across the ceiling, maybe the wine, gives a weird dreamy feeling, like he's a giant.

'Alright, Becs. Good to see you up and about again. How you doing?' he says.

'Good, thanks, Dan. You?'

'Yeah. Knackered, you know. I'm telling you don't ever have—'

Jeannie clears her throat to cut him off.

Dan offloads Sam onto Jeannie and he stops crying almost straight away. She tuts and puts him into the rocker chair near the sofa, looking at her watch. 'Well, that's screwed any chance of me getting any sleep then. Routine blown.'

'Sorry, I shouldn't have come round. I'm getting in your way.'
I make a gesture at getting my coat.

'God, don't be daft and don't go! It's just what he's like some-times. Sam, that is.' She shoots a smile at Dan and rocks the chair gently with her bare foot.

Dan goes upstairs and closes a door behind him loudly.

We sit for a while both looking at the baby.

'Look, Becs,' Jeannie says eventually, 'I didn't know whether to say anything about the vigil.' She's shifting in her seat, hold-ing her wine glass up and looking into it as she swirls it around, pretending to concentrate. She looks towards the baby. Sam, I remind myself again, it's Sam.

I feel my throat tense and my lips wobble. Stupidly, I some-how didn't think of the vigil being public knowledge. Jeannie squeezes my hand. 'Come on,' she says. 'Don't.'

Is that impatience? Am I making her uncomfortable? She has enough to contend with with a crying baby, I bet that's what she's thinking. It's not her fault. She just doesn't know what to say anymore, what to do with me.

I've learnt with people, since all this happened, that you have to support them through it, as much as the other way around. To be fair, though, how could they ever really help? They offer you little bits of solace that you have to swallow, or they just can't face it.

'At least you and your mum are so close,' people said at my dad's wake, mouths full of egg sandwiches from the buffet, half cut on the cheap booze at the social club. But we weren't actually all that close, not then, and so what? We didn't need to be – she was independent then. She had Dad. And my dad was still dead, so what difference would it make either way?

With Chris, they struggled to say anything at first. Everyone around me was on edge. But as time passed they'd say I was look-ing better or it might be nice to have a day out sometime soon.

Because they need me to be. Now I know to just nod and smile. They can't even acknowledge the abyss, let alone stare straight into it. And I can't blame them. Before all this happened, I couldn't have contemplated the blackness of it either.

Texts from friends tapered off after a few weeks. It was hard to tell if they believed the media speculation, didn't want to be guilty by association, or they just didn't know what else to say anymore.

I stare at the grey dots cast by the chandelier on the ceiling. Jeannie and I used to be able to hold a comfortable silence. Not anymore.

'How do you know about the vigil?' I fill my glass again, Jeannie eyeing me.

'Well, for one thing I've got a TV – you might have noticed. But actually, a couple of the mams were talking about it at the group the other day.'

'Right. Which one was it this time?' We joke about Jeannie's packed social schedule, with all her kiddy clubs, as I call them. Baby massage. Baby sing and sign. Baby art.

'Just a boring old coffee morning this time,' she beams. 'No wonder I am stacking it on,' she says, patting her tummy. 'You eat a lot more cake when you have a baby. Don't we? Yes, we do.' She switches to a cutesy voice and pinches Sam's cheeks lightly. He gurgles and kicks his feet.

I don't ask but Jeannie tells me that Sam is eating better now and sleeping right through the night.

'So we need to have a night out soon, me and you,' she says. 'Go for a meal or something. Dan can have Sam for the night; it's about time. And my birthday is coming up of course…'

I drink my wine back. It is starting to taste syrupy and sickly, my head getting woolly.

Jeannie is making faces at the baby, making him giggle. She looks pale and tired, purple under her eyes, small tyre round her middle visible under her thin top. I feel a wave of affection towards her.

'Yeah, maybe… Let's see how it goes.'

The stair creaks again. Ellen comes downstairs in a polka-dot onesie and pink dressing gown.

'Well, hello there,' says Jeannie. 'Thought you were doing your homework and getting your stuff sorted for tomorrow.'

Ellen tuts. 'I'm just getting a drink, Mum – and I wanted to say hi to Aunty Beccy.'

I love that she calls me that.

'Anyway, Dad's computer game is distracting me and when I knocked he said I couldn't go in.'

'For God's sake! Get yourself some juice – I'm going to talk to your dad. Then you can finish your homework and get ready for bed at a decent time. And you too!' she says to Sam, who gurgles again.

Ellen flops down on the sofa next to me and slurps on some orange juice, looking at me over the rim. She looks at the wine. I like her. I like most kids, but I don't know what to say to them. I feel on edge around them. Although with Ellen it's comfortable. I don't feel the need to try to entertain her or impress her. I think she's too intelligent for that.

Jeannie and the girls could never get their heads round the fact that Chris and I hadn't had kids yet; that we weren't 'trying'. 'You'll be a great mum,' Jeannie always said, as if it's inevitable. Not lately of course.

Ellen's twelve, only a little younger than Kayleigh. She's growing up fast. 'She's got more clothes than me!' Jeannie always says. And you can see it in her face too, the plumpness hollowing out. She pulls the belt of her pale pink dressing gown around her small waist tightly.

'How are you? Are you feeling better now?' asks Ellen, mimicking a grown-up. I feel a rush of love for her that she would even think to ask me that; that she senses or registers that I might not be. She must get it from Jeannie.

The room feels like it's swimming a little now, a queasy feeling swirling slowly in my stomach. Ellen swishes the orange juice around her mouth as if it's mouthwash.

'That's no good for your teeth to do that,' I say. She looks panicked and swallows it, rubbing at her teeth with her finger.

'How's school?' I ask. The ultimate boring adult question.

'It's OK. You know.'

I hear Jeannie's voice raised slightly upstairs. 'It's a bloody game!' she says.

I know that I shouldn't but I also know I don't have much time. I might not get another chance.

'Ellen,' I say. The sweetness in my voice sounds fake to me. I don't mean it to.

She looks at me attentively.

'Can I ask you a question?'

'Yeah. 'Course you can.' But she looks cautious. She knows the conversation, the approach, is not usual. Her eyes are shiny, staring at me intently, waiting to see where this is going.

'You go to the same school as Kayleigh, don't you?'

'Kayleigh…?' She looks up towards the stairs. Checking whether Jeannie is coming, or hoping that she is?

'Kayleigh Jackson. You know the girl who…'

'The missing girl.'

'Yeah, that's right.' I hate myself for doing this. 'Do you know Kayleigh?'

'No, she… she's above me at school.'

'Yeah, I know. It's an awful situation, isn't it? So you don't know anything about her?'

'She hangs around with a girl with blue hair. That's all I know.' She shrugs.

'Blue hair?'

'Yeah, it's dyed like a silvery blue colour. All the lads in my year fancy her.'

'Kayleigh?'

'Both of them.'

'You're allowed blue hair at school?'

'Dunno. She has blue hair. Silvery blue, like I said.' She shrugs. 'Mum won't let me dye mine.'

'You don't need to. It's lovely as it is. Does she hang around with anyone else, Kayleigh?' I realise I am being careful to use the present tense.

'A few other lasses. And some boys, I don't know their names.' She's blushing now.

'So, what are people saying at school? I remember when I was at school. There must be all sorts of rumours and stuff.'

She stares down at her lap, twisting the pink dressing-gown belt in her hands. Her shoulders are hunched, turning in on herself.

She just shakes her head. 'Sorry, I don't know what they're saying. I don't pay any attention to that stuff.'

'Yeah, you do right.' I hate myself for manipulating her like this but I can't stop myself. 'Do they say things about Chris?'

She looks at me. *Please don't do this*, her eyes are saying.

'My Chris.' I try to sound cheerful.

'Sometimes,' she answers so quietly I can barely hear.

'And what do you think?'

'I told you, I try not to pay attention. Mum said to ignore them.'

'So you know Chris?' I begin. I could drop this right now. I should. I've drunk too much and I will regret this, I know it. But I can't stop myself.

'Ye-es, of course I know him, silly.' She's trying to change the tone but she already looks stiffer, more guarded. 'Is he... is he back?'

'No, not yet, unfortunately not. What has your mum told you about him? You know, him being missing.'

She shrugs again. 'Just that we don't know what's happened and that he's just missing... And... and that you're upset.'

'That's right. But I'm OK. Don't worry about me. Honest.' I touch her hand lightly and she looks back up again. I try to smile encouragingly.

I gulp the last of my wine down. It's warm now. Sam starts to grizzle but I talk over him. 'Now, listen. I just need to ask you a question. OK? And there isn't a right or wrong answer. I just need you to be honest. OK?'

She stares back at me, stricken. Sam lets out another squawk, and she starts to go to him but I put my arm out so she stays sitting down. Like ripping off a plaster, I have to just do this.

'Did Chris ever touch you?' I can hear myself slurring.

Ellen looks at me confused, a little startled. I stroke her hair. This is all wrong. I shouldn't have started this.

'Just answer me.' My voice sounds strained. 'Did Uncle Chris ever touch you anywhere he shouldn't?'

She is starting to cry but there is this compulsion in me that needs to hear an answer. I shake her – only a little, grabbing onto her by the sleeve of her dressing gown. My grip is tight, but I think it is just the fabric that I have hold of, not the flesh. I can hear a voice getting louder. It feels detached. 'Just tell me! Tell me if he ever touched you!' I realise that the voice is mine. The baby is screaming now too, an angry, guttural screech.

Then, like a slap across the face: 'What on earth are you doing, Becs?' Jeannie is looking through the gaps in the bannister, then coming down the stairs as fast as she can. 'What is going on?' She's clutching at her hair and Dan is coming down the stairs now too. Ellen and Sam are still crying.

'I'msorryI'msorryI'msorry,' comes out of my mouth. 'I don't know what I'm doing.' I go to get up and accidentally kick over the wine glass, invisible shards exploding across the laminate floor.

'For fuck's sake.' Jeannie's cheeks are bright red. She looks set to explode, her finger raised to point at me, trembling, but then she pauses and swallows it down again.

Dan helps Ellen to hop over the broken glass and pulls her sobbing face into his ribs to comfort her. 'Come on, love – get upstairs to bed. I'll be up in a minute.'

Ellen starts up the stairs, still sniffling.

'I'm sorry, Ellen,' I say, pathetically. 'I didn't mean anything by it.' She looks back once but I can't read her expression.

I step forward to speak, to give Dan and Jeannie another pointless apology, but I feel a sharp pain at the ball of my foot, followed by warm moisture. I look down and there's blood on the beige floor. 'Oh Christ. Becs, are you OK?' Jeannie asks. 'Is it deep? Get some pressure on it.'

The chandelier shadow is wobbling again, watery.

I hop through to the kitchen and remove my sock, dabbing my foot with a tea towel. Used. It's not deep, but every time I clear the blood, it stays clean for a second before a fresh surge seeps out again.

'Do you think it needs looking at? Do you need to go to hospital?'

'No, honestly, it's fine. It looks worse than it is. There's just loads of blood. It's not deep.'

'Are you sure? I'm just going to…' She gestures into the living room with a dustpan and brush and some kitchen roll, and hands me a tin. 'Put some antiseptic and a dressing on it. And give it a bit of a prod – check if there's anything inside, just to be sure.'

At first the blood keeps making the plasters slide off but eventually, with two plasters crossed and a cotton wool square held in place with tape, it feels secure and the bleeding seems to be slowing.

Dan's voice filters into the kitchen, a low rumble. I open the door, approaching it as quietly as possible, turning the handle lightly to prevent the catch making a sound.

Jeannie is bent down searching for bits of broken glass, Dan stooped over her. 'No wonder he'd started...' I can't quite catch what he says so I carefully open the door a bit more. 'She's off her bloody head! It's no wonder...'

Jeannie looks up from the glass to answer him and spots me standing in the doorway. Dan looks over too.

'Rebecca, please, I am so sorry. I did not mean that.' He looks genuine but maybe he just knows what a bollocking he is in for from Jeannie after I leave.

'Becs...' Jeannie says.

'Rebecca, please, I feel awful. I was just blowing off steam because Ellen was upset. Honestly. I know this whole situation is terrible for you. She's just a little girl though, you know? My little girl.'

'It's fine, Dan. Really. What were you saying about Chris, just then? No wonder he what?'

'Dan, go upstairs and see to Ellen, will you? And take Sam with you.' Jeannie throws me my shoes. 'Put these on before you slash the other one open.'

Dan disappears upstairs, apologising twice more as he goes. Jeannie and I sit on the sofa.

Dan and Chris played football together sometimes. I think Jeannie encouraged him to invite Chris along, take him to the pub after. They got along well enough but it was mainly through me and Jeannie.

'What was he saying?'

'Nothing, Becs. He's just... just worried about Ellen. He's worried about you too. Do you want to sleep down here? I've got bedding and stuff.'

'Nah, I better get back.'

'Why? For what?'

'I just should. Aren't you angry with me?'

Jeannie shrugs, picking up the other wine glass and the bottle of wine. She's probably worried about me drinking the rest. She inhales through her nose. 'I can't say I'm pleased but – these things happen. You can't go on like that. But I understand… OK, understand isn't the right word. Of course I don't, but I know where you were coming from. I think.'

I let her give me a hug for once. Usually I shrink away, but I squeeze her back.

'Thanks for having me round, Jeannie. I know I'm horrible at the moment, but I do appreciate you looking after me – you're a star. I don't know where I'd be without you. I'll try to make it for your birthday, promise.'

She rubs the tops of my arms.

'Will she be OK?' I gesture upstairs.

'She'll be fine. She's a bright girl. She's sensitive and she thinks the world of you. She doesn't know all the details, but in her own way she knows you're going through a tough time. She'll probably forget about it tomorrow.'

I know Jeannie is lying about that last bit.

She calls a taxi and I begin to gather my things. A car soon pulls up and beeps outside.

'Wow, that was quick. You usually have to wait ages.'

'Jeannie. I really am sorry. I didn't mean to upset Ellen. I am just a bit up and down at the moment.' I stuff my scarf into my bag and search my pockets for my keys.

'Becs?'

I look up to face Jeannie.

'Did Ellen answer you?'

'What?'

'Sorry, I shouldn't ask. I am just checking she said no to what you were asking her.'

She definitely did hear me then.

I can see that she's cringing. 'I mean I know she would have; I just need to check. I just need to hear it.'

Jeannie has always stood by me, when we were younger and she still does now. She helped organise everything when my dad died. She always stuck up for me at school. She didn't think I should move to the caravan park but she still brought the car round and helped me take my stuff over, and she talked Dan into helping me move in and get set up.

'You don't know until you know,' I heard him whispering to Jeannie while we were moving things out and when he thought I was out of earshot. 'The guy deserves the benefit of the doubt.' This wasn't something I needed persuading of – perhaps just re-minding of from time to time. I thought she was on my side. She is, but this showed me that even Jeannie wasn't sure about Chris.

'He didn't touch her, Jeannie.'

She shakes her head. 'I'm sorry. Text me when you get in.'

She tries to stuff a £5 note into my hand as I leave but I run out for the taxi.

I've never told Jeannie, but the police, they asked me about Ellen. If they asked Jeannie too, she never said anything to me either. Because Chris had pictures on his computer. He liked photography, had a new camera. We'd been out for the day a few weeks before he disappeared; a walk on the beach with Jeannie, Dan, Sam and Ellen. Fish and chips for tea. It had been a good day, the way I'd envisaged our life here.

I'd seen the pictures already, when he took them. The police dug them out again. *Who is this girl? What relation is she to you?* There were pictures of us all – Dan giving Jeannie a piggy back, me eating chips, Ellen doing cartwheels on the damp sand. They were innocent pictures. The police were just twisting things, looking for something that wasn't there because of Kayleigh's disappearance.

CHAPTER NINE

Monday, 9 November

I lean my head against the cool glass of the taxi window, opening it a crack at the top. The wind blows my hair around violently. In the mirror, there's just a strip of the driver's eyes, like some weird masquerade ball mask, and every time I glance at the mirror, his gaze is directed at me. He's probably looking out for traffic behind, but it looks like he's looking right at me.

'Cheer up, love. Might never happen.'

It already has.

'I'm fine,' I say. 'I'm just tired.'

'Good night?'

'Yes. Not bad, thanks. Just visiting a friend.'

I try to focus on looking out of the window to avoid him chatting to me further, and to take my mind off how ill I feel. The toxic mixture of the wine and how I treated Ellen and upset Jeannie.

The empty streets whizz past; people secure in their houses: lights on, curtains closed. We go past defunct hotels – grand old buildings being left to crumble away.

On the seafront, almost everything is closed except a few takeaways. The metal shutters are down on the arcades, the restaurants have probably closed early due to it being a slow night mid-week.

I open the window a bit further to let more freezing air onto my face. The smoothness of the road and the newish car are making the nausea catch in the back of my throat.

His eyes flick to me again, like a ventriloquist's doll.

'You sure you're alright back there, love?'

'Fine,' I say, between deep breaths.

'I'm not being funny, love, but it is £25 if you're sick in here. And I would need to charge you, else it comes out of my pocket.'

'I'll be fine, honestly.' I want to add: 'If you would please just shut up and stop talking to me.'

He puts the radio on and begins to whistle along to some dance tune. The abrasiveness and unpredictable beat is making me feel more ill, and my throat contracts once suddenly but then relaxes again.

'You need to let me out.'

'Sorry, what, love?' He tries to turn to address me but doesn't want to take his eyes off the road.

'Please, you need to let me out.'

'It'll not be long before we get there – sorry, pet, I'm doing my best but with all these flaming roadworks… and we seem to've hit every red light tonight.'

'I just don't feel well. Please stop the car.'

The car jerks as he swerves it quickly inwards. He cranes his head around now to speak to me, a vein like a spiral telephone wire straining at his temple. 'Do you want to just have a minute?'

'No, it's fine. I'll get out here and walk the rest of the way. The air will do me good.'

'Well, I don't like to leave you at this time of night. Not round here. I'd rather drop you off, love.'

'Please, I will be fine.' I'm already getting out of the car. I talk to him through the front window now. 'How much?'

'Just six pounds, please, love. You be careful. You don't know who's about round here.' But I am already walking away and he drives off.

When he's gone, I stop and sit on the curb for a few minutes, my head between my knees, waiting for the nausea to subside.

I am almost certain I put one of Chris's missing posters on the lamp post here. But when I look up now all that's there is a flyer for a missing cat.

I think about what Jeannie said about me moping around, living in a bubble. She's right. I am out of bed. I've got that far, but it isn't enough. I can't just wait for things to happen. I know where I am going to go now.

It's after 10 p.m.: the high street is deserted. Some of the windows are still lit; mannequins with blank faces, no features, staring out. I take a deep breath before I go in. There's someone at the desk signing something, getting his wallet and keys back from a plastic tray. I sit on the bench and wait.

'I hope for your sake we won't be seeing you here again,' the police officer says to the man.

'Whatever, mate,' he says, shoving his items into the pockets of his leather jacket. 'Laters.' He raises his hand in a wave as he walks away, arguably giving the policeman the middle finger for a second or two.

'What are you looking at?' he says to me on the way out.

'Oi!' the policeman shouts, shaking his head, but it's half-hearted. 'Right, love, what can I do for you?'

'I'd like to speak to Detective Fisher. Please.'

He looks up now, less distracted. 'Concerning?'

'I'd rather not say.'

'Because…?' He has a bald head and smooth skin with bright pink cheeks, almost like a cartoon police officer.

'Because she knows me and I'd rather not go through all the details with you, if you don't mind.'

'Your name is?'

'Rebecca. Pendle.'

His eyes do a small twitch and he pauses. Do they all know my name here? Does the case still come up in the morning meeting where they decide on priorities? Is my picture up on some noticeboard in the offices, perhaps with red string or pen lines connecting me to various facts and times and places, like on TV cop shows? Or is it forgotten now, shelved?

He sighs and there's a beeping sound on the computer, diverting his attention for a few seconds, and he makes a few clicks.

'Are you here regarding new information on a crime, miss?'

'Sort of.'

'Sort of, or yes?' A sigh of impatience escapes from him.

A uniformed female officer comes behind the counter and whispers to him. He looks at his watch and nods.

'Sorry, where were we?'

'I'm here to see Detective Fisher. Is she here?'

He looks up at the clock. 'She is as it goes, but I'm not sure she'll see you. If she's still here it means she's got too much to do. And if you won't tell me what it's about …'

'Well, I am not leaving until she sees me. She will know what it's about.'

He raises his eyebrows and puts his hand on the telephone receiver.

'Right. What's your name again?'

'Pendle. Rebecca Pendle.'

He nods his head, gesturing for me to sit back on the seats near the door. He picks up the receiver and turns away from the counter, cupping his hand around his mouth when he speaks. Eventually he spins his chair back round and puts the phone down.

'You're in luck. She'll be down in a minute. Just hang on there.'

He turns back towards his computer and starts typing and clicking away.

Eventually, Detective Fisher comes down, the double doors clattering as she comes through.

She sits on the seat next to me with a blank notebook and pen in her hand, like a theatre prop. She doesn't say anything for a while, presumably waiting for me to speak. But then she gives in. 'Rebecca. Everything... alright?'

I have started to sober up a bit now; I don't feel so wired, and the determination I felt has started to diminish. I want to go to bed. But I am here now, I have to go through with it; I'd look foolish otherwise.

She is wearing the same cheap grey trouser suit she always wears. It's the only thing I can ever remember seeing her in. Perhaps she just has two or three of them so she never has to think about what to put on in the morning. It clings on her thighs and bunches up around her crotch. Looks like static would crackle off it if you touched it. She brushes her hand back through her cropped hair, grown out, style-less. Her cheeks are ruddy, no make-up.

She said I could call her Jane a while ago. I was wary at first. Was it a trap? Was she trying to get me onside 'woman to woman', trying a new angle on me? But I have nothing to hide so there's nothing to be afraid of. That's what I tell myself.

'I'm fine. I just... I just wanted to ask you a few questions, that's all.'

'Ask *me* a few questions? She looks at her watch and purses her lips before slapping her hands down onto her thighs. 'Alright then. Do you want to come through?'

We go through to one of the interview rooms. I was never arrested before, when this all happened, but I was 'invited to come in to the station for questioning'. I wasn't sure what that meant really, but I took it to mean that whatever happened, I was going to the police station.

She sits heavily on one of the plastic chairs and gestures for me to do the same. All the interview rooms must look identical. Windowless, marine-blue walls, thin, utilitarian carpets and black plastic chairs. A safety thing, probably. I think of all the people who have sat in here – guilty, innocent, bewildered, scared. The beginning of the end for some of them.

My heart is fluttering. It's just being in here sets me off. Detective Fisher, Jane, doesn't turn the tape on or anything. She's sitting less formally too. This is just a casual chat. *I came here of my own accord,* I remind myself.

'So…?' She glances up at the clock again. Perhaps she is due to finish work soon. Her eyes look tired, like she's been staring at a screen all day. Red-rimmed, the light outline of bags.

'I-I-I just wondered if there is any news at all? Any update?'

She raises her eyebrows at me. 'News?'

'About Chris. Or anything.'

'Do *you* have any news to report, Rebecca?'

'No.'

'Well, I would of course be in touch if there was any news to report that is pertinent to yourself.'

It's 'you' not 'yourself', I think but I don't say anything. I can feel myself hardening again.

'Rebecca, you seem a little… this evening.' She doesn't fill in the blank but waves her hands near her head, wiggling her fingers. 'Are you OK? Can I get you something? Water? Coffee?'

'No, I'm fine. Thanks.'

'Well, I have had a hell of a day and I am dead on my feet. Mind if I get a quick coffee?'

I just shrug.

She leaves the room. From the chair, I look around, scanning the corners for cameras. They don't look as if they are switched on but it's hard to tell. Could there be other hidden ones too? I wonder if someone is watching me now. If Detective Fisher is recording me, assessing my behaviour, talking about me with colleagues in another room. I don't know what to do with myself so I just stare at the floor. But I keep noticing that my legs are jiggling.

A few minutes later she comes back in, pushing the door open with her backside. She has two beige plastic disposable cups in her hands and a packet of crisps in her mouth.

She puts the cups down and blows on her hands. 'Bloody hell. Talk about bad design!'

She pushes one of the cups towards me – it has some sort of creamy vegetable soup in it. I can't remember the last time I ate powdered soup before all this. Now I can't seem to move for it.

She takes a slurp of her coffee and pulls a face. 'Ugh. Vile stuff. So, what is all this about, Rebecca? Why are you here now?' She looks at the clock again. 'We've not seen you for a while.'

'I was... I wasn't well.'

She raises her eyebrows, waiting for more information, but I hold out. I don't tell her that I've hardly been out of bed for weeks, sleeping away as many hours as possible.

She tips her head slightly to the side, but I get the impression that maybe it wouldn't be news to her; that she already knows everything that's been going on. Would she have access to my doctor's records? The therapist?

'I wasn't feeling great, but I'm here now and I've been thinking.'

'Uh-oh. Here comes trouble.' Her tone is neutral, lighthearted, and she follows it up with an 'out with it then' smile.

'I'd like an update on where things stand with the case; with the search for Chris.'

'Oh, you would, would you?' A flicker of amusement. She is licking salt from her fingers.

I take a sip of the soup because I feel nauseous again. My arm is wobbling a little and some of the scalding liquid spills out onto my hand, but I refuse to react. It tastes completely synthetic – savoury, liquid plastic. I think of it coating my insides, setting hard inside me.

'I'm sorry, Rebecca, but there are no new developments I can tell you about at the moment. I'm sorry – I can see how difficult this all is for you.'

I feel a flash of shame at that. That it's so obvious.

'So does that mean there are no new developments? Or that there are no new developments that you can tell me about?'

'As I say, there are no new developments relevant to you, at the moment.'

'But you don't tell me anything! Ever!'

'Could you please not shout, Rebecca? There's really no need.'

'Can I take some of Chris's things back?'

'What things?'

'His computer. Clothes.'

'Why do you want his computer?'

'It's got loads of our photos on. From holidays and that,' I quickly add. 'Why do you need to keep it?'

She takes a deep breath. 'Rebecca. No, you absolutely cannot have any of your husband's "things" returned at this stage. And frankly, I am not sure why you are asking. This is an ongoing investigation.'

'Investigation into *what*, though?'

'Into the disappearance of Miss Jackson, as you well know.' Her voice is still even, quite soft. She never shouts – she is completely unreadable. 'And your husband.'

'You don't have anything to connect them, though! You should be out looking for Chris in his own right! Not like some sort of criminal. You need to search again. He could be…'

Like a sharp headache, I picture him dead; skin waxy. Stabbed. Did someone kick him 'like his head was a football', like you read in the papers? Left to die? Did he slip and fall on the rocks by the beach? But we'd know by now, wouldn't we? Someone would have found him by now.

'I just don't understand why you're not out there looking.'

She doesn't say anything. I drink the rest of the soup, just for something to do to break the silence, and I almost gag when the slime from the bottom of the cup hits my throat.

'We're doing all we can to find Kayleigh Jackson. And your husband, Rebecca. I have shared with you all the information that is pertinent.' I hate it when she uses such official language.

'Did you find anything on the laptop? There's no evidence. None at all. Yet everyone is saying the worst things someone could ever imagine hearing about their husband. I haven't done anything and I'm tainted. It isn't fair. Did you find anything then?'

I always have to keep pushing, don't I?

'Find anything such as…?'

'I don't know, do I? That's why I'm asking you. If you didn't find anything, you should release his stuff.'

'Is there anything in particular you are expecting us to find on the computer, Rebecca? Because if you do know something, it isn't too late to share it with me. I just want the truth, Rebecca, that's all. Don't you?'

You can't handle the truth. The line from a film comes into my head.

Then Detective Fisher's calm voice again. So deceptively neutral, I was always scared I would miss the details of what she was saying, get lulled into something.

'I think we better get you home, eh? You seem like you've had a rough night. Tomorrow's another day.'

'I know what you're looking for. I know what everyone is saying and it isn't true!'

She sits calmly and waits.

It bursts out of me. 'I know you'll find porn on the laptop but it doesn't mean anything!'

I expect Detective Fisher to flinch but she remains impassive.

Another mental cramp. Before he left. In the spring? I had come down the stairs one night when I couldn't sleep and he wasn't there next to me. He hadn't come to bed yet. The laptop, the glow from the screen on his face, the fist in the groin. He scrambled when he realised I was there, almost dropping the laptop.

'I'm just coming up to bed now.' The clatter of his belt as he fumbled with it; the forced lightness in his voice. But what was on the screen? I didn't see the screen, did I?

I didn't know how to feel at the time. Should I care? Something in me did care, but lots of people look at porn, don't they? It depends on what was on the screen, though... I didn't even really think about that then – it was just the principle. Now I think about it a lot.

I realise I am pulling at the hair on the sides of my head to try to clear the latest seizure.

'Why do you say that, Rebecca?'

'Because loads of people look at porn! You'll try to read something into it. Like the photos he took. But it doesn't mean anything. It doesn't mean what people are saying!'

I think I detect a look of pity – or is it revulsion? – across Detective Fisher's face now, but she quickly recovers herself.

'Rebecca, I can assure you we will keep you abreast of any developments that concern you. But I have to be very clear here; this is an ongoing investigation and we have to keep all avenues open at the moment until Kayleigh is found. And that includes the possible connection with your husband's disappearance. As I have done to date, I will tell you everything I can. I realise this is hard for you. But to be blunt, it's more important that you share with me anything that you know, rather than the other way around.'

I can't meet her eye. I am scratching at a ridge in the table, tiny wood shavings collecting under my nail.

'Rebecca? Is there anything else or...? Can I get one of the lads to take you home?'

'Don't worry about it, thanks. I'm sorry I came. I'm just…'

'It's fine – really.' She looks me directly in the eye, leaning forward slightly.

I'd rather walk home on my own. It's clear I am on my own, after all. The police won't share anything with me. And if Julie sees me arriving in a police car, she won't like it.

'Look, I insist, alright, Rebecca? I'll ring you a taxi – you can't go home on your own like this. It's probably more than my job's worth.'

I don't think that last part is true. But I am tired now, and the foot that I cut earlier at Jeannie's is throbbing from the walk.

'You still staying at the caravan park?'

'Yes, why?' I refocus again, a reminder that I shouldn't let my guard down. I don't believe that Jane – Detective Fisher – doesn't know where I am living. But I am a little taken aback that she thinks I am so naïve. Not that I have really given her any reason to think that I'm not. I often wonder if they're monitoring my phone, my whereabouts, in case Chris contacts me. If I had moved, I am sure she'd know about it.

'So I can ring you a taxi then? I'll get you some more water before you leave, eh?'

I take three sleeping pills when I get back to the caravan, the bitter sediment burning the back of my throat. Eventually I feel the pleasing heaviness. Thank God, I am finally going under.

CHAPTER TEN

Tuesday, 10 November

I don't wake up until 11 a.m. I am relieved that it is so late; that a decent amount of the day is already gone. I can hardly open my eyes, or barely keep them open, they are so heavy. My head is throbbing too and feels like it's been stuffed with cotton wool. I lie still for a while, staring at the ceiling in the caravan and enjoying the silence. My nose is freezing and my teeth are chattering.

Unfortunately, I still have a very clear memory of being at the police station; of confronting Detective Fisher. I don't know what gets into me sometimes. I feel terrible about Ellen too, what I said to her, how hard I was gripping her arm.

I search for my phone to text Jeannie.

The caravan is a mess. Damp, musty-smelling clothes draped over the backs of all the chairs. Cups and used bowls in the sink, dust gathering along the edge of the windows. I need to try to clear it up later on. Julie might not like it if she saw the caravan in this state. She might think I am being ungrateful. It would probably be easier for her not to have me here; I don't want to give her any reasons to consider that. I'll wait until it's warmer in here, though. The duvet feels warm and soft against my bare legs when I jump back under the covers with my phone.

'I'm so sorry about last night. How's Ellen? Is she OK?'

I tap and send. I thought Jeannie might make me sweat on it all day like she sometimes does, but it isn't long before the phone beeps, making me jump.

'It's OK. Really. How's your foot?'
'Knacks actually! I deserve it. I know I need to sort myself out – sorry.'
'xxx come over soon.'

A text isn't enough, though. I know I've gone too far this time. I feel like I am falling again, back into the danger zone of staying in bed all day, my head under the covers, drinking, not answering the phone. Or would I even do worse this time?

I can't go back there again so soon. It isn't fair on Jeannie for one thing. Or Mum. I need to stay busy. I need to find some answers – it's obvious from speaking to Detective Fisher that no one else is going to give me any.

I sit upstairs on the bus. There's no one else up there. My head is still floaty from the sleeping pills, and I rest it against the window. The rain is creating a film across the glass, making the outside a blur, like a watercolour painting. Trees brushing against the window and roof of the bus give me a start.

When I get to the house, I pause in the entrance again, but not for too long. If I sit down or turn around, I won't be able to do this. *In through the nose, out through the mouth. Breathe.* I put my hand on the handle and turn it, pushing the door open in one swift move.

There are dust particles in the air, zipping around because of the movement from the door.

I head straight for the stairs, avoiding looking in the front room just yet. I'm not ready. Thinking of our evenings there, the indoor picnic we had on the rug on Valentine's Day.

But there on the step is the letter I left for Chris; I can't ignore that. It's in a closed envelope on the second stair. I left it on the day I moved to the caravan; the last thing I did before leaving the house. Inside on a slip of paper, it just says: *Dear Chris, I've just popped out. Phone me. Becs x.*

A few short lines but it took so long to write. How many kisses? *Love Becs* or just *Becs*? Hard to strike the right tone.

There's something a bit pathetic about it now, I know. But it felt much more possible then that there would be a simple explanation. That it would be a short-term thing. If you'd have asked me, I'd have said all this would be behind us now. We'd have moved on or we'd be working through the gambling, the job situation, the going AWOL. Kayleigh wouldn't be part of the equation because he'd be back – and hopefully she would be too. He'd be shocked to know the two things had been linked; full of apologies about the trouble he'd caused.

I can't bring myself to move the letter now; afraid of what that would mean. I can't rewrite it because I don't know what I would say.

I take deep breaths again and go straight upstairs. When I pull the loft ladder down, a light shower of dust falls onto my face and mouth, onto the cheap beige carpet. The loft hatch is stuck and suddenly gives way. I never really came up here – even though it's a new house, I still find it creepy.

I hated Chris coming up here so much; afraid he'd fall down the stairs. He said he'd started work on the loft, sorting things out. He was up here enough. Whole evenings, long weekend afternoons. He said he was reading, playing video games. There's even an old sleeping bag strewn across the floor. I played along with the idea of a den. But now I wonder what he did up here.

His guitar is propped up against the wall. £1,000 and barely played. It taunts me now and I think it taunted him too, that he hadn't learned how to play it. Ambitions not realised, money wasted. There's the chip on the base from the Sunday when he dropped it on the ground in frustration.

I can't see any signs of anything having been done. It's full of clutter. Boxes from London that we haven't even unpacked yet. It makes me feel sick to be surrounded by all this unused stuff. The money spent on it; the wasted time and effort buying it, carrying it from one place to another. But I couldn't persuade Chris to part with a lot of it. He said it had sentimental value, 'might come in handy one day'. And, of course, I can't get rid of it now.

It's dusty and I can only stand up halfway in most places because of the low ceiling slopes. There are cobwebs hanging in the corners in some places already. We've only had the house since last summer. You wouldn't expect it to age; the scum and detritus to accumulate so quickly. Boxes full of random crockery that we've long since replaced with new, matching stuff. But most of it was Mum and Dad's – what's left of the blue, floral set they got for their wedding present. We only used to use it at Christmas and birthdays when we were young. I'll never use it again but I can't bring myself to throw it out.

There's a box with a projector in too – all this stuff I've forgotten about already. We got it at a junk shop in London. Chris bought it, an old cine film projector and some old Super 8 films, unlabelled. We joked about having probably found someone's home-made porn stash or a snuff film.

One was a home movie; a chubby baby in a knitted blue cardigan and a nappy, a woman supporting him in case he fell, her body cut off by the camera from the knees up. The faded colours and clothing style make it look like the 1970s, like old pictures of Dad and me in the paddling pool in the yard, or out on day trips. It took Chris ages to get the projector all set up, and we sat with wine and crisps in the dark in the unfurnished back bedroom. But the film only played for a few seconds before bubbles started appearing, then a big black burn as if someone put a cigarette through the film. It spun faster on the projector, like a broken bike chain, and eventually the screen was completely black, the film destroyed. We tried a second one too – at an air-show, the old-fashioned planes flying in formation, the camera pointing at the sky on a bright sunny day. But again, the film burned up quickly. I thought of planes exploding and falling out of the sky.

I try to remember where the photos are, the ones Simon asked me to bring for Mum. There's a chest of cheap drawers that we had couriered from London for no good reason other than we were bringing loads of other stuff and we couldn't be bothered to deal with it at the time.

I check the bottom drawer, shunting and yanking it to get it to glide along the runners, sticking due to all the stuff rammed inside. There are Chris's old drawing books – the charcoal has smudged so much, though, that it blurs the pictures. I told him to hairspray them. Most are from the life-drawing class. I find pictures of nudes quite ugly but he said they were fun to draw – the shapes, light and shade. Even the idea of this makes me cringe now; I question the motive.

I always wished I could draw like Chris; have a talent like that. When I tried to draw, people's hands and legs would always look withered, everything out of proportion. Chris would say you have to look again, draw what you actually see, not what you think you can see. The mind can play tricks. It fills in the blanks.

There's a coloured picture poking out so I take a better look and see it's of the beach here in Shawmouth, done in coloured pencils – windsurfers can be seen in the distance. The sparseness of the picture, the smallness of the boats and surfers, gives it a sadness somehow. It has more of a childlike quality than his usual stuff, but maybe it's just because of the soft colours.

I consider taking the picture back to the caravan, maybe framing it, putting it up. But what am I even thinking? Am I trying to torture myself? As if I could bear to look at it.

In the top drawer, among old birthday cards, CDs for long-discarded computers and old notebooks, I find the photo album. The corners are bashed, some of the protective film over the white-framed photos is missing, but most of them are still held in place by the corners. Pictures of Mum on the beach, bleached-out colour, a red halter-neck swimsuit. I can't imagine her like that, in that life. There's Mum and Dad's wedding picture too, Mum's dress high-necked, long-sleeved, simple lace. A small flower crown on the top of her head, a chiffon veil spilling over her shoulders. Dad in a sturdy-looking dark suit, a matching flower in the lapel. I put the album into my rucksack. There's one box near the loft opening that isn't sealed at the top like the others. I know what's in it.

I asked Dan to put the box here when I moved to the caravan, after he and Jeannie cleared the glass up from the brick, got the window fixed. I'm surprised she didn't just tell him to sling it out. I can picture it now, him asking her if she's sure he should chuck it out. 'Oh, for fuck's sake, just stick it up in the loft, Dan!' she'll have said, exasperated. I take a deep breath. I was hysterical then, in a black hole. But I am stronger now, aren't I?

I look inside – the newspapers look older now already, like artefacts from another decade, a different life. Curled edges, faded print. But it's just a few months. I tip the box out, starting to feel hot and dizzy straight away as I remember the early weeks of confusion, panic, sickness. The feelings haven't gone away. It's less sharp but the pain runs deeper, to the bone now. Looking at the papers, the articles flood in all at once. I can almost remember them word for word.

14-YEAR-OLD SHAWMOUTH GIRL MISSING
Concerns grow for Shawmouth teenager: missing 3 days
Fears grow over missing teenager and Shawmouth man
Kayleigh Jackson still missing: not seen for 14 days

I pick one up to read

POLICE HUNT FOR MISSING MAN AND 14-YEAR-OLD
GIRL WHO WENT MISSING ON SAME DAY

Police are still looking for information relating to the disappearance of Shawmouth 14-year-old Kayleigh Jackson, who has not been seen since 17 July. Kayleigh left her family home at 8.30 p.m. to meet friends locally but did not arrive. She has not been seen since.

Police are also looking for a local man, 37-year-old Chris Harding, who is understood to have gone missing on the same day from his home in the seaside town, which he shares with his wife.

Police declined to comment on whether the two cases are connected, saying in a statement: 'It's important to be clear that police remain open to all lines of enquiry.'

Did I expect the information to change? The answer to leap out at me?

I try to push them out of my line of sight but my eye is drawn to the pictures in the article, as if magnetically. Kayleigh in her school uniform. No make-up in this one. She looks even younger. And then a smaller one of Chris – another of the photos they have in rotation. It looks like it's been taken on a night out, other people cropped out. Was I there that night, I try to remember? Eventually I have to prise my gaze away because it's burning the image of them, Chris and Kayleigh, together into my mind.

CHAPTER ELEVEN

Tuesday, 10 November

I sit on the bench opposite the school, a blue railing separating me from the disused train track behind, flanked by thick undergrowth, dense with rubbish thrown over, knotted into the undergrowth now. I stuff my hands down in my pockets and jiggle my feet to try to keep warm.

First one or two, then a small group, swelling into a shoal of blazer-clad boys and girls, spilling out of the school. The gates create a temporary bottleneck, encouraging pushing, shouting, jostling. No teachers to be seen. I don't know what made me come here. Talking to Ellen, maybe the newspaper articles. I knew I was coming though. I went to the caravan after being at the house, put my hair up in a bun, dressed in a vaguely smart outfit – black trousers and a slightly bobbly pink V-neck jumper from the bedroom. All my clothes are just piled on the bed. I smudged chalky concealer to cover my dark circles and scribbled a sheer lip colour across my cheeks and mouth.

Kayleigh's friends are one of the only links I have to try to get some answers. I've talked to all Chris's friends, here and in London; I can tell they don't want to hear from me anymore. Especially not after all this time – they want to get on with their lives, distance themselves from all this. I've been into the betting shops – there's nothing to tell. Some of them vaguely remember Chris coming in 'once or twice'; most just shrugged. Detective

Fisher won't tell me anything. I can't very well go round to Janice's house again. I wince, picturing her flying at me, hands in a claw shape, nails first. I can't blame her.

I've thought about it for a long time, held off. But I'm afraid I'm becoming more numb now. And I can't let that happen. Trying to get closer to Kayleigh is the only option I have left.

None of the school kids are paying me any attention. Perhaps they think I'm an embarrassing overprotective mother. I'm looking for a sign among the sea of young faces.

Two girls come towards me; they look about the right age. They're walking along but engrossed in the phone one of them is holding, laughing and pointing at the screen. The phone is covered in sickly-coloured, stick-on plastic jewels. I think of the rainbow drops sweets I used to eat when I was younger. The girl holding the phone has leftover red varnish in the centre of her nails, chipped off round the edges.

I stand up, clear my throat. 'Excuse me. Girls. Could I have a quick chat with you?'

They stop and look up from the phone – the muffled sound from a video they must have been playing is still crackling out from it. One of them looks me up and down.

'I'm a reporter from the *Courier*. It's about Kayleigh Jackson. We're covering the case, you know, since they announced the vigil.'

They look at each other.

'So, did you know Kayleigh?'

'Yeah, course we knew her,' one of the girls says. She is wearing teeth braces.

'So, like I say, we want to make sure Kayleigh's story stays in the public eye.' I hate myself for that last bit.

'She's in the year above. But, yeah, we know her,' says the smaller friend, reaching up to split her high blonde ponytail and pull it tighter against her head.

The girl with the braces nudges her, hissing, 'Remember what Mrs Whittaker said about talking to people?'

But she shrugs her off. 'I want to be a journalist when I get older,' says the blonde one. 'Not round here, of course. Down London or Manchester or something. I wanna work on like *Heat* or for a proper newspaper or something. Miss says she's gonna try and get me some work experience.'

'Sounds good. I'm sure you'll be good at it.' It's a chance to get them onside. I hold myself back from offering to put in a good word for her.

'Don't you need a notebook or a recorder or something? Or you recording it with your phone?'

'Er... when you've been doing it as long as I have you get a pretty good memory. And, yeah, I've got my phone to record stuff if I need to.'

'Cool. So what did you study and that?'

I change the subject. 'What are your names, if you don't mind me asking?'

'I'm Abbie,' says the blonde one, stretching her ponytail again. 'This is Jess.'

'OK, great. Let's talk a bit about Kayleigh for now, if you don't mind?'

'If you say so,' says the one with the braces, checking her phone.

'So can you tell me what she's like, Kayleigh?'

'She's pretty,' says the blonde one. 'Everyone fancies her. All the lads. Lucky cow.'

'Mm-hmmm. And have you talked to her or...?'

'Only a bit. She gets on my bus. Well she did. She seems nice. She ain't a bitch like some of them she hangs about with.'

'And – what are people at school saying about her disappearance?'

'Hang on, Abs. Hey, are you gonna put our names in this like? Miss will have a fit. You know what she said,' Jess says to Abbie.

'No, no, nothing like that. It can all be anonymous. No problem. So what are people saying about Kayleigh's disappearance, off the record?'

'Well…' says Abbie, looking at her friend for reassurance. 'I heard that it weren't the first time she'd gone missing. That there were a couple of other times and all and her mum had been worried about her. Her and Paige, who she hangs about with – bit of a cow – they'd been in trouble at school for twagging some lessons as well.'

'And that was recent?'

'Yeah, I think so, but I just heard it so I dunno.'

'And did Kayleigh have a boyfriend or…?'

'Well, she went out with some older lad called Adam but I think they'd finished. He works in town at the phone shop in the arcade. I think she likes older lads because she looks older herself – I think so anyway. That's why all the lads like her. But then they said it looks like something was going on with this bloke – the one who's missing 'n' all. And he's like in his thirties so…' She screws her face up in disgust and trails off.

'Anyway, sorry, I go on too much. These lot know her, like. Jack! Come over here.' She shouts to a group of boys walking down the road.

There's a small crowd gathering behind Abbie and Jess now. Two boys play-fighting in the road, another two standing closer.

'Who's she?' says one of the boys.

'She's a reporter,' says Abbie. 'She's asking about Kayleigh.'

'Are we gonna be on telly?' he asks.

'Do you see a camera? You dick.'

'I'm Jack,' he says. 'I was meant to meet Kayleigh in the park that night but she never came. We told the police all this.'

'I'm sure. And how had she been in the days and weeks leading up to her disappearance? Did you notice anything unusual? I'm just trying to build up a picture. Of Kayleigh, and of the time around her disappearance. See if we can jog anyone's memory.'

Another boy chips in from behind, standing slightly on tiptoes to be seen over Jess's shoulder. 'She was seeing someone.'

'The boy from the phone shop? Adam, was it?' I look to Abbie for confirmation.

'Nah, not him,' the boy says. 'They'd finished. He's alright. Bit of a knob but nah, someone else.'

Jack chips in. 'She'd been meeting that fella, hadn't she? He were ringing her up all the time.'

'What man?' I say.

'I dunno. She wouldn't say. Must have been that Chris bloke.'

'Maybe she was pregnant!' shouts one of the other boys, then laughs.

My stomach churns. 'But you don't know who he was exactly?'

'Like I said, it must have been that Chris. I tried to look at her phone a few times when it rang or she texted. But it was just a number. No name.'

'Here. Reporter lady – Nicky Blackett fancies you. Says you've got nice tits. Put that in the paper,' one of the boys shouts. Another boy punches him hard in the arm.

'Oi! What the fuck are you talking to her for?' A stocky girl with a heavy, straightened fringe and thick black eyeliner is coming over, with a smaller, delicate-looking girl with hair with a metallic tinge. *The blue hair.*

'Paige,' says Abbie. She looks nervous and readjusts her backpack. 'This is a reporter from the *Courier*. She's just asking some questions about Kayleigh. To get the campaign to find her going again.'

There's a crowd gathering round now. I can just see the identical green and yellow stripe of the tie wherever I look.

'Oh, shut up, you thick bitch,' says Paige. She has a dark foundation tidemark along her jawline.

Abbie looks taken aback. 'Paige, I wasn't saying anything; I was just telling her that Kayleigh was popular and how nice she is, that's all…'

Paige goes up close to her face, pointing. She's wearing a pink watch with sparkly stones around the face, brown marks on her hands from fake tan. 'She's not a reporter, you stupid little cow. She's that pervert's wife. Chris Harding's wife.' She knocks hard on the side of Abbie's head.

The girl with the blue hair touches her shoulder. 'Paige, there's no need to be so—'

But Paige shakes her off. 'Get off me, Kat. Not now, right. What are you doing here asking questions for?' Paige is jabbing a finger at me.

'I'm… I'm just trying to get to the bottom of things, that's all.'

'Well, I have heard all about your husband,' Paige says. 'Everyone knows about your husband, you know. Maybe I will tell a real journalist all about it, about what I know, shall I?'

'Tell them what? What are you talking about?'

She looks down and hesitates for a second, and I think she's going to back off, it's all hot air. But she hasn't lost her nerve at all; she's just gathering herself. When she looks up her face is all hard edges again. She fixes me with a stare.

'He got sacked from Green Point for looking at dodgy stuff on the work computer. My uncle told me; he works there in the factory. Probably kiddy porn.'

Stomach bile, hot and acidic, shoots into my mouth.

A few nervous laughs from those crowded round.

'That isn't true!' My voice sounds shrill. I can feel them all looking at me. There are probably only around seven but it feels like hundreds.

'So he didn't get sacked? You need to stop lying. And you need to stop thinking you even have the right to say Kayleigh's name.'

'Yes, but not like that. It isn't like that!'

She mimics my voice, 'It isn't like that.'

Detective Fisher clearly said he had been sacked for gambling on the computer. That's all. Why wouldn't she tell me everything if there was more?

Chris struggled to find work when we came here. Temped here and there for a bit. He eventually got taken on at Green Point, Shawmouth, a wind-farm plant just opened on the edge of the town. He was excited about it. I wondered if he just tried to be. He was interested in green technology, he said. It was just admin for now: raising invoices and POs, that kind of thing, but there was potential, he said, if you got in there at the start because it was so fast-growing.

'It's the only bloody hope for this town,' my dad had said. 'Over a thousand jobs have been promised for the factory alone. Skilled bloody jobs as well. Industry! It's what we need – we can't just send it all abroad.' He'd get quite heated about it, slide into casual racism if you let him run with it long enough.

You can see the wind turbines in the distance when you stand on the seafront, spinning round silently. I like them. The smooth swiftness is calming somehow. I try to think of them now; to block out Paige and this crowd around me. To erase what Paige just said.

She soon yanks me out of it. 'You're fucking deluded, love. I feel sorry for you. You're a joke! And not a very funny one.'

The other girl, Kat, twists strands of her hair around her hand. It's almost down to her waist.

'And,' Paige starts again, 'if you're so convinced that he's innocent, your precious husband, why have you changed you name back so you don't have the same name as him anymore? Embarrassed, are you? You should be.'

'No, actually. I never changed my name when we got married. There's no law that you have to, you know. Ever heard of feminism? Equal rights? Choice?'

Paige screws her face up, deep grooves appearing in her forehead. 'Well, what's the point in that? Why bother getting married? Not surprised you don't want to be associated with him. But the fact is, you fucking well are.'

A woman is striding across the road towards us now, looking puzzled.

'Hey! What's going on here?'

'Miss, miss,' says Paige, her tone entirely different. 'There's a lady outside the school gates acting suspiciously.' She emphasises the syllables of the last word, parroting the warnings they've had to report anything strange. The teacher already has a mobile phone up to her ear and she doesn't stop, checking for traffic as she powers over the road.

'Just stay away from me, OK. Stay away from my… home.' I stop myself saying caravan, just in case. 'I know you've been throwing fireworks and stuff. Just leave me alone, OK?' I say it to Paige, but then look around the rest of the group.

'Stay away or what?'

I push through the two boys behind me and start to run.

I hear Paige say something and someone replies, 'I didn't know it was her, did I?'

'Excuse me. Madam. Excuse ME.' An adult voice. The teacher is calling after me now but I don't look back or slow down until I get back to the seafront.

I am out of breath when I reach the end of the road. My foot hurts where I cut it at Jeannie's, and there's a warm wetness in my sock. Blood again.

When I look back, the teacher has stopped chasing me. She's just looking down the road after me.

I think about the phone calls. Kayleigh texting and talking to a man. Could Chris really have been calling her, huddled up in the loft? Pretending to nip out to the shops? Going out to play football? While I was out visiting Mum?

I close my eyes and breathe deeply to try to block out the images in my head.

CHAPTER TWELVE

Tuesday, 10 November

Julie lets me use the pool some evenings, even though it's officially closed out of season. I try not to think too closely about whether it's still being cleaned properly or not. I think the staff, what's left of them in the winter, have parties in here. I've seen bottles under the loungers and once a piece of foamy white bread floating in the pool.

I don't know exactly what they do on the site out of season, apart from drink in the bar sometimes, but I see them flitting between the vans still in their uniforms – cheap, faded red polo shirts with a yellow logo, staggering with buckets of soapy water or carrying straining bin bags. Perhaps they just have nowhere to go back to in the winter months. I think maybe Julie just keeps them on because they need a job. 'Julie's waifs and strays,' I've heard people in the bar say. I suppose I'm one of them.

Swimming helps to clear my head, and it feels like something of a luxury having a pool on-site and mostly to myself. I wouldn't come in if anyone else was in here.

I pick up my costume from the back of the chair; still damp from my last swim. I wash everything in the tiny kitchen sink but nothing dries properly in this caravan. All of my clothes have a musty smell to them. I should use the launderette in town. I wrap the costume in an equally damp towel that I pull from the mountain of the clothes monster on the bed – arms of jumpers tangled and knotted up with the legs from tights that I never wear.

I roll the costume in my towel and shove it under my arm, heading over to Barnacles to get the pool key from Julie. It's dark right across the site now, I can barely see where I am going. An almost imperceptible drizzle is fizzing in the air.

Something makes me jump. As my eyes adjust, I think I see something out of the corner of my eye, disappearing around the side of the van. I am aware of my breathing: shallow, loud. It makes me think of The Watchers' video again.

I stop still and hold my breath. There's nothing, no sound. I know I shouldn't, but I am drawn to look – I can't risk anyone damaging the caravan while I am out, setting a trap. I turn the corner quickly, ripping the plaster of fear off, hitting my shin on something sharp and metal at the back of the caravan. The pain against my bone makes my eyes water. I hear a rustle. My own coat, the wind swirling around me.

I dart between the caravans, but then I am out in the open again, alone. Nobody there. A light goes on somewhere – a caravan or a torch? Creeping around the side, I see it now, another caravan about three along from my bay; I haven't seen anyone around here before. I can hear muted sound coming from it, the walls are so thin. I cup my hands around my eyes and strain to see who's inside, but can only make out a bulky shadow, the TV a flickering square blur. Craning my head around, there's a crack behind the curtains, the sliver of a bulky man, work boots, oily jeans. I strain further, then panic when the brick I am balanced on for height topples and falls away, scraping against my ankle and causing me to automatically claw at the plasticky glass of the caravan window. I see his feet stop in their tracks, and he lunges for the window so I cower down against the side of the van in the dark, trying not to breathe. The door opens and a torch beam searches the grass. 'Hello. Who's there?'

Crawling along the ground to make the least possible sound, I manage to get to the far end of the caravan as he is at the other end, shining his torch in the opposite direction. Still on all-fours, plotting my moment to get up and get back on the path, I see something move again – but it's a few caravans away, obscured in the wheels and wires and shadows. Another pair of legs. They're outside my caravan. And they don't belong to the man whose caravan I just peered inside, because he's still there, shining his torch. I hold my breath and duck my head down again as I sense him move towards me, but he heads back inside the caravan. I check he isn't looking out of his windows, but the curtains remain still. The legs outside my caravan have gone.

And now I can't piece it together. Maybe I got confused in the panic, between the man's feet and the feet outside my caravan. I'm so tired – maybe I just mixed things up again. But I don't think so. I consider running back into the caravan, locking the door, but decide a swim will clear my head. I pick up my towel and costume where I dropped them, try to wipe off the mud.

The bar is empty and Julie eyes me suspiciously when I ask for the pool keys. 'You've not been drinking, have you?' she asks. 'You can't go in there when you've been drinking.'

'I've not had a drop all day,' I tell her. 'Just gallons of tea.' And it's true. Although I could do with one now.

I let myself into the pool house. It's a small pool, just for kids for messing around really. I imagine it's packed in the summer; I can almost hear the screeches and yelps reverberating around the place, toddlers staggering along the poolside in their arm bands.

I don't smell chlorine, certainly not as much as I would like. Is it clean, or stagnant and dank until the summer? There's grey water gathering on the tiles at the edge of the pool. With the bright lights on, beyond the glass is complete blackness and all I can see when I look out is myself reflected back. Even when I cup my hands up to the window I can't see anything except the November night. I half laugh to myself. Usually in films when people are in pools alone after dark, it's for some kind of love scene.

I don't bother using the changing room to get changed. There's no one around and it feels creepy in there, like you're hemmed in, backed into a corner. Instead, I contort my limbs to get my swimming costume on and remove my clothes without revealing anything, just in case. I pull the costume over the top of my leggings, then I wangle them out leg by leg, along with my underwear. I can hear some of the stitches give way at being stretched so far. There's blood on my ankle bone from falling at the caravan, and my shin is already starting to bruise. I twist my shoulder painfully, whipping my bra out from under the costume.

My clothes are piled on a white plastic chair under a brightly coloured umbrella. The water is completely still, with a few beach balls and foam floats puncturing the surface. Dipping my foot in, the water is freezing. It's too shallow to jump in but I have to force myself to climb straight in and put my whole body under or I will never take the plunge. I put my head under to slick my hair back before rising to the surface, gasping in the air. The water already feels warmer.

I swim breast stroke then front crawl for a few laps. Last time I did twenty without stopping, so I force myself to push through to twenty-two, my chest heaving. I am seriously unfit.

Clutching a striped beach ball, I lie on my back, staring at the pointed, glass-paned roof. I can see myself floating in the blackness, serene and weightless. I lie there for what feels like fifteen or twenty minutes, thinking about nothing except how light my limbs are, how good it feels to do nothing after the effort of the laps. It almost makes me wonder if I have drifted off to sleep.

It reminds me of Chris and me lying on the beach here at Shawmouth earlier this summer. It must have been in June. A sudden warm day so everyone swarmed outside. We shared a pair of headphones, one earbud each, and crammed together onto one towel. We were tipsy after a picnic of cava and crisps, looking up at the clouds, listening to John Cale's 'Half Past France'. The beach was overcrowded with families and groups of teenagers on a rare hot day, but we really did feel miles away from them all. I commented to Chris that it felt like the song fitted so perfectly. He said, smiling, that's why he'd put it on. 'D'uh.'

Even remembering the good times together brings me more pain than comfort. I try not to let the past creep in, but the smallest thing can trigger the deepest cut: a turn of phrase, a flash of someone's facial expression. A kind of déjà vu.

I need to go out again tomorrow; be busy; ask more questions.

My floating is broken by a sound. Maybe it's just the sound of the pool water sploshing by. But I am tense, on edge now, scanning the big screen of the glass ceiling for signs of movement. Then again. This time, I know it's definitely something. The door rattling? Someone trying to get in? I grasp to try to get upright – the serene picture in the glass is fractured, my mouth and nose filling with water, choking me for a few seconds.

I look up again at the reflection for clues – a faster way to see who's there, but the water is making everything in the picture move now like a hall of mirrors. After a lot of splashing, obscuring the origin of the noise, my feet find the scratchy floor. I scrape my big toe on the rough surface, trying to pull it round, and a faint wisp of blood curls up in the water. I freeze when I hear the next noise; the door rattling. I look towards it. A flash of colour. Or was it just the speed at which I moved my head, the shock? It's gone. Then the echoing of the door slamming. Did I close it properly? Has it caught on the wind? Like Mum's door that time she went missing.

I walk over to the metal steps to climb out of the pool. I can't seem to move fast enough, the water getting heavier and heavier in front of me. I eventually climb out, slipping off the metal step and bashing my shin again. I grab my towel, but it's wet through straight away, making me feel even colder. Pressing my face against the glass, I cup my hands around my eyes to try to see out, but I can't see anything. Shivering, I pull my clothes on over my wet skin and swimming costume. They stick to me, dragging against my skin. I turn out the lights but I can hardly lock the door for looking behind me and because my hands are shaking with the cold. Outside, I listen for the sound of anything but I can't separate the sound of the wind from the possibility that it's someone moving around. I make a blind run for it towards the light in the doorway of Barnacles.

When I get inside, in the brightly lit foyer, I can see that dark stains of water are seeping through to my clothes. My wet hair is dripping onto my back and the floor, freezing white droplets appearing on the strands.

In the bar, Julie is serving. She looks up and sees me straight away, a puzzled look appearing on her face. 'Everything alright?' she mouths. She is pulling a pint for someone. I nod but I just dangle the keys on my finger, putting them on the end of the bar in an exaggerated manner, making sure she sees they are there. I am stretching out like I am crossing a body of water, as if one foot has to stay on land. As soon as I drop the keys, I make a run for the door before Julie asks any more questions. I see her do a small shake of her head and raise her eyebrows.

It is so cold, my teeth are chattering uncontrollably when I get back outside. Back at the caravan with the gas fire on, I can feel the moisture in the air from my clothes. I barely sleep at all, listening out for every little noise.

CHAPTER THIRTEEN

Wednesday, 11 November

It's busy in the town. I wouldn't usually come in now in the daytime. Young children skip ahead of their parents down the pedestrianised shopping area, swinging bags or clinging on to the handles of pushchairs, gabbling away about their day at school. A cloying, overpowering smell and heat floats out of the bakers, where a queue to the door is forming.

I am hyper alert. It feels like I am somewhere where the music is turned up too loud. It's times like these that I'll think I catch a glimpse of Chris in a crowd. I consider turning back, waiting until later, but I am dressed now. I am ready. I need to push on.

Then I see her. Shit, it's Amanda from work – she's coming out of Marks & Spencer with another woman and she's headed right towards me. She must have the day off. She came to see me at the house just after Chris went missing. Brought flowers and chocolates and a card signed by everyone at work. It was painful: a fishing expedition. She'd either been asked by Mike, the boss, to scope out whether I was likely to be back soon, or she was looking for dirt she could share with her cronies over their Ryvitas and *Heat* magazines in the lunchroom at work. I tried to go to the kitchen to make coffee just to get away from her, to cut off her incessant yapping, but she followed me everywhere, poking and prodding me, asking questions in a sugary, mawkish tone. *How was I feeling? What had happened? Was I coping?* I pull up the collar on my coat across the bottom part of my face and put my head down, focusing on the smooth, grey concrete and powering forward to try to get past her as quickly as I can, without her noticing me.

'Oops, sorry, I wasn't looking where I was going!' It comes out automatically, though I'm too dazed to work out what's happened. I expect it to be Amanda but it's someone else.

The woman smiles back at me serenely, her frizzy grey hair catching on the wind. She's got a waterproof outdoors coat on and walking boots. Hand-knit fingerless gloves. 'Come, come, my dear. Please.' She guides me towards a cluster of chairs, as small as those you sit on in primary school. My buttocks are spilling over the edge of the chair; it feels like it could collapse. The woman sits on a low stool in front of me. 'I'm Mary,' she says. There's something unnerving to me about the slow, calm way she delivers her words and the blankness on her face.

Close by, other people are plonked on these chairs too, their carrier bags from JD Sports, fruit and veg from the market clustered around their feet. One man is crying, while a woman clutches his head at the sides. Her eyes are closed and she's saying something to herself under her breath.

'What's your name?' Mary asks me but I don't answer her.

'I sense that you have great pain in your life,' she says to me. Again, I don't reply.

'In the name of Jesus, we believe that God loves you and He can heal you,' Mary says, her voice as matter-of-fact as before.

Amanda is parallel to us now, so I can't draw any attention to myself by running away. I put my head down. Mary is kneeling in front of me, her hands are on the top of my bowed head. She's chuntering something under her breath. Nausea is welling up inside me; I feel choked, claustrophobic. The chair scrapes and falls behind me, and Mary stumbles backwards. She doesn't fall but the commotion means people turn to look.

Amanda's face screws up, then starts to change shape again. 'Is that you, Rebecca?' She stops for a moment to think and changes direction to come back towards me – telling her friend to wait. So I run, kicking the chair out of my path. My field of vision is taken up by a group of people – they must be some sort of religious nuts anyway – crowded around a young boy and his mum. They turn to stare at me and I run right through their little circle, the mother leaping out of the way.

People are stopping to stare at me. They probably think I'm a shoplifter.

I slow my run to a fast walk and duck into the shopping centre through the glass doors, drab spa-type music piping in so quiet you can hardly hear it. Inside, it's dead. A woman manning a stand-alone make-up stall twiddles with her phone. She's obviously given up on the commission and just wants to go home. I look purposeful to avoid a man hunting around for someone to pounce on about a cable TV subscription.

'Do you watch TV, love?' he calls after me half-heartedly.

I see the shop I am looking for, the reason I came into town, and go inside and pretend to look at phones, tapping at the screens. There are a couple of other customers in the shop. An old woman complaining about a bill she has received that isn't accurate, and a man with a glazed expression as he tries to take in all the information about data and minutes and models that the assistant is reeling off.

'But will I be able to send a picture message to my daughter? That's what I want to know. She lives abroad, you see.'

This re-energises the assistant even more and she flicks through the catalogue again, telling the man about video messaging and apps where he can draw on his photos.

'Can I help you, madam?'

I jolt. 'I'm just browsing, thanks.'

'Well, I'm Adam, and if you need anything in store today just give me a shout, yeah?'

I am surprised at how deep the voice is and to see that he is so much taller than me. I have to look up to meet his eye. His hair is brushed forward and gelled, like the teeth of a rake.

'Actually I'm a journalist from the *Courier*. I'm er...' That came out easier last time.

'Right. You looking for a phone with plenty storage then, for videos and that?'

'Not exactly. I was wondering if we could have a quick word.'

'Alright, yeah; is there like a specific type of phone you're after or something? A tablet?'

'It's about Kayleigh. Kayleigh Jackson.'

His manner changes from the polite sales pitch. He speaks more quietly, pretending to tidy and straighten up the display phones. 'Why? What do you want to talk to me for? What's been said?'

'Nothing. I'm just, you know, gathering some details to keep the campaign going. Do you have a moment?'

'Well, not really, no. I'm working.'

I look at my wrist, but I'm not actually wearing a watch. His eyes follow my hand.

'No one wears them anymore, do they?' I say, breezy. 'When do you finish? I could wait for you; or I could come back.'

He looks over his shoulder towards the rest of the shop, then back to me. 'Look, I'll meet you out front in a minute, right.'

He shouts down to his colleague. 'Mark? Am nipping out for me break while it's quiet, right?'

'Well, actually it's not really a good time, mate,' his colleague says.

I go out and wait on the bench outside.

He comes out of the shop pulling a hooded top over his head. He doesn't come over to the bench but turns right and keeps walking. So I follow him, half jogging to catch up.

'You can buy us a drink then. I've not sat down all day.'

We go into Costa Coffee and Adam sits down on a stool at the window bench looking out into the shopping centre.

'I'll have a large mocha with cream. And a brownie. Chocolate. Cheers, you can put it on your expenses, can't you? Can't wait till I get a job where I can claim expenses, me. And get a car.'

I order for him and buy a tea for myself, clenching my fists and pushing my nails into the palm of my hand as I make the card payment, praying it won't be declined.

He rubs his hands together as I pass him his drink; so big that it has two handles.

'Have we talked before?' Adam asks. 'You look familiar.'

'Erm… yeah, I think we did. A while ago now. When… well, you know, when all this first happened.'

'Because I ain't never talked to the papers before. That's all. No one asked me, to be honest. I don't read the papers anyway. Especially not after all this. My dad says I should. But it's all so depressing, isn't it? I'd rather not know.'

'Yeah, you're not wrong there. Hmmm… maybe you've seen me in the shop then, I don't know. I'm always losing my phone or breaking things. And it's such a small town anyway, isn't it?'

He frowns and seems to scrutinise my face. 'So what's this about then? Why you wanting to talk to me now?'

'Well, you know, with the vigil and everything. Kayleigh's birthday coming up… I just wanted to revisit things. Make sure people remember Kayleigh, yeah?'

He scoops cream out from the cup with his finger.

'So, I understand you used to go out with Kayleigh?'

'Yeah, but we split up. Not long before she went missing. But… but that don't mean nothing. Don't write that.'

I don't say anything; I just look at him, willing him to continue. The less I say, the better.

'Look I'm not a suspect or nothing so you better not print that. I've told the police everything and it's all above board.'

'Don't worry. That's not what I am getting at at all. I'm just trying to build up a picture of Kayleigh. Who she really was. Those last few weeks before she went missing. Jog people's memories, you know?'

'OK.' He looks unsure but shoves almost half the brownie in his mouth at once, using the thin wooden stirrer to load it with cream first.

'So, were you and Kayleigh together long?'

His eyes are fixed while he chews and it seems to take forever for him to swallow. I wonder if he is playing for time. 'Erm, quite a while, like a month or six weeks or something. I liked her but she were a lot to handle, you know.'

It's sweet that he classes a month as 'quite a while' in relationship terms. It is when you're a teenager.

'How do you mean, "a lot to handle"?'

'Sometimes she didn't turn up to meet me and she wouldn't say why. And she wanted to go fancy places – like clubbing or buying stuff in town. Trainers, games, clothes and that. I'm working full time but I don't have the money. I'm saving up for a car.'

'OK. How old are you, Adam?'

'I'm seventeen. So, listen, I don't want my name in the paper, right? I'm trusting you because I want to find her – after all this time, we need to do more. But I want to apply to go in the army. I can't risk my chances with anything like this.'

'OK, that's fine. I don't have to name names. Hey, I don't even know your last name and I am not going to ask. So Kayleigh wanted you to buy her stuff?'

'Nah, it weren't really that – she had money herself. I dunno where she was getting the money but I can't have my girlfriend paying for everything. I felt like I had to try to keep up with her.'

'And that's why you broke up?'

'That was part of it, but it weren't just that. She went home late one night, her mum hadn't been able to get her on her phone.

Sometimes I couldn't neither. It weren't nothing to do with me, though. I live with my mum – I can't have girls back at mine or nothing like that. I mean, please. Ugh.' He screws his face up at the idea. 'But her mum came into the shop shouting the odds at me and to keep away from her daughter. Kayleigh told her she had been with me. But she weren't.'

'What do you mean? So Kayleigh went missing before?'

'Well, she weren't *missing* missing. Not like now. More like she was off the radar when she wanted to be. Her mum was worried. And I'm thinking she's saying she's with me but she ain't, so where is she? I just thought, I don't need it, you know? I didn't want to get involved. I ain't getting blamed for that shit. I'm going in the army, that's what I'm focused on now.'

We both look out of the window for a while. A few schoolkids wander past but the centre is emptying out now, people heading home for tea.

His phrasing 'off the radar when she wanted to be' catches in my mind. I hadn't been able to put my finger on it before, but that's how I'd sometimes felt with Chris too. His battery was often gone on his phone – straight to voicemail. Or he'd go out for the day to work or to football, or saying he was going to take pictures, and leave his phone at home. It annoyed me, but it almost became a running joke about him being scatty. Doesn't feel so funny now.

'I didn't like it. I just thought… it weren't going to be worth it, you know?'

I take a sip of my tea, gone cold now.

'I mean it's a shame. She's a really nice girl and that. Just dead sound.'

'And… you didn't think she was too young for you?'

He straightens his back at this, bristling.

'Well, she said she was sixteen. I believed her.'

He drains the rest of his drink and checks his phone. 'Nothing happened though like… you know, like that. Nah nah nah. I swear. I only knew she was younger when all this came out when she went missing. We just met up in town a few times on a night and at the weekend and that, and that was it. It weren't serious but I thought she was nice. I liked her. She was funny and stuff.'

'And you didn't see her again before she went missing?'

'No. That was it. I'm upset, don't get me wrong. I hope she's alright and she's found. Or maybe she's happy or whatever, I don't know. I mean, it's pretty fucked up however you look at it. But I just want to put it behind me, you know?'

'I understand.'

'Listen, I better go. I'm gonna be late back. My boss already hates me and my mum will have me if I get sacked.'

'OK, thanks, Adam. Take it easy.'

He looks back at me again and shakes his head. 'I'm sure I do recognise you from somewhere.'

Back out on the high street, some of the shops are already starting to close. There are lights off in some; in others people are cashing up or hoovering, ready for tomorrow.

I head to the seafront and sit there on a bench for over an hour. The waves are hypnotic. But something keeps pulling me out of the trance I'd prefer to be in. It's the money. Adam said Kayleigh had money. A knot in my mind. The day we went to the beach with Jeannie and Dan. Ellen tried to give Chris the change from the chips. They were standing a little way off and he dropped it back into her pink beaded purse. She grinned and flushed. Every memory gets poisoned.

The idea that Chris could have been giving Kayleigh money keeps pushing in. Our money, my money – all of it – gone. And my dad's voice is stirred up from somewhere, how he always used to say, 'You don't get anything for nothing.'

CHAPTER FOURTEEN

Wednesday, 11 November

Everyone round here calls the street I am standing on now 'Cheap Street' because it's full of pound shops, Cash Converters, a food weigh house, charity shops. There are two dodgy pubs and a Tesco Express. I pop in there to buy teabags and tins of soup. The white strip lighting in the store is harsh and bright. Outside, it's dark now, starting to rain, so I put up the hood on my coat and pull the tie around my face. The lights from the shops create blurred, coloured ribbons across the puddles on the street.

There are people crowded outside The Grapes pub smoking, despite the weather. A paper sign in the window advertises the cheapest drinks in town. Inside it already looks busy: men in hi-vis jackets and boots stand at the bar, the after-work drinkers. 'She Loves You' by The Beatles blares out. It's the bright blue that gets my attention. Someone is drinking something the shade of a highlighter pen. The pop of colour catches my eye against the grey drizzle. It's Paige.

She has the hood of her jersey top up but she's arranged her hair carefully at the front, tendrils framing her face. She's leaning against the wall, one leg bent up, engrossed in her phone. I think about going over, trying to smooth things out from the other day at the school, see if she's willing to talk any more now that she's on her own. But before I can make a decision, a man goes over to her and claps his hands in front of her face. She jumps a little.

She holds the straw to her mouth and drinks while he talks to her. She seems detached, disinterested.

After a while, Paige tips her head to the side and gestures to the man to walk with her. He follows with his hands in his pockets and his step has a bounce to it.

I go after them, a safe distance behind. We go past the pound shop, toilet rolls and tubs of fat balls for birds stacked in the window. Past the bookies, the bright lights glowing around the edge of the window, but what's going on inside is hidden by digital screens explaining the latest odds. It's one of the betting shops I went into after I found out about Chris's gambling from Detective Fisher. The police probably checked the CCTV from all the betting shops too. In some of the gambling places, they told me they remembered him. But so what? He gambled – after the shock of initially finding that out, him being seen in a bookie's didn't really tell me anything new.

We pass the other pub on the street, and the man high-fives someone drinking in the doorway. After he and Paige have passed, he turns round and walks backwards for a few paces. 'Y'alright, mate? Aye, aye, sound, mate, sound.' Even from here I can see his cheekbones jut out through his skin.

Every so often Paige adjusts her hood. I worry that she is going to turn round and see me, but she doesn't. What would she do? It's hard to tell if they are chatting, like friends, or walking in silence. I can't risk getting close enough to find out.

They walk up one of the alleys towards the seafront – the street is narrow, I could too easily be seen, so I decide to go up the parallel one. I don't really know why I am following them. *Closer to the truth about Kayleigh, closer to the truth about Chris.* It makes me want to turn and go back again.

I run quickly up the side street; I don't want to lose them. All the shops are closed and it's eerily quiet, badly lit. They're nowhere to be seen when I reach the top. I think they must have got away. *Got away*. Listen to me, running around Shawmouth like I'm in a 1970s detective show.

But when I look down the alley, they've stopped; they look like they're having a row. He tries to walk away, back the way they came, but she grabs his sleeve and pulls him back. They're coming up the alley again, faster now, so I move away and stand in a doorway, shrinking into my hood, pretending to look at my phone. They cross the street, waiting in the middle for the traffic to pass, her gripping on to the sleeve of his jacket. I think they must be heading for the bus but they walk the other way from the stop. They turn to go down the steps to the beach. I cross too and reach the top of the steps.

There's a level between the beach and the road because it's so far down. Down the first flight of stairs is a concrete stretch and some benches under a wooden canopy. Elderly people often sit here to watch the sea. When I've been here for an early-morning walk, I've seen tramps lying on the benches under newspapers, empty bottles nearby.

I can't follow them down because it would be too obvious, but I stand as close as I can without being seen. I can hear them talking, but over the waves and the wind the sound cuts in and out, just broken words. The man's voice sounds raised, a whiney edge to it, but maybe it's just the way the sound is carrying.

A woman comes along walking her dog, a fluffy white husky type. She lets it run on a long, extendable lead for a while but when she sees Paige and the man she calls, 'Come on, Sheba, come on, girl,' and pulls the lead back in, looking back a couple of times as she goes up the steps.

I chance a look, and Paige and the man have their backs to me now. They're going into the disabled toilet. She looks out before closing the door but she doesn't see me. From my vantage point I can just see a corner of the floor in the toilet, covered in muddy footprints. Bile shoots into my mouth, hot and acidic.

I wait. A couple of people walk past, eyeing me suspiciously, so I return to pretending to look at my phone until I hear the lock click again. I cross over the road to watch from the doorway.

When they get to the top of the steps, they exchange a few words. The man comes over the road towards me. I notice again how hollow his cheeks are, his eyes sunken. I think of the Mexican Day of the Dead festival, a Halloween house party Chris and I once went to. I look right at him but he doesn't notice. He goes back down a side street, probably towards town again. Paige is sitting on the railing, one leg hooked over, talking on the phone, and fighting against her hair blowing across her face. I wince to think of her falling backwards. A long drop to the concrete ground below. Eventually, she hops off and crosses the road. She doesn't see me.

She goes back down the side street she came up with the man. I keep a safe distance and go to follow her, but she goes inside the only building with its lights on. I stand and wait for a while but she doesn't come back out. I walk past; it's a takeaway. A white cube in the otherwise darkened street. There's just one man, his back to me, agitating the fryers. Paige is nowhere to be seen.

I recognise the place now that I'm standing in front of it. Dirty windows, starving drunks. We saw a fight in there once when we were walking past on the way home from a night out. A group of lads. The place exploded in arms and legs flying everywhere, blood splattered across the white wall tiles. I remember dragging Chris away by his arm, saying we shouldn't get involved. Selfishness, really.

The wind is freezing now, causing my eyes to water. It's making a howling and whistling sound, clattering empty cans along the side of the road and sending crisp packets swirling into the air.

The walk back to the caravan park seems to take ages and my shopping bag is beginning to cut into my fingers.

I decide to go to Barnacles when I get back. The lights are bright; there's a table of men playing dominoes, two men having a game of pool, and a man and woman sitting at the end of the bar. The man's wearing a sports jacket and the woman has a French pleat in her black hair, like they got dressed up for a night out. Maybe they're going somewhere else later. The woman is perched on a stool and he stands to the side of her, his hand on her back, but they're not talking. She sips white wine from a small, round glass.

Julie is sitting on a stool at the end of the bar, reading the paper and eating crisps.

'Eh up! Look who it is. How are you, love? Come and sit with me, will you.' She pats her hand on one of the bar stools.

'I'm bored shitless in here tonight,' she says, when I get a bit closer. 'Sent Beth home, it were that dead. No point in us both standing about doing nowt all night, eh? What are you having?'

'Erm… brandy, please.' I spread coins out in my hand, counting the change.

She bats her hand at me. 'Bit posh for you. Don't worry about it. It's on the house. You'd be doing me a favour.' She pushes the glass into the optic. 'Might join you, actually.'

She reaches for another glass. 'So, what've you been up to? Out and about anywhere nice?'

'Just er… been into town for a bit, that's all.'

'Eeh, you don't give much away you, do you? Well, good for you, petal. Do you good to get out and about a bit, eh? Listen to me – I sound like a right patronising old bat, don't I?'

The sound of snooker balls clacking together in the background and the whir of a fruit machine is the only other noise.

She throws me a packet of crisps. 'Go mad. Treat yourself,' she says, and winks at me.

The woman on the stool is tapping her feet but there isn't any music on. They're still not talking.

'Julie?'

'That's me, love.'

'Do you know Lisle Street?'

'Lisle Street? Off the seafront? Let me think… I usually do know because I used to do the taxis. Not driving. Switchboard. Good laugh, shit hours. Same as here! I don't learn, do I?' She lets out a chesty laugh and pulls her T-shirt down over the back of her hips where it had ridden up.

'There's a takeaway there.'

'Yeah, think it's a pizza place. I remember now. Star Pizza. We used to pick people up there pissed at kicking-out time. They'd always want to scoff their bloody kebabs in the back of the taxi.'

'Did you ever pick up any young people – you know, like teenagers?'

She tips her chin down and looks at me over invisible glasses.

'Rebecca. I said I had a good memory. I don't have a super-power! I can't remember that. We're talking years ago, woman!'

'Yeah, right, sorry.' I sip the brandy and it warms my insides.

'Why do you want to know that, anyway?'

'No reason.'

'Bollocks. There's never no reason. Especially not with you, given that you hardly say two words.'

'Well, it's just that— No, really, it's nothing.'

She raises her eyebrow. She's signalling it won't drop. She's waiting for an answer.

'Well, I don't know; I just saw something, that's all. And I was just wondering. Being nosey, I suppose.'

There's a clatter of dominoes and a small cheer from the table of men behind.

'Jesus wept. It's a bit exciting in here tonight! Another drink, lads?' She starts to pull pints for the men.

I sip the rest of my brandy and Julie tops it up again.

'Want my advice?'

'Always, Julie.' I give her my best attempt at a cheeky smile.

'Turn a blind eye. Don't get involved. You've got enough on your plate. Leave it to the neighbourhood watch brigade or whoever. You need to look after number one right now.' She jabs a finger at me.

'I know, just ignore me.' I offer her a crisp and she reaches in with her maroon-chipped talon.

But I can't get Paige out of my mind, the man she was with near the beach. I keep seeing Chris's face with his eyes sunken in like that too. In that filthy toilet cubicle. The crisps repeat on me, rancid oil, and I push them away.

'Here,' Julie says to the glamorous lady and the man she's with. 'Stick a song on the jukebox or something, will you? And make it something lively too, for God's sake.'

CHAPTER FIFTEEN

Thursday, 12 November

'Thought it was my turn to come and see you.' Jeannie beams as I open the caravan door. I am still not dressed even though it's almost midday but my nightwear involves bundling up so much perhaps she won't notice.

Jeannie makes a point of shivering, rubbing her hands together and jiggling the baby's pram. I realise that I have just been standing there, leaning out of the door, looking at her.

'Erm, did you want something? Sorry... I wasn't expecting you.'

She flinches. 'I just wanted to pop round and see you. Don't worry about it; I can just go if you're busy.' She is subtly straining to look behind me. 'You got company or something?'

'Like who?! Ignore me; I'm sorry.' I gesture for her to come in. 'I'm just tired. Please... but you'll have to ignore the mess.'

'God, don't worry about it – my place is always a total mess with this one!' She gestures at Sam.

The house always looks pretty pristine to me. I help her lift the bulky buggy through the door. It almost looks like it isn't going to fit. Once we're all inside with the buggy, it feels like there's very little room to move. The windows steam up within a few minutes, once I put the gas fire on, so I open the window a small crack.

Jeannie unclips a wriggling Sam from his buggy and releases him from the bulky, hooded snowsuit that he's wearing. He seems to like the caravan. I am sure it's a novelty for him, like it was for me when we went on holiday when I was little, and he crawls quickly backwards and forwards along the bench by the table, squealing with delight. It's undeniable that he is pretty cute.

'Jesus Christ!' Jeannie jumps when my phone suddenly rings, the vibration making it shuffle across the table. A high-pitched ring. I need to change the ringtone; something less abrasive.

I snatch it up. 'Unknown number' the phone says.

She's already seen it. 'Ignore it, Becs. If they're legit, they'll leave a message.'

When Chris first went missing, it was non-stop. Journalists, mostly, wanting an interview or a 'quick quote'. Other times it was people giving me abuse, people calling me a 'cunt' or 'a paedo lover' down the phone. A few were just silence. There were pranksters too; people saying they knew where he was but then they'd say he'd run away with the circus and burst out laughing, or that he'd been abducted by aliens. One time, even, a medium rang. She meant well. She said she'd had a vision of Chris and that he was still alive – he was happy, somewhere, somewhere sunny, but wanted me to know he was 'sorry'. I almost followed it up until she told me she accepted payments by card and cash, or cheque. She even took PayPal. They all got the number from the Facebook page. I won't take the number down, though. The idea of missing out on something that would help to find Chris is worse than what they say.

It's all been quiet recently anyway, until now. Now it feels like everything is repeating itself. Maybe it's because of the fresh leaflets I posted, with my number at the bottom. The phone is still ringing. Sam puts his hands over his ears, shaking his head. The vigil announcement, the TV coverage, it's got everyone worked up all over again. They want fresh blood.

I snap myself round. I have to answer; you never know when it might be a clue, maybe even Chris.

'Hello.' I try to sound decisive, assertive; approachable.

Jeannie tuts and shakes her head. She focuses on Sam's coat, pretending not to listen.

I wait for the insult to be spat at me. Or the journalist to talk as fast as possible, trying to get their spiel out before I cut them off: *How do you feel about the vigil, Ms Pendle? Is there any message you'd like to give to the Jackson family?* But the line is silent, a few breaths close to the mouthpiece. 'Hello?' I repeat. I wait but there's nothing, just the low hum of the line. Then a click and the line goes dead. It's unsettling; a tingle goes over my skin.

'Who was that?' Jeannie forces a lightness into her tone.

'Wrong number, I think. No one there.' I shrug.

She purses her lips.

'So, how's it going?' Jeannie can't help casting an eye around the place. I see her notice the half-empty vodka bottle near the sink, but she doesn't say anything.

'Oh, you know.'

'I'm not being funny, Becs, but you look terrible. Sorry, I just mean really pale.'

'What's new there then?'

'You're beautiful, babes, and you always will be. I just mean you look tired. Are you OK?'

'You mean even more tired than usual?'

'Well… yeah.'

'I'm fine, honestly.' I try not to sound petulant. 'It's nice to see you both.' I gesture with a spoon and an open coffee jar, and she nods.

I turn my back to make the coffee.

'Got any biscuits?' she asks from behind me. I don't – I have a few jelly sweets left, so I offer her those. She looks amused and puts them to one side behind her bag, out of Sam's sight, no doubt. Is he old enough for jelly sweets or could he choke? No wonder she never leaves him with me.

When I turn to put the coffee cups down, Jeannie is looking at my laptop. I should have closed it when I went to answer the door.

I see her click between the tabs. News stories about Chris and Kayleigh. Kayleigh's Facebook page.

'Jeannie. Do you mind?'

'Sorry. I just—'

'I don't go through your stuff when I come round, do I?'

'I wouldn't really mind if you did, but sorry; I know that's not the point. Why are you looking at all this stuff again now, Becs? This isn't good.'

'This *is* good, though, Jeannie! Can't you see that? I was in bed for all those weeks. It was wasted time. Time I could have been going over everything. Finding Chris – clearing his name.'

I think about telling her about Paige, down near the beach. That it's worth it doing my own research.

'You've not been out with the leaflets again, have you? Tell me that you haven't.'

I don't answer. Mentioning Paige will only make her more worried. And worse, she might interfere, try to stop me.

'Becs, I get where you're coming from but we've talked about this. Tensions are high around here. Things had calmed down a bit… but, this vigil. It could stir things up again. It's almost like you're… provoking people. I really think you should lie low.'

'Provoking people! What do you expect me to do, Jeannie? Sit around? Do nothing, say nothing and focus all my energies on not upsetting anyone at all?'

'That isn't what I am saying. You know it isn't. You need to focus on looking after yourself and letting the police do their job.'

'OK, Jeannie. Yes, miss, no, miss, three bags full, miss.'

'Becs, please.'

'Can we talk about something else now?'

'After the other night and everything, round mine, I'm worried about you, Becs. You're not yourself.'

I shrug at her and gesture around the caravan. 'Hello-oh! I do have quite a lot going on, if you hadn't noticed?'

She sighs, exasperated. 'I *know* that. I just mean you seem to be… getting worse. Again. God, sorry, you know me, I've never been that tactful. I know you hate me for nagging you, Becs, but you have to look after yourself and you have to talk to someone – if not me, someone else, about what's going on in your head. I'm not surprised you're having a hard time. I bloody would be.'

She covers her mouth and quickly fakes a sing-songy voice to distract Sam from the fact she swore. He hasn't noticed. How much does he take in? What does he understand?

'Look, all I'm saying is what you went through is not to be taken lightly. You've got to take care of yourself.'

'What I'm *still* going through, I think you'll find, Jeannie.'

'I don't just mean that. Becs. You had a nervous breakdown. I mean, bloody hell…' She half-heartedly covers her mouth again, but doesn't bother addressing Sam this time.

'Did I? Don't be so dramatic.'

'Come on. You just said yourself you hardly got up for a month.'

'I was just… you know… '

'Well, whatever you want to call it, you can't go back there.'

I want to tell her this is different. What tipped me over the edge last time wasn't so much the escalation of the attacks, the comments. More the opposite. Kayleigh's disappearance slipped down the news agenda, then off it altogether. More bad things in the world surpassed it – there isn't space for them all. People weren't looking for her anymore and therefore there was no interest in Chris either. And I felt Chris – everything we had together, all those years, our whole future – sliding away, a paper boat towards a waterfall.

'I know' – I manage to get in before she continues – 'I'm not going to.'

'It was painful to see, Becs. You hardly knew – or cared – what day it was.' She's welling up.

'I wasn't that bad!'

She just raises her eyebrows at me.

I change the subject. 'Sorry. I feel guilty I have nothing for Sam.'

She smiles and sniffs the tears back. Sam looks at her, worried. 'Oh, he's OK with his sippy cup, aren't you?' She strokes his fat rosy cheek and he giggles again.

'Was Dan pissed off the other night then? After I was at yours? Sorry.'

'Dan? No, he's alright.'

'Liar,' I say. I can hear it in her voice.

She rolls her eyes. 'Yeah, he was a bit, but he's over it now. He does understand, you know. He liked Chris.' I see her flinch at the past tense, but she doesn't correct it, avoiding drawing more attention.

'Does he ever say anything to you… about Chris? When they were at football and stuff?'

Jeannie bristles. It's unmistakable.

'Jeannie?'

She doesn't answer.

'He knows something, doesn't he?'

'It isn't anything big.'

'What is it?'

She chews at some loose skin on the edge of her nail. 'He said Chris hadn't been turning up sometimes. To football. That's all.'

Air escapes from me.

'Why the fuck have you not said anything?'

I bang a cup down, and Sam looks startled.

'Presumed you knew from the police and, well, it's never come up, OK? You never asked me and I didn't think it would help. You've asked me now outright and I've told you. What does it change?'

'What does it change? How could Dan not say anything?'

Jeannie's head snaps up, her eyes fixed.

'You never said anything at the time. Used to Dan lying, are you?'

'Becs, do not go there. Seriously – let's not do this, right?'

'But you—'

'I didn't know anything at the time.' Her voice is raised again. 'He told Dan he was working, told you he was at football. It's not like we talked about football, is it? I wouldn't hide something like that from you, Becs. Never.'

Wednesday nights. I would paint my nails, batch cook for the freezer, watch *The Apprentice*. Chris always took a shower as soon as he got in.

'He might have been gambling again.'

'Exactly,' Jeannie says, but she doesn't sound convinced. 'I didn't say anything because I didn't want to pile it on, but now you've asked me and I've told you.'

She looks shattered in the light in here and it makes my anger at her subside. I hate that all this is taking such a toll on her. She always takes things to heart too much; takes other people's problems on as her own.

'You keep too much in,' she says, picking at something that isn't there on the table.

'I don't really know what you want me to say, Jeannie. I am feeling a little on edge with the vigil approaching. Of course I am. But what do you want me to say?'

'I just want to know what's going on. We need to get you out of here, out of this caravan. Back in the house. You can't live like this. The police should be offering you some support or protection.'

'I am fine – honestly. I really quite like it here.'

She looks around, bemused.

'I mean, obviously it's not like my dream home or anything. But in the circumstances, you know...'

I think it's the combination of the term 'dream home', the fusty-smelling washing and the rain that has started – making it 'feel like we're inside a drum', as my mum always used to say on caravan holidays – that makes us both start laughing. Sam looks confused, but then he joins in and starts to laugh as well.

The laughing fit breaks the ice between us a bit. Jeannie's never been afraid of a little gallows humour.

But Sam is making me tense, touching things, tipping cups so they teeter and almost spill. Jeannie is still recovering from her laughing fit, unaware of or ignoring what he's doing. I look obviously between her and Sam, willing her to intervene.

Jeannie rifles in her bag, probably for some tissue or breadsticks for Sam. She's always producing plastic tubs of food for him from nowhere. Then I see him reach for it. But I am too late. He grabs the corner of the picture of me and Chris. The Brooklyn Bridge is behind us, the sun low. The honeymoon. It's in a faux vintage gold frame. It looks out of place in the style-less caravan, but it sort of fitted in with the look we – mainly I – were going for in the house. Each time I look at the picture, I can almost feel the warmth of the week, walking around bookshops in Brooklyn, cocktails in the West Village.

The frame rocks back and forward, slow motion. My reaction is too late. I reach out and almost grab it, but I feel the air whip between my fingertips, and it falls backwards and smashes. Sam screeches with laughter and bunches his fingers up around his mouth. He squeals and points at Chris in the picture. 'Dada,' he shouts, laughing with glee. 'Da! Hahahahaha.'

Jeannie is horrified. 'Sam! No!'

'Dada hahahahahahaha.'

Before I can say anything, she says, 'He's going through a weird phase; he's saying that to every man he sees!'

'Is he? That's weird... Why would he say that?' I know I sound accusatory.

Silence hangs between us while she registers. The penny drops.

'Becs, come on! As if Chris would do anything like that; as if *I* would. Christ's sake! I don't know what the hell is wrong with you!'

Her voice is raised now, the blood has rushed to her face.

'Wouldn't he? Wouldn't he do that?' I ask. I sound like I am trying to start a fight.

'Get a bloody grip of yourself, Becs. Sam is just a baby, he doesn't know what he's saying.' She shakes her head. 'Honest to fucking God, I put up with too much from you sometimes, really. And I seriously need to stop swearing if I don't want this one to grow up to be a delinquent.'

Sam is wriggling and whining, trying to be upset that he got told off, but his heart isn't really in it. Calmer, Jeannie says, 'I'm sorry about the frame. I'll get you a new one.'

'It's fine, honestly. It was just cheap.'

She looks upset, resigned. 'I'm sorry for shouting. Again. Can we just take it down a notch, yeah?'

Sam is still whimpering half-heartedly. I suppose he can read the mood, the change in the atmosphere. She starts to bundle him back into his spaceman-like coat. I wince at his little arms staying straight, the awkwardness as she tries to force them into the sleeves.

I don't want her to leave yet, not on this note. I don't want to have ruined it all again.

'I know you don't approve but I do still love him, you know?'

'Don't say I don't approve. Please. It isn't as simple as that. I can't begin to understand what you're going through but I care. I do care.' She has stopped fussing with the coat. She probably still wants to leave, but it would seem tactless. 'I can empathise, you know – to an extent.'

I raise my eyebrows. *Can you really?*

'Not like that. But because I know *you*,' she adds.

Jeannie doesn't say anything for a while.

Then she says, 'I just don't know what to think, you know? No one does… do they?'

She knows she's on dangerous ground.

'Do you think *I* do, Jeannie? Do you think *I* know what to think? How to handle all this? All I know is that, deep down, I just know he wasn't like that. He *isn't* like that. He wouldn't be involved with a teenage girl. He's not that stupid. And he just… wouldn't… couldn't have.' My voice is cracking now.

She shoots a look at the baby. I remember how upset I used to get when I was little if an adult cried, and I force a smile at Sam.

'You didn't think he'd lie to you about work and about the gambling, though, did you?'

This again.

'No, I didn't. But gambling… Jacking your job in… It isn't abduction, is it?' I don't want to say the next but I force it out. 'It isn't grooming or paedophilia!'

She's rattled by what I have said, taken aback to hear the word out in the wild like that.

'And we were happy, Jeannie. Really, we were. So that's why I just can't understand all this. And why I have to try to.' My voice is really going now but I take deep breaths. 'We had some good times, didn't we? Me and Chris, you and Dan. Didn't we?'

'Yeah, we did.' There's warmth in her voice now. 'Do you remember Tenerife?' she asks

'No, I have forgotten a whole week of my life, Jeannie,' I say, but she knows it isn't real sarcasm.

'I wouldn't be surprised, the amount we drank! Ugh, I am gagging even now at the thought of that peach Schnapps we were necking every night. It was like sugary perfume.'

'Ha! God, I know. Well, we had to do something to get through and block out that place, didn't we? That hotel was such a shithole!'

'It's all coming back to me now. Remember that awful singer? Singing "Lady in Red" every night?'

'Oh, yeah! And his wife at the end of the bar. How the hell did she put up with that every night? You'd go mad!'

'I can think of worse things,' I say. 'Getting pissed on cocktails by the sea every night while your husband does a few karaoke songs. No stress!'

I used to say to Chris that's how I wanted us to be when we got older. Me glammed up, and him charming the grannies. My throat is throbbing again at the memory.

Jeannie touches my hand again. 'No one would know what to do in this situation, Becs. You're doing fine.'

'Are *you* happy?' I ask Jeannie.

'Christ! We usually need a few wines before we get going with this stuff,' she says. But the tone is amiable. 'Yeah, 'course we are.' She ruffles Sam's hair.

'How do you know, though?'

'I just know.'

'Right. And I just know too that Chris wouldn't do what they've said he's done.'

At least, I think I do.

CHAPTER SIXTEEN

Thursday, 12 November

I am sitting across the road from Star Pizza, where I watched Paige go the other night. I'm in the bus stand on the seafront, shivering in the cold, but sheltered from the full icy blast of the wind so I can wait and watch who comes and goes.

It's 6.30 now, a little early for people to be getting a takeaway from somewhere like this. You need to be pretty desperate; that specific gnawing need for greasy food that only a stomachful of alcohol gives. A couple of people come and go, polystyrene boxes tucked under their arms.

There are two girls coming along, arms linked. They must be around fourteen, fifteen. The bus stop is filling up so I pretend to read the bus timetable, peeping out every now and then as if I am looking for the bus, but really checking over the road. The cold is starting to numb my toes. Eventually, in a slow shuffle, heads down after a long day, everyone files into a brightly lit bus and it moves away. Nothing, the girls are gone now. But a girl with an older man is coming up the side street and they turn left into the takeaway.

I know I shouldn't be here. I should listen to what Julie said and stop stalking teenagers like some weirdo. Not just teenagers; the teenage friends of the girl my husband is supposed to have run off with… or taken. I feel a fresh twist of nausea. But still, I am looking side to side, crossing the street, then find myself walking down towards Star Pizza, everything tensed up.

The darkness of the side street gives way to the white glow of the takeaway and the scramble of techno music blaring out. I take a deep breath and walk past, facing ahead at first but my head automatically turning to look into the takeaway. I see the two girls I saw earlier whose arms were linked. No other customers. I don't see the other girl and the older man who went in too. There are a few men. I can't count how many – two, three? – behind the counter, leaning on it, talking and laughing. And there's one in a navy and white apron playing on a punchball machine. He pulls his fist back and smashes it into the red leather ball, screaming out as he does. One of the men behind the counter notices me and our eyes lock for a second, his gaze seeming to get narrower. Then whooping from the others, but by then I have already walked past.

I stop in the alley to breathe deeply, taking in the cold air and leaning against the wall, trying to let my heart rate return to normal. The sky is white. 'It's trying to snow,' as my dad would say. I stand and watch for a while to see who comes and goes. A light goes on upstairs in the flat above the shop. But I can't see anything except dark shapes beyond the grubby lace curtains. Eventually, I can't stop myself and I walk past the takeaway one more time.

I try to take a sideways glance without turning my head, and I hold my phone out in front of me, as if engrossed in a text or looking online for directions. The man in the apron is pretending to jab and spar like a boxer, probably preparing to hit the punchbag again.

'You want a kebab, love?' the voice shouts. 'Yes, you. You've walked past enough times. You want some meat, love?' They all laugh, the girls and the men.

As soon as I am past the shop I break into a run, not daring to look back to see whether anyone came out or followed me. I don't stop until I reach the top of the alley again. My cheeks are burning and I am out of breath. I crouch down and wait for a while.

Eventually the two girls come out and start walking towards me. I stand up, trying to look casual, straightening my jeans. I hadn't intended to but I am blocking off their exit. They look at each other then try to pass, but automatically I go in the same direction. Without trying, without even thinking about it, I am more nimble on my feet than I realise. My body has moved before my mind has made a decision. I think of The Watchers video, the men in the masks.

'What the fuck is this?' one of them says. Her smooth, high ponytail is immaculate, scalp tight. You can see the hair follicles pulling near her temples. There's a school tie peeping through the top of her coat. Maroon and blue – not St Augustine's, though. Theirs is yellow and green.

'What are you doing hanging out here?' I ask. I am expecting to get a load of lip but the girls just look between themselves.

'We're just getting some chips to warm us up. Eating's not a crime now, is it? Are you a copper? We've finished school now, you know. I've been today; you can check with them. We can do what we like, can't we?'

'Alright,' says the other girl, nodding her head in recognition of someone behind me. Another girl their age and a teenage boy. The boy's hair is shaved almost to the scalp round the back and sides, leaving a textureless shading on the skin that almost looks painted on. The mop of dark hair on the top brings to mind a comedy toupee. His features are hard. The girl is wearing ice-pink lip gloss, slathered on thickly.

'What's going on? You two alright?' the boy asks, sizing me up.

'Yeah, yeah, no bother, we're fine. We'll see you in a bit, yeah?'

'Who's this old wifey?' he asks, gesturing at me.

'Shut up, Maz. We'll catch up with you in a bit, like I said.'

'You not sitting in?' He gestures down the alley. 'It's proper brass monkeys outside.'

The boy and girl walk on into the alley, looking back every few steps, suspicious of me.

'So is there something you want like? Can we get past, please?' The girl with the tight ponytail nudges her friend.

'Do you know a girl called Paige?'

'Yeah, we know her from round and about.'

'And her friend, Kayleigh Jackson?'

They look at each other again.

'We know her. We're not like bezzie mates or nothing. Everyone says they were best mates with her since she went missing. But yeah, we know her. It's a small place, round here.'

'Did she used to come round here? Hang round at the takeaway?'

'Sometimes. I think so, yeah. They do good chips. Ashy lets us sit inside, as long as we buy stuff every now and again. It's better than freezing your tits off out here.' She rubs her gloved hands together and stamps her feet lightly to warm up.

'Are you safe?' I ask. I notice the other girl looking at the floor, kicking her battered Converse shoes at pebbles.

'Safe? We're eating chips, missus, that's it. Is that something else we're not allowed to do now?'

The girls' attention is drawn down the alley. One of the men from behind the counter is walking up towards us.

'Let's go.' The girl yanks at her friend's arm to pull her away. 'I need to get home or my mam will kick off.'

'Here!' shouts the man – but the girls have already ducked into an amusement arcade. I look the other way. I don't know why but I don't want him to know which way they've gone.

'What was all that about?' he asks me. His face is pock-marked, a greasy sheen to his skin and hair. Under the street light it makes him look waxy. His white T-shirt has faint brown stains on it.

'All what?' I say, being careful to stand my ground.

'Why are you hanging around here, asking questions?'

His colleague is coming up the alley too now. I look around but the seafront is deserted.

'We've got a nosey one here,' the greasy one says to the new arrival, a short, pasty-faced man. Early forties, I reckon. 'We hear you're asking questions – harassing my customers. Didn't we, Daz?'

'Yeah.'

My legs are wobbling but I make a point of standing straight, pushing my shoulders back. 'I was just asking about Kayleigh Jackson actually. The missing girl.'

'What the fuck has that got to do with me and my shop?' He steps forward. I don't move.

'Ashy, cool it, mate, yeah? Come on.' Daz pulls him back slightly.

I don't think they recognise me or know who I am.

'What's this Hayley to you?' says the one called Ashy, looking me up and down.

'Kayleigh. It's Kayleigh. I just want to find her like everyone else round here. She's only fourteen so, you know, I am concerned for her well-being.'

'Well, don't come around here pointing the finger at us.'

'I don't believe I've made any accusations, have I?'

Ashy repeats my words in a mock posh accent and Daz smirks.

My temper flares. 'Why have you got so many young girls hanging around your little establishment anyway?'

'Huh,' he pretends to give a mocking laugh. 'Dunno what you're talking about, do you, Daz? Ain't any girls in there now.'

'Uh-uh.' He shakes his head.

'I'm not stupid; I've just watched them coming and going.'

'Oh, so you're watching us now, are you? I let them sit in the shop if they want. It's freezing, if you hadn't noticed. They're just kids; they get bored. They need somewhere to go. They meet their mates here, eat chips, go home – I make money, they stay warm. That alright with you? Who the fuck are you anyway?'

'I just wanted to see they were OK, that's all. And ask if you knew anything about Kayleigh. I'm asking around everywhere.'

'Just what do you think we know about this Katie? Should we be running to the police? "Ooh excuse me, Officer. I'm worried little Katie might have been eating chips. Do something: it's an emergency, Officer, I've seen some teenage girls eating chips."'

His friend Daz forces a laugh. *Arse-licker*, I think to myself.

'You won't mind them knowing then, will you, just in case that you "saw Kayleigh Jackson eating chips"?'

He shrugs. I could easily slap him for the disgusting, cocky look on his face. My temple is pulsing.

'You won't mind me telling them about girls going upstairs either then, will you?'

His eyes flash. 'What girls?'

'I saw a girl go in tonight. With a bloke. She didn't come out again. Then I saw them upstairs through the window. She couldn't have been more than fourteen or fifteen. The police might be interested, mightn't they?'

I hold his stare and refuse to look away. I hope his face will give something away, confirm that I'm right about the girl but he just looks calm, cocky like before.

Ashy whirls his finger near his temple.

'Well, they might be, but I doubt it. You're deluded, love. Simple as. Is a dad not allowed to buy his daughter a pizza for her tea?'

'But – no – I saw them go in and not come out. I saw people upstairs.'

'Yeah, there's a flat above the takeaway. I let the staff use it on their breaks. I'm nice like that.'

'I didn't see her come back out, though.'

'Not my problem, babe. I know her dad. Know where they live if you want to go round. I'll give them a ring, will I? See if they'll save you a slice of pizza.'

My heartbeat pulses in my ears.

'What did you think we've done with this mystery girl, put her on a pizza?' He looks to Daz for the obligatory laugh. 'Hehe!'

My stomach rolls.

'I mean, they are pretty tasty some of the girls round here, right, Daz?' He rolls his tongue across his teeth, making my stomach churn again.

They both snigger.

'Look, fuck off, alright, Miss Marple? We don't know nothing about this Hayley, Katie, whatever her name is. Just don't come back round here, alright?'

'Or what?'

'Just don't.' Rubbing his hands together. 'Come on, Daz, we've got kebabs to make. Crazy bitch,' he hisses under his breath as they walk away.

CHAPTER SEVENTEEN

Thursday, 12 November

I go to Barnacles when I get back to the caravan park. I need to calm down after my run-in with Ashy and Daz. It feels like I am looking at the situation through frosted glass. The shape and colours are there but I can't make sense of the details. I need to get to the details if I'm ever to get any answers. I think about Paige at the school, near the beach. What she said about Chris's job, about his computer. I have to drink most of the half of lager down in one to push out the mental flash that has invaded again.

I sit near the door at the edge of the bar because Julie's running a bingo night. It's draughty but the tables further in are full, mostly older people but a few young ones too. Everyone is hunched over, marker pens at the ready, far too engrossed to pay me any attention.

Julie raises a plate of pie and peas to me from the other side of the room, but I shake my head.

One of the young lads I sometimes see around the park is doing the bingo. He spins the little metal cage and lines up the balls. No one speaks. Julie comes by and wipes the tables. 'Deadly serious about it, this lot,' she says quietly. 'Still, nice little earner for me. Good to see it packed, eh?'

'Yeah, great.'

'You don't fancy a game? I can get you a card.'

'No, you're alright, thanks.'

'Well, give us a shout if you want a go.'

'Unlucky for one some… number thirteen,' says the bingo caller. A murmur goes through the room, people conferring on their numbers. 'Key of the door… twenty-one.'

'I made him learn all the proper names. I've been testing him behind the bar. Doing alright, isn't he? Eh, think on, I'm doing fish and chips every Friday so pop in.'

I check my phone and see I have six missed calls from Sandra, Chris's mum. That's all I need. I'll ring her when I get back to the caravan. A sense of unease is creeping in. Has something happened to Geoff? She doesn't ring that much anymore, not like she used to. So why is she ringing me six times?

'Legs eleven, number eleven.' A few people wolf whistle and a ripple of laughter drifts around the room.

The lad reading out the numbers keeps his eye down, embarrassed. 'Droopy drawers, number forty-four.'

'Line!' a woman shouts, jumping up out of her seat and knocking over a drink. Julie goes over and checks her card, but eventually she looks over at the caller and shakes her head. The woman's made a mistake.

Boos from the tables.

'OK, eyes down everyone for the rest of the game. Please only raise your hand if you have a line or a full house.'

'Never been kissed… sweet sixteen.'

'You'll be lucky round here,' a man shouts, and his wife slaps him on the forearm.

I need to get back to the caravan to think in silence. I drink down the dregs of my lager.

* * *

I am making a strong coffee in the caravan when there is a loud rap at the door, making the crockery rattle again. I am not expecting visitors; I never am.

'Who is it?'

'It's Detective Fisher, Rebecca. Can we have a quick word?' she shouts.

Every time the police come round, it brings back the feeling in the pit of my stomach, that day, when they first came over.

I open the door and they're looking up at me. I don't recognise her partner. They tend to change but it's always been her, although we rarely speak now compared to the early days. I wonder if she's here to talk to me about the vigil, or to check up on me after the other night. But why the colleague?

'Hi, erm, yes, I suppose so.' I beckon Fisher and her sidekick in. She takes off her coat and scarf without me inviting her to. It's still freezing in the caravan as I haven't put the gas fire on yet.

'Tea?' I ask her, keen to both delay and move the conversation on at the same time.

'Yeah, why not? You get home alright the other night?' She moves the bedding out of the way and sits down.

'Oh, yeah – fine, thanks. Sorry about that.'

'No bother. Nothing to apologise for.' Her tone makes it clear the matter is closed, for now at least. It isn't why she is here.

'This is PC Lyons,' Fisher says, gesturing at her colleague. He looks young and I wonder if he is new, just getting started.

He hovers awkwardly and I gesture for him to sit. 'If you can find a bit of space. Sorry there isn't much room in here.'

I notice Detective Fisher surveying the caravan, looking up and down for anything suspicious. Or maybe just looking around. To be fair, she probably does it automatically. It's her job.

'You may already be aware of the latest developments?'

'The vigil, you mean?'

Lyons flips the front of his ring-bound notepad over and poises his pen. It's only a tiny flicker but it looks like she's rolling her eyes at him.

'Um, no, I did want to talk to you about that but it's… something else. I thought you might have seen it. You haven't been online today, Rebecca? Or read the paper? No one has contacted you?'

'No, I've been busy. I've been out… Why?'

'Anywhere nice?'

'Not really, no. Just out.'

'OK… I am sure this is going to come as a little bit of a shock to you, Rebecca. You'll probably want to sit down.' I didn't realise I was still standing up. I think of all the missed calls, Sandra ringing me. Trying to reach me over and over.

It's painful when I swallow. The wait for Detective Fisher to speak seems endless.

'Have you found him? Please just tell me.' But I know that's not it. I'd be able to feel it in some way, I'm sure of it.

She shakes her head. 'I'm afraid not.'

'Is it Kayleigh? Is she home?'

She purses her lips. 'It isn't that, Rebecca.'

'So, what is it? Please – I can't stand this!' I wish I didn't sound quite so desperate.

She gears herself up to speak. It's obvious she's uncomfortable; she doesn't want to. I wonder why she doesn't send one of her lackeys to do it. Or get Lyons to do it now.

There's another pause. Then she blurts it. 'There's been another allegation against Chris.'

I feel the wind knocked out of me.

'Your husband,' she adds, as if I don't know. As if he is no longer the first person that springs to mind when I hear the name.

My ears are ringing. 'What do you mean, allegation?' I am still clinging on to the hope that this may not be as bad as I know it will be.

'Another female has come forward, stating that Chris, your husband, made... advances towards her. In the time leading up to his disappearance and the disappearance of Kayleigh Jackson.'

'What "female"?'

'I'm afraid I can't say much more at this stage, but since this has unfortunately been leaked to the press without my authorisation, I feel it is only fair that I confirm to you that the female in question is also fourteen years old.'

My intestines twist. 'And is it true? I mean, what exactly are they saying happened? And who's saying it?'

'I can't go into the details, Rebecca, I am sorry – we've discussed that side of things the other night, if you remember. We just wanted to ask you a few questions.'

The room feels like it's spinning. I think of the cyclone scene from *The Wizard of Oz*; the music, Miss Gulch cycling past the window.

'Wait, they're saying this happened now? I don't understand, Detective?'

'Get her some water, will you? Look lively,' she says to Lyons, clicking her fingers quickly at him.

He clatters around at the sink, knocking some cups off, and Detective Fisher shoots him a scathing look.

'It's not an allegation about now, no. It dates from the spring. Before Chris went missing. But it has just come to light now. Rebecca, are you OK?'

I am guzzling down the water, missing my mouth most of the time, cold water dribbling off my chin and shocking the skin on my chest. I suddenly feel very hot, although I know it's still cold in here because I can see my breath in the air.

'I wanted to let you know since this has appeared in the papers. And it's been going round online, I'm afraid.'

'Can you tell me if you at least think it's credible, what this new girl is saying. I mean, why wouldn't she have come forward before?'

'We have to take all leads and information we receive seriously, Rebecca. We are concerned it could suggest a, well, a "pattern", but I really can't say any more on the specifics of the allegation at this stage. It's out of my hands.'

'Oh, so you can tell the newspapers but you can't tell me anything, is that right? Is that fair, Detective Fisher?'

'Rebecca, I sincerely apologise to you and to the family of Kayleigh Jackson that this was leaked to the press, and I can assure you we will have an internal investigation to identify the source of this leak and shut it down.'

'Yeah, right.'

'So, I just want to run through a few questions with you. Nothing new, just clarifications, confirmations for my records, really.'

'Whatever.' I sound twelve.

'So, Chris was formerly a teacher when you were living in London.'

'Is that a question? You know that already.' I shift in my seat and Detective Fisher doesn't take her eyes off me.

'But here he was working up at Green Point?'

'Yes.'

'Good job, was it?'

'Not especially, no.'

'Interesting,' she says, matter-of-fact.

'Is it? Is it interesting, *Jane*? Is it so amazingly fascinating to you that someone in Shawmouth has a shit job? Because the last time I looked, there weren't that many of the other kind.'

She raises her eyebrows. 'And he left teaching because…?'

'As we both know I have told you before; because we moved here. And because he was getting ground down by the job. Teaching. The hours, the hassle, the stress. Ask any teacher what it's like. They mostly all say the same.'

She puts on a puzzled expression. 'So it was both things at the same time? Moving here, hating the job. Not one that led to the other?'

I tut involuntarily; exasperation spilling over. 'My mother is ill. Really ill. Deteriorating, actually. I believe I have said. So we needed to move back here. Seemed like a good time for Chris to get out of teaching, make a new start.'

'He didn't look for teaching jobs up here, then?'

My teeth grind. 'No, like I said. We wanted to make a fresh start. He was looking to change career.'

'You don't think there were any other factors that led to his decision? Anything that might have happened at school? In London?'

I don't like the change in the tone of the conversation; the neutrality in her voice sounds forced now.

'Well, of course it was related to something that happened at school. How you feel about your job is usually based on, you know, what happens at work – no?' My tone is aggressive. I'm lashing out, I know.

She puts her hands together, intertwining her fingers. 'OK, let's try to look at this in a slightly different way. Think about anything that might have happened at the school before Chris left. Related to recent events? What we have been talking about today?'

'No! I don't know what you're...' Then it hits me; what she might be driving at. I feel backed into a corner. I need space, time to think. 'No, there is nothing I can think of that is *relevant*.' I try to make the last word sound sarcastic. Throw her off.

'OK, have it your way. I will cut to the chase then, because unfortunately you'll be able to read about it yourself in the paper anyway.'

And so will everyone else. The whole town. Petrol on the fire. *They'll say he's a serial predator.*

'We have spoken to the school where Chris worked in London. We spoke to the headteacher there.' She checks her notes, or pretends to. 'A Mrs Grange. Have you met her?'

'No.'

'Well, she made us aware of an incident in which your husband was reprimanded regarding physical contact with a female student.'

She blurts it out then just looks at me, letting it hang in the air. It's clear that she expects me to be the one who speaks next.

My mouth is dry, my tongue and lips catching on my teeth. 'I… I… I don't know what you're talking about.'

'No?' She opens her own notebook again and flips over some pages. There's definitely writing in there now. 'In March 2014, only last year in fact, Chris was warned to refrain from touching a student.' Very matter-of-fact again.

'No! That isn't what happened. That isn't it.'

'I thought you weren't sure of the situation I was referring to?'

This feels like the part in a film where the person demands to see a lawyer. When I speak, my voice is getting higher pitched.

'I didn't think of it before. But it wasn't like that. Not what you are saying.'

'Well, then; why don't you tell me about it in your own words?'

'There *was* a girl at school…'

She gives me a blank, unreadable half-smile. They have both stopped taking notes.

'Mmm-hmmm, yes, we know that much.'

'Well, she was upset and—'

'And the girl was how old, did you say?'

I didn't.

'She was fourteen… fifteen… I don't know. One of the older ones. The year before the last one, I think. I'm not sure. He didn't say.'

'You didn't ask?'

'Why would I?'

'So, go on. What happened?'

'Well she was upset. She had some stuff going on at home. Her mum was ill. She was upset about that. She'd been misbehaving in the lesson. He said it was out of character for her. So, he kept her back after.'

'Go on.'

My voice is trembling. I suddenly feel exposed.

'Well, there isn't a lot more to it. After a while she told him what was happening. Why she'd been acting up. What was going on at home… and she got upset. She was crying.'

'Right?'

'And he comforted her. He put his arm around her or hugged her or something – she was really upset. She didn't complain about him or anything like that.'

'No one is saying that she did.' Blank-voiced again.

'Mrs Grange just had a word with him, but it was for his own protection.'

'A word… about?'

'She was saying he should be careful about being on his own in a classroom with the door closed with a female pupil.'

'Anything else?'

'No…'

'You're sure?'

'Yes.'

'Mrs Grange told me she had warned him about making physical contact with students.'

'It wasn't like that. It wasn't a *warning* warning.'

'No?'

'It was for his protection. To avoid situations like this!'

'So he had mentioned this to you?'

'Yes, of course. But only because he was really annoyed. He said he'd turned a corner with the girl and managed to get out of her what was going on at home; why she was struggling at school, and he said it felt like a kick in the teeth for Mrs Grange to say that. He said he felt…'

'He felt…?'

'He said he felt accused.' I put my hand up to my face. It is hot to the touch.

'I see.'

'But there was nothing in it. Nothing at all. It didn't go any further than that. Mrs Grange said to him it was for his own good, that's all. It was the same for all teachers. She was always reminding the teachers to be careful on social media and all that sort of stuff. It's a big problem these days, that kind of thing.'

'Oh, yes, we know that. Believe me.'

'It was this sort of stuff that made him want to leave teaching. They put CCTV in some of the classrooms. They were even thinking of getting a police officer in the school, like a security guard or something.'

This raises a faint smile to her face but she kills it off again.

'Fancy that, eh.' She exchanges a glance with Lyons.

'The teachers, they always feel on edge. I thought you said you spoke to Mrs Grange? She didn't say there was more to it, did she? Did she not say the same as me?'

'More or less. It just struck me, I suppose, with this new allegation that has been made, that she had thought to mention it and you hadn't.'

'Because it's not relevant. The fact that she only "remembered" this now proves that it wasn't significant, doesn't it?'

'I wouldn't say it "proves" anything. We can't really say at this stage.' Detective Fisher's voice is softer. 'Look, I'm not trying to have a go, Rebecca. I am just trying to get to the bottom of things. And I need your help to do that. OK?'

'Feels like you're trying to trick me.'

'Well, I'm really not. I don't have time for that type of thing, even if I was so inclined. I just want all the facts I can get a hold of, that's all. And I want to know that you're being straight with me.'

'I am.'

'Good. So, just a few more questions, Rebecca?'

'Do I have any choice?'

'We're just looking to find Kayleigh. And your husband, Rebecca.'

'I'll get you that tea.'

I flip on the kettle to finally make tea, giving myself a chance to turn away from Detective Fisher for a moment. When I catch my reflection in the window, it looks like I am on the outside looking in. A ghost, an apparition.

'Rebecca?' I can hear Detective Fisher's voice but she sounds distant.

When the kettle boils I let the steam burn my arm for a second or two before I pull it away. It snaps me out of it.

'Ask away then, if you must.'

'So, cast your mind back to the day Chris went missing, if you can.'

'Oh, wait a moment. I can't remember that day very clearly. They all blur into one.' I shoot her a snide smile, passing out the two cups of tea and sitting back down again.

'Please, Rebecca... this isn't helping anyone.'

'Sorry, I know, I'm sorry.' I feel a wave of embarrassment at being so immature. I know it isn't Detective Fisher's fault. I can't help myself sometimes.

'So he left for work in the morning, as usual?'

'Well, yeah, but he wasn't going to work, was he – as we all know now.'

'OK, Rebecca – we'll get to that – but he left at the usual time anyway and you understood him to be going to work?'

'Yes, he left about 7.45. He had to leave earlier because the buses are so crap where we live, lived… on the estate, anyway.'

I think of that morning now, and the memory burns up like the old film reels, blackening and crackling.

'OK, and then you didn't hear from him again that day?'

'Right.' I don't know why I am talking like an American. Mimicking what they say on TV.

'You received some texts, did you not?'

'Yes, sorry.'

'Saying…?'

'Saying that he loved me, that's all.' I have to take a deep breath to avoid getting upset.

'And you no longer have the texts… Is that right?'

'Yes.'

'You deleted them straight away? Any reason for that?'

'Erm, I think my phone was just getting a little full. Or maybe I did it by accident. It's habit when I have read stuff.'

I take a deep breath to push a wave of threatening tears back down. I'd give anything to get those texts back now.

'You still don't remember?'

'No. Do you remember all your phone admin in detail?'

'No, I suppose not. Those phones tend to have a lot of storage though, don't they?' She tips her head towards my phone, which is face down on the counter, and pats her pocket. 'Don't recall ever having to delete old texts on mine. I've got them from years back. I was just having a look on the way over here. I tend to just let them all rack up.'

She writes something down. I imagine she already has all the phone records.

'Right, well…'

'And you didn't think there was anything unusual about the texts?'

'Not really, no. Do you?'

'Not really or no?'

'No, I didn't think there was anything unusual about the texts.'

She looks at me hard, for longer than usual, then cuts away. 'OK, anything else spring to mind? Anything odd, out of the ordinary? You went to work like usual that day?'

'Yes, everything just seemed normal.'

'And you went to work?'

That stops me in my tracks.

'No, I was off sick that day. And the day before, remember?'

'Ah-ha that's right, of course. I do remember now.'

Detective Fisher doesn't forget things; she never mixes them up.

'You just stayed in bed then, most of the day?'

'Yes.'

'You didn't see a doctor?'

'No, it was just a virus.'

'OK. And did Chris say anything else. Besides that he loved you, of course?' She gives me a smile like a curtsy after that little dig.

'He just said, you know, 'bye and he'd see me that night.'

'Just a few more questions then we'll be on our way, but it is important.'

Lyons is scribbling away. How can they still be writing this down? Don't they have iPads or recorders or something for this stuff these days?

'And – I'm sorry, I know you have mentioned this – but just to be clear, you say that you didn't realise your husband had lost his job? He hadn't told you this?'

I shake my head. That still stings. 'I had no idea, honestly. I was still making his sandwiches every day, for Christ's sake. What a mug, eh?'

'It happens.' Detective Fisher shrugs. 'And at the time, were you aware at all of any problems at work he was having? Or personal issues?'

'No. We have been through all of this!'

Lyons jumps a little, startled. He avoids catching my eye.

'OK, Rebecca – just a couple of other things. You'll understand that we need to keep looking at things afresh, especially in the light of any new information. And new information is so crucial—' I open my mouth to speak, but she cuts me off, '—whatever the nature of that intelligence may be. We need to revisit the facts of the case in the light of this.'

I shoot her back a forced 'of course' smile.

'So, once more with feeling. We came to see you on...' She consults her notebook but I can't help feeling that it's all show, she knows the lines.

'That was the Monday we came to see you, when we were doing a door to door, wasn't it? And you hadn't yet reported that Chris, your husband, was missing. Missing since Friday. Why was that again?'

They had knocked as I was getting ready for work. When I first saw them, my stomach dropped, afraid that something had happened to Chris. Little did I know what was coming next.

A few general questions. *Had I seen anything? Who else lived there? Where was he now? When had I last seen him?* The questions started speeding up, they wanted to come inside. Then one of the officers left the room, made a call. Everything snowballed...

'I told you, I just thought maybe he'd had a few too many with his friends and was sleeping it off somewhere. Maybe he knew he'd be in my bad books so he was delaying coming home.'

'You didn't ring round friends? See if they'd seen him? Call the hospitals?'

'I did call the hospitals. Check with them – I'm sure you already have.' I shoot her one of her own false smiles back. 'I didn't ring his friends. As I've said, I suppose I didn't want to seem like a nagging wife, suspicious, like I was keeping tabs on him. You know how people are. They never forget about stuff like that and they don't let you either. Stupid, really.'

'Mmm-hmm.' She and Lyons catch each other's eyes but I can't read their secret language.

'So, no unexpected stays away from home, late nights, that type of thing?'

'Well, there were a few late nights.'

'Go on, Rebecca.'

'There's nothing to "go on" about. He'd sometimes go for a pint after football or work or whatever. Doesn't your husband?'

She doesn't answer, but I notice she isn't wearing a ring.

'Forgive me, Rebecca, but something still doesn't add up here.'

This is new. The silence reverberates around the caravan.

'Sorry, you've lost me.' I try to buy myself some time.

'I mean, this is what you told me when we first met. But you've had more time to think now, distance. It's just, your husband, who you say everything's fine with, doesn't show up at home for three days and you don't call us? I'm having problems marrying that with you and everything else you've told me.'

I focus on my breathing. When I am confident my voice is steady, I speak.

'Well, that's up to you. Maybe it sounds a bit unusual but it's the way it is. Not illegal, is it?'

Her face tightens then relaxes again.

'Have it your way. Perhaps we'll pick it up another time. And think back again, please. Do you remember anything unusual around that time? Anything at all? Please, think hard about the details.'

I remember the day he went missing – *they* went missing – as clearly as if it were yesterday, of course, although I didn't know everything had gone so wrong at the time. At least I think I remember it. But the time leading up to it... I can't recall the details as precisely as I need to. I have run over them so many times.

Have I accidentally embroidered, rearranged, blurred things? It's all these questions posed in ten different ways that makes it hard to remember clearly.

I still run it all over and over in my head most days. It used to be all day every day at first. A fingertip search of the field of my memory, our life, looking for new clues. I wince to remember the details of his face, and already sometimes I can't. I'd looked at it every day for the last twelve years. Sometimes studied it head-on for minutes at a time, yet when I try to summon it now, it often distorts. It blurs and zips just out of view, the details of the features aren't there.

Chris had been a bit distracted, though, hadn't he? Taking his phone everywhere with him. But that could have been just the gambling, I know now. Or it could have been Kayleigh. Everything is skewed through the new lens.

'Everything was just normal. That's what I don't get.'

At least she hasn't asked me about our sex life this time... yet... like she did in the early days. 'How were things in that department? I'm sorry but we do have to ask, given the nature of our concerns here.'

'Fine,' I'd told her. The truth is 'things in that department', as she put it, were non-existent over the last year or so. But I was stressed with Mum. I was going to bed early. Visiting Mum every evening and weekend at first, while she adjusted, and to soothe my guilt for putting her in the home. Chris'd stay up late on the computer. He was looking for jobs, he said. Or playing computer games. He couldn't sleep. It was just something we had to get through; a temporary thing. And it isn't relevant. I won't give them that. One more undignified slight on our relationship.

'You OK, Rebecca?'

I feel the cramp again. The porn on the computer. But so what? It doesn't mean anything. It can't.

'Yeah, fine, sorry. Bit of a headache. Not sleeping great.'

'Right, OK. That's us for today, I think.' Chirpiness back in her voice. 'There's just one other quick thing.'

'I have a question for you, actually,' I tell her.

She looks taken aback but quickly rearranges her face into a placid expression. 'Fire away, by all means.'

'Kayleigh.'

She flinches again. Barely perceptible but it's there, a tiny flicker in her face.

'Have you investigated... well, are you investigating the take-away off the seafront?'

Lyons's pen stops writing in the notebook but he leaves the nib on the page.

'You'll need to elaborate.'

'I heard someone talking... saying that teenage girls hang around there, that there's dodgy stuff going on.'

'What sort of "dodgy stuff", Rebecca? Who have you been talking to?'

'No one. I haven't. I overheard someone. Just on the bus. Chatting about it. I just thought it was worth mentioning.'

'Right, thanks for passing that on.' She's shifting to get up and leave.

'It's Star Pizza, the takeaway they were on about – down Lisle Street?' I notice she hasn't asked for the details. Is she discounting the information or does she already know?

'OK, good, thanks.'

Lyons makes a small scribble.

'And what about Kayleigh's ex, Adam? Did you talk to him?'

She lets out a slow breath. 'Of course we did, Rebecca. We are conducting a serious investigation here, you know. We're not messing around.' She is sterner now. The atmosphere between us has stiffened again. 'I don't know where all this is coming from, but I can't say I appreciate the way you are going about things here. It concerns me, if I am honest.'

'Kayleigh. She had some money from somewhere. Adam said he didn't know where she was getting it from. And that she'd been staying out late at night. Her parents were worried.'

'And you know this how?'

'Never mind that. But have you explored it?'

'Never mind that nothing. Funny you should bring this up now, don't you think?' She glances at Lyons. He doesn't react.

'What's that supposed to mean?'

'Nothing. Just seems a bit odd, that's all. We come with some new information that doesn't cast Chris in a good light, and boom.'

'I'm just trying to help.'

'Let's not forget, Rebecca, your husband was withdrawing large lump sums of cash from a joint bank account without your knowledge, was he not? And Kayleigh suddenly had some money from somewhere. I think you should be careful just what accusations you're throwing around about other people here, don't you?'

That's how it is with Detective Fisher. One minute she'll be pally with you; the next, she can just slap you right down.

She relents again. 'Look, Rebecca. I get that you're trying to make sense of this and you're looking for answers, right? I really do. But you need to let us do that – because you could end up adding two and two and getting five. We need to be objective about this, and that's why you need to leave it to the experts.'

I feel a flash of rage. 'But we're not getting anywhere,' I say, my voice raised again. 'That's the problem! We're no further forward. Nearly four months.'

'That isn't true, Rebecca. For obvious reasons you're not privy to the full investigation.'

I shake my head. There is no point saying anything else to her.

She scratches her cheek lightly. She's standing up and ready to leave now. 'Before we go—'

'I know about the vigil; I saw that on the news and in the paper too.'

'Right, yes, I thought you would have. Not thinking of going, are you?' She takes a big glug of the tea, now it's cooled a little. Forced casual.

'I won't be going.' But I don't know if that's true. 'How are they? The family,' I ask Detective Fisher.

She tightens. 'Oh, you know… frantic, exhausted…'

Generic, she isn't comfortable talking about it to me, she probably isn't allowed.

Fisher inspects her hands. They are plump and dry, her nails uneven, no polish.

'Anyway, we better get off. Still got a few things to do before I finish my shift.' She cocks her head, gesturing to Lyons to get a move on. As she pulls her coat on, the buttons gape open, exposing a small flash of the chubby white of her torso. She looks round the caravan again and seems to stop for a moment. *What is she looking for?*

Lyons has already stepped outside when Detective Fisher turns to me again. 'Oh, that quick thing I mentioned – stay away from the school, yes? I don't want to have to come round here with a Harassment Warning. Seriously.'

I go to answer her, but she cuts me off.

'Let's not say anything else on the matter, OK? If anything comes to mind, anything at all, think on – you've got my number. Use it. Ring me.'

I can't tell if she sounds supportive or threatening.

The Watchers' video runs through my mind, the sound of the tyres on the gravel, the glare on the man's glasses. But now it feels as if the one in the trap is me.

CHAPTER EIGHTEEN

Thursday, 12 November

After Detective Fisher leaves, I sit in silence in the caravan. I have to work up my nerve to turn the laptop on, my hands shaking as I load up the *Courier* website. I hoped I had dreamt her visit, that she'd made a mistake, that the article had been taken down.

Fresh allegation against missing Chris Harding

Another local teenager has come forward claiming that missing man Chris Harding had approached her, the *Courier* has learnt.

A source close to the police, who did not wish to be named, said that the allegation had recently come to light and would be considered closely in the investigation to find missing 14-year-old Kayleigh Jackson.

The fresh allegation comes at the same time as further worrying details about Harding's past emerge. Reports detail how last spring Harding was apparently warned about his conduct with a female pupil – he was working as a secondary school teacher at the time. No further details were available at the time of writing, and the school did not respond to a request for comment.

Neither Chris Harding nor Kayleigh Jackson has been seen since 17 July. It is not clear if or how their disappearances are connected. Police say they are pursuing multiple lines of enquiry and urging anyone with information to come forward as soon as possible.

On Sunday, Kayleigh Jackson's family will hold a vigil on what will be their daughter's 15th birthday.

I snap the laptop shut, wincing to think of Chris's mum, Sandra, reading the story, linking things up in her head. Reluctantly, I pick up my phone and call her back. I can't put it off any more. She answers within two rings, so has clearly been waiting next to the phone.

She fires her sentences out at me in one long string; no gaps between the words. 'Rebecca! Where have you been? What is going on? We saw the article online. Christine, our neighbour, sent it to me. It's dreadful.'

'Give her a chance, Sand,' I hear Geoff say in the background, always the calmer one.

'Hi, Sandra. Sorry, I missed your calls. The police have just been over. They've confirmed there has been an allegation, I'm afraid.'

'Oh, oh! Geoff!' She's getting upset, hysterical already. Can't blame her really, but I can feel myself closing up, hardening.

'Calm down, love. Please.'

Geoff's voice is clearer now. I'm on speakerphone. I can picture them in their chintzy, pristine living room in the semi-detached in Peterborough where Chris grew up. They'll be crowded round the phone, Sandra perched on the edge of the sofa. Everything cream-coloured, spotless, with framed photos of Chris everywhere. Sandra spends most of the day cleaning and tidying mess that isn't there. She's always been 'a bit bad with her nerves', Geoff would say in hushed tones. She's worse now, I'm sure.

'What does it mean, Rebecca? What's happening?'

'I don't know what it *means*, Sandra. You'll have to judge for yourself.' I sound snappy, voice slightly raised.

Sandra sobs again.

'I'm sorry, Sandra. I'm really sorry. I'm just tired.' I wish I was in the living room with them. That what I mean to say wouldn't become warped and harsh between my brain and my mouth.

'I just don't understand all this,' she says again.

It's usually me like this, but the more upset Sandra gets, the more detached I feel. Like I'm floating above, watching myself have the conversation.

Geoff now, more matter-of-fact. 'Have you had any other information, Rebecca? Did they tell you anything else? Are you alright, love?' His breathing crackles on the line.

I feel softer towards them now. I know he'll have his arm around her shoulder. I sometimes resented them – for the way they interfered in things, always having to have a say on the house and wedding because they put the money in. But they've been good to me. They mean a lot to Chris. He missed them, I know he did. Sandra won't sleep again for weeks. She won't leave the house. Maybe I recoil because I know I could easily be like Sandra. I've been there only recently.

'That's all they said, Geoff. Same story as always. They can't tell us anymore.'

I hear Geoff tut and Sandra whimper. 'Bloody ridiculous, it is,' he says.

'I can't understand it, Rebecca.' A hoarse Sandra again. 'I hadn't seen Chris in a while. He hadn't visited, had he? He wasn't ringing like he used to. We thought you might be expecting. That you might be wanting to keep it to yourselves. So he was keeping quiet until you'd had the scans and everything.'

There's silence between us on the line. I think she's still half hoping I will say that's true, that there's a baby.

'It can't be what they're saying, Rebecca. It can't. You must know that.'

'I know, Sandra. I haven't given up.'

'We saw Phil, you know. He was visiting his mum and dad the other weekend.'

'Oh.' Phil is Chris's friend from Peterborough. They went to school together. We still used to see him and his wife Rachel in London, but the contact tailed off between me and Rachel when we moved here. I was busy and there just seemed nothing to talk about. Nothing warranting an email, certainly not a call… a Christmas card, perhaps. And anyway, the connection was really between Chris and Phil.

'How is he?'

'Oh, he's well, love.' She sniffs and blows her nose lightly. 'Busy at work like all you young people. He said he hadn't heard from Chris either before he went missing. Said they organised a visit but Chris cancelled it and that's the last time he talked to him.'

I didn't know that. I would have encouraged him to go down to London for the weekend. Or even better, invite friends up here.

'He feels terrible, love; you should give him a ring. He kept saying how he should have kept in touch better. He feels awful, love.'

Well, maybe he should have kept in touch better, I think, but don't say.

'Come on, Sandra, love. Don't.' I bet Geoff is stroking her hair. I hope so. I wish I could offer her more comfort.

'Have you rung round all his friends again, Rebecca?' asks Sandra.

I take a pause to avoid snapping at her. She is fragile.

'Sandra, I've already done all that. There's nothing there – they don't know anything. If they think of something, they'll ring me. I think most of them already think I'm a bit nuts. There's no point in me calling again.'

'Well, we're just waiting and waiting! It's unbearable!'

'I know, I do know. I'll try to come and visit, Sandra. Maybe in a few weeks.'

This seems to calm her a little.

'Don't you worry about us, love. You look after yourself, petal. And your mum. We'd love to see you, of course, though,' says Geoff.

'We're on the same side, you know. I haven't given up on Chris. I don't intend to.'

But the new allegation about Chris, what Detective Fisher said about the school, scratches at my brain and churns around in my stomach. Could I really not have seen something like that? Living in the same house? Sharing a bed? And yet, something is still telling me that it can't be true. Not Chris. Maybe I'm just refusing to see.

CHAPTER NINETEEN

Thursday, 12 November

After Detective Fisher's visit and talking to Sandra and Geoff, I know I won't sleep, at least not yet. I go to Barnacles to catch Julie before she closes. The place is almost empty now and she has already started to clean up. She's wiping down the bar.

'Jesus Christ, you nearly gave me a heart attack! You shouldn't sneak up on someone my age.'

'Sorry, Julie. Thought you'd seen me.'

'You back in here again? We can't get rid of you tonight, eh? You OK, love?'

'Yeah, bit of er… bad news, that's all.'

'Your mum alright, is she?'

'Yes, she's fine. It's not that.'

She sits down on one of the bar stools and pauses her spraying and polishing. 'I did hear a few people talking in here earlier about what's been in the paper. Not seen it myself, mind.'

'Yeah, it's… I wasn't expecting it. It's still all a bit of a bad dream, to be honest.'

'I bet. You just don't need it, do you? Chin up, love. I've told you before. You're not responsible for what he's done. Or not done,' she adds on. 'My ex-husband was a complete twat as well – I mean, not a twat like that.' She clears her throat. 'But he was still a wanker and I was still devastated when we split up. But it gets better, is my point. It won't feel like it right now but it will. "This too shall pass," my old mum used to say.'

I know she means well but I can't face hearing this right now.

'You wanting a drink, love?'

'I was hoping to use the pool, if I could?' I pat the rolled towel under my arm.

She looks up at the clock. 'It's a bit late, isn't it?'

'I won't be too noisy, I promise.'

'Well, it's not that. I mean, Christ, who are you going to wake up?' She looks at the clock again. 'I don't know; it's just a bit... Oh, balls to it; you've had a rough old day. If the lights are off when you're done, stick these through the letter box, will you?' She unhooks the keys from behind the bar and hands them to me.

'Thanks, Julie. Really appreciate it.'

I swim as many lengths as I can. I don't even count; I just push myself as hard as possible until my chest burns.

As soon as my breathing starts to level out again, I make myself do some more lengths – front crawl as fast and hard as I can. I feel almost sick when I come up for air again. My arms are tingling too – they should hurt tomorrow, but in a good way.

I pull one of the floats into the pool – a pink foam fish. I try to stand on it; push the weight of the water down until the foam explodes up out of the water again. The muscles in my thighs pull and contract as I push it down.

I'm starting to feel more tired now. Perhaps I'll be able to get some sleep, but I doubt it. Pulling the top of my body onto the float, my legs dangling in the water, I rest my chin on my hands and let myself bob around, weightless in the silence.

I must have fallen asleep, because I jump at a sound and the fish launches up into the air. A click against the glass like gravel.

Another. Then a loud bang – the door. Cold air. It takes me a moment to understand what's happening, but there's someone at the door and someone darting along the poolside too. Two boys.

'Hey. It's closed to the public!' I shout, and it has that weird, swimming-pool echo. Then their laughing echoes too.

He's wearing a woollen hat pulled down to his eyes but I recognise the boy on the poolside – he's been at the bus shelter near the caravan park. The other has his hood up and he's holding the door open.

'Hey! You can't be in here. It isn't open to the public. You need to leave!'

'You gonna make me from in there, are you?'

I start to walk towards the stepladder to get out on the opposite side of the pool. A splash as my shoe is thrown in, then the other, the water blackening from the mud. The boy is gathering up my clothes. He throws my bra into the pool. It's old and greying, chewing-gum white, floating on the surface. I think he'll just throw them all in, but he's heading towards the door now, with my towel too, his mate egging him on and laughing.

'Stop! Please! Don't… please!' I know it's futile and he's already outside, gone.

I'm freezing, teeth chattering as soon as I get out of the pool. I look around for something to cover myself with but there's nothing. How can there not be something? I do a quick check in the changing rooms but they're totally empty too.

The icy blast hits my soaked skin as soon as I open the door; almost painful. And they're standing outside – I can hear them laughing and talking low.

The light from the pool casts a wide, white spotlight on the group, like we're on a film set.

'What do you think about your husband now? Not so innocent now, is he, that's what they're saying in the papers.' I can't see her yet but it's Paige; I recognise the voice.

I can hardly speak, I'm shivering so much. I'm still in nothing but my swimsuit – my ten-year-old swimming costume. Navy blue, round neck, luminous yellow and pink swooshes up the sides. It's utilitarian, no support built in. It makes my breasts look squashed and low.

'I said, what do you think about your precious husband now? Kayleigh ain't the only one he went after. Dirty get!'

'Nothing's been confirmed or proved. You can't believe everything that's in the papers.'

'You would say that. Why do you think everyone's lying but your husband?'

They're standing around me now in a semicircle. One of the boys is looking me up and down. My arms are twisted, trying, failing to cover myself up. He is looking at my thighs and whispers something to Paige. She takes her phone out and points it at me. I hear the click. She's taking a picture of me, then another, or is it a video?

The flash goes off this time and I put my hands to my face. I think of Chris at the laptop, the photos of Ellen, the computer at the police station. The Watchers.

My body is shaking quite violently now with the cold.

'You a bit chilly?' It's Paige again. She holds out my towel to me. I am scared of stepping in something on the grass, and walking is painful on my feet, especially from the glass cut at Jeannie's. I reach out for the towel but she throws it to someone else. I try again but they do the same. I don't go to the next boy because I know the same thing will happen again.

'Don't you want it, then? You warm enough now?'

I don't answer. He is staring straight at my chest, making it obvious.

He throws the towel towards me. I bend to pick it up and I hear the phone camera click again; this time right behind me. My backside; the cellulite on the back of my thighs. Paige is laughing and showing the picture to her friend.

I reach down to snatch up my towel, but one of the boys runs in and kicks it just out of my reach. He picks it up and throws it to Kat.

She doesn't meet my eye. Head down, she comes over and hands it to me. I don't dare to reach out for it at first but she doesn't snatch it away. I grab it and wrap it around myself straight away. It's damp and covered in mud and doesn't make me any warmer at all.

'You're so fucking boring, Kat!'

'Piss off and grow up,' Kat replies, almost under her breath.

'Maybe I'll put these on the internet, shall I? Let someone perv over you like your husband did, shall I?' Paige waggles the phone around.

She looks at the screen. 'Although not sure many people will be interested, to be honest.'

Two of the boys gather round to get a better look at the pictures on the phone.

'Oi! What is going on here?'

It's Julie. I can't see her yet but her voice is getting closer.

'Rebecca, love? You alright?'

I can't answer, can't stop shaking from the cold.

'Shit!' one of the boys says.

Julie's out in the light now. She's still in her miniskirt and flip-flops, but she has a long brown cardigan on, tied at the waist.

'What you stood here like that for?' She looks at me, then looks around, realising that they have my clothes.

She clicks her fingers. 'Hand them over. Now.'

When she gets closer to Paige, Paige pretends to hand her the clothes but then puts her arm out to the side and drops them all.

'Get off my caravan park, you nasty little shits. You should be bloody ashamed of yourselves. I don't see how any of this helps your friend. Remember your friend, Kayleigh? You'd be better off out looking for her than terrorising other people. You hear me?'

No one says anything. The boys and Kat look at the floor. Paige looks at Julie right in the eye but she doesn't say anything.

'Jack Wilsden, I know your mother as well. And I know where she drinks. I'll be having words with her if you don't all piss off. NOW!'

She shouts on the 'now' and they all jump, me included.

The group troops towards the exit. Paige lifts her phone up and waves it at me again.

'You alright, love?'

'I'm alright; just freezing.'

'Honestly, they're vicious little twats. Here, get in the bar, will you, and let's get you sorted out. I'm freezing too, and I've got clothes on.'

CHAPTER TWENTY

Thursday, 12 November

Julie fished my stuff out of the pool and gave me a cup of tea and some dry clothes to put on. She even said I could stay with her for the night if I wanted, but I said no. I always assumed she lived on the caravan park but she told me she's got a house in town. She sometimes ends up staying on the site if she finishes late, or if she's 'had a few'.

I didn't tell her about the previous attacks and she didn't say anything either, so I assume she doesn't know. I don't want her to think I am bringing trouble to the caravan park. She might ask me to leave.

I am sitting in the caravan with the crockery on the chair in front of the door again, but I know I'm not going to be able to sleep. And I still can't warm up properly; I don't even feel dry.

I start clearing the pile of clothes off the bed and consider trying to sleep in there instead, but I get frustrated straight away. You can't even stand head on at the side of the bed. You have to stand sideways because the bed takes up most of the room. And there's a thin current of draught coming through the window. Now I remember why I don't sleep in here. I used to wake up with my head like a block of ice; and that's even before it got properly cold.

* * *

I give up on sleep and decide to walk to see Mum. It's not visiting time: it's late, too late. But I want to see her, be with her. Looking behind me again, I double-check that I am not being followed. I'd hate them to know where Mum is.

When I arrive at the nursing home, most of the rooms are in darkness, but the main living room is still brightly lit. Through the window, I see there are a couple of residents staring listlessly at the TV. The rest are probably in bed already or pottering around in their rooms.

I don't expect the front door to just open but it does. I look around for someone near reception but there's no one, so I head down the corridor to Mum's, past the TV room, the news blaring out. I run my nails loosely down the bottle-green Artexed walls. The darkness makes the corridor feel narrower, more oppressive. I am hoping to bump into Simon on the way, but to avoid everyone else. I start to walk slower near the staff room as I haven't seen him yet, but there's no one around at all.

The place is eerily still and quiet, the TV just a distant murmur now. I imagine it when it was a hotel, full of families returning from a day at the beach or heading downstairs dressed up for an evening of entertainment in the bar.

I press my ear to Mum's door to listen out for the TV or for her still shuffling around. Nothing. I let myself in anyway. Aren't they locked? Perhaps it isn't safe to lock them in. A fire hazard.

Will an alarm sound when I enter? Will she scream?

But nothing happens. The click of the door, then silence. It's completely dark in Mum's room. It takes my eyes some time to adjust to it. The room is toasty like always, cosy and comforting after being freezing outside the pool. There's a low hum and click from the radiator; the carriage clock ticks.

As my eyes become accustomed, I can see the outline of the frill on Mum's nighty. She looks peaceful. How much peace does she actually get, though? She stirs slightly. I want to crawl in with her, hold her and fall asleep, but I don't want to wake her, so I settle down in her armchair and pull the checked, knitted blanket over me, and put a cushion under my head. I feel calmer, safer in here in the darkness and silence, with Mum. I can feel myself floating off.

I'm violently yanked out of my almost-sleep when my phone rings. Mum stirs, but she doesn't wake. I answer the phone quickly, but I don't speak. Nor does the person on the other end of the line, yet again. I can just hear slow breathing, some shuffling around in the background. After about thirty seconds, the quiet of the dark room, the breathing, the line goes dead. Could it be Chris, trying to contact me?

It's light when I next wake and my neck is stiff. I am sweating under the blanket now so I wriggle out and stretch, trying not to make any noise so as not to wake Mum yet. Simon says she needs as much rest as she can get as she is often agitated, especially at night. This must have been a good night. Maybe she somehow sensed that I was here, and was comforted. Probably not. I seem to cause her distress these days.

The room is covered in pictures of me and Dad – birthdays, nights out, day trips. There's that wedding picture of me and Chris again. It has pride of place on the dressing table. The same picture they always used of me in the papers, in my wedding dress. Peterborough Town Hall. At first I wondered if it was a good thing, relatively speaking. Maybe people would be less likely to recognise me. I barely looked like myself that day. I wanted an up-do for my hair. It's what everyone said would look best with the dress. I thought it looked vintage, but it ended up just looking old-fashioned, and the 1940s make-up aged me too.

'You want to look like yourself, don't you?' the make-up artist had said. Stupid to book one really. Not me. But looking back at the photos, I didn't really look like me. I didn't think so anyway. I looked stiff and uncomfortable, the strapless dress a little too snug on the waist but too big at the top. It stuck out like armour when I sat down and I was yanking it up all day. Little rolls of fat that I didn't even know were there under my arms, splurging over.

The truth is I didn't really enjoy my wedding day. I couldn't admit it to myself at the time, and I could never admit it to anyone else. But I was uncomfortable in my skin; I hate to have my photo taken, and all day I had to smile and talk to aunts I didn't know in garish skirt suits and ridiculous hats. I barely saw Chris – he was doing his own rounds so that we could get to see everyone. I was peeved at the night do when he loosened his tie and drank too much, treating it like a night out in town with his mates, I thought. But they looked happy too, genuinely jubilant on the dance floor, arms around each other, grey suits flecked with spots of colour from the disco lights.

I had wanted a small wedding, but Sandra insisted that certain people had to be invited, because they'd invited Sandra and Geoff to their children's weddings. It would look terrible if these people didn't receive invitations, Sandra said. The planning went on and on, mushrooming. 'You can't not have a photographer. You can't just have a buffet – it needs to be a proper sit-down meal. You have to get covers for the chairs…' And Sandra and Geoff were paying for most of it, so we went along with their plans. Chris and I didn't have any money and my parents didn't have much.

I tried to prod at the idea with friends. Maybe they'd felt the same, it was normal – we'd laugh and roll our eyes knowingly at the strain of it all. I can't help but wonder now, if it was a warning sign even then. But even Jeannie toed the line, cooing, 'Are you having the best day of your life? Treasure it!'

But, I truly did want to get married more than anything; to form our own two-person family. Maybe I was already worrying about what would happen when Mum and Dad slipped away from me, although I didn't know it would be so soon. But as for the wedding – I just wanted it to be over; to get on with being married and together. But you're not allowed to say that, are you?

The papers said we didn't look happy in the photos. But we *were* happy. They cherry-picked the worst ones, where we're squinting at the sun, looking in opposite directions. And one where Chris is kissing me, yet it looks like I am pulling away, but I wasn't. People put all their photos up on Facebook. I had meant to, but never got around to untagging the unflattering ones, updating my privacy settings. I have now, of course.

I feel like a burglar, checking Mum's jewellery box again, turning to check that the tinkling hasn't disturbed her. The ring still isn't there. On the dresser, there's also a doily and a few of the ornaments from my parents' old house: a small yellow ceramic dog that was my grandma's, a little glass bear full of coloured sand, a money box shaped like a cottage. I shake it and it still has some coins inside. I can't remember now why we chose these specific things to bring from the house. We gave everything else away. They don't seem to add up to very much now, but it took so long to sort everything out, to decide what Mum should keep, what would fit in this little room. They'd lived in the house their whole married lives – forty years of knick-knacks, things saved 'just in case'.

In the dressing-table mirror, I see Mum stirring. She opens her eyes and it takes a few seconds for her to adjust and then notice me.

I look like her. You can see it in the bone structure, the shape of the lips. Sometimes I fear that I will lose my mind too; maybe I already am. Mum was only sixty-four when it started. I remember reading on the internet that it can run in families, especially when it starts quite early.

Her eyes dart around. I expect she's searching her mind for the information on who I am and why I am there, unable to trust her instinct that something is different, possibly wrong. She is fidgeting, beginning to panic. I don't want to make any sudden moves. Is it really so alarming to see such a familiar face here? Her own daughter. I suppose it is and I should be glad that she is at least able to recognise that something is different than usual. After all, I could be anyone.

I walk towards her slowly so I don't startle her any more. 'It's just me, Mum. Rebecca,' I say, holding my hands ahead of me to placate her. I stroke her hair when I get close enough. 'Sshhhhh, everything's fine.'

This seems to soothe her somewhat, although she still looks bewildered.

I pull the drawer out from under the bed and take out one of her *The Way We Were* magazines. She enjoys looking at the pictures of the area back in the 1940s and '50s. She seems to be more comfortable with the world in the pictures, less frightened by it.

I think about going in search of a cup of tea for Mum, but decide against it. Officially, I shouldn't be here for at least another few hours yet. I fetch a glass of water from the sink by the window instead. The sink is so small – child-sized – I can barely fit the glass into the bowl underneath the tap. The water splutters out in bursts, icy spray dampening my sleeve.

Mum turns the pages carefully, touching each picture, fascinated. Does she still think this is the world now? The world outside this room?

In one of the magazines we once came across a picture of Mum as a girl. She'd been the gala queen that year, and there she was. It didn't seem real. It was strange that I recognised her so easily. The picture was in black and white but something about the face was unmistakable. She was in a lacy white dress, on a float, a crown of flowers in her hair. Sure enough, in the caption there was her name, Averil Richards. Some people in the photo were simply named as 'unknown'.

Do you know the people in this picture? Is it you? Get in touch.

When Chris and I pointed it out to Mum and said it was her, she couldn't grasp it and kept pointing at me, even when I showed her the name. I suppose it did look like me when I was younger too.

'Chris,' Mum suddenly says, dropping the magazine onto the duvet in front of her and sitting bolt upright. She pulls a copy of the *Courier* out from the drawer next to her bed, folded open at the article from yesterday, with Chris's picture. I turn it face down again and she seems to lose her chain of thought, drifting back to the magazine.

She's come across a photo of Prospect Park in the magazine. We used to take her there on Sundays, when she was well enough to go out and about more often. We'd eat ice cream by the small lake and sometimes watch sprightly old men in white outfits playing bowls on the perfectly manicured lawn.

'Chris,' she points again, this time at the magazine. But she looks confused.

'Yes, Chris used to take us there, didn't he?' I silently berate myself for the baby-talk voice that keeps slipping in.

'Chris, here,' she says, pointing emphatically as if to say 'right here on this spot'. And she reaches for the newspaper again, but I snatch it away and put it out of view.

'Yes, we used to come, didn't we?' That stupid baby-talk voice again. 'Chris is busy with work at the minute, Mum, you know that. But he'll come again soon.'

I feel uneasy – about lying to Mum, about talking about Chris, about the fact she has even brought this up.

But Mum is shaking her head furiously. 'No, Chris came here!'

I try to hide my sigh, not to sound snappy. 'Yes, he comes to visit, doesn't he? But he hasn't been in a while because he's been busy with work.'

'No!' Her voice is rising to a shout now. 'He came here tomorrow!' She is shaking her head again and clutching at her hair with exasperation. She starts to jiggle up and down in the bed. She gets like this when she can't explain herself properly.

'You mean when me and Chris came together on a Sunday and we took you out to the park for the day?' I point at the magazine picture again, trying to distract her. 'And then we brought you back here, didn't we?'

'No, not you.' She shoos me away. 'Only Chris. He was here tomorrow.' She is getting angrier now, pointing backwards, over her head behind her when she says tomorrow. Her eyes are searching for something.

Chris only ever came here with me. He wouldn't have come alone, he found it far too awkward. Too upsetting seeing my mum like that, he said.

Deep breaths. 'Yesterday? Mum, he didn't come yesterday.' She nods at this. 'He came a while ago, with me, and he will be back again soon. I'm sure. Please.'

'He was here yesterday.' She is emphatic, with a defiant look. She refuses to give in. 'He took my ring.' Her speech is much more decisive now.

'No, Mum. You're just getting confused. Please. You're mixed up. Your ring is temporarily lost – God knows what you've done with it. And you've seen Chris in the paper. Please don't say things like that about Chris!' I can hear that I am shouting now too.

'Where's Kayleigh?' Mum's eyes dart side to side, panicked.

I am holding both Mum's hands down so that she can't keep waving them around, jabbing her fingers.

The door handle turns. It's Simon.

He is surprised, struggling to weigh up the situation. 'Oh, well, hello. What's going on in here? You're early.'

His tone is even, purposefully measured. He doesn't sound annoyed or suspicious. You probably get good at that, working here. Confused residents, bereaved families.

I glance at the clock. It's 8 a.m.; visiting isn't usually allowed until after 10.30.

'Yes, I couldn't sleep. I woke up early so I came in to see Mum.' I don't want to get Simon into trouble. Or draw attention to myself. I stand in front of the chair, and try to bundle the blanket away.

Simon shoots a knowing look so I realise he has seen it, and he turns his attention to Mum.

'Now then, Averil, shall we get you a cup of tea and some breakfast? You can have it in here with Rebecca today, if you'd like?'

Mum gives a serene smile and nods, although I can't tell if she knows what he is asking her. Is she pretending or is her train of thought still on Chris? The ring? Or just derailed altogether? I open the curtains and the window and Mum shields her eyes, pulling the covers up around her neck. She eyes me cautiously.

Simon returns with tea, porridge and toast. I notice there are two bowls of porridge, more than enough toast for us all and three cups.

'Haven't had time for my own breakfast yet.' He winks. 'I'm Hank Marvin here.'

We eat and drink in silence for a while, a strange picnic around Mum's bed. Silence except for the chomping and slurping noises Mum's making. She has food around her mouth and on her nighty.

'She's enjoying that then,' I joke feebly.

'We'll soon clean you up after, won't we, Averil?' Simon says. 'No harm done.'

Mum shoots a huge smile at Simon. 'Where's my ring?'

The smile drops from his face.

'You took it,' Mum says, jabbing the back of Simon's hand, leaving a small indentation with her nail. 'He took it,' she whispers to me.

Simon's face flushes. 'I wouldn't worry too much. I expect we will find it.' His voice is breezy. 'These things happen quite a lot. And she hasn't been out anywhere. Obviously not alone, anyway. So it can't have gone far, can it, Averil?'

'She said Chris took it a minute ago.'

He gives me a quizzical look. 'Your Chris? Well, that's a new one on me.'

I clear my throat, unsure how this is going to go. 'She said Chris was here. Recently. Like really recently. After-he-went-missing recently.'

Simon looks startled. 'What do you mean?'

'I think she was trying to say he was here yesterday.'

Something flashes across his face. Irritation? Pity?

Mum is turning her head between us like she's watching a game of tennis.

'What, is Chris back? I don't understand, Rebecca?'

'I don't know... no, he isn't back. Well, I don't think so... but Mum is saying he was here yesterday... I think. So now I just don't know. Is that possible?'

'No, Rebecca. Surely you know it isn't possible. Well, I mean... of course anything's possible. But you know your mum says things. She isn't well. And I mean, you haven't quite been yourself, have you, Rebecca?'

'Please stop saying my name like I am a child, will you?'

Simon looks weary, resigned, and puts his toast down. Put off. I have broken the atmosphere. I shouldn't have said anything.

'To the best of my knowledge, Rebecca, he wasn't here.'

I can't tell if he's making a point of saying my name to show me he won't be shouted down by me, or if the flicker on his face means he forgot.

'You know that he can't have been here. Apart from anything else...' He stops there, clearly wishing he hadn't drawn attention

to the 'anything else'. But he decides to finish his thought anyway, 'I would have seen him; I'd have seen his name in the book.'

'I don't always sign the book,' I say, petulant.

'Well, you should. It's a health and safety thing. It's probably a
bloody legal thing! We'd have seen him, Rebecca – you know he
can't have been here. I mean… you'd know if he was back, right?
Someone would know. And most likely that would be you.'

'Well, you'd hope, wouldn't you? But, seriously, who does
know anything anymore?' I try the closed window, rattling it,
jabbing at the locks and pushing at it. It's stiff with paint and
old wood. Eventually it comes loose. 'Maybe he got in through
here.'

Simon's jaw clenches. 'Rebecca, seriously, what is going on?
What is this about? Why would he come here now? And why the
hell would he break in through a window? I think we'd notice
that, don't you?'

'Well, you tell me. I'm beginning to wonder.' I already regret
saying that. 'Has he ever been here? Without me?'

'Well…' He thinks for a while. 'I don't know?' I can hear the
exasperation in his voice. 'Yes, I am pretty sure sometime in the
summer, he was here, yes. I will look in the book.'

I throw my hands down onto the bed, raising my voice, startling Mum. 'Well, why have you never said anything about this?'

'Why would I? He's a relative, isn't he? He's allowed to come
here, isn't he? What's wrong with that? I don't see what you're
getting at.'

I am exasperated now, clutching at the duvet, grinding my
teeth. 'Mum, when was he here? Tell Simon what you told me.
MUM!'

Tears wobble in Mum's eyes and she looks to Simon for a clue
on what she should do next. She begins to cry and pulls the covers up to hide her face.

'Mum!' I am shaking her now, grabbing her arm tight through the duvet. I am only shaking her lightly – it won't hurt her – but I catch myself mid-action. I shouldn't be doing this.

'Rebecca!' Simon speaks sharply as if to slap me out of it.

He is standing up now, official. 'I am sorry but you just cannot come here and upset your mother. Your mum isn't equipped to deal with these situations.'

I pull the duvet down from Mum's face but she still tugs against it.

'I'm sorry, Mum, I'm sorry. Just forget it, yes? I'm sorry.' My voice sounds pleading and desperate.

Warily, she brings her hands back down onto the bed and looks sheepishly at me, waiting for the storm to pass.

'Look, don't worry about it,' Simon says, shooting a smile at Mum. 'Tensions are high all round at the moment. I understand why you're upset, you know. But, as I say, you can't come here doing this. And… well, you can't take everything your mum says on face value. She's very confused.'

I am stroking Mum's veiny hand, full of guilt, trying to calm her down.

Simon's voice has softened now. 'Maybe you better go, Rebecca. It's time to get you showered and dressed, isn't it, Averil?'

'Yeah, 'course.'

I give Mum a long hug and kiss her on the top of the head. She looks happy enough when I turn to take a final look before I leave, raising her arms obediently to be undressed and washed, completely open, trusting.

The idea of Chris being here alone, never mentioning it, pinballs in my mind. The ring is sitting somewhere, stupid and inanimate, glinting in the dark in a drawer or a pocket. Or sparkling in the outside world on someone else's finger. Mum gets mixed up but she hasn't said anything like that before. Accusing Simon too. My guts clench, a phantom pain where my instinct used to be, telling me what to do, showing me the way. Now the needle just spins and spins.

A sense of unease sits like oil that won't dissolve in my thoughts, polluting everything.

CHAPTER TWENTY-ONE

'I'd like to speak to Mrs Grange, please.'

'Do you have an appointment?'

'No.'

'I'm afraid she's probably otherwise engaged.'

'Can you check?'

Almost straight away she says, 'She's busy right now. Can I take a message?'

Not enough time to really check. I can hear the receptionist typing.

'I don't want to leave a message, no. I'm Chris Harding's wife. I'd like to speak to Mrs Grange.'

A pause.

'One moment. Hold the line, please.'

A click, then silence.

Eventually she comes back. 'I'm putting you through now.'

Being Chris's wife at least opens some doors for me these days. I decided to ring the school where Chris used to work in London, after what Detective Fisher said the other day. I know I won't get a straight answer from her.

'Mrs Harding?'

'It's Pendle, actually. Ms Pendle.'

'Oh, but I thought…' She moves the phone away and shouts, 'Marie!'

'I am Chris's wife, though. Chris Harding's wife.'

She moves the phone away again. 'Never mind, Marie. Close the door, would you?'

I picture Marie, pressing her ear up to the door, listening in.

'So, Ms… Pendle. What can I help you with?' There's a definite edge, a brittleness to her voice. If I was there in the room with her, she might have one finger on the panic button under the desk.

I woke up agitated after I fell asleep again when I got back from Mum's. My jaw was aching. I must have been grinding my teeth. I'd been going over the newspaper article, the new allegation, in my mind, trying to think of an answer, something that could redress the balance.

'I want you to make a statement about Chris.'

'A statement?' The way she says it reminds me of Lady Bracknell's 'A handbag?'– arch, aghast at the idea.

'I think if the school were to make a comment about Chris, in the media, it would help. It's all very one-sided at the moment. These latest allegations. It's no good from me, but someone impartial like you… it could help.'

'Ms Pendle, I—'

'It doesn't have to be anything big, just that when he was at the school there were no issues. A clean record. That kind of thing.'

'I'm afraid I can't do that, Ms Pendle.'

'Why?'

Mrs Grange has never met me; I'm just a voice on the end of the line to her. Someone she wants to get rid of.

'Because… well, we have taken professional advice on the matter and we've been advised not to make any comment on the issue. At all. We have to protect the reputation of the school, you'll understand. It's not appropriate for us to… to draw attention to ourselves any further.'

'What about Chris's reputation, Mrs Grange?'

'Believe me, this pains me greatly, but the children and the school – and Kayleigh Jackson, frankly – are the matter at hand here, Ms Pendle.'

I wish she would stop saying my name like I am one of her pupils.

'I understand you must be in a very difficult position right now. Really I do. And I wish I could do more to help. But I can't, I'm afraid.'

'The police, they said you had mentioned the incident with the student.'

Silence. Just her breathing.

'When the girl... when she was upset and you'd said he shouldn't be alone in the classroom.'

'It's standard practice, Ms Pendle.'

'But was there anything more to it?'

'Ms Pendle, it's my duty as headteacher of this school to be transparent – I stated the facts to the officers that I spoke to and, frankly, I would rather that we were not having this conversation about it. I don't think it's appropriate. It is beyond what I am comfortable doing.'

Her voice is nothing but official now. The wall is completely up.

'Is that all, Ms Pendle? I'm very sorry. Really, I am.'

I click to end the call.

After the call with the school, I'm still a ball of energy. My nails push into my hands, jaw flexed. It didn't help. Didn't get me anywhere at all. Everywhere I go I just get a hand in the face, locked out. No one is interested in finding Chris, or helping me to.

CHAPTER TWENTY-TWO

Friday, 13 November

Jeannie and I sit in the seafront café, surrounded by the minty green walls and the high ceiling that make it feel even colder indoors than it is. The glass doors at the front of the café look out to the grey sea. I can't warm up after the blustery walk over so I leave my coat on. Jeannie's been texting me non-stop since the newspaper article. She pretty much demanded to meet.

Pictures of poolside beauty contests in the 1950s line the walls in cheap, black plastic frames – the women look coiffed and pristine in close-fitting shorts or voluminous skirts and halter-neck tops. A fake, romanticised version of real life, surely. How will they represent our era, I wonder?

The foam wobbles as Jeannie puts two cappuccinos down, and two scones.

Before I can refuse, Jeannie gets in there first. 'Do me a favour and just eat it, will you, Becs? I've got an hour on my own to have a coffee without someone swinging off me or demanding food. Just go with it, for me.'

I stir the coffee and break a small piece off the scone. Jeannie slathers hers with a thick layer of butter.

'So, I have finally got a hold of you then.'

'Sorry, I was visiting Mum and stuff.'

'How is she?'

'Same.'

'Bless her. Give her my love. I'll bring Sam and Ellen in to see her again soon.'

'She'll like that.'

'So the thing in the paper then…'

I take a gulp of the coffee and it burns my throat. Good.

'There's nothing to say that it's true.'

'Becs—'

'There isn't!'

'Have you spoken to the police? Detective Whatsherface.'

'Fisher. Yeah. She came round.'

'And what's her take on it?'

'Same old. She doesn't give much away. They have to investigate blah blah blah.'

'Well, at least she's giving you a bit of information for once. But she didn't say she didn't think it was true?'

'No, but she wouldn't say that, would she? What are you trying to say, Jeannie?' I put my cup down and it clatters a bit too loudly. People turn and look.

Jeannie lowers her voice. 'I'm just saying… well, I'm just trying to find out how you feel about it. Because the thing with Ellen the other day; at my place. The questions you were asking her. I was… well, I was wondering if you were having your doubts.'

I push the barely touched scone away. 'I've never had anything but doubts, Jeannie. This hasn't changed my mind about anything.'

The mental cramps, the spasms; they've been getting worse. When I'm trying to get to sleep or just sitting around, they come in so vividly from nowhere. The images of Chris and Kayleigh. But I don't tell her that.

'Will you not come and stay with us for a few days? Ellen would love it, I know she would.'

'How is she? After the other day? I'm so sorry, Jeannie. Really, I am.'

She bats the air away in front of her. 'Honestly, she's fine. Please let's just forget about it. You're under a lot of pressure.'

But her manner is too breezy. It's obvious it's a 'thing'. Dan's probably had a word with her about it.

'I'm fine at the caravan. Really, I am. I prefer to be on my own.'

Jeannie sighs and takes a big bite of the scone, talking with her mouth full. 'Well, I don't really get why, but whatever. I'm not going to rope you into babysitting, you know.'

'You'd never let me babysit your kids.'

'Don't be daft.' But she looks uncomfortable. 'Becs, just promise me you'll lie low. You'll knock it off with the leaflets and hashing over the stories on the Internet again. Please. People will be on edge right now with all this. So just keep a low profile.'

'We wouldn't want to upset anyone, would we?'

'You know what I mean.'

'Yeah, I know. Does going out for your birthday count as lying low, then?'

'I said lie low, not roll over and bloody die. I'm saying don't provoke people. You're allowed to go out and have a laugh.'

'I'll see how I feel. I'm really not up for going out at the minute. Sorry.'

'You're coming out. End of, Becs. It's my birthday and you have never not come out for my birthday. It's happening.'

Jeannie looks out at the sea, drinking her coffee without blinking.

'Jeannie, I want to ask you something.'

She lowers her cup. 'You don't need permission.'

'You won't like it.'

'Out with it,' she says, clattering the cup onto the saucer.

'The other night. Dan. What was he saying?'

'Not this again. I don't want another row, Becs.'

'It's not that.'

'What then?' I suspect she knows what I'm referring to but evading it.

'He said "no wonder" something about Chris.'

Jeannie lets out a sigh and turns to the waves again. 'You really want to do this? OK, it wasn't just about Chris.'

'What do you mean?'

She puts her hands out in surrender. 'He said no wonder you were always arguing.'

'What? That isn't true. Why would he say that?'

She takes a sip from the cup, even though it's empty. 'Look, Becs, the last few times we'd seen you, things seemed a bit… tense between you?'

'No.' I can't keep the defensiveness out of my voice. 'It was more that I had a lot on with Mum and everything and sometimes it just got a bit much for us.'

'What about that day at the beach? Ellen said you had a row.'

'It was stupid.'

'OK. You don't have to tell me.'

'I was trying to tell him to try to get an exhibition of his pictures at one of the cafés in town and he lost his temper a bit with me. He felt like they weren't good enough. Or maybe he was offended that I suggested an exhibition somewhere so small. I don't remember now. It was nothing.'

'Alright, Becs. Fine.'

'Then why are you looking at me like you don't believe me?'

'Becs, I just want you to take the rose-tinted specs off a bit. I think maybe it will help you deal with all this a bit better.'

We sit in silence for a bit after that. She tries to make chit-chat with me but I give her one-word answers. We say a frosty goodbye after a while, and Jeannie watches me walk away until

I'm out of view. It's like I said to Detective Fisher – people fix-
ate on the cracks and the flaws in other people's relationships.

'See you tomorrow!' she shouts after me.

I need to go round to the house before I go out, to get something
to wear for tomorrow night, and to check for a credit card – just
one more, in case one of the others gets stopped.

I take the bus to the house, as close as it will take me anyway.
It's almost empty, just a group of boys at the back. I try not to
look at them, not be noticed. In case it's any of the ones who
have been to the caravan park.

I sit close to the front and watch myself on the CCTV screen,
grainy, then the picture switches. I can't get a clear view of the
boys because there's a delay. The footage jerks. There's a whoop
and laughing from behind and it's a physical effort not to turn
round. They're on the camera again, coming down the aisle towards me. I tense up. No longer able to stop it, I crane my head
round but they're already past me and out onto the street. They're
only about twelve years old, laughing and joking among themselves, not interested in me at all.

As we approach the estate, I notice how strange the newly laid
roads look, how much they stand out for their perfect straight-
ness, and the emptiness on either side. Just fields and swathes of
wasteland where they said they would build. There's no sign of
anyone, like always; the show home placard still there, the houses
uniform, bland, boxy.

I keep my head down between the bus and the house, just in case
anyone is around.

As I open the door, letters collect behind it in a snowdrift. I
can't look at them now. Most will probably be telling me how

much money I owe, others will be offering me more credit. I will need those ones, later on.

I lock the front door behind me and stand in the entrance breathing in through my nose and out through my mouth, with my hand on the handle of the door to the front room. My stomach is contracting. I close my eyes and push, forcing them open after a few moments in the room. This time I don't run upstairs – I force myself to look.

Everything looks and feels just the same, as if I've just been out to work or popped to the shops, like the letter I left for Chris suggests I have done. As if he and I are still living here as normal. At least, I think it feels the same. It's hard to focus on a solid memory of what it was actually like, but I can so clearly picture Chris, about to pop his head out of the kitchen, wearing rubber gloves or an apron, getting started on tea or the washing up when he got in from work. There'd be music or comedy on the radio or a CD playing. Here, now, it's completely silent, except for a tap dripping in the kitchen.

I survey the room more slowly now, try to stop my mind doing an auto-fill. Sometimes I think, *Maybe I should just move back here. Why pay twice? Especially when I have so little money anyway.* But I can't. My stomach is twisting, throat tight already at just being so close to him, yet so far away. I am better at the caravan.

I take a slow walk around the house, and already the tears are rising. It's too much. This is why I don't come here; it's my way to block things out. I can see now, cold-eyed, that it looks like a house but not a home. Maybe it's just because he's not here, it's not lived-in. Because it *was* cosy when we were here: the mornings with tea and toast on the sofa with a blanket, the nights watching films.

But now, the pictures we have up look cheap and anonymous. We said we were going to get some of Chris's photos blown up, but we hadn't got around to it. The cushions that I bought from the supermarket looked fun when I saw them – parakeets on one, coloured houses on the other – pink, mint, yellow, powder blue. They look tatty and washed out already.

Deep breaths. There's some vodka in the fridge. Someone left it after we had them round for a meal and board games. A couple – Chris plays football with the husband – it's bad that I can't remember their names now. *Ashley* rings a bell. Was that her or him?

The fridge is empty except for the vodka, but it still smells foisty. Sealed for too long. I don't remember clearing it out before I left. I can't imagine I would have, but a lot of things from around then are a blur. I take a swig. It's icy cold, which makes it easier to swallow; it burns less. One more, since I need to go upstairs to the bedroom.

I should really turn off the fridge, save what little money I have. But, pathetically, that feels too final. Part of me wants to leave everything as it is so we could just pick up as we left off tomorrow – as if nothing has happened.

Buoyed by the hit of vodka, I go up to our room to find something to wear later. I just want to get this over with now. All our clothes are still hanging there, lifeless. His in the wardrobe on his side of the bed; mine in the one on my side. His side. My side.

I open my wardrobe. The colours, patterns and shapes; each reminds me of the old me, my old life, our old life. Places I have worn them, days out we had together. Jeannie's wedding, my last birthday. The flowery anniversary dress I opened with a cava breakfast in bed – two sizes too small – his face fell before we laughed about that. I take out a jumper of Chris's from the drawers on his side of the bed and lie down with it, breathing it in, its softness against my face. The need to hold Chris, to touch him and be near him is physical; it's overwhelming. I would give anything, really anything, for just one minute together. I hold a pillow and drape the soft jumper over it. The blinds are slightly open and the winter sun is beaming through. I close my eyes, and for two minutes, I allow myself to imagine we're lying there together. I don't let anything else, the truth, in at all for that short time. I am getting good at that. I am completely calm for those moments. I almost feel as if we are actually here.

But soon this feeling will be replaced by the anger again – the rage that he's just abandoned me here; that he might have betrayed me in one of the worst ways I could ever imagine. The shame he's made me feel for something I haven't done.

I wake with a start. Being back here in the bedroom, I dreamt Chris and I were lying here, intertwined. But I turned into Kayleigh somehow. In that way you can in dreams, I was both Kayleigh and I was me, outside of it all, watching them in horror. I was trying to shout at them, at us, but no sound would come out.

Even though there is no one to see me, I suddenly feel foolish clutching the pillow and the jumper. I feel exposed somehow and I push them both away.

I lie there for some time, just in the blankness, focusing on the feeling of the softness of the bed underneath me, the weight of my limbs.

I don't know how long I have been here, but the time is getting on. The alarm clock blinks red. It's 4 p.m. already.

The light outside is changing. Eventually, I force myself up to find something to wear for this stupid night out. I no longer feel like going, but it would upset Jeannie if I didn't. And she's right: I can't slip back to where I was before.

I am unenthusiastic about the clothing selection, scraping the hangers along the rail and discounting each option immediately. Once, I would have spent hours picking out the right outfit, trying things on, getting a new lipstick, doing a trial run with my hair. In the end, I decide on blue jeans, a cheap black vest with subtle sequins around the edges, ballet flats and a long black cardigan. The type of thing I would once have worn for an average day – to the supermarket, even. Not for a night out. But I have no interest in looking 'nice'; it's for Jeannie's benefit. I don't want to drag her night down.

Something in me keeps feeling that making an effort would be inappropriate, that it would be frowned on.

When Dad died, before Mum really deteriorated, she fretted for days about what to wear to his funeral. Should it be bright, in celebration of his life, or dark and sombre? It was Mum's friends who had mentioned the 'celebration of life' approach. But, really, we're not that kind of family. It's too modern. We're a fire and brimstone, all in black, get-pissed-at-the-wake type of family. She went for dark grey in the end and I wore an old black dress.

The outfit I have picked out won't draw too much attention. It's suitably nothing.

I go downstairs and take one last look back into the living room; another twinge. I can't put my finger on it – this niggling feeling that something is off or out of place, not quite the way it should be.

CHAPTER TWENTY-THREE

Back in town, I wander aimlessly for a while, looking into the arcades, peering into empty pubs as I go, before drifting into the town centre and past the betting shops. I think about going in again, asking around, but what would be the point? I wonder if the woman would remember me, from throwing me out the last time, guiding me by the elbow. She said I was 'harassing her customers'.

On the high street, the shops and cafés are already starting to close. There are lights off in some; in others people are cashing up or hoovering, ready for tomorrow. Further along the seafront, the traffic peters out to almost nothing.

There's a narrow road that leads to the caravan park. As I approach the turning, a parked car suddenly flicks its lights on and starts the engine. No one has got in, though. They must have been sitting, waiting. Waiting to collect someone, perhaps, passing the time with a newspaper. Or pulled over to make a phone call.

The red car gets a little ahead of me, then drops back again, parallel. It makes me think of the dog, Polly, that Mum and Dad had after I moved out. The trainer told Dad the dog should never be allowed to get ahead of you when you're out walking. If you want to show it who's boss, it should always be next to you or a little behind. '*You're* walking the dog; don't let it walk you,' she'd said.

I slow down slightly. The car's engine runs at a low hum. It's going slower than it should on this stretch of road, but there are no other cars around now. I try to look quickly into the car but all I can see is my own reflection.

I speed up again to turn into the narrow lane to access the caravan park. It's poorly lit, only a few street lamps too far spaced out, high walls and huge trees on both sides, making it feel even darker. I realise the car is in the lane too. *Just a coincidence*, I tell myself. I take out my phone, flashing on the light, making it clear that I can contact someone, call for help. Reaching into my bag, I position my key in the fist in my hand – the point poking out, a makeshift stabbing device, like they tell you to do for self-defence.

The car is behind me now, its headlights switched low. I stop and wait for it to pass, the engine gently growling at me. My plan is to make a run for it back up the lane. I know it's probably nothing, but my anxiety levels are high. I just need to get out of the situation. It'll take the car a while to turn round on a lane this narrow.

But it's getting closer and closer, pushing me into the wall. It's deliberate. I press myself back against the wall, feeling the cold, slimy green moss under my hands. The front wheel of the car mounts the slope, it's close to my knee, spinning in the dirt. I fumble to light up my phone again, finding the main button, but the icons are swimming in front of me, my thumb refusing to carry out the actions my brain is already visualising. The car's engine revs. I momentarily consider jumping onto the bonnet. But then the beam comes on, shocking my eyes at first. I have found the phone torch and quickly turn it round and shine it into the car. Before my eyes have time to recover, the engine revs harder and the lights blare on again. The front wheel spins close to my leg and I'm on tiptoes. My eyes are starting to adjust to the shape of a person driving the car, maybe two people in the front, but it's reversing up now, preparing to pull away. I push out my left hand and feel the key drag along the paintwork of the car as it speeds up. When I pull it away, a fine curl of metallic paint falls into my hand.

I run straight to the caravan and sit inside, wrapped in the duvet for warmth. But I don't dare to turn the lights on.

After a while, when I feel sure no one has followed me, I pore over the stories online again. I can't stop myself. I search Kayleigh's and Chris's names under news, like I have done so many times before. After the early barrage, when they first disappeared, the updates thinned out; only the odd mention since mid-September. Now there is a fresh flurry, regurgitating the new allegations about Chris, recycling and rewording all the previous stories again. It feels like an endless pattern, repeating as far as the eye can see.

And it's obviously getting people stirred up again, reheating all that hate. It's not even 7 p.m. yet but I try to sleep anyway, just to escape, but it won't come, my mind like a cooking pot on the stove, bubbles and blisters puncturing the surface.

CHAPTER TWENTY-FOUR

Saturday, 14 November

I told myself I was going for a walk, to get some morning air. Maybe I'd walk on the beach. But I knew where I would really end up. I am standing at the top of the alley again, where Star Pizza is. But there's nothing happening. No one coming and going at all. I walk down the street and look into the shop. The door is open, radio playing, but I can't see anyone. No girls, no men, no one working. Nothing at all. They're probably just setting up for the day.

But parked a little up the street from the takeaway, a red car is there. The red car from last night? My stomach contracts, an image of the narrow road to the caravan park, being pressed against the wall. Mixing in with the video of The Watchers, the characters all jumbling up.

Did I imagine it? Maybe just a car passing, me overreacting… but I put my hand in my pocket and the red curl of paint from the car is still wedged down in the corner, retaining a certain stiffness. I roll it between my fingers.

It's a compulsion to have one quick look. At first I don't think it's there, I don't see the scratch on the side of the car. Maybe I was wrong. I look inside the car. Rubbish is strewn on the back seat – coke bottles, polystyrene takeaway boxes.

There's an old duvet crumpled in the back seat, the cover looks stained with brown liquid, the grubby foam poking out at

one end. Walking slowly around, I look at the other door and I
see it's there. The scratch I made with my key. Shallow, but fresh,
unmistakable. I run my middle finger over the groove.

'We must stop meeting like this, love.'

It takes me a second to make sense of everything. His crotch
is pressed hard against my backside and I spin round, but he
doesn't move. Ashy is right in my face, a leer across his mouth.

'What can I do for you?' he asks, not moving backwards. 'I
don't know why you are suddenly so interested in me. Sorry, love,
I'm seeing someone, and to be honest you're not really my type.
You know what I'm saying, Rebecca?'

He pushes his crotch into me harder and I shove him back. He
holds up his hands, palms open then rubs them down on his jeans.

I hadn't told him my name.

'Why are you looking in my car and sniffing around my business?'

'What happened to your car then? Nasty scratch there.'

He screws up his face and inspects the car, then shrugs. 'Must
have scraped it.'

'Where?'

'I don't know, do I? Out – what's it got to do with you?'

I reach into my pocket, looking for the curl of paint, but it's
gone. I search both pockets and my jeans too, casting around on
the floor.

'Lost something?'

My mind is spinning now. I am still rooting in my pockets,
digging right in the corners. I feel woozy and sick.

Ashy smirks at me.

'Why have you got a duvet in your car?'

He lets out an exaggerated laugh and looks up at the sky.
'Because I've got a dog and I don't want hair and shit all over
the back of my car. I don't know why I am answering all these

questions or what this is all about. I am just trying to run a restaurant.'

'Restaurant! That's stretching it a bit.'

'And I don't want any trouble round here, Rebecca. It isn't
good for business. I feel like you're trying to bring me trouble,
Rebecca Pendle. I thought I warned you, but maybe you didn't
get the message.'

'Warned me?'

'The last time you paid us a visit here, remember? Not that
long ago. You can't seem to stay away.'

'You tried to run me over.'

His expression looks like true shock, confusion, then it breaks
into a smile. He shakes his head.

'You came to where I live last night.'

He raises an eyebrow. 'Where's that then?'

'You know where.'

'My car has been sitting there since yesterday morning, babe.'

'No.'

'Look, what are you doing here? What do you want?' He
looks at his watch and gestures towards the shop. 'I've got stuff
to do, you know?'

Daz appears at the door. 'You alright, mate?'

'Daz, mate. Where was I last night?'

'Here. Where else?'

'Exactly. Where else? And where has my car been?'

Daz points to where it's parked.

'Thank you – now fuck off back inside, will you?'

Daz shoots me a dirty look, then his head is down and he
shuffles away.

Ashy turns his attention back to me. I dig in my pocket for
the metal scraping again but it isn't there. Nothing fits together
right. I'm watching him closely, alert for sudden movements.

'If you're here about Kayleigh Jackson again you need to look a bit closer to home, love. Chris Harding's your man, is what I hear, in more ways than one.' He spits to one side. 'It is what it is, babe. You'll have to face it and stop acting like some crazy woman.' He throws his hands up. 'Sorry, but it ain't my problem.'

Something surges up in me. What Ashy has said has struck a raw nerve. It feels like salt in a wound, hearing it from his mouth. I'm angry at myself for finding myself here. I feel myself lunging forward towards him, and he grabs me by the wrists, hard.

'Don't you say my husband's name; you don't know anything about us, about any of it.'

He lets go, white finger marks with a red outline on my skin. 'You don't like it, do you? Get your own house in order.' He jabs at the air in front of my face. 'Get away from here and keep away from me and my business.'

He's already walking towards the takeaway, jangling the keys in his hand. He bats the other hand back at me – not listening anymore. His hair is kind of the same colour as Chris's, I notice now, has that dark brown wave in the back. I try to drive out the association, but Chris is everywhere again now, and nowhere too.

There's a large, smooth pebble on the floor at the curb. I picture myself throwing it at Ashy, cracking the back of his head, or launching it at the window, the glass breaking out like a spider's web.

My neck pulses. Here, now, in the bright winter daylight, everything looks different to when I was here the other night. It looks normal. The sun bounces off the car, showing up a few small scratches on the paintwork, old ones and new ones. The kind you get on any car when you've had it a while. Ashy and Daz busy themselves in the shop, wiping things down and fiddling with the fryers. I start to walk away and Ashy waves at me sarcastically, whistling along to the radio.

CHAPTER TWENTY-FIVE

Saturday, 14 November

I am churned up after the run-in with Ashy so I am glad that when I arrive at the restaurant the girls are already seated. They're Jeannie's friends, really. Angela and Shelley went to school with me and Jeannie, but we stopped being in touch directly a while after I moved away. The novelty of writing long emails at work wore off; we got busy. 'What have you been up to?' became too much of an open-ended question. It's still nice to see them, though. Gemma is one of Jeannie's 'mum friends', as she calls them, a circle I can't be part of. We've been on a few nights out since I've been back and when I used to visit from London. I like Gemma. She's quick-witted, with a dry sense of humour.

Jeannie's been texting me since this morning to make sure I wouldn't drop out. She would have sulked a bit if I had, but, deep down, she wouldn't have been surprised. She would have forgiven me; she always does. That's why I am here.

She's booked a cheap Italian place on the seafront. Rosa's. Chris and I used to come here sometimes for a mid-week tea or for lunch on the weekends. He'd always get the calzone, chips on the side. I am a little hurt that Jeannie doesn't remember this. Why would she? But I thought I noted a flicker of recognition between us when she told me the name of the restaurant. I think she remembered then, but it was too late. Most places around here have memories for me. So what difference does it make?

In the end, I couldn't say why exactly, I did feel like going out after all, getting out of that tiny caravan, seeing the girls for a bit. I wanted a night off from it all, from my life. To go to the restaurant and smell the warm, savoury scent of garlic, like we've done so many Saturday nights before. Let the wine take the edge off, listen to them talk.

I am purposely a bit late, as I don't like the idea of sitting there on my own waiting for them. Once I wouldn't have minded, but not now. I sat in the caravan for a while after I got dressed, coat on, working myself up to coming out. Jeannie puts on a show of being pleased to see me when I get there, standing up and giving me a hug. We are not huggy friends and never have been, but I know she is trying to be nice and reassure me, so I go along with it.

'You look lush!' she says, looking me up and down, although I haven't even removed my Puffa coat yet.

I see the other girls smiling politely, that early point in the night before everyone has thawed out.

'I've not seen you for ages. You look really well,' Angela says timidly.

I have straightened my hair, put on a little make-up and some earrings, so to be fair maybe they do genuinely mean it.

Angela fills my glass of wine straight away and I notice Jeannie staring directly at her, purposefully. They must have talked in advance about how they all need to keep an eye on how much I drink tonight. Angela notices and stops at half a glass. I drink most of it down in one mouthful, partly to be defiant and partly to take the edge off. Everyone else takes a silent sip too. We get through the awkwardness by chattering about the menu and what everyone is having.

'Sod the diet,' says Gemma, 'I'm having a big fat pizza.'

'You do right,' says Shelley.

I say I'll have a carbonara and shut the menu without looking at it.

'What about your starter? You've got to have a starter,' Jeannie says

'No, I'm fine, honestly.'

'I'll order some for the table, for us all to share, eh?'

The girls nod obediently, letting Jeannie lead them, since she dragged us all here and nobody else has any idea how to handle things.

The restaurant is how it always was, why we liked it, Chris and I. Old-fashioned, red-checked tablecloths and warm, white fairy lights strung from the ceiling. The candles on the table in wine bottles with fountains of melted wax.

I nibble on garlic bread, when it arrives, to look busy, and listen to the girls chat, mainly about children. Jeannie says that Ellen is doing well at judo and is going for her orange belt. She looks at me uncertainly as she mentions her. I don't react.

Shelley starts on about her husband's new job, but eventually tails off as she senses the freeze-over from the rest of the table. Of course I don't really mind if she talks about her husband. It's not as if he bears any significance to Chris, other than being married and being a man. My temper is starting to fray, so I glug back my drink and fill the glass up again.

Jeannie eyes me up while I knock back another glass of the dense, yellowy wine, shuddering as it hits the back of my throat.

The waiter comes over. 'Another bottle, ladies?'

Jeannie and I say, 'No, we're fine, thanks,' and, 'Yes, please,' on top of each other.

'We'll have another – it is a special occasion after all.' I force a lighthearted tone.

Jeannie is too embarrassed to argue in front of the waiter and I know it. She does a sharp intake of breath and presses her lips together so they're white at the edges.

'So, what have you been up to today?' Gemma asks Jeannie, and for a second I think Jeannie looks panicked.

'Oh, just getting ready, you know.' Something about her tone is off. She probably doesn't want to brag about how Dan did something thoughtful for her birthday because she thinks it will set me off.

'Ooh, I love your nails, Jeannie,' Angela pipes up.

Jeannie looks relieved and wiggles them out in front of everyone, sickly pink and glittery. 'Did them myself,' she says, admiring them.

She isn't usually so girly-girl like this. She is obviously trying to make the best of the situation, but it's getting on my nerves. My jaw feels tight. It isn't Jeannie's fault, it's just me.

'I'm just a magpie for anything twinkly, but Dan reckons I look like a twelve-year-old girl with these nails.' She's already trailing off before she finishes the sentence. The atmosphere stiffens. Everyone looks at their wine; Gemma fingers her knife, polishing away imaginary scuffs.

'Pah! What does he know, eh?' Jeannie looks for back-up around the table and the other girls oblige, nodding – a theatrical eye-roll for good measure.

I stare away from the table out of the window at nothing, pressure and anger trying to break out of me for no good reason. Sometimes, even more so lately, I just want to needle people, push their buttons, see how far it will go. That's why I rang Mrs Grange, and why I went to Star Pizza again. I needed some reaction.

In the window reflection, I notice Jeannie shoot me a look, but I can't read it. Probably just her usual concern. Eventually, I drift back into the conversation to hear Angela talking about her new bathroom and how stressful it's going to be when they start installing it. 'Evie's going to have to stay at Tom's mum's,' she says. Jeannie looks glazed, bored. This makes me smile to myself. I love Jeannie, really.

I don't feel like it's anyone's real loss if I chip in now. I glug back more wine and Jeannie tenses. 'Well, there's no news on

Chris. Thanks everyone for asking.' It comes out even worse than I intended it to.

Everyone looks at Jeannie for guidance. She shakes her head, which incenses me even more.

'And it's not getting better, if you must know, as inconvenient as that is for everybody!' I can feel the tears start to prickle. The waiter is looking over, intrigued, a little worried too. He was bringing over a jug of water, at Jeannie's request, but hangs back when he sees the tension.

'You're not being fair,' says Jeannie.

I know she's right. 'I'm sorry. I'm really sorry. This is all a bit much for me. I shouldn't have come.' And I mean it. 'I don't want to spoil your night. I should go.' I get up to leave, the chair making an abrasive scraping noise that I feel in my teeth. The other diners I hadn't noticed arrive look around now.

Jeannie puts her hand over her eyes and sighs. I feel worse.

Shelley looks up at me, pleading. 'Don't say that. Don't go, Becs, please. Sit down a sec, will you?'

I don't know why, but I do.

She puts her hand on mine. 'Please stay. We want you to stay. Really. I don't know about everyone else but I only didn't ask because I don't know if you want to talk about it. I didn't know if it's the right time and I didn't want to upset you.' It's a sweet gesture – I can tell that she's sincere.

Angela and Gemma nod in agreement, pulling 'there, there' faces. Jeannie doesn't say anything.

'Come on, stay. Please. I don't want to stay out if you don't,' Shelley says.

I don't really want to go home and I appreciate Shelley's honesty. I sit down and mumble. 'I'm really sorry, everyone.'

Gemma says not to worry about it and Jeannie is shooting me a small but reassuring smile. I relent, but I feel awkward and in the spotlight so I'm relieved when Angela pipes up, 'So, who is watching *First Dates*?' The table erupts into squeals and ohmy-gods and we are thankfully moving on.

Chris and I always used to say how great the food was here but my pasta is pale and tasteless, the sauce creamy and claggy, drying out. I move it round the bowl, not eating much. Mainly I'm knocking back the yellow, vinegary wine, keeping a careful eye on everyone else's glasses, trying to keep a pace I can get away with. Luckily for me, and despite the pep talk Jeannie obviously gave everyone earlier, it looks like they're all out to get hammered, as they are downing the drinks pretty quickly, too, Jeannie included.

We're seated in an alcove in the corner. I'm glad of it but suspicious. Did Jeannie plan it this way on purpose, in case anyone were to see us? Would she ask the waiter to seat us out of the way? She might have told him, 'We could be a bit rowdy,' or something. I consider asking her but, *Choose your battles*, I remind myself.

When the main courses are finished, sparkly bags with coloured rosettes and cards start appearing on the table, whipped from below. Brightly coloured wrapping paper. It dawns on me that I have completely forgotten to get Jeannie anything – a card or a present. Not that I have any spare money or a single idea in my head of what I would get her. I don't think anyone has noticed that I didn't add anything into the pile.

Jeannie smiles and I nod approvingly as she displays cheap, dangly earrings in her hand and opens vouchers, holding them up for me to see. I smile, raise my eyebrows and nod. She looks relieved that I am playing the game again.

Everyone has dressed up for the occasion. One-shoulder dresses, jumpsuits, fake tan, heels, lots of mascara. In my old dowdy clothes and pale skin, I actually blend in less than I had hoped.

The girls share puddings, despite having garlic-bread starters and huge pizzas or bowls of pasta. The waiter brings Jeannie over some profiteroles with a coloured sparkler in the top and they force the whole restaurant to sing 'Happy Birthday'. Jeannie feigns embarrassment. I think the waiter keeps looking at me, but I can't be sure. Does he know? Does he recognise me? I lose track of how many bottles of wine have been taken away and replaced. The supply seemed endless and there is a numbness in my mouth as if I have been gargling with strong mouthwash. I start to think about the cost and whether I have enough money to cover it.

When I come back from the bathroom everyone is putting on their coats. They are talking but they wrap it up when they see me. Jeannie gathers up her bouquet of gift bags.

'How much do I owe?' I ask, but Jeannie shoos me away and says not to worry about it, and everyone else pretends not to hear.

When we leave the restaurant, I am glad to be outside, the cool air a welcome relief against my burning cheeks. I'm hoping that's it; that I can go home after this, but Jeannie has already hooked arms with me.

'Where to, girls?'

Everyone except me is staggering along the pavement in spiked heels. We walk up towards the bars off The Parades. The image of Chris, the CCTV, flickers in my mind and I scrunch my eyes closed, pushing it out again.

'In here?' Angela says, beckoning us into a bar with fake flames outside, belting out loud pop music that I don't recognise.

'I'm going to go,' I say, but I know I won't get away with it yet, and they all start squealing and pleading.

'Not yet.'

'Just one drink.'

'Come on, come on, come on, pleaaaase.'

I feel guilty leaving now since they paid for my food, so I give in.

The bar is called Xanthe, but it used to have a different name the last time I was here, years ago. The decor is all silver and purple inside, with swirling coloured lights that make me feel unsteady on my feet. They've probably spent a fair bit of money on the place, but it's already lost its sheen. Posters on the wall are peeling, and parts of the sparkly floor feel sticky underfoot.

I haven't been to a place like this in ages. I can't say I miss it, but, in truth, I do miss having nights out, seeing friends. I feel awkward standing on the edge of the dance floor and I'm relieved when we sit down in a semicircular booth with padded, sofa-style seats.

Jeannie is already on her way back from the bar, carrying an unsteady-looking tray with two round fishbowls on the top, straws bobbing around in the liquid. One is full of a bright, gem-green-coloured drink, the other a Cadbury's purple-coloured concoction. They seem to want to get even drunker than me. We all crowd round with a straw each and drink the sickly sweet cocktail, uncertain at first. Everyone sits back and holds the drink in their mouths for a second, thinking and assessing, as if we were at a high-end wine tasting. It doesn't taste like alcohol at all at first, just sugary pop, but you can tell it's strong by the way it catches on your throat, the heat after you swallow.

A few more people are trickling in now. Skinny girls, their tans glowing against tiny Lycra dresses, white or neon, under the UV light. It makes their eyes look other-worldly. I don't recognise much of the music yet. It's too loud to talk, and it's making everyone drink even faster.

Angela looks woozy. She leans over to me to talk; I can see right down her top and try to look away. 'So do you think he did it then?' she slurs. I freeze, stunned. I can't believe she'd be so blunt. But maybe it's refreshing too – people aren't usually so honest.

I take a long drink of the purple stuff.

She gives me a strange look, a forced, fixed smile.

The drink is hitting me now, my head buzzing. My brain says, *I don't know anything anymore.* My mouth snaps, 'Of course not. Why, do you?'

Angela looks confused. She moves closer now, raising her voice to shout right in my ear. I can smell her perfume, mixed with booze and garlic. 'Alright, keep your hair on. I just came when it opened.' My ear is vibrating. 'Not been for yonks. Not really my sort of place, you know? I don't get out a lot now. The kids and that.'

I quickly try to recover myself, cringing at my mistake. Of course she wouldn't ask me that. 'Yeah, me neither. It's OK – we're getting a bit old anyway, eh?' I shrug, over-exaggerating my words and movements.

More drinks come after that, but no one will let me go to the bar when I offer. Not that I could afford it. Gemma brings cocktails that she shouts are called lemon bombs, and the thought of the sourness, the tartness of the smell, makes my tongue contract even before I drink any. Seemingly, no sooner have we started drinking those than Shelley brings shot glasses of something that looks dark and thick. 'Jaeger!' she shouts, handing the shots out and instructing us all, shouting over the music, to drink it 'down in one!'.

I sniff it: liquorice, sugar. I knock it back after three like everyone else, retching, feeling all the liquid swimming in my stomach. The mixture of drinks and fatty food is making me feel queasy, and my head is pounding.

Then it comes on. That 'Cheerleader' song. Kayleigh in the park, the roundabout. A girl jumps up and down clapping on the dance floor.

I need to go outside, and I push through people to get to the door.

The cool air, the escape from the music is a relief when I get outside. There are people standing in groups, smoking, talking too loudly because they're drunk, women shivering in tiny dresses.

I'm not sure it's him at first, as he has his head down, but when he looks up he catches my eye. He looks stunned, but he quickly rearranges his face. It's Sean, someone Chris used to work with at Green Point.

He's sitting at one of the round tables with an umbrella branded by some alcohol company. The wood looks old, grey and flaky, chunks missing.

'Heeeeeey! Rebecca, how are you?' He's smoking and offers me one, but I refuse. His eyes are glassy. Definitely had a few.

He gestures for me to sit down and I have to climb over as the seat is attached to the bench.

'What are you up to then?'

'Ugh, lads' night out, you know. Too old for this shit. You?'

'Same. Girls' night out. Best mate's birthday or I wouldn't, you know… I don't even know why I'm out.' I feel like I need to add that, for some reason.

'Listen, Rebecca, I'm really sorry I never replied to your texts or emails.' He places his hand on his chest as he apologises. 'I… I… I didn't know what to say and so I kept thinking I'd reply after and I just – I still didn't know what to say.' His words have a slur to them.

'Don't worry about it. I get it.'

'D'you want a drink?'

'No, fine thanks. Having a break.'

'Wise. Very wise. I'm going to suffer for this tomorrow for sure.'

'Where's all this come from?' I pinch my chin with my fingers and he mirrors me, ruffling his beard. I haven't seen him with one before.

'I'm getting old now,' he says. 'It's obligatory to have a beard! Tattoos next. Hipster trend finally hits Shawmouth – just the decade later.'

I appreciate him trying to act normal.

Sean works in IT at Green Point. We'd been out with him and his wife Nicola a couple of times, met up after work or for a meal on weekends, but it didn't really take off. He and Chris used to have the occasional pint, though, text each other about football and video games, eat lunch together. I joked about their 'bromance'. I was glad he had met someone, hoped he'd miss his friends in London a bit less.

'How's everything at work?'

'You know, same old, same old. Anyway, bollocks to that. How you doing?' Sean asks.

I shrug. 'Ah, you know. Same old here too.'

'You working?'

I shake my head and he takes big gulps from his lager. Pleasantries are drying up now. He's probably wondering whether he can go back inside yet. Find his mates. Now's my chance to rip the plaster off. Ask the questions that have been swimming round my head.

'I haven't been all that well, to be honest,' I offer. 'Just coming round really. Well, sort of.'

'Oh, sorry, I didn't realise – on top of everything else. Wow.'

'Well, not ill exactly. But just with everything that's been going on; it's hit me hard, you know.'

'Can totally imagine. I'll tell Nicola I saw you. She'll be pleased. We've… we've wondered about you, you know. Didn't want to intrude, though. Sorry, I should have emailed you back.' He shakes his head at himself.

'Nicola not out tonight?'

He doesn't meet my eye. 'She's with the kids. No sitter. She wouldn't want to go out with this lot anyway. You wouldn't catch her dead in here. You sure you don't fancy a bevvy? I'm taking advantage of a rare chance to get out.'

'No, I'm right, thanks.'

'Last one I'll have in a while. We're expecting again, Nicola and me.'

'Congratulations.'

He is wondering if he shouldn't have told me that, but it really makes no difference. I'm happy for them.

'Anyway, I'm glad I've seen you.' He looks startled and on edge again. Thinking of a way to leave.

I push on. 'The reason I was texting you before, why I wanted to meet up... Well, now that I'm getting my head out of my arse a bit, I'm just, I'm trying to get a clearer picture of what happened. You know, with Chris. Police don't tell me much.' I shrug. 'Suppose they can't, really, when it's all ongoing.'

He looks a bit uneasy now, plays with his beard again. There are white flecks in it.

'So, work. How was Chris doing, you know? Was there anything unusual before he went missing? We didn't really talk about his job that much. It's all a bit of a blur, to be honest. I am just trying to get things straight in my head; see if it jogs my memory or something, you know. I don't want people to just... give up.'

'Well, he, he...'

'Don't worry, I've been told he'd lost his job.'

'Right, yeah.'

'Wasn't aware at the time though.'

He shakes his head, looks as bemused at the idea as me. 'I've told the police everything, just so you know. I want to be totally upfront with you.' He raises his palms to me.

'It's fine. I'm not asking you to tell me anything you shouldn't. But if it was Nicola, you'd need the details too, wouldn't you?'

He scowls. Two deep lines appearing between his eyes. 'Well, I don't really think she er...'

'I know he lost his job, but I don't have any other details.'

'I don't know, I...'

A girl in the group next to us screeches and staggers into the table, but one of her friends grabs her by the arm and pulls her back into the group.

'Honestly, I'm not going to go storming up there shouting the odds with Big Boss Bernie or anything. I just need to understand for myself.'

He smiles over his pint. 'I would love to see you having a go at Bernie. What a prick.' His face softens again now.

'Imagine how you'd feel if Nicola was just gone one day. Just like that.'

He winces at this.

'You'd want to have all the details, wouldn't you?'

'Well, it's not really the same thing but…'

'Can you just tell me? Please?'

'It might be better if you were to come into the office, talk to someone in charge. I could set that up for you.'

'I'd rather talk to you. At least I've talked to you a bit before. A friendly face. I'd rather hear it from someone I've been out for a curry with than some bloke I have never met, but have heard on good authority – from more than one person – is a bit of a wanker.'

'Ooh, curry – I could murder a vindaloo after all this.' He lifts his half-empty pint glass.

'I'm not going to take it further, it's purely for my own sanity, like I said. Although I think that ship has pretty much sailed.'

'Don't say that, Rebecca.'

'I'm totally in the dark here.'

'OK, I'll do what I can. What do you want to know?' He scratches his head. He looks knackered now.

'Why did Chris get sacked? Really?'

He rubs at his forehead and takes a large drink, his throat contracting twice to let the liquid flow down. A deep breath. 'He came into the office one lunchtime. I say lunchtime, it was like… two thirty, three or something. Quite a way after the hour that we're meant to take. You still clock in and out up there, so they know. Ian, his line manager, had been looking for him. He was meant to be in a meeting or something.'

'Go on, please – it's already more than anyone has told me. I just need to get a picture of those last days.'

'Well, I'm sorry, it wasn't pretty. He stank of booze. I'd noticed that once before and I remember thinking on that day that I was going to have a word with him after work, you know – tell him he should watch it. Or have a quiet word with him over the phone or on a weekend or something. I didn't want to ambush him at work. Anyway, that day when he came in late… he was talking loudly. Slurring. Knocking stuff over. He wasn't plastered but he had an edge to him. I didn't like to see him like that.'

I nod.

'Well, Ian came over. Asked him where he'd been, what was going on? He'd missed a scheduled meeting. Ian's pretty hot on that kind of thing. Chris just said he'd been "out". He wouldn't answer Ian's questions.'

I can't picture it. Chris behaving like this. At work of all places. I'd always had him down as a rule-follower. But then, you don't really see your friends or family at work. They might be someone else there.

'Anyway, Chris just ended up laughing and telling Ian to fuck off. Ian sent him home. He was properly furious – looked like he was going to explode. You could have heard a pin drop in the office.'

'So he got sacked there and then?'

'No, not there and then. I went to see Ian later. I said let me talk to Chris. He said he'd think about it.'

'Right… so…? I don't get it.'

He bites at his lip.

'There were meetings, closed doors. Anyway, IT were asked to look at his computer. Next thing we know we get an email round from Bernie saying Chris was no longer with the company and to direct any queries to HR. Usual business bullshit speak, you know, you can't get a straight answer from anyone.'

'So they didn't give details on the reason for the sacking?'

'Well, not exactly, but I think the thing with Ian would have been enough. Being pissed. Telling his boss to fuck off?'

The image of this is still boggling my mind. 'Right, but you said Ian seemed to be open to you having a word with him. So something with the computer?'

'Have the police not told you any of this? They were in the office a fair few times at first. Much to Uncle Bernie's displeasure, I can tell you.'

'They have. But broad brush strokes, like I said. Need-to-know basis. But I do need to know the details; I really do. I can't... move forwards... otherwise.' I can't quite bring myself to say 'move on'.

'Well, when people just go like that – it's happened a few times. I mean not quite as spectacularly as that, but when people get made redundant and that, they don't tend to give us the dirt. Just the blanket announcement. They don't want the workers getting ruffled, now, do they?'

'So you don't know the details of what happened then?'

'Well, look – and seriously, please do not quote me on this or I will probably be out the door myself.'

Everything tightens. *Please don't say what I think you're going to say.*

'The email just said all the usual stuff. But then a reminder about "prohibited activities" on work computers being taken seriously. We all had to sign to say we'd read the policy again. We've had a firewall to rival China's put in since then – can't access Facebook or owt now. Thanks, Chris.' He cringes at his own joke. 'Maybe they were looking for justification; maybe they found something, I don't know. They're pretty strict about that stuff. Modern branding and all that, but pretty old-fashioned set-up behind the scenes. Bernie can't even get his head around me taking paternity leave.'

'So the computer stuff, you don't know anything more?' That familiar squirming sensation in my stomach. This bit pains him, it's obvious.

'People were talking. God knows they do – I mean it's that boring up there. They love a bit of scandal to break the day up. First I heard, when he was sacked, it was gambling.'

I relax a bit at that, but not for long. Your life has come to something when that's the good news.

He sucks air in.

'At first…?' I push him on.

'Well, then there were rumours about what they found on the computer.'

'Rumours about what?'

'Dodgy stuff, you know. Underage stuff.' He can't meet my eye now.

'When did they start saying that, that it was more than gambling?' I remember what Paige said, at the school.

'Was it after the news about Kayleigh?'

He nods then shakes his head straight after. 'Maybe, I really don't recall, sorry.' He shrugs his shoulders, defeated. He takes a big drink, leaving a thin line of foam along his beard on the top of his lip.

A lump forms in my throat, a throbbing agony straight away.

He quickly follows up. 'But, like I said, I haven't been told anything for sure, and as far as I know, no one else up there has either – and I've said to people, when I've heard them gossiping, to get their facts straight or not say anything at all. It's only fair.'

'Thanks.' I nod, trying to take it in.

'You getting stick, are you? Heard you'd had a bit.'

'Some. Nothing I can't handle. People are upset. I get that.'

He just shakes his head. 'Can't believe it, me.'

'So anything else? Before this… this… explosion? Honestly I just can't get my head around Chris being like that. But I'm just his wife, aren't I? How did he seem in general?'

'To be honest, he was a bit off. Hard to know if you just think that looking back, though, isn't it? I'm sure people are weird all the time, me included. You just don't pay attention.'

'What do you mean "he was off"?'

'He kept… well, he was late a lot. The lunchtime thing wasn't the first time he was late or had been having a bit of a liquid lunch. But he got away with it. And he was always getting phone calls and texts – more than usual all of a sudden. Sometimes he'd answer, but usually he'd just ignore them, but you could tell the calls had rattled him. I said to Nicola after it all kicked off, I said, "I think there is something going on with him." But, like I said, I said it after – not at the time. So, I'm not sure. Honestly, I'm not.'

'Do you think he was seeing someone? Kayleigh?'

He jumps a little. 'You can't ask me that. There's no way for me to be able to answer that. I am just telling you what I know. I mean, I did kind of wonder – he didn't want to go for a drink anymore, had to pop out at lunchtime. Seemed like he always had somewhere to be. But I honestly have no idea. It wasn't like I really knew him well enough to judge, you know?'

'And did you ask him? If anything was going on?'

He drains the rest of his glass now. 'I didn't.' He shakes his head a little. 'I mean, we were just work friends.'

The lump again, pulsating in my throat. He's distancing himself, doesn't want to be associated.

'I'm sorry, that's not really true – it's not fair of me to say that, about just being work friends, I mean. To be honest, I just feel shitty about it. I didn't ask him before because we never really talked about "stuff". I didn't want to pry. Nicola says it's a man thing.'

I give a small laugh.

'But after what happened in the office, when he got sacked; I was worried about him. I texted him, but he didn't reply. I was going to phone. In a while. I just thought maybe he was a bit embarrassed. I figured I'd give it a bit longer, then give him a ring or an email. But then... Well, you know how it is. Time got on and...well I didn't do it, did I.'

He looks up, behind me.

'Jesus, there you are, Becs. I was worried about you.' It's Jeannie, wrapping her arms around herself from the cold.

'Sorry, I just needed some air. Sean, this is Jeannie. Birthday girl. Jeannie, Sean worked with Chris.'

'Happy birthday.' Sean raises his empty pint glass.

Jeannie eyes him suspiciously. 'Right... You coming back inside? It's freezing out here.'

I disentangle myself from the bench. Sean runs his hand through his hair. He seems more sober now. 'You coming in?'

'Nah, think I'm about done, to be honest. I'll probably head off.'

'Well, nice to see you, and thanks.'

'No worries. You too. We'll have to meet up. With Nicola and the kids.'

'Yeah, sounds good,' I say. I know we won't. I watch him walk away up the street, zigzagging across the pavement.

CHAPTER TWENTY-SIX

Saturday, 14 November

Gemma brings more drinks but everyone's enthusiasm is waning now – they probably can't stomach much more booze. No one is showing any signs of wanting to actually leave yet, though.

Jeannie, Angela, Gemma and Shelley seem to be deep in conversation, crowded together in the booth, shouting at each other over the din. I stand and drink for a while, hoping the fizziness will start to cut through how full and bloated I feel. The strobe lights on the dance floor make it look like a weird kaleidoscope: arms, legs, colours.

I battle my way to the bathroom. The place has filled up and I am jostling against drunk girls, dancing and gyrating without looking around them, and gangs of raucous lads standing round the edge of the dance floor and by the bar, pushing each other around.

Luckily, there is no queue, and I hang my head over the silver toilet, the floor covered in grey, slimy tissue and dirty footprints. I try to be sick but there's nothing to come up except sugary, foamy saliva, dangling from my mouth. It doesn't make me feel any better. It's not just the alcohol, it's what Sean said… picturing Chris at work, the 'prohibited activities' on the computer.

I sit on the toilet with the lid down for a good few minutes, enjoying the respite. I could almost fall asleep, but I know Jeannie will be in to look for me soon enough.

Outside, a toilet attendant in a winter coat wordlessly offers me perfume from a collection of bottles. 'Or a lollipop instead, miss?' She rattles a tray of money.

I shake my head, moving towards the taps to splash some water on my face. I try to look down and avoid eye contact with the other people in the queue, but there's something I recognise about one of the girls – perhaps her voice. She is chatting to her friend, but I hadn't registered the words. It's Paige and Kat from the school. Paige is wearing a dress that is too tight, belly rolls visible under the Lycra. I look up; she's wearing too much make-up, harsh black liner rimming her bottom lashes, making her eyes look hard. Kat's hair looks even bluer under the strip light over the sink. It reminds me of an old glass Christmas decoration. Her eyeshadow is metallic purple and her eyelashes spike out like Kayleigh's in the now-famous picture. A flash of slim, toned midriff peeps out from under denim shirt and boob tube.

'Excuse me, can I just…' I gesture at the sink. My heart is vibrating in my chest.

But Paige doesn't move. I go to use the other sink, but she slides along and blocks that too. Instinctively, I try the other one again, but she does the same thing. I can't look at her directly so I stare down, cheeks blazing.

'Here. You looking at my tits? She's looking at my tits, K.' She nudges Kat.

'Don't be ridiculous.' I couldn't sound more school ma'am-ish if I tried.

Paige mimics me. 'Don't be ridiculous.'

She laughs, but Kat just looks at the ground, fidgeting with her hair.

'Maybe she's a bit of a perv, like her husband, eh?'

The toilet attendant's radio crackles. She rearranges her perfumes, trying to look busy. She's probably used to quickly getting out of the way when fights break out.

'What you're saying is slanderous and you need to stop. You don't have any proof.' I take a sharp breath and look her in the eyes this time. She doesn't look away.

'More than you think.' She taps her nose. 'Eh, Kat?'

Kat still looks at her feet, glancing at the toilet attendant to see if she will step in.

'We haven't seen you in here before, that's all. Have you, K?'

Kat shakes her head but doesn't look up.

'You're too young to be in here. Far too young.'

'Your husband wouldn't mind that, would he?' She nudges Kat again.

I wipe my hands against my jeans, even though they're not wet, and go to leave.

'You've not washed your hands, you scruff!' she shouts after me, laughing, as I push the door to go back into the bar. The lights dazzle my eyes, disorientating me, and my head pounds.

Barging through the crowd, I reach Jeannie and shout in her ear, 'I want to go. Now. I mean it, Jeannie.'

Jeannie is oblivious to the fact that I'm upset, that anything has happened. She's drunk now.

'Uh-uh. Not before we've had a dance, Becs.' She is shouting right in my ear, spit spraying onto the side of my face. 'It is my birthday and I've got the night off. And we are out together for the first time in forever. You are not going yet!' I try to protest but she's already dragging me onto the floor, spinning round and looping under my arm as she does, bashing me into people.

Chesney Hawkes's 'I Am the One and Only' is blasting out. We've moved into the cheesy music section of the night – I remember the format now. A few of the younger people are leaving the dance floor. At least I know this one. Gemma, Angela, Shelley and Jeannie jump up and down, and Jeannie throws her handbag into the middle of the circle. They all twirl and shout and mouth the words to a blast from our shared youth. Younger girls stand at the edge of the dance floor, sucking Vodka Red Bull through straws: tiny waists, sculpted cheeks, lots of hair. The whole bar smells of sweat and the smoke machine and the sugary energy drink. I stand there shifting awkwardly from foot to foot, refusing to dance. A man with gelled hair is looking over at me – sneering or sleazing, I can't quite tell.

Then, I'm surging forward, shoved from behind. Paige and Kat again.

'Oi, watch what you're doing,' says Jeannie, as she recovers herself from almost falling over. But I tell her to leave it and move us along, mingling between the next group of friends. I try to look out for Paige, but it's impossible with the moving lights and the crowd.

We get through 'Summer of '69', 'Disco 2000' and 'Smells Like Teen Spirit', which brings a group of men onto the dance floor standing in a circle, arms round each other. On the chorus they all shout out the words and jump up and down, meaning everyone else has to get out of their way, unless they want to get pushed over and trampled on.

Finally, Angela says she's had enough. 'I'm ready for off?' she mouths, pointing to the door. The others agree. Finally. They carry on dancing as we leave the bar, conga-ing towards the door before collapsing into laughter when we get outside.

Shelley rubs her feet before putting her shoes back on – they are black on the soles. Under the street lights outside the club, everyone looks tired – me too, no doubt. I feel exhausted, but strangely proud of myself for surviving the night out. Jeannie's mascara is smeared under her eyes, making her look quite startling. Everyone looks pale and glassy-eyed compared to the pristine sheen they started out with at the restaurant.

'Chips!' shouts Jeannie, clapping with excitement. 'Chips, chips, chips!'

'You must be joking,' I say. 'We've just had a massive meal!' It's the most I've eaten in one go in weeks, and even though I didn't eat most of it, my stomach still feels uncomfortably bloated, the garlic repeating on me and congealing with the brightly coloured booze.

'Pah! That was ages ago!' Shelley says. 'I'm starving. Cheesy chips!'

We walk towards the seafront, and the cool air makes me feel cleaner after the sweat and fake smoke of the club. I realise where we are heading. 'I'm just going to walk back from here, I'll be fine, honest.'

Jeannie is more sober now. 'Becs, no. Give me ten minutes to get some frigging chips will you, and I will put you in a taxi myself. You can't be walking around on your own at this time of night. It's pitch dark round by the caravan park. You don't know who's about.'

We are walking up the alley now, the neon Star Pizza sign coming into view.

'Well, I am waiting outside. I can't eat anything and I don't feel great. I drank too much.'

'If you say so. It's bloody freezing, though. I'll get you a can of full-fat pop. That'll sort you out,' Jeannie says as she goes inside.

I pace up and down the pavement for a while, willing Jeannie and the girls to hurry up. I consider leaving and just going back to the caravan. I could text Jeannie. But I know it's not fair. I've got this far – no point in spoiling her night now.

I can hear them laughing and messing about inside the takeaway. But a big group of lads is coming down the alley. An array of coloured shirts, jumping around and shouting, pushing each other.

'Oi oi, bird ahead,' shouts one of them. 'Alright, love? You looking for the last chance saloon?'

I go inside the shop to avoid them.

'Don't go, darling, don't go,' one of the group half sings at me.

They bang hard on the window when they go past, and when we look, a couple of them grab and thrust their crotches. Jeannie waggles her little finger at them, and Gemma, Angela and Shelley burst out laughing.

'You're all dogs anyway!' one of the men shouts when they're out of view.

'Right, the booze is wearing off now, let's hurry up and get this over with and get home,' says Jeannie. 'That's it until next year.'

The takeaway is surgically lit. It shows up the grubby sole prints on the floor and the greasy smears across the table, dried-on ketchup. I catch sight of myself in the mirror and my skin looks haggard – dry, make-up collecting in the lines around my eyes. I pinch my cheeks to try and wake myself up a little, sliding into a plastic seat. They're all locked together with the table and other chairs for maximum inconvenience and discomfort.

I can't hear what's being said but Jeannie and the girls giggle at the man behind the counter. He pretends to pass Shelley her takeaway ticket, then snatches it away again. What are we, ten? I cringe at them lapping it up. Thankfully, though, it isn't Ashy or Daz. There's a younger man in tonight who I don't recognise. Tall, soft-featured, a crop of angry spots along the hollows of his cheeks and his jawline.

I can't see Ashy and Daz anywhere so I begin to relax a bit. It's almost over. Jeannie, Gemma, Shelley and Angela go to sit with me but I cover my nose with my sleeve and point to the next table along, trying to restrain a look of disgust as they gobble their food. Jeannie offers me a tray of grey kebab meat, hanging in strips like old, dead skin, and cardboardy chips drowning in so much vinegar it catches in your throat. I refuse and stare at the tiled wall.

Eventually, they start to shove their empty, greasy, white polystyrene boxes into the bins. Finally, we are ready to leave. Bed and the solitude of the caravan are in sight. As I angle myself out of the stupid plastic seat, I feel something hit my hair. I reach up and it's a chip. Turning to look, it's Paige and Kat again. I didn't see them come in.

'You dirty cow. You didn't even wash your hands in the bathroom.' Paige, of course.

I try to leave, but I can see Jeannie calculating, starting to react.

'Who the hell do you think you are?' she says half laughing. 'You're about twelve. Becs, who are these clowns? Clowns with the appalling make-up to match.' Jeannie looks Paige up and down and scoffs.

'They're no one; just leave it.'

'Piss off. You're the no one,' says Paige, genuine venom. 'Your pervy husband didn't mind about people only looking twelve, did he?'

I feel sick, frozen to the spot. I know this will incense Jeannie even more.

'Look, you little bitch… You don't know what you are talking about and you've got no right talking to her like th—'

There's a crack as Paige smacks Jeannie across the face from the side. There's already blood. The panic is rising. I see a flash in the corner of my eye. I am terrified it's a knife but it's just Paige's gold ring.

Someone runs from behind the counter. 'Hey, ladies! Please.' It's Daz.

'Don't patronise me. You need to ring the police on this little psycho,' says Jeannie, shaking him off as he grabs her arm.

The two girls stand close to the counter, laughing with the younger man behind it. Jeannie and the girls talk among themselves, shaking their heads and fussing over Jeannie's bloody mouth.

'You heard the latest about her husband?' Paige shouts over, stopping the chatter dead.

'Just leave it, you vindictive little bitch.' Jeannie is dabbing at her mouth with a serviette, bright red blotches on the paper.

My teeth are pressed together.

'Wonder where they are now, him and Kayleigh. He's probably got her locked away in some basement somewhere as his sex slave. Eurgh! You can't have been very good in bed, love.'

'Fuck you!' I can hear myself screaming. 'And what is it that you're doing in here?'

I take a step towards her.

'Calm down, love. Just eating chips, like you.' But she flinches.

'Are you, though? Are you just eating chips? Why are you always hanging around here? Did Kayleigh hang around in here, did she? I saw you, Paige. On the beach.'

'No, you didn't.'

'I saw you meet a man and go into the disabled toilets.'

Her face drops.

'Becs. Leave it,' Jeannie says but she sounds far away.

'What's this? Paige?' It's the younger man from behind the counter.

'It's nothing. Leave it, yeah. She don't know what she's on about. You following me or something?'

I feel something hot on my neck. Then the voice I recognise. 'Are you causing more trouble in my shop?' It's Ashy.

I spin round and his sallow-skinned face is right up close to mine. 'It's not me. I didn't even want to come in here. It's your younger friends you need to worry about. In more ways than one.'

'I've already told you to mind your own business, haven't I?' There's a loud crack in my ear as he claps his hands loudly next to it. 'Ladies, please. If you can't be civilised I am afraid I will have to ask you to leave.'

'We're going, don't you worry,' says Jeannie. 'But it's these little teeny bops you should be chucking out, not us.'

Paige does a fake sweet smile and waggles her fingers at us in a wave. ''Bye, ladies.'

'Ladies, come,' says Ashy, ushering me out, his hand on the top of my back. I shrug him off but he grips my shoulder for a few seconds, hard. It will leave a fingerprint.

I hear them laughing, then the smell of vinegar and then the chips fly over. I am sprayed with it and probably grease, but the chips mostly land on Jeannie, sticking in her hair and down her top.

She turns and her face is twisted in anger. Everything happens so fast, but I see Gemma and Angela restraining her from going back into the shop again. 'It's not worth it, Jeannie, let's just go.'

'Girls, girls, can I get you some more chips? A drink?' I hear Ashy say to Paige and Kat as we leave.

I watch as he goes back in. The younger one is lifting up the hatch to allow them behind the counter. He and Paige look like they're having a row.

Outside, we all gather around Jeannie. 'Little bitches. Can you believe that?' she says.

Fresh red blood blooms on her lip.

'Shit, do you think you need it looked at?' I touch her arm, feeling responsible.

'It's fine, it's just bust, I think.'

'Are you sure? There's a lot of blood.'

'Honestly, it's fine. I've had worse.' But I can see she's starting to cry. I brush chips out of the back of her hair and she forces a laugh. 'Well, it's been eventful. Happy birthday to me, eh?' She sniffs back tears.

'Right, taxis!' Gemma's already heading to the rank a few streets away.

'I'm going to walk,' I say. I could do with the sea air. I feel queasy from the drinks and I am wired. There's no way I will sleep.

'I'm not asking you, I am telling you – you're coming to get a taxi,' Jeannie says, stopping in the street and dabbing her lip. I don't argue. 'And we will talk tomorrow about what that was all about.'

When we get to the caravan park, she makes the taxi wait, lights turned down, engine running, until she sees me get into the caravan and I've put the lights on to let her know they can go.

Finally, I am in bed, enveloped in the darkness. The seagulls overhead sound like babies wailing or women screaming. Often I've been so convinced it was a human cry, I've looked out of the window of the caravan into the blackness or tentatively opened the door to hear more clearly.

Something is niggling at me – like I've forgotten or misplaced something; it's shifting out of view. 'It's on the tip of my brain,' my dad used to say.

I keep thinking of the house. Is there a bill that I need to pay? A renewal date coming up that I haven't remembered? One false move there and I could get another card blocked and future applications denied. Is it something Sean said about what happened at Chris's work?

I drift in and out of sleep, exhausted but restless – my mind is working over something.

Pushing the covers back, sweating, it comes into my mind and I can barely keep a hold of it. It *is* the house.

I try to concentrate on the sound of the wind and gulls squawking overhead to quell the nausea rolling in my stomach – from the alcohol and the food and the sense of unease about everything: Chris, Kayleigh, the takeaway, the house. The stuff Sean told me. The room spins.

Something wasn't quite right at the house. The envelope on the stairs was facing backwards. The letter I left for Chris for when he comes back. It has his name on the front – with some hearts doodled around it. We always used to do that in little notes to each other. I left that side facing out, so he would know it's from me, recognise it straight away and know that I love him;

that I am open to hearing what he has to say. But I can see it clearly now.

When I went round earlier, it was facing the other way.

CHAPTER TWENTY-SEVEN

Sunday, 15 November

I dreamt of Chris again. I'm not sure I'd call it a dream, or a nightmare. It's like seeing Chris, being there with him again. All the details that I often can't recall these days are there. The light lines across his forehead. The gestures he uses with his hands as he speaks. But I wake covered in cold sweat. Because in the dream I'll be banging on a window, but he can't hear me trying to call after him on a packed high street, winding in and out of the crowds of people, and he keeps disappearing out of view.

Maybe it's because today is Kayleigh's vigil. She would have been fifteen. I think of myself at fifteen – Jeannie and me, 'thick as thieves', full of plans. We weren't so different. We hung around in the park and on the seafront, we tried to get into the pubs. I think of Ellen. Of how broken Jeannie would be if anything ever happened to her.

I shouldn't go to the vigil, I know. I could be attacked; I don't want to upset Janice any more than she already will be. But still, there's a magnetic pull there, like I might not be able to stop myself drifting towards it this evening.

It's freezing outside, my breath forming clouds in front of me, the grass glittery with frost. I hurry off the caravan park, anxious to avoid running into anyone or getting held up.

It's before seven and the streets are mostly empty and still, curtains drawn, only a few lights on. People are sleeping in, huddled up to their loved ones. I walk to the house, barely passing anyone else except a dogwalker or two. When I get there, I sit on the low wall outside for a while, taking deep breaths to try to steady the palpitations. I almost can't make myself go inside; maybe I'm not ready for anything to change.

I push the heels of my hands into my eyes and watch the colours come – dots of purple, yellow, green and blue beneath my lids.

Fumbling in my bag for my keys, my fingers are too cold to get a proper grip.

The electronic drone from my mobile makes me tense up. Unknown number again. This is the earliest call yet. I've started to ignore them sometimes. Straight after the night out too. The confrontation at the pizza place. Ashy's sweating, snarling face. Paige.

The anxiety, alcohol and lack of sleep are making me nauseous and restless. It feels like all my bones and muscles need to be stretched out, to get some kind of release. Snatching the phone out of my bag, my finger catches on the zip, drawing blood right down the side of my nail. The pain makes me squeeze my eyes together. The phone is still needling at me, a low insistent rumble. I press the screen hard.

'What do you want from me?' It sounds more shrill than the no-nonsense approach I had intended. I don't wait for an answer. 'I am not scared of you and I will go to the police.'

'Rebecca? Are you alright?' the male voice asks, throwing me off. I can't connect things up quickly enough. 'Rebecca?' It's Simon.

'Shit, Simon. Sorry, I thought it was someone else. Shit, is Mum alright? It's early. What's going on? What's up with Mum?'

'Calm down, Rebecca, please. Don't worry.' Why is everyone always saying my name? Like a dog that needs to be trained. 'Now, don't panic. Your mum just had a little fall last night, that's all. She's completely fine, I promise. I just thought you'd want to know and maybe pop in to see her later.'

'Oh God, what happened? Is she alright?'

'She's fine. Minor cuts and bruises, bit shaken up, that's all. Doctor's looked her over. Given the all clear. You'll both feel better if you come and see her, I'm sure.'

'Right, yeah, 'course. I'll be in soon.'

'OK, I'll be in. Erm... is everything alright, Rebecca? What's all the stuff about the police?'

'Oh, nothing. Trust me, you don't want to know.'

I kick the new mound of post out of the way. Everything is as still and lifeless as ever. I stop to take it in. It doesn't have the air of a place completely undisturbed, does it? I can't put my finger on it. When we cleared things out of Mum's house, it was obvious she had only been using her room upstairs. The windowsill and blind slats were thick with dust, cobwebs collecting in the corners. When we took the pictures down, darker squares remained, the edges of the shape sun-bleached because the blinds were always left open.

I think I can detect a faint scent of something on the air – a cleaning product or furniture polish. Or is it something else? Paint? Aftershave? Nothing?

The cushions in the living room look plumped, arranged, like someone has been sitting there and then replaced them with care. I thought I'd closed the door the last time too. I always do, I am sure. But today it was open.

I can't keep the information in my mind; I need something to compare it to. I can't face the thing I know I must look at just yet, so I survey the rest of the house first. My stomach is churning and clenching.

On automatic, I head to the kitchen for a swig of the chilled vodka to take the edge off. *It's 8 a.m.*, I think to myself. But just one sharp shot; I need to stay focused. Reaching in and grasping... but there's nothing there – it's gone. I give my eyes a second to adjust. I know it was here before, I'm certain, aren't I? I was swigging from it just two days ago. My eyes dart around the room, panic rising. The red label of the vodka bottle jumps out at me on the draining board of the sink. It's empty, but I raise it to my nose anyway, the blank smell suggesting it's been rinsed out. My head swims. Did I finish the bottle the other day? I did sleep for a while… Or did I pour it away in a fit of renewed enthusiasm to stop drinking? The memories wash around my mind. I just remember lying down and falling asleep on the bed. That's the last thing I can picture. I had a couple of swigs (at most, didn't I?), found some clothes in the wardrobe and lay down for an hour or two on the bed. Isn't that what happened? It was just on Friday. I hold on to the kitchen worktop for balance, feeling faint, breathing in slowly through my nose. I feel like I am losing my grip again.

I go upstairs, stepping over the letter, averting my eyes, for now. The bathroom looks tidier, I am sure of it. I remember smelling Chris's aftershave when I was here last, spraying some on my scarf. I dropped the cap. I couldn't find it so I left it off, but it has been returned to the bottle. I feel out of body, like I'm watching over myself again. In the bedroom, I look around – there are far fewer clothes on the floor. The top I hugged in bed the other day is gone. I don't remember putting it away again, in the drawers or wardrobe. I know that I didn't, but I scrabble through anyway, swiping the hangers quickly each time. I look in the drawers, Chris's drawers. And the jumper is there, neatly folded. Who else would move Chris's clothes? Touch his after-shave? Could it be possible? Has he been to the house…? I can't hold the information, the possibilities, straight in my head. I think of computers, crunching and processing all that data, spitting information back out.

Swallowing hard, my mouth is so dry that my throat constricts and the saliva pools on my tongue. I can't ignore what I came here for any longer. Slowly, I lower myself down the stairs, holding on to the banister for support, as if I am elderly and frail, until I reach the bottom step and force myself to turn round.

There it is, the letter. I was right; it is facing backwards and the flap is neatly opened but stuck down again gently, not quickly torn like a birthday card or an ominous, official-looking letter. I know that I sealed it down, remember the sickly sweetness when I licked the sugary edge. My breath is uneven and my hands are shaking, but I see that the letter is still there. Still there but read? So if he was here – could he really have been? – he knows I am waiting for him, open to seeing him again. The spark of hope that there's still a chance for us is rekindled, then snuffed out again, replaced by the gnawing, the terror at getting closer to the truth.

But what if… what if…

What if he *is* connected to Kayleigh?

CHAPTER TWENTY-EIGHT

Sunday, 15 November

A horn blares in my ear before the screech of tyres. I turn zombie-like, jolted from a trance. A bearded man leans out of his car window. 'Watch what you're doing, you daft bitch! You'll get yourself killed – or some fucker else.' He shakes his head and beeps the horn again, this time signalling for me to get out of the way.

I am in the middle of the road on the seafront, traffic snaking along around me. My legs are wobbly underneath me, mind foggy, trying to think what I should do next.

When I get to Mum's room, I knock lightly and push the door.

Simon is putting something into the drawer by Mum's bed and doesn't see me at first.

He presses his finger to his lips then beckons me in.

'You nearly gave me a heart attack,' he whispers.

Mum is propped up in bed by pillows, but she's sleeping. There's a dark black ring under her right eye, purple on the edges. I hear myself sharply intake breath.

'It looks worse than it is. I promise,' Simon whispers. 'Let's go and get a coffee. Let your mum sleep?'

* * *

When Simon passes me the weak instant coffee, it is wobbling in the cup, my wedding ring clanking against the handle.

'Rebecca.' Simon clicks his fingers in front of my face. 'You're drip white. I'd give you a nip of something stronger if I had it. She's going to be alright, you know.'

'Thanks for looking after her. What happened? Really?'

'She just had a bad night, Rebecca. It happens. She was very confused last night and she just got upset. Ended up falling over. We were looking out for her, honest.'

'I know. I'm not blaming anyone.'

'I took a bit of a beating myself. Surprised I don't have a shiner.' He smiles.

'Oh God, really? Shit. Sorry.'

'Not your fault, remember.' Simon holds his hand up to stop me apologising.

'What was she upset about?'

'Nothing major. She was stressing about her ring again. It was just one of those nights.'

'And she hit you over the ring?'

'Yes... well, just in general.' He looks guarded.

'Why is she so adamant you have the ring?'

'Because she's confused.' His voice has a warning tone, that I shouldn't push any further. 'She was really confused in the evening. Honestly the ring's got to be about somewhere. It's a right old head scratcher.'

'And Chris?'

Simon stares into his cup. 'She was on about that again, yes. But, as I said before, it's just stuff that's going on: she's jumbling things up. The papers, the news, she probably senses you're upset.'

'She's deteriorating, isn't she?'

'I can't really answer that, you know that. It could be a phase. It isn't that predictable.'

'Is she going to have to move to a different home?'

'We don't need to think about that just now.'

Simon swirls the tea from side to side in the mug.

'You trying to read the tea leaves?' I joke feebly. 'Look for a sign? Give me one, will you?'

He laughs, but he looks tired.

'Does it get you down working here? Seeing people suffering, not being able to look after themselves? People dying every week?'

'Not everyone's like that. And mostly, no, it doesn't get me down. The opposite, actually.'

'The opposite? How?'

'Dunno,' he shrugs. 'I'll try not to be too Miss World about it and wang on about how I like helping people and making a difference. But, apart from that, I genuinely like the residents here and the people I meet. They make me laugh. They're interesting. And, I dunno, I just like it.' He shrugs again, looking a little embarrassed. He adds, 'I tell you what – I don't do it for the money, that's for sure.'

I start picking up my coat and bag but he looks up then.

'There is one other thing,' he says, hesitant. 'I had a look through the visitor records. For Chris's name. I couldn't find anything at first, but it's there: the fifteenth of July.'

'You're sure it was the fifteenth? That's two days before…'

'I had a good look through. Don't see any other references. Not on his own anyway. A couple with you.'

Probably not that many with me. 'Hmmm. And none since then?'

'Since? Well… no,' says Simon, flustered.

'Well, I suppose he wouldn't be likely to sign in, would he?'

'I don't follow.'

I think of the house, the signs of life. He might have just sneaked in to see Mum, like she said. Why would he come here first, though?

'And if he *was* here? If he *was* back?' he asks.

I shake my head. *Who knows?*

'I'm going to sit with Mum for a while longer before I go. I'm going to look for the ring again.'

I wince afresh, picturing the tender purple skin around Mum's eye. Standing in the doorway, I turn to look at Simon once more. He's sitting at the table with his back to me, hunched over his cup. And it strikes me then, an ugly thought. That maybe he decided to tell me about Chris visiting to distract me from Mum's fall.

'Simon,' I say. His shoulders jump and he turns. 'Can I see the book?'

He looks surprised, then confused.

'The guestbook with Chris's visit in?'

A look of recognition and I wonder if he's forcing it on. 'Oh, right, yeah, 'course. No bother. I can't get into the office right now – someone's in there. But next time, remind me.'

'I definitely will,' I say, emphasising the words.

CHAPTER TWENTY-NINE

Barnacles looks even more shabby by day – chipped tables, stained carpet, browning net curtains. I was jittery at the van, needed a change of scene to try to pass the time. A girl I haven't seen before is still taking stools down and wiping tables. She looks annoyed that I have dared come in so early. Her leggings are thin, bobbling and stretched – you can see the flesh colour pushing through.

I sip a lime and soda with ice, enjoying the refreshing tang and the fizz burn at the back of my throat. I need to think about what I am going to do. If Chris is back, when will he let me know?

Maybe I should stay at the house for a few days, wait for him there. He wouldn't know where to look for me at the caravan. Perhaps he wants to see me in person, rather than calling.

The smell of my chicken dinner arrives before the food itself: savoury, piled high on the plate.

'Try this for me, will you?' It's Julie. 'New chef. You can be my guinea pig. If you live, he can stay.' She slaps the back of her hand across my arm. 'I'm just kidding. Just let me know if it's alright.'

When she hands it to me, the plate tips to one side it's so heavy: gloopy mash causing the whole thing to almost flip over. A little gravy sludges onto the table, blending into the shade of the wood.

'Thanks, Julie.' I don't want the food really, but I don't want to hurt her feelings.

'Enjoy.' She shoots me a smile, patting her maroon, chipped nails on my shoulder, skin wrinkling in folds at the knuckles, gold bracelets jangling together. She waves to a couple of men at the bar waiting to be served, gesturing that she'll be over. The place is getting busier now.

Jeannie jokes that she wouldn't mess with Julie, wouldn't like to meet her in a dark alley, but she's been good to me. I feel a wave of gratitude to her. One day I will tell her, make sure she knows how much she's helped me these past months. It strikes me that for the first time, I am daring to look ahead, think of the future.

The gravy is thick and salty and the chicken skin is gristly and rubbery in my mouth, slicking my lips with grease. But it tastes good anyway. I'm even enjoying the over-boiled cabbage, giving off a pungent smell, and the dense roast potatoes that burn my mouth.

Physically, I feel a little better after the food.

The bar has filled up. I was the first one in when it was just opening. There's been a steady trickle of people since then. There's shouting and jeering from the bar, patting on the back, gullets contracting as beer goes down.

As I am thinking about leaving, there's a commotion at the bar. Something about it catches my attention. A half-caught word, a shift in the tone. It isn't about the sport on the TV or a game of pool. Over the chatter, I strain to make out the words, 'Hey, have you heard? They've found a body in the river, a few miles out.'

My ears tune in to the conversation now.

'Is it her?'

Her.

Julie and one of the men are coming towards me, faces unreadable. I grip my glass in my hand. Would I really be capable of using it as a weapon? The man stands up on the padded stool just next to me and I cower down, covering my head with my hand. But the next thing I hear is the TV. I chance a look through the crook in my elbow and see that the man is changing the channel on the TV above my head. I allow myself to unfold and see Julie is staring at me, arms crossed. I can't tell if she is looking at me with pity or disapproval.

'I was worried the TV might fall...' I offer, obviously lying.

'I'd get out of the way if I were you,' she says, raising her eyebrow and over-emphasising her words as if to get a message across.

I'm standing now; I'm not sure if she means because I am blocking the TV or I need to get out of the bar.

I should. I should get out of Barnacles. And right out of the way in general. I move from my seat and turn round so I can see the screen, and don't have to look at the faces of the crowd of people gathering behind me to watch the news. I know I should leave, but I am rooted to the spot. I need to see what the news is. All of it.

A reporter stands at the edge of the river. I don't recognise the spot. An industrial area. You can hear the water rushing behind him. The wind is whipping his collar around his face. In the distance, police tape wobbles, not stretched taut. A white cloth tent in the background, people milling around in forensics suits.

'Police here in Shawmouth have today confirmed that the body of a young woman has been found in the River Swathe. The body was found ten miles outside of the seaside town of Shawmouth, but investigators say it could have been swept downstream. Police report injuries consistent with being dragged through a rocky, fast-flowing waterway. It is still unclear the exact location or circumstances in which she entered the water.'

He looks at the camera for a few moments, sombre-faced, before going on, 'Local teenager Kayleigh Jackson is still missing.

The fourteen-year-old schoolgirl has been at the heart of a four-month police investigation after she disappeared on the last day of term at St Augustine's School on 17 July. Police stress that they are yet to confirm the identity of the body found today.'

Fifteen, I think. She's *fifteen* now.

As I run from Barnacles, crashing a table of drinks onto the floor with my bag, I hear Julie call after me, but I don't look back. I can't bear to see the faces staring at me. I need to think, to get back to the safety of the caravan.

I am trying to compute all the information at once, and an ugly picture is starting to emerge. The last sighting of Chris on the CCTV – at the top of The Parades. Close to the river. His ghostly grey figure. And I remember, too, something that the police said at the time, something that has always puzzled me. It niggled at me then, something so small. But now it feels like it could be the missing piece of the puzzle that I hoped I wouldn't find.

Could Chris really be involved? And whatever 'it' is, it looks like it could be the worst possible scenario. A murderer too? The thought of them being somewhere together is horrific enough.

But it might not be Kayleigh. It might be some other poor girl. Someone drunk who fell in. Someone who wanted to die. Other people's lives ruined. Not mine this time, not mine.

When he first went missing, I answered their questions, hours and hours on end in that bleak, square, windowless room. There was nothing I could tell them that they didn't already know.

But then there was that moment of dread. When they came back again the next day. I recognised the knock on the door, the pattern becoming all too familiar. Three quick knocks and one for good luck. They had 'a few more questions', Detective Fisher had said.

'Tell me,' Detective Fisher was testing the waters then. 'Tell me, where do you think your husband – Chris – would have gone? When he said he was going to work but, you know, wasn't?'

I remember that I thought I could detect a note of mirth or mockery when she said this last part, but having got to know her a bit better now, perhaps not after all.

I shrugged. I was defensive, tired of being poked and prodded. 'Ms Pendle?'

She wouldn't let it go. She was driving at something specific. Not just fishing like before. That made me panicky. I felt like I had something to hide, like I needed to choose my words carefully, but I wasn't sure why. It was a strain, racking my brains, trying to think ahead to the next step, the next question – and keeping a calm, impassive face. I didn't want to give anything away, create the wrong impression. Even now I can still remember clearly the tense silence that hung in the air. It felt like a power game.

I cracked first. 'Seriously, how do you expect me to know?' I was trying but failing to sound calm. The persuasive, decisive tone I was going for was coming out shrill. 'I was too stupid to even realise he wasn't going to work. I clearly know nothing at all about the man!'

'I understand this is upsetting for you, Ms Pendle. But please try to think. It's important that we try to piece together Chris's whereabouts before he went missing.'

I lost it then. 'Answer me this.' I knew I was being too cocky at that point. 'Would you really care about any of this, about Chris, if it wasn't for this teenager as well? Would you?' It was spiteful of me, I hated myself straight after for refusing to use Kayleigh's name.

I think I went down in Detective Fisher's estimations. She looked disappointed in me.

It was the opacity I found the most frustrating. I still do. Not knowing anyone else's hand. I obviously hadn't known Chris's and I definitely didn't know the police's. I couldn't even guess what they knew, what their assumptions were – where their questions were leading, what my answers might suggest.

'I am guessing he was going to the arcades, the bookies,' I told Detective Fisher. 'I mean, I'm guessing – with what you've told me about the gambling and everything. Maybe in the next town along to get out of the way. I am sorry, but I really don't know.'

Sadly, it was the truth. I didn't know. I *still* don't know. Trying to picture him, not being at work, lying to me each day. I can't visualise that... maybe I just don't want to. Where *would* he go? Where would *I* go?

One of the awful images that keeps coming into my head, creeping around in the shadows, then leaping in all at once, is him and her in one of Shawmouth's cheap little B&Bs – ugly 1970s bedspreads, plastic under the sheets.

Then the police dropped the bombshell, the one that's firing off shrapnel now.

'We have intelligence, Ms Pendle, that Chris had been seen close to the river around the days of Kayleigh's disappearance. Close to The Cut. Do you know the area?'

Now I am trying to remember the exact words. Did she say *the day of* or *the days around*? It was the word *intelligence* that stood out. So official, the cool distance. Does it even matter? He was seen there. And now a body has been found in the river. *Ten miles out*, I remind myself again – it might not be her. Swept downstream. But still miles out.

Should I go to the police, now someone has been found? Let them know about the house? No, I need to stay calm, do nothing. They'll come and find me. I'm just a bit-part character in all this. It might not be Kayleigh. *Please don't be Kayleigh.*

I am humming with anxiety, my teeth clenched, pacing the caravan, but there's nothing practical at all that I can do. A nausea is coming over me. Would I really cover for him? Is that what I am doing?

But I am trapped here in this hellish purgatory. Even now with this latest evidence 'presented' to me – a body – something in me won't allow me to be totally sure. But something has definitely shifted, hardened.

I picture what he might have done, and I am repulsed. I picture his face, our time together, and I am full of warmth and love and yearning for him and what we had, our life together.

I take a swipe at the drying rack, sending all the crockery flying onto the floor, but it doesn't break. One of the cups even bounces. I let out a scream, as loud as I can until it burns my throat, frustration and anger welling up inside me. I am grabbing clumps of hair at the side of my head and pulling until the pain sears, coloured dots popping in front of my eyes, temples hot and pulsating, a vein throbbing.

I tire myself out after a while and I sit in the corner on the floor, pull my knees in and make myself as small as I can. I wait like that for I don't know how long, expecting the police to knock at any moment.

CHAPTER THIRTY

Sunday, 15 November

My phone rings and I pull it out straight away. I hope that it's Detective Fisher. I decided to call her in the end; just to get an update. But she hasn't been available or answered her mobile yet. She hasn't called me back either. Is that a good sign or a bad one?

But the number is Sandra and Geoff's house. It's 3 p.m. My first strange thought is how Sandra would have started making the Sunday dinner earlier like she always does. How she'll have let it burn or go cold now. I feel guilty, but I let it ring and ring. I just can't do it right now. I'm only just holding it together as it is, if I am even doing that.

My body is all tension; I can't just wait at the caravan. It's unbearable.

I've just been walking around the town. I don't know for how long or where I have been. I just have to keep moving. I keep thinking to myself, if it is Kayleigh, or even if it's someone else, now would be the time, Chris – whatever's happened – to come back, to explain everything, to rescue your reputation. To show that it wasn't you.

He wouldn't know to come to the caravan. So I'm standing now near the top of The Parades. Near the river. A sudden headache and my thoughts start spinning again.

He was near the river. The body is in the river. Chris grabbing Kayleigh; a fight at the edge. Or maybe... maybe it could be that Kayleigh was in trouble and Chris went in after her to try to save her? Then I see his face, water-bloated, like a horror film. *Will he be found next? Please, no.*

But he's been to the house. I feel more sure now. *That's where he'd go, isn't it? He'd look for me there. Surely he'd try to reach me.* My hands are shaking and I take my phone out again. More missed calls and a text from Sandra. *Ignore.* I try Chris's phone again. The first time in a while. The wait seems to take forever; the little clicking sound as the number dials. I don't think I breathe.

'Sorry, the number you are calling is not available.'

Same as always. I feel like screaming at the top of my voice again.

The area around The Parades is quite busy today. Daytime drinkers, squeezing the last out of the weekend. It surprises me somehow – that the whole town isn't indoors crowded round their TVs, waiting for news of Kayleigh. It reminds me how small my world has become. Some people won't have heard yet, others will only care on a distant level. For everybody else, life goes on; it's background noise. Upsetting but not central.

I think of Janice, Kayleigh's mum, what she must be going through. Is she at the police station? Or sitting in her living room, curtains closed, coiled like a spring, jumping at the slightest noise or movement? Maybe she's already had more news; she'd be the first to know, surely.

When I see it, I think my heart stops for a second.

It can't be him – he's walking down the street with the pubs and bars on, where I was out for Jeannie's birthday. Was it just last night? It already feels like weeks ago.

I know it can't be him. *But it is. It is him.* Even the trainers with the navy-blue stripes. They're the same. The parka. The specific way he walks. The height. He's further down the road from me. I can't shout. Would he run? Is he on the way to the house? Or the police station to explain everything?

I speed up to a slow jog – a couple of people smoking outside one of the bars smirk at me, probably for running in the street. I'm trying to catch my breath and calm myself at the same time. I'm sweating, a cold film around my hairline.

As I get closer, he turns into one of the pubs at the bottom – an old man's pub – I've been in before. All wood beams, ship paraphernalia everywhere. Yes, he used to drink in here, didn't he? With Sean. With football lads after practice.

There are bouncers on the door when I get there, but they're busy talking to two women standing to the side of the door. They don't notice me. Why would he come here? I don't want him to get attacked. Everything has to be brought out into the open first before he can just waltz into a pub here. Maybe, somehow, he doesn't realise the strength of feeling around here. Could he not have heard what's happened?

I feel sick, my jaw is clenched.

Inside, the pub is rammed. There's a football match on the big screen. Groups everywhere, standing, leaning over the backs of seats, kneeling on stools. Everyone is melding into the next person; I can't see anyone clearly. Glasses clinking, the sound of money clattering. There's a goal; the whole place erupts and I get jostled around, beer spills down my front.

When the commotion settles, Chris is there at the front. Drinking a pint, looking up at the TV. *Deep breath.* Maybe he needed Dutch courage to come and see me. We just have to get out of here, go somewhere that we can talk.

My legs are carrying me over there. I stand behind him for what feels like over a minute. People are starting to notice. Then my finger goes out, jabs him gently on the back. I wait for it, I want to really feel and experience that moment that I see him face to face again.

When he turns round, he's scowling.

It isn't Chris.

'I'm… I'm sorry; I thought you were… someone else.'

He looks sideways at me and shakes his head, wiping the beer I caused him to spill from the sleeve of his jacket. The people sitting at the table nearby are laughing between themselves.

Then, I am pushing people out of the way. I feel claustrophobic in here, need to get outside.

'You alright, darling?' the bouncer asks me, smirking.

I don't answer him. I walk away, dazed. I need to keep my wits about me here. I'm spinning off: of course he wouldn't just go to the pub in town. And he wouldn't go to the river. He would be at the house, it's the safest place to be. And the place he'd be most likely to find me.

The bus waited for ages at the previous stop, trying to get back onto a regular schedule most likely. I couldn't stand it any longer so I jumped off and tried to speed-walk the rest of the way, although I have a stitch now. How can something so minor be so painful? I stop and lean on a fence, doubling over to try to manage the stabbing pain in my side. The house isn't in view yet.

But I hear the low rumble, a car again to my left. Everything tenses. Has someone followed me? Is it the police? I have to get to the house. Get inside. See if Chris is there. This is my last chance.

I break into a run, my feet stumbling over each other before I am crashing down to the pavement, a hole tearing in my jeans as I scrape along the pavement. A car door slams. My hands instinctively come up to my head to protect it. Someone is coming over.

'Becs, Becs, what's the matter with you? What's going on?' It's Jeannie's voice. Her hand is on my shoulder now.

I don't want to look up.

Her voice is a little softer now. 'Becs. What are you doing?'

I try to get up, staggering a little, and she helps me, a stricken look on her face, a vein popping out at her temple.

'Are you OK, Becs? Becs? Oh fuck! Your knee's bleeding.'

'Can we just sit in the car for a minute?'

'Yeah, if that's what you want. Come on.'

The windows in the car start to steam up once we're inside. I realise I am panting. Jeannie takes the keys out of the ignition.

'So what's going on? We are not leaving this car until you tell me what is going on,' she says, after what seems like a long time. The car door locks click into place. 'Why haven't you replied to my texts or rung me back? I wanted to see if you were OK. I heard about the body. You look like death warmed up, by the way.' She puts her cold hand on mine.

'Sorry. I'm all over the place.'

'I've been looking right across the bloody town for you.'

'I just had a bit of a shock, that's all.'

'You've heard then?'

'Yes, but I was just in town and I thought I saw Chris. I went over and… it wasn't him.'

'Oh, Becs. But listen, you need to be really really careful right now.'

'What do you mean?'

'Becs… there's a body. It's a girl… People are already saying things.'

I look at her blankly. 'Where's Sam?' drifts out of my mouth, distant.

She shakes her head, impatient or exasperated. 'Dan's got him. Why are you here, Becs? The house, it's not a good place for you to be. And why were you so scared when I pulled up in the car?'

I don't answer. I am closing up, curling inwards, so when Jeannie shouts, it makes me jump.

'Becs! Becs!' She clicks her fingers in front of my face. 'What the hell is going on?'

'I think he's back, Jeannie. I need to see him.'

'Who? What? Who's back?'

'Listen... you're not going to believe this, Jeannie. But just hear me out, OK? Just promise me that you won't react. You honestly can't go straight to the police. OK?'

'OK... I'm listening. And that's all I am agreeing to for now.' She puts the keys down in her lap.

I take a sharp breath in through my nose. *Here goes.*

'I hope you haven't done anything stupid, Becs.'

'I think Chris is back.'

She lets out the breath slowly. 'Fuck.'

'I think he's been to the house. I think he's trying to reach me, thinking about coming back, maybe. And now... the body... I need to see him. Give him a chance to explain.'

There's something like terror in Jeannie's eyes, and she lifts her hand to her mouth but she doesn't say anything. Her throat contracts with a swallow. 'And that's why you rushed back here?'

I nod.

'Becs – I really think we should think about going back to the doctor's again – like today, now. You got like this before.'

'I am fine.' *At least I will be, as soon as I see Chris.*

'So, he's back here. You're going to come back and meet him and what? All live happily ever after. You need to call the police. Apart from anything else, you could be putting yourself in danger. It won't look good if you don't let them know. Really.'

'He's not dangerous to me, Jeannie. It isn't like that. I think he's back to clear his name.'

'Becs, a girl has just turned up dead in a river. And Chris left without a word, cleaned out your bank account, lied to you about getting sacked. Is that normal? You don't know what he's capable of.' Her voice cracks.

'I just need to see him, Jeannie, and have a chance to talk to him.'

'Well, where is he then?'

'He's been at the house, Jeannie. I know it's him.'

She looks at the ceiling. 'I can't do this all the time, you know. You're stressing me out too. You need to go back to the doctor's. I will come with you.' Jeannie presses the heels of her hands into her eyes. 'For God's sake, Becs.'

I can picture in my head the coloured dots she will be seeing now.

'Listen.' I grab at her sleeve. I'm not helping myself or calming her fears, I know. 'Some of his clothes have gone from the bedroom. And his aftershave has had the lid returned.'

I realise how feeble this last one sounds now, out loud. But her head snaps towards me, more interested.

'There's other things too. I had a bottle of vodka in the fridge. I know, I know. But it's been either drunk or poured away. And not by me. Only Chris and I live there, Jeannie.'

I have her attention now. Finally. She's looking right at me, actually listening. I feel vindicated so I go on, speaking faster.

'I've been getting calls – there's no one speaking but I think he's trying to reach me, Jeannie. I really do.'

She's biting at her lip, thinking.

'I left a letter for Chris on the stairs, Jeannie, and it's been opened. He's read it. I don't know where he's been, or what's going to happen when he gets back, but I know it's him.'

Jeannie stares at me.

I am panicking now, my heart is fluttering. 'Please, Jeannie. Please don't go to the police. Not yet. I just need to hear the truth and then I will report him myself. Please, Jeannie. I am not mad; I know this is real. I have seen it all at the house with my own eyes.'

She takes a deep breath. I see a flicker of her eye. Something kicks in.

'Do you know something, Jeannie? Is something going on? *Youhavetotellmenow.*' I am tugging on the sleeve of her coat.

'No. Not really. Sort of. It isn't what you think. It really isn't.' Jeannie looks tearful.

It feels like she is speaking in slow motion.

'Tell me. Please, Jeannie. I can't bear this.'

My mind races with what it could be. Has Chris been to see her or contacted her? Sworn her to secrecy? Maybe he wanted to sound her out for how I would react. Maybe he's been in touch with Dan. But why wouldn't she tell me? Why would she wait for me to come to her?

'It isn't Chris, Becs. You've got this all wrong.'

'I KNEW you'd react like this. I just knew it. Why do you have to treat me like some kind of idiot all of the time?'

I go to open the car door and get out. It's locked anyway but Jeannie grabs at my wrist, scratching me with her nail accidentally. Her grip is firm and my shoulder twists painfully.

We are face to face now.

'It wasn't Chris, Becs. It was me.'

It takes time for the information to sink in. At first I think she means it was her who had something to do with Kayleigh's disappearance. My stomach and chest are frozen.

She is rummaging for something. I imagine her pulling out an incriminating photo or a message from Chris perhaps. Finally, she pulls it from her bag. A bunch of keys. She separates it out.

My spare house key.

I feel the tension break, like I've been holding my breath underwater. Everything crashes down at once. Of course… I gave her a key after the house was attacked with the brick. Dan was cleaning up. *Dan will sort it all out.*

A surge of anger at Jeannie interfering is quickly replaced by a flood of disappointment, full of floating debris, false hopes.

'But… the clothes? The letter?' I am trying to piece it all together now, but the information swims. 'I don't understand, Jeannie. I can't…'

'I poured the vodka away, Becs. I'm sorry. It isn't good for you. I can't bear to think of you round there, off your face, getting so upset. We wanted to get the place a bit cleaned up for you. I know you're struggling paying double rent. I thought you might want to consider moving back in soon or, you know, selling it maybe, making a fresh start. It was getting dusty and run down; I wanted to help you.'

'But the letter? What about the letter?'

'I'm so, so sorry.' She covers her eyes with her hand. 'I shouldn't have – but I opened it. I don't know what's going on in your head, Becs. You are all over the place. I was just trying to look out for you. I shouldn't have opened it; I know that. I didn't even read what was inside. I felt bad straight away and I just put it back. I swear, Becs. I'm sorry.'

I pull my arm away again, her nails scraping on my forearm.

'I just wanted to know what was going on!'

She is saying something else but I am not listening anymore. I stare at the steamed-up windows. I feel like I am at high altitude; that my ears need to pop. I want to curl into a ball right there in the car, for Jeannie and everything else to just disappear.

'I am so stupid. I just wanted it to be him.' I say it over and over again.

We sit in the car for a long time. Jeannie puts the heater on and lets her head fall back on the headrest. The atmosphere is gradually seeping away and I am just numb.

'Becs, there are journalists everywhere. Outside your house. Right now. You can't be here.'

'Journalists. But why?'

Jeannie just shakes her head and starts the engine.

CHAPTER THIRTY-ONE

Sunday, 15 November

My face is pressed into the earth, the taste of blood and gritty dirt filling my mouth. Initially, I can't work out where I am. Have I been locked up somewhere, beaten, left for dead? I remember Jeannie bringing me back to the caravan. Eventually, I persuaded her to leave, that I'd be OK. I checked online again, tried Detective Fisher's phone a few more times. But there was still no news on the body in the river. More missed calls from Sandra and Geoff.

I managed to sleep for a while. Someone knocked. I went outside. I can't make sense of being here, on the ground.

Still in the silence, scared to move, my senses tell me it isn't that bad. But my head is foggy. Maybe I blacked out. Tentatively I raise my head and lift myself up from the floor, allowing my eyes to adjust to where I am. Gradually, dark outlines reveal themselves in the night sky. I can move, nothing is broken. Pressing my lips together, they feel swollen and bruised, but running my tongue over my mouth, my teeth are not jagged or broken, as I feared.

Everything is on its side. I'm outside the caravan, on the ground at the bottom of the steps. I stepped out to get some air... Did I faint due to the stress? The caravan door is still open. I fumble in my pocket and my mobile is there. I use the light to see if someone is inside. I don't see it at first but it's clearly there, dark shapes outside on either side of the door. I don't understand. I push myself up off the ground, dirt collecting under my nails as I struggle to stand up. I touch the shapes; electrical tape. Feeling around reveals a wire across the door to trip me up when I left the caravan. Not an accident, then.

The blood in my mouth, Jeannie dashing my hopes, the body being found. I have this sensation of being in free fall. Something snaps. I'm not going to let them do this to me anymore. I'm going to go to them for once, confront them.

I don't feel afraid as I walk out of the caravan park. My mouth is metallic, lip bulbous. The seafront is dead, no one around – clear road. The bus shelter is deserted, too, so I turn off and head towards the next place they could be.

Through the stone pillars, street lamps light either side of the pathway, but the rest of the park is in complete blackness. My eyes are adjusted now though, the landscape emerging from the dark. It should have been Kayleigh's vigil tonight, here in the park. Her fifteenth birthday too. It must have been cancelled because they found the body. Too much for Janice, no doubt. What she must be going through now, waiting for news. Or does it mean that she knows something? An announcement coming soon to shatter everything for good?

I head for the playground area. Jeannie and I used to hang out there when we were teenagers, drinking, wasting time. They said in the paper that Kayleigh was supposed to meet her friends at the park, but she never showed up.

The cool silence in the air is broken by the odd laugh, the low murmur of chatter, the squeak of a swing. Getting closer, I can hear them now, but I can't see them yet. The sky is vast and clear above the park, an indigo blue.

I think about hanging back, seeing what they are up to, listening in, but I don't want to lose my nerve. Their silhouettes are starting to take shape and make sense now. There are a few lights dotted around the edge of the play area. I'm in the darkness but they are lit up, exposed. Can they see me yet? There seem to be around eight of them – I count them as my eyes adjust – sitting on the roundabout and the swings, occasionally darting around.

'Someone's coming,' I hear one of them say.

Then, louder: 'Is that you, Deano?'

A girl. I recognise the voice. Good. I don't answer.

'Hey, who is it?' someone else asks.

Another makes a ghost noise.

'It's me,' I say. 'You've been to my home plenty of times. I thought it's time I came to you.' For once, I do manage to sound blank, unemotional. Not the usual wobble that comes out.

'Oh fuck,' I hear one of them say, but they're stifling a laugh too. I wait to see which one of them is going to take the lead.

'It's her,' another one whispers. More awkward giggles. 'It's his wife.'

There's jostling; a boy spins the roundabout lazily through his hands, slowly, trying to look unruffled. It creaks loudly. The same roundabout Kayleigh is on in the video. They're closing in on me now, coming forwards for a closer look.

'Here! What have you done to your face? Slipped with your lipstick?' one of the boys says.

Many, not all, of them snigger.

My legs are wobbling and the volume in his voice is cutting in and out. My vision blurs too, like I am looking through a bubble of water. I must be more tired than I think, or perhaps it's the fall.

I breathe the cold air into my lungs to try to wake up. Forcing calmness, pronouncing each word fully and carefully. 'I had a nasty accident, actually.' My voice sounds disconnected, like it's in the air around me, warping.

'You should be more careful.' He's saying something else now but he sounds like a record on the wrong speed; words too long and drawn out, all running together.

'I know it was you lot. I want to know what you want from me,' I hear someone say. I think it's me. Have I been drugged?

'Are you drunk, missus? Oi, where's your husband then? You hidin' him? Coverin' for him?'

The faces and the park feel like they're spinning around me, I'm slipping into a dream. Kayleigh on the roundabout. That song. I feel a fresh wave of shock that such a young girl has disappeared, a beautiful young girl. And that I am part of the equation in any way. And that now there's a body.

'Oi, where's your husband, I said.' Someone claps in front of my face, focus sharpening again.

I expect to see Ashy, to be back in the takeaway. Jeannie's night out. It takes me a moment, feels like it's in slow motion. It reminds me of when I took magic mushrooms at university. That echoey feeling, heart buzzing. The sharp hand-clap again.

Paige.

'Why are you protecting him? Why are you here? Your husband is a murdering bastard and an old perv and you shagged him. And now you have to live with that for the rest of your life.'

'He isn't anything to do with this.' Even I can hear the lack of conviction in my voice compared to before. I push on to something more certain. 'We don't know anything for sure yet. It might not be Kayleigh.'

'Ooh, do you think there's a serial kidnapper and murderer in Shawmouth?'

The veins in Paige's neck are strained. The words and the venom in her voice shock me into some clarity again.

'We're innocent until proven guilty in this country. Don't they teach you that at school anymore?'

Paige pushes me against my chest, right on the breastbone. I stumble backwards slightly.

'Someone else said he tried to crack onto them, remember?'

'It's an allegation, that's all. We don't know.'

'Don't we? You calling my friend a liar?' This renews her enthusiasm. She has smelt fresh blood.

I try to catch my breath.

'That's shut you up, hasn't it?' She folds her arms, triumphant.

'Wha—what do you mean?'

'Tell her, Kat.'

'Paige, just leave it, will you?' one of the boys says.

'Tell her, Kat.' She says it louder this time, pulling Kat forward a little by the arm.

She doesn't look up. Paige nudges her again.

'It was me. He was talking to me.' Kat speaks down into her own chest so I have to strain to hear.

'When? What did he say? What do you mean by "talking"?'

She is starting to cry, her small shoulders shuddering. I think I am going to be sick.

'You should not be sticking by him. You need to face it, love,' Paige butts in.

Kat steps back again, covering most of her face with the sleeve of her coat.

'Your mate enjoy her chips the other night, did she?' Paige is coming towards me again.

I take a step forward too. 'Why are you hanging around in there anyway?'

Paige stops still. 'Ha! What has it got to do with you? You're taking the absolute piss now.'

I sense I've gained a little ground of my own. 'You just need to be careful.'

'What do you know about it?' She jabs at my face with her finger.

'I know enough.'

'What does that mean?' Paige says.

I don't answer her.

'My boyfriend works there, you stupid cow,' she says, pride in her voice.

'Your boyfriend?' I think of the younger lad working in there the other night.

'You hanging out with your greasy boyfriend again? Owt for free chips!' one of the boys shouts over, and the others laugh.

'Fuck off, dickhead! Why don't you get a job and some money? Then come back and take the piss out of me, yeah? And you're not complaining when you get free stuff out of it, are you?'

'Look.' I need to change tack, stop this escalating. 'I just want you to leave me alone. Stop coming to my home. There's nothing I can do. I'm truly sorry for what's happened. It's terrible but it isn't my fault.'

No answer.

'And stop following me and calling me. Or I will go to the police.'

'Don't flatter yourself, love. No one's following you. You're not that important. I'm pretty sure you'll be hearing from the police again yourself soon.' Paige laughs and looks round but no one else is laughing this time.

'Oh boo hoo,' says Paige, putting her face close to mine.

'Leave it, P. Please just leave it, yeah?' Kat puts her hand on Paige's arm.

'Why should I leave it? Why should I? And why are you crying?' The last question is directed at me. Paige's shoulder is pulled back like she's thinking about hitting me. 'You didn't know Kayleigh. What's it to you all of a sudden?' She waits for an answer.

'How can it not be anything to me after all this, the past few weeks and months? How can it not? You've made it about me!' I realise I am pointing.

'Yeah, well, like I said, you don't know her, so don't talk about her, yeah? It's none of your business.'

A low voice from the back of the group, barely discernible. 'Says you.'

Silence.

Paige slowly turns her head around to the side. 'You fucking what?' Her face is an ugly grimace, the branch of a tree casting a shadow across it, fracturing her features.

Kat is breathing quickly, panicky. I can see white clouds puffing from her mouth. '*Please-please-please* just leave it. Everyone just stop it.' She stares straight down at her feet, shuffling them from side to side.

The voice, a boy, less aggressive. 'You're causing all this drama, Paige, but you've only just started hanging out with us this year. We've grown up with her. So let's just leave it, yeah? Kayleigh's still gone, and well, it don't look good, does it, after today, and none of this is going to change it. She don't need this and neither do we.'

I can't tell if 'she' is me or Kayleigh.

'Oh, shut the fuck up, dickhead! Was she your girlfriend or something? Or did you just want her to be?' But there's a tone to Paige's voice. Something has struck a chord.

'He's jealous of your husband.' She gestures back with her thumb, coming towards me again.

The boy starts to walk away, back towards the swings. 'She might have been dragged from the river today. Show some fucking respect, Paige.'

I can see him shake his bowed head, kicking his feet into the ground. Kat follows him in silence and the others start to drift towards their friends, murmuring among themselves. They're not interested in me anymore, and they're backing away from one of their own.

Quietly, I address Paige so the others can't hear. 'I saw you at the beach, remember. I haven't forgotten.'

She takes a step towards me but then stops.

I go right up to her, can feel her breath on my face. 'Just leave me alone, Paige. I don't want any trouble, but just leave me alone.'

I walk away, reluctant to turn my back, but I have to do it anyway. I'm getting away. It's over. Then, something wet hits the back of my head. I reach up; it's just a clod of earth, wet and slimy.

'Pisshead,' I hear her say. I realise I am snaking from side to side when I walk. But I haven't been drinking at all. I just need to lie down.

I look back and Paige is already walking away, back towards the group. I can't hear any of them speaking now. They're disappearing into the darkness again.

CHAPTER THIRTY-TWO

Monday, 16 November

I try to open my eyes, but there's only a chink of light getting in somehow. I can't see anything but bright white. I wonder momentarily if I am dead or dying, and a panic sets in. A hand on mine, soft and warm; in an instant I have time to process that it's a woman's hand. Not Chris's.

But I still delay opening my eyes. I must have been drinking, fallen asleep at Mum's. Another of the carers at Mum's home must have come in. I can feel that my legs are bare and I am under the covers. I've gone too far. My hand instinctively goes to my head and there's fabric there, a bandage.

'Becs, it's me, Jeannie. Everything's OK. You're in the hospital but I'm here with Julie. From the caravan park.'

I open my eyes and try to prop myself up on my hands, but the light's too bright and my head is throbbing.

'Shhhhh, you need to rest,' says Jeannie. The figures emerge now.

'What's going on?' I finally manage to say. I see Julie wincing at me. My face must be a mess.

'Well,' Jeannie looks at Julie for reassurance. 'I think you, er, fell. Well... we don't know. That's what we need to establish, but Julie found you near the entrance to the park and you were unconscious, on the ground.' She puts her hand to her mouth, restraining tears.

'How are you feeling, love?' Julie offers me one of the plastic cups of tea that she's holding in her hands. I refuse, but Jeannie has already jumped in to try to stop me taking it.

'A bit soon, I think.' I force a weak smile.

I'm able to pull myself up a little better now, pushing through the pain to get upright. Jeannie fusses and plumps the pillow.

'What happened?' She's staring intently at me, waiting for an answer, giving me no space to think. I remember now, being at the park with Paige and Kat, and the other teenagers, then walking home. Arriving at the caravan park.

The fog lifts and I remember what happened yesterday.

'Is there any news? On the body?'

Julie opens her mouth to speak but Jeannie shuts her down with a look.

Then Jeannie just looks down at me, shaking her head. 'How have you come to be in this state, Becs?'

'I'm just really tired, I guess. I think I fainted. Sorry. I was feeling a bit woozy earlier in the day. I probably didn't eat enough – you know what I'm like. Sorry.'

Julie presses her lips together. She knows that's not true: she served me the chicken dinner.

Maybe I fainted from hitting my head after the fall at the caravan. Or maybe Paige came after me, followed me to the caravan park.

'Don't be sorry, love,' Julie says. 'Had you been drinking? Taking something? I mean, Jesus Christ, you don't just fall down in the street. Or in the caravan park, in your case, as luck would have it.' She looks across at Jeannie. 'You could have got run over or anything.'

Jeannie's shaking her head again. I can't tell her where I was; what happened. She'll think I've lost it again. 'Chasing shadows' was what she said before. It stuck with me. I don't answer her anyway, feigning another wave of headache. 'You couldn't get me some water, could you, Jeannie?'

'Um, yeah, I guess. Hang on, let me check with the nurse whether you're allowed anything. Don't drink anything until I've checked with her, right? Right.' She points at Julie this time, before heading out into the hall to stalk a nurse down.

Julie rolls her eyes at Jeannie but in good humour. 'You sure you're alright?' she says, sitting down and slurping one of the teas, looking at me over the rim. 'Are you sick of being asked that already?'

'I'm fine. Sorry for the commotion. I'm sure you've got stuff to be doing at the caravan park.'

'Not really. 'S dead this time of year anyway, as you know.' She rolls the gum she's chewing over her teeth with her tongue.

The thought of the tea and the chewing gum together makes me queasy.

'You gave me a right old scare, you did. I thought you were a goner when I saw you lying there. Was just nipping out to the all-night garage. You could've caught hypothermia lying there like that.' She adds, trying to sound casual, 'Did you have some trouble with someone? On the park? Or wherever?'

'No, sorry, Julie. Nothing like that. Like I said, I was knackered and I'm probably not looking after myself as well as I could. I mean, you know what I'm like. I'm sorry; I don't want to cause any trouble at the caravan site for you. I really appreciate you letting me stay there. Honestly, I do. I had a couple of drinks and I probably shouldn't when I'm feeling like that.'

'Did you?' She narrows her eyes. 'I noticed you've not been drinking as much lately, that's all.'

'I have my blips.'

She's still twisting the gum and has an eyebrow raised at me. I can tell she doesn't believe me. Maybe she saw the wire at the caravan, across the door. Perhaps people have been talking in the club.

She snaps out of something. 'Suit yourself. I'm not having a go at you, love. This isn't about the bloody caravan park. There's barely anyone stopping there but you anyway.' She's rocking back in the plastic chair now, balancing it on two legs. 'I just thought it was funny how you'd managed to somehow fall and hit your face and the back of your head. I mean, how do you manage that? Hey, I've been as pissed as the best of them, but I either end up flat on my face or flat on my arse – both is a bit of a feat!'

'I'm an idiot, Julie. Sorry, it won't happen again.'

'What's that, then? You won't pass out again? Or you won't get clobbered again? Not sure you're quite in control of either of those things, are you? You come to me if you need anything, you hear me? And stop saying bloody sorry, will you! I feel like a flaming priest.'

Jeannie's back now, carrying a small cup of water. 'You're fine as long as you sip it. Don't guzzle it, the nurse said; you might be sick.'

Julie's getting up to go. Jeannie's probably getting on her nerves, fussing around. 'I'm going to get off, girls. And think on what I said, yeah? Pop into the club and see me when you get back on the park, right.' She winks at Jeannie. 'Don't worry, I'll only give her a lemonade, I promise.'

'What's she on about?' Jeannie says, after Julie's left.

'Come on, she's alright really. She looks out for me.'

'Right. And don't be going in there getting pissed again when you get back, right? Well, you'll be staying with me anyway, so that solves that.'

I hear someone tut from behind the curtain in the next bed. 'Language, please,' an elderly man's voice says.

Jeannie and I both stifle a laugh.

Jeannie sits reading a magazine. She offers one to me, but I couldn't focus. I'm on edge. About the body they found in the river. About how I ended up here.

'Are you alright?' Jeannie lowers the magazine to her lap. She shoves a grey pulp sick bowl at me.

I bat it away. 'I know you mean well, but will you just leave it?'

She looks hurt, but makes light of it and pretends to read the magazine.

'Never mind me. Are you alright anyway? After the other night? At the takeaway.' I try to inspect her lip from afar, but there's no sign of swelling or bruising now. I feel shame that I didn't even think of it when I saw her at the house yesterday. 'I did mean to ask, I meant to send a text, Jeannie. Sorry.'

Usually, she'd berate me for this, freeze me out for a bit, but she relents. 'Hey, don't worry about it; it wasn't much in the end. Little cow.'

'What did Dan say?'

'I told him Angela headbutted me by accident when we were dancing about and being daft.'

We both laugh.

'Hey, and while we are on the subject, since you don't reply to my texts… What was all that about in the takeaway? Do you know those lasses? You seemed to know the owners?'

'Please. Not now, Jeannie. I feel like death warmed up. I can't think straight with all this going on.'

Jeannie shifts her tone. 'I could have gone to the police, you know.'

'They're just daft kids, Jeannie.'

'Still.'

'Why didn't you, then?'

She looks up at me. 'Because I know you don't want me to.'

'Correct.'

Jeannie doesn't let things lie. 'But after this, Becs, I mean – it could be connected.'

'What, me falling over?'

'Yeah, you "falling over".' She does quote marks with her fingers in the air.

'They're kids, I've told you. It's nothing.'

Jeannie tuts and goes back to her magazine. 'To be continued,' she says.

She knows not to push it just now.

Could it really have been Paige? I picture her face, twisted with aggression and spite. She was so angry.

I remember the argument with Paige; the mud hitting my head. I remember feeling weird in the park, like I'd been drugged. The fall outside the caravan. The sound of a car, headlights, tyres on gravel. Or is that everything running together? My memory is gloopy. I have a hazy memory of a push to the back, something hitting the back of my head. Am I confusing this with what happened at the park?

'Jeannie, I'm sorry for worrying you. I'd had a few drinks; I'm sorry for all this.' My voice is cracking. If I tell her I had been drinking, she will be less suspicious.

Her phone beeps in her pocket.

'Shit, that'll be Dan. Not meant to have these on in here, are you...' She reads the message; her hand goes up to her mouth. She looks at me and straight away jumps out of her seat and hugs me, clutching tightly at the back of the nightgown I am wearing. For once I don't mind and I put my arms around her too.

After what seems like a long time, she takes a breath. I don't want her to speak.

'It's her, Becs. I'm so sorry, but the body... it's Kayleigh.'

At first we just sit there for a few minutes. Neither of us wants to face it; what it means, what happens now.

I grab her phone and load up the *Courier* news site. It's slow, the wheel spinning and spinning.

CONFIRMED: RIVER BODY IS KAYLEIGH JACKSON

The headline is the first thing that screams out at me. Jeannie manages to get the cardboard sick bowl in front of me just in time to catch most of the vomit that bursts out.

I play the video anyway while she faffs with the bowl and shouts for a nurse, before she can stop me.

The police tape again, the tents, the white suits. The same reporter.

'The police have been informed that a body found in the river yesterday, in an industrial area on the edge of Shawmouth, is that of missing teenager Kayleigh Jackson.'

His eyes stare into the camera, out at me.

The script is a familiar one; I've heard it countless times before on TV, the radio, in the paper. I feel like I am watching a play that I've seen rehearsed over and over again, so I know the next line in my head. I fill it in in advance. But the line is wrong. Instead of saying, 'Police say there are no suspicious circumstances surrounding the death,' the newsreader says, 'Police are still appealing for witnesses to come forward as they continue their enquiries into the disappearance, and now death, of Kayleigh Jackson.'

I can't get the image of her out of my head. Floating in the water. Or left there, dumped on the side of the river? Would she have decomposed? I close my eyes, but the picture just gets clearer: white, bloated skin, chunks missing, hair floating or tangled in weeds.

I am sobbing in great heaves into Jeannie's chest, my breath causing my face to overheat.

'Sh-sh-sh-sh. I know. I know.' She strokes my hair, carefully avoiding the wound at the back of my head.

'She was just young, Jeannie. Remember when we were that age? Ellen, Ellen.'

She squeezes me even tighter then, so that it almost starts to hurt.

'What did he do, Jeannie? What did he do?'

CHAPTER THIRTY-THREE

Wednesday, 18 November

They gave me some sleeping pills at the hospital and I took one, sometimes two, every time I woke up. I switched my phone off. I don't know if I dreamt all the knocking at the caravan door, so hard it rocked. If there were really journalists banging at the window, shouting my name.

I dreamt of being at the river, where Kayleigh was found. I was trying to save her, but we were being dragged towards rapids. She got pulled under, her head hitting a rock. I couldn't breathe in the dream or when I woke up. I couldn't get to her in time.

Julie used her key to let Jeannie in in the end. It would take a lot for Julie to agree to that. I think they thought I was dead. Jeannie put me in the shower physically, force-fed me coffee and toast. She wants me to go and stay with her. I've told her I'll think about it.

My legs feel weak. But the sleeping pills are wearing off now. I'm coming round. The sickness and anger are coming back.

I am walking towards the house. There are a few cars parked there, journalists I assume, leaning on them. I expected there to be more. They've probably been called back to the office now, given up or had their budgets cut, another story demanding their attention.

Someone's thrown red paint across the windows, drying in plasticky rivulets down the glass.

Three journalists crowd around when I am opening the door, but I zone out. It's not hard anymore. It doesn't feel as if they're really there.

'Rebecca, do you have any comment to make?' 'Do you have a message for Kayleigh Jackson's family?' 'Who do you think did this to your house?' 'Is your husband guilty, Rebecca?' 'Rebecca! We can offer you a fee for your story.'

I stop to take some deep breaths when I get into the house, my back against the door. But they're slapping it hard from the outside, so I go into the living room. I don't put the lights on and I make sure the blinds have no gaps.

The house feels emptier than ever; there is a grey, lifeless tinge to everything. I expected to collapse into tears when I got inside. But it's something else that is welling inside me. My teeth grating, everything tensing up. I feel like I could explode, smash. How could this have happened? Hiding away in a caravan and cowering in my own home?

The letter taunts me on the stairs. I tear it into two, then four, finally letting out a scream that shreds and burns the back of my throat. I feel better for a second. I wonder if they heard it outside. Let them report it; I don't care anymore.

I take the picture of me and Chris off the windowsill. We're on the beach, bundled up against the weather. The rage swells again and I throw it as hard as I can against the back wall. It's not heavy, but the corner hits the plaster with a dull thud, creating a dent before bouncing down onto the floor. The clean sound of glass smashing is pleasing. Then it's cups, plates, anything I can get my hands on. Most of the cups don't break, but the plates smash into thousands of tiny pieces and splinters that could lodge in your eye or sink into your foot, impossible to get out again. I don't care if they hear me outside. They'll write what they want anyway.

I go upstairs now, into the bedroom, dragging Chris's clothes out of the wardrobe and throwing them on to the floor, pulling at the sleeves. The effort, the pain of trying to tear the tightly woven fabric of the shirts gives me some release.

I can still hear the journalists outside, shouting my name. I look out of the window, and one of them is pressed up to the living-room window, another one standing further back, his camera angled up towards me. I jump back.

I barely wait for the ladder to be in place before climbing up to the loft, pushing the hatch open with a shove so that it slams open onto the loft floor. I don't use any of the usual caution, striding up the ladder quickly, not bothering to check my footing.

There's no escape up here though. This room taunts me too. The queasiness creeps in again. What did Chris do up here all those nights? Nights while I was in the house downstairs, oblivious. I've tried to stop it, to hold the line, but something in me has given way. You read about these houses and hotels built on cliffs. The sea is eroding the foundations, bit by bit, day by day. The people won't move out, though. Then one day the buildings go. They are hurtling towards the rocks below.

There wasn't anything to connect Kayleigh and Chris before, but now the facts look stark, there are fewer places to hide. Chris and Kayleigh were both at the river. Kayleigh died in it. Now when I see Chris's face, it's all hard lines, that almost-sneer I'd sometimes catch during a row.

I pull out a drawer from the chest and launch the contents across the loft, old phone chargers, random photographs, pens clattering across the wooden floor. *Why do we have all this stupid, useless shit?* I think to myself, tension collecting again in my jaw.

I splay the photos out on the floor but they're nothing. Days out in London, the weekend we took to Berlin. Chris's parents' wedding anniversary.

Pulling out the bottom drawer, I lose my grip. It's heavy with old papers, tapes and empty CD cases. The corner falls to the floor and strikes me on the bridge of my foot. The pain radiates out and I stagger backwards.

I sit on the floor of the loft, exhausted from the outburst. Now that they are still, my upper arms feel stretched and strained from the weight of the drawers. I can feel the blood pumping around my body, the rhythm calming me down.

Catching my breath, I pull out my phone and switch it back on. Missed calls, texts, voicemails start to beep in. My heart rate starts to slow down again.

Would any of this have happened if we hadn't come here? If I hadn't made Chris leave London? He'd always joked about how awful Shawmouth was: the arcades, the grotty pubs, the lack of anything much to do. 'You floaters,' he'd say, after a weekend visit or a Christmas trip, 'you're a funny lot.' Jokes about in-breeding…

But I picture him now as we left London on the train, rattling past glass skyscrapers, cement-grey balconies crowded with over-spills from tiny flats – washing racks, bikes, makeshift gardens – eventually giving way to big houses, gardens with trampolines. He wasn't smiling anymore. There was genuine sadness. But it's not enough for this. It doesn't explain this. Could anything?

The phone rings and it's Sandra and Geoff. They must have been trying constantly. I can't avoid them anymore; it isn't fair.

Sandra lets out a sigh and starts speaking as soon as I pick up. 'Oh my God, Rebecca – where have you been? What's going on? We've been trying to reach you!'

'Go easy on the lass,' I hear Geoff say.

'I'm sorry, Sandra. I've just been, you know, trying to deal with all this.'

'We've seen the news, the police rang. How awful. That poor girl and her family.' The panic is rising in her voice.

'Are you OK, Sandra? You need to take some deep breaths.'

She puts Geoff on the phone.

'Don't worry, pet. I'm doing my best to look after her. Not bearing up so well myself.'

'Geoff…'

'Please don't, love. Not right now.'

'I can't do it either. But she's going to have to come to terms with the fact that… well, it looks bad, Geoff. He'd been seen at the river. She was in the river. Geoff?'

'Geoff, what's going on? What's she saying? What have the police said to her? Does she know something?' Sandra in the background, bubble not yet burst.

She comes back on the phone. 'It's not right what they're saying. There's no proof he did this!'

'Sandra, it looks—'

'He saved someone's life once, you know.'

She always likes to tell this story. I don't have the heart to stop her now.

'Do you remember he told you about it?'

'I do, Sandra.' But I know she'll tell me about it again anyway. I think it soothes her, the repetition of things.

'He was working in a restaurant. More of a pub, really. A weekend job – while he was at college, before university. And this young lad just dropped to the floor. Like a stone, Chris said. They said he had a heart condition, the young lad.'

Her voice has drifted off now, become more wistful. I have to let her finish.

'Chris did CPR. Learned it in the Scouts. Kept him alive until the ambulance came. We've still got the thank-you card the lad's mother sent, haven't we, Geoff?'

'We have, love,' he says in the background.

She's sobbing now, struggling to get her breath. 'Which thing do you think people will remember, Rebecca? It's not going to be that he saved someone's life, is it? They don't write that in any of their stories now, do they?'

Geoff takes the phone back off Sandra. 'We best get off now, Rebecca, love. Keep in touch. Please. We'd appreciate that.'

'I will, Geoff. I'll call soon, I promise.'

As I put the phone down, something on the floor catches my eye. It must have been stuck behind one of the drawers I pulled out. A large envelope, ripped open across the top. I shuffle over on the floor and pick it up to look more closely. The envelope is unbranded but from a business – one of the ones with a cellophane window for the address.

I tip out the contents onto the floor. Mostly official letters, folded neatly. A letter about the failure to repay a payday loan of £1,000 in May. I think back to May. Did I notice anything around that time? Was he on edge? Did we row? All I remember is that we did the garden up – Chris's parents helped us – we all went to the garden centre together. It was a nice weekend. I remember a row too, I think. I don't know exactly the month but it was spring because the nights were light. I said he never made any effort, that we didn't do anything together anymore. We had become boring. I didn't mean it, though. I just meant that I was bored that day. I wanted to get out of the house, see other people. For him to arrange something for once. I went to bed at 7 p.m.

There's a letter from a Marshall Collection Services about a debt that had been passed to them. A notification from a credit card company that his limit had been increased to £10,000. I feel my chest tighten at the thought of my own mountain of credit card debt, rising and rising. Then there's a credit card statement – from June of this year. My eyes dart around the page, desperate for clues that might tell me where he had been, but there's nothing. Just large transfers to his bank account – £300, £500, and cash withdrawals listed as being from here in Shawmouth. How did I not know?

There's one more letter that is different to the rest. The headed paper says Powell & Sons. 'Jewellers and pawnbrokers since 1840.' My stomach clenches. I can't take everything in; all the information in the different boxes. A serial number. Chris's name. Our address. Description: *14 KT gold brown topaz diamond ring*. Date: 15 July. He got £100 for it.

I feel winded. Gut-punched afresh. My mind is clawing around the edges, looking for an explanation, but there's nothing. Not this time. Why should I still be surprised? Chris stole my ill mother's wedding ring and sold it for £100.

I take out my phone again and go to the video. Chris on the grass, the sun beaming down. I've watched it every day since he left. I think for a second, but not for long. I don't want to remember those times now, the happy times. They make me feel almost as sick as the other thoughts now. Me, the stupid wife, unsuspecting, smiling.

I delete the video. *Are you sure?* the phone asks.

The journalists are gone when I eventually come outside. The housing estate looks stark: completely still and deserted, the street lamps putting each empty house into its own little spotlight. I walk all the way back to the caravan park.

Along the seafront there is just the odd car every now and then. I tense up each time. I sit on a bench for a while, listening to the waves. There's nothing to see; just blackness.

CHAPTER THIRTY-FOUR

Thursday, 19 November

They're treating Kayleigh's death as 'unexplained'. There are going to be more tests. But I think I know enough already. I can't cling on to false hope anymore. A small part of me still does, but mostly there's a sense of inevitability. Maybe there always was.

The blue glow from the laptop. The cursor has been hovering here for over half an hour now. *Are you sure you want to delete this page?* I take a deep breath and delete the 'Find Chris Harding' Facebook page. I expect something to happen, something to lift, but there's nothing, just the unbroken silence. I've sat in it at the caravan all day, a strange calmness.

I flip-close the laptop and lie down under the blankets. It's almost 10 p.m. But then I hear it: the shuffling. I knew they'd come; I just thought it would be sooner. Maybe this time they will really do some damage: to me, to the caravan. But I am strangely calm.

The sound is coming from the window closest to the sofa, a scuffling sound. But it doesn't sound like there is a group this time. An animal? A cat? I don't put the light on but I pull on my jeans and a jumper and grab the torch, feel the weight of it – am I taking it for light or protection?

I shine the light out of the kitchen window, but I can't see anything except my reflection. Kneeling on the sofa bed, I look out of the side window opposite, placing the torch next to me, letting the beam cast light upwards. My hands are shaking as I cup them around my face to look out of the window. At first I am confused, thinking it's my reflection staring back at me, but I am too close. It's someone else's face looking in at me. A shock of terror runs through me and I close the curtain again, my heart bursting in my chest.

I throw open the caravan door and use the torch like a search-light. But there's only one silhouette running away towards the exit. I recognise who it is. I switch the torch off before she has a chance to turn round.

I open my mouth to call out to her, but I think better of it. It is Kat. Chris approached her too. Jeannie's words run through my head: *Sometimes you have to give yourself closure. You can't wait for other people.* I have my chance right here. I don't think following teenage girls was what she had in mind, though. I quickly find my coat and boots.

Her silhouette looks small, fragile and childlike. She shouldn't be out this late, alone. And alone, why would she come here *alone*? They always come together. I'm walking after her, keeping a safe distance behind. She walks along the seafront, the blue in her hair suddenly showing each time she passes under the street lights.

She stops every now and then, taking her phone from her pocket to check it – the screen glowing a white rectangle. She looks around from time to time too. Does she know I am follow-ing her, or is it just the natural nervousness of any woman out walking on her own on a dark night, in a town like this?

Eventually she turns down the alley where Star Pizza is. It's in total darkness downstairs tonight, an early finish. But upstairs, the lights are on. She stops and looks up, like she's thinking about something. Going in? Ringing? I wait at the top of the alley. But then she's on the move again.

I wait a while and follow her from further behind, staying close to the walls where it's darkest. At one point, she stops and turns. Perhaps she's heard my shoes or my breathing. But I turn my face slowly to the wall and stand still and silent, disappearing into the darkness. I chance a look. She's getting away.

We're weaving down some back streets I haven't been down for years, since I was a teenager myself. The backs of takeaways and arcades – just bins and closed back gates. Eventually, the shops give way to the backs of houses. I never go this way, but I think I realise where we're going, heading up towards the station. Or – my stomach flips over – maybe the river. I think again of what they said about Kayleigh, and I wince. 'Injuries consistent with being dragged through a rocky, fast-flowing waterway.'

Kat turns into a snicket, looking about her more than ever. The passage overlooks gardens with swings and plastic slides. Greenhouses, rusting gas barbecues bought in a wave of optimism one sunny day, not uncovered for years. I can see her more clearly now as the alleyway is quite well lit, a half-arsed concession to safety after an old woman was robbed last winter, her bag stolen for just the £3 that was in it. She was on the front of the newspaper a week later, her cheek bruised and purple, the white part of her eye turned solid red.

I put my hood up, making a point to hide my face. Why? A shiver of fear – what am I thinking of doing? If she tells me about what happened with Chris, him approaching her, what will I do? I have lost my grip on what anyone is capable of these days. But at the same time, I have to know. I can't look away anymore.

I hold back until she clears the snicket. I could go back now. I *should* go back. What am I doing, stalking a teenage girl? But it was Kat who started this; she came to me for a reason.

She comes back into view, crossing the street; I pick up the pace so as not to lose her. As I come out into the clearing, I recognise where we are now. Right at the top of The Parades.

I am closer now, but I jump and freeze when the electronic song from her phone blares out. She ignores it and puts it back in her pocket.

The football field is floodlit but empty. As we get closer, the sound of the river hissing and rushing is getting louder, making it harder to keep a sense of my bearings.

The lighting is petering out – I can't see her now apart from the odd glimpse of a silhouette. I hold my breath.

As we edge into the darkness, I have to speed up again because I am losing her.

Then we are in a clearing. The sound of the river rushing is very close.

I stand on something and it releases a loud snap.

'Who is it?' I can hear in the movement of her voice that she has spun round. 'Who is it? Paige, is it you?'

I don't say anything straight away.

'Who is it?' she asks again, the panic clear in her voice.

'Hey. Hey!' I call out, trying to stay reassuring, non-threatening. 'Please stop. I need to talk to you.'

But I can't hear anything over the rushing river. And my eyes haven't properly adjusted to the new level of darkness yet. I wait and listen, worried that I have frightened her away.

Then there's a small voice, very close, although I can't see her yet. It must be Kat. She sounds frightened. 'Who is it? What do you want?'

'You came to my house; my caravan. Just now.' My eyes are adjusting. She's less than an arm's length in front of me. Touching distance.

'What caravan? I don't know what you're on about. Why are you following me?'

I hadn't noticed before, but her accent has a soft cockney lilt; she's not from around here. I reach out to grab her by the shoulder, but I misjudge the distance and grasp at the air. 'I know you know who I am. I know you are Kat. You knew Kayleigh.'

'Look, I don't know what you want but, please, just leave me alone.' She's trying to sound tougher than she is, but I can hear the crack in her voice too.

'What are you doing up here by the river at this time of night? It isn't safe.'

'I am going home. It's quicker this way. You should do the same. Please go away.' I know she's trying to be forceful, but her voice is wobbling.

I can't see her again now so I spin round – she must have moved further away.

I shout out; I think I am shouting forwards, where I expect her to be. 'I saw you. You were looking into my caravan.'

Her phone rings again, sounding unnatural in this environment. She takes it out and the glow helps me get my bearings.

'Fuck,' she says, looking at it, but she doesn't answer.

A text beeps through almost straight away.

'You really need to just leave it. Like I said. You shouldn't have followed me. But you really, really need to just leave it.'

'Kat?'

'Please, please, please just go away and leave me alone. I can't do this.' I can hear her breathing fast or starting to cry.

'It's OK, Kat.' I try to mimic the tone people used with me. The doctor, the police, the therapist, Jeannie in the early days. I can't sound hostile to her. No sudden moves.

'OK, Kat. Like I said, I just want to know, why did you come to my caravan tonight? Were you going to attack me again?'

'No! That ain't me. I just wanted to... I wanted to check you were alright. After the other night. At the park. I thought you might be injured or... And the news about Kayleigh. I was worried you might... I dunno, do something, hurt yourself.'

'Why do you suddenly care so much about me?'

'Don't say that.' She's snivelling now. 'The way we've treated you lately. It isn't right. I felt bad for you. I'm sorry.' Her voice cracks now.

She's closer. I don't know if she moved or me. I can see her face now. She's looking down at the floor, biting her lip, I think.

'It's OK.' I take a deep breath. 'I understand that you're upset because of what he did to Kayleigh... And you.'

There's a jolt of shock in her. 'What— what do you mean?'

I don't want to say it out loud, but I have to. 'I can see now what has happened. And I'm sorry I tried to protect Chris. I'm sorry for what he did to you. And Kayleigh.'

She's biting her nails, shifting her feet on the muddy ground. It has started to rain, the earth already beginning to shift and liquefy.

'Don't say that!' Her voice is louder now. It startles me.

'What do you mean? I thought this is what you wanted.'

'Arrrrrgggghh... just please go away. I came here to think; to be on my own. I need you to just go.'

'I can't leave you here like this.'

'I came to the caravan to talk to you. I've been trying to talk to you!'

'What do you mean, trying to talk to me? When have you been trying to talk to me?'

'Just forget it. OK? I have to go.'

'Kat, I need to know what you are talking about. Please.'

'Stop saying my name. It's too late. I've been trying to tell you for weeks. I rang you and I came to the caravan park, but I just... I couldn't. It's just a huge fucking mess.'

'Do you know something about Chris? About what he did? You can tell me. I can help you. We can go to the police together.'

'Go to the police?'

'If you know more about him, you have to tell them. Don't be scared. We just have to get to the truth now, Kat. It's all I want. It's best for everyone. For Kayleigh.'

Her voice sounds burnt or scraped now... raw. 'Don't you get it? Don't you see? It wasn't Chris, OK? But you really, really need to just leave it. I can't say any more. You need to leave it alone.'

'Kat, what are you talking about? How do you know all this?'

She goes to run away but I grab her wrist, yanking her round. It's tiny and bony in my hand.

'Because it was me!' she screeches.

CHAPTER THIRTY-FIVE

Thursday, 19 November

Kat's voice is clear now, even over the sound of the river and the wind. Before, I was straining to hear it.

She is trying to pull away but I don't let go of her, my nails are digging in. 'Oh fuck, what am I doing? I didn't mean that. Just forget it, OK? Fuckfuckfuck!'

'Kat, you know I can't just leave it.' My voice sounds automated. I put my other hand on her shoulder instinctively. One hand giving comfort, the other holding her back. But I have to get to the bottom of this right now, or it's not going to happen.

She's crying, becoming hysterical. 'It was us, it was me, OK? It's all my fucking fault.'

The rain is coming down more heavily now, falling in rivulets off the trees overhead.

'Follow me,' she says. 'We can't talk here.' She pushes black make-up streaks off her cheeks.

I hardly care where she's taking me. As if I could walk away now, if I even wanted to. She uses her mobile phone to lead the way; the light intermittently cuts out before she presses it on again. I can hear her breathing heavily, psyching herself up, trying to regain her composure. She's walking purposefully; she knows where she's going.

Suddenly, she speeds up and I am disorientated, in blackness. 'Hey, wait.' I brace for a blunt force to the back of the head or a hard shove onto the ground. But a light comes on and I can see she's in a clearing, some kind of den. There's a large upturned torch flooding the space with light. It's the size of a small room. She beckons me to come in.

I hesitate, looking behind me. 'Is this a trick? Is someone in here?'

Kat doesn't answer me and kicks at the ground, clearing plastic alcohol bottles out of the way. A blue 2-litre white cider bottle, bright yellow cans. She sits on an upside-down milk crate and gestures for me to do the same. We could almost be in a suburban sitting room somewhere, drinking tea. The thicket canopy, surprisingly, shields us from the wind and rain.

'Nice place you've got here.' It sounds ridiculous. 'Is this where you hang out, then?' I have to keep her on side. Calm her down.

She nods her head slightly. 'Sometimes. Me and Kayleigh used to.'

'I didn't even know it was here.'

We both jump when her phone rings again, the light shining through the fabric of her coat.

'You wouldn't. It's why I like it here.'

We sit in silence, just the sound of the water rushing. It's more distant now. The rain or the river, or both.

'What did you mean before when you said about Kayleigh, that it was you?'

She drops her head into her hands again, crying. When she looks up, her nose is red, lips swelling slightly from the tears. She takes a tall can from her pocket, the same brand that is strewn around the den, cracks it open and takes a swig. Her hands are trembling.

She tips the can at me. I think about refusing, but instead take a large swig. It's cheap, sweet stuff, an after-taste of ash. I go to hand it back to her, but she's already taken another one from the other pocket.

When I had something on my mind as a teenager, I would sometimes lie awake in the night for hours, worrying. It might be a boy or schoolwork or someone calling me fat, festering away at me. But in the end I'd have to get up and get it out, talk to someone. I was the same with Chris. Waking him up in the early hours. 'Are we OK?' I'd ask, needing reassurance. I can tell Kat has something she needs to talk about. It's teetering on the edge.

Finally, she says, 'I didn't mean it to happen.'

I don't even dare to breathe in case it breaks things, makes her clam up again. The truth is so close I feel like I could almost grab it.

'It was here,' she says. 'I come up here to be on my own now, to think about stuff. We used to come here with Kayleigh too. It was like our den; us lasses. Me, Kayleigh and… anyway.'

She's getting hysterical again, making whooping sounds as she struggles to catch her breath. I used to get like this when I was young, even over small things. And I've been like this recently, many nights since Chris has been gone.

'We're here now. I know something's happened. You'll feel better if you get it out. I know you will.'

I feel a twinge of guilt, coaxing her like that, but I push it away. Why should I feel bad? And anyway, it feels like it's going to hurt me as much as her.

She lets out a heaving sob, her face sodden with tears. 'I just wish I could go back. It wasn't supposed to happen like that. I'm sorry. I'm sorry.' Her voice is thick, sound fading in and out. She blurts, 'We chased her.' Blue strands are pasted to her cheeks now, like veins.

'Kayleigh?' I ask.

It hardly needs saying, but I need to keep her talking. But this just sets off a fresh wave of sobbing.

'You chased her where? I can see this is hard for you, but it will be better.' I reach to touch her jean-clad knee but she's just out of reach.

She's shouting now. 'Here! We chased her here! We chased her and she tried to get away. She fell in! She fell in the fucking river.'

'In here?' I gesture around the den.

I think she is shaking her head, but I can't be sure.

'I think she tried to get across the stepping stones. She was trying to get away, but we didn't push her, I promise, we didn't push her. She fell – but who would believe us? We shouldn't have been chasing her.'

'OK,' I say, trying to control the tremor in my voice. 'Who's we? Who chased Kayleigh?'

'It was me.'

'It wasn't just you, was it, Kat?'

She just snivels and cries, refusing to look at me.

'It was Paige who was with you, wasn't it?'

She's rocking slightly now, a catatonic look about her.

'But why?'

She flinches at this then shrugs. 'Me and Paige came up here after the park to see if Kayleigh was here. Because she didn't show up.'

She puts her hand on her forehead, shakes her head. 'I was drunk. I can't sort it clearly in my head. But Paige and Kayleigh, they got into a huge row. Because Paige thought Kayleigh was making moves on her boyfriend. Someone told her that. They got into a row and Kayleigh even had a go at me. She was lashing out. She felt like we were ganging up on her. She thought I'd turned on her.'

'So you…?'

'Her and Paige got into a fight. It was so stupid! Kayleigh was pulling her hair and everything and Paige chased her. I was trying to split them up, I know I was.' She punches herself hard in the head three times, and I wince.

'Kat, don't do that.' I stand up and reach out but then sit back down again. I need to keep my distance.

'It's just all so hazy. But I was trying to break it up. I couldn't have been going after her too. I couldn't. I wouldn't. God, I fucking hate myself. I hate myself.' She's shaking her head side to side quickly, clawing at a handful of her blue hair.

'Over a boy? And some gossip? All this over that? All this…?'

'I know how disgusting I am, I do, you know that? You know, I don't think Paige even wanted to catch her. I didn't. Paige probably wouldn't have done anything more neither. She would never have pushed her in. Her pride was just hurt. I drank too much. *Aaaaaarrrrggggggh! Why why why?* I should have just stopped it. I could have.'

'But why didn't you say anything after? It was an accident, wasn't it?' Another stupid question, no doubt.

She flinches again at this. Maybe I am pointing out the obvious; the things she doesn't want to think about.

'I just couldn't. You really don't understand. I couldn't. And anyway, who would believe me that it was an accident? We shouldn't have been chasing her. Once we'd said the lie once, that was it – we couldn't go back. We said she was meant to meet us and she didn't show up – that part is true – and people believed it. I don't know how, but it just ran on. Kayleigh, she must have wanted to be on her own too. That's why she was here. We knew that's where we'd find her. Paige was determined to find her and have it out.'

I am struggling to process what she's saying but can't risk cutting off the flow. 'So who else knows? All of you?'

'Just… just Paige. We were all totally out of it at the park. No one remembers clearly who was where when. People just come and go on nights out, you know? I think they all feel guilty they can't clearly remember who left when. They probably don't even remember whether Kayleigh came to the park or not. Who knows? Half the lads were on cider and skunk and stuff. We're all fucking idiots.'

I expect to feel relief or more tears or something, but I just feel lightheaded. Maybe it's the beer; I realise I've swigged most of the can.

'You could have just told the police.'

'I honestly thought they'd work it out. I can't believe it's gone this far, I really can't. I just remember hearing her shouting, "Leave me alone. Please!" She sounded really scared. Then there was this weird silence and I heard the splash. I just knew. I'm sure I heard it. It's the nothingness followed by the splash; I just can't get it out of my head.'

She is calmer now. 'It was weird, you know, because there was no scream then. Not when she fell in.'

I shudder.

'Paige said Kayleigh had got away, she'd gone home. And I didn't say anything. I went along with it. It's my fault. Paige knew too, she must have heard the splash. But she didn't say anything.' Kat looks dazed, drugged, disbelieving of what she's saying. 'She said, "We'll sort it out with her when we next see her."'

She wraps her arms around herself, 'But then she said, "If any-one asks, we didn't see Kayleigh, she didn't turn up to the park, right?"…We knew. We both knew Kayleigh had fallen in at The Cut. We didn't want it to be true, but it was. And we just went home. That was it.'

I feel queasy.

'Then later it was like we thought we could make it true that it was Chris and not us.'

I feel sorry for Kat, but that snaps me out of it and then it hits me.

'But why did you say that Chris made advances on you?'

She seems to ignore me, spaced out again, but then she says, 'I did see him, you know? I wasn't lying about that.'

'Chris?' My mouth is dry, whole body braced for what is coming.

'Yeah. I came here after school. We got out early because it was the last day. And he was sitting in here. Reading a book.'

'Reading a book? But what was he doing here?'

'Dunno, he just got his stuff together when he saw me and scarpered off.'

'Didn't you ask him?'

'Nah, I thought it was a bit weird but, you know. Free country.' She shrugs.

'But what did he say to you? Did he do something?'

'No, that's it; he just left when I got here.'

I think of him on the CCTV. The last time he was seen. He must have been on his way to the river then. To here. It's a physical pain to think of him all alone here.

'But I don't understand. Why did you say that to the police? Just recently?'

She's shaking again, trying to contain herself. 'Because Paige told me to. When his name came up in the papers, I told her that I'd seen him here and she just jumped on it. I shouldn't have told her. I can't blame her though, 'cos it was me that did it. You came to the school and you were asking questions and stuff. Then the police interviewed us again and Paige said we had to do something.'

'But he didn't? You know... try to...?'

'No! He didn't do nothing. He just left, I told you that.'

'But where did he go? After you saw him?'

'I dunno. I didn't really take no notice. Until after, until I saw him on the news and in the paper.'

'You must have seen which way he went? You could have told the police all this.'

'I know. I'm sorry.' It comes out as a kind of howl. You can hear the pain in it.

I soften my tone. 'So why did you come to my caravan?'

'I wish I never had now. I can't do this. I just felt bad for you. I seen you in the paper and that, and round about, and you look really... just... you know. I feel bad for what we've done to you. Letting you think that about your husband. Letting everyone think it. It's not right. I've seen you around and it isn't fair.'

Something clicks into place. 'It's you, isn't it. Have you been phoning me and following me?'

She nods, looking down. 'I told you that before. I needed to see how you were doing. I thought you were going to top yourself or something.'

'I've thought about it, believe me.'

'I know.' She's crying again, strings of snot hanging from her nose. She drags the back of her sleeve across it. 'It was too easy. When we found out he was missing too. It just happened, you know?'

'No, I don't know.' There's a hot current of something else running through the shock now. The lies they told about Chris, the things I let myself think about him.

'People were blaming him and we just went along with it. I think we wanted to believe that too. Sometimes it even felt like I did believe it. It didn't seem real. Do you hate me?'

It reminds me how young she is, such a childish thing to say, needing the reassurance. I can't answer. Do I hate her? You'd think it would be easy to answer, but it isn't.

'I just kept wanting to reach you, you know. To let you know it wasn't him. I should have just left it.'

'No, you shouldn't! How dare you? No, you shouldn't have let me fucking think my husband is God knows what!' The anger catches and flares.

'I feel terrible, I am just so sorry.'

I believe her.

Kat looks up at me now. 'So you really just don't know where he is then, your husband?'

'No.'

'It must be horrible.'

'It's horrific. They could have been looking for him as a person. Not as – as what you've all been calling him. You've destroyed his reputation. He can't get that back. Mud sticks. Some people will always have him down as a paedophile now, I hope you know that.'

I spit the word at her. She starts to cry hysterically again. The rage that swelled up recedes just as quickly, knocked out of me. Nothing had to be this way. Kayleigh is gone. Chris seems further away than ever.

Something catches my eye then. There's more light coming from outside the bush. Kat notices too, panic in her eyes.

'Fuck. You need to go.'

'Kat? Kat what are you doing, mate?'

I recognise the girl's voice. It's Paige.

'Oh shit, you've got to go. I've got to go. Just go away,' she hisses.

'Where am I going to go?' There's only one way out of the clearing.

'I've been ringing you, K. I thought you'd be here. What's up? Why you ignoring my calls?' Paige's voice is getting so close now.

'I'm coming, Paige. I'll come over now.' She tries to sound normal but her voice cracks with alarm.

'Who are you talking to, Kat? I'll come in there, you daft cow, it's slashing down.'

'No one, Paige, I'm just on the phone to my mam.'

'You need to leave,' she hisses at me and then shouts to Paige again. 'I'm coming over, Paige. Just stay there – I've got something to show you.'

'Nah, mate. I'm piss wet through. You can show me in there.'

Suddenly, the torch beam swings round like a lighthouse, into the bush. It is right in my face.

'What the fuck is she doing here?' Paige says, digging her teeth into her bottom lip.

'Paige! How long have you been out there?' Kat looks at Paige, startled, panic flickering behind her eyes.

'Long enough.' It's impossible to tell if Paige is bluffing.

No one says anything.

'We're just talking, aren't we?' I explain.

'What did you tell her?' Paige says to Kat. 'Why are you talking to her?'

'I didn't say anything, I promise,' Kat says.

My heart feels like it's stopped.

'Alright, pervert's wife. How are you?'

The spite in Paige's voice makes up my mind. 'I am his wife, yes. But we both know the rest isn't true, don't we?'

'What the fuck have you said, Kat?' Paige's eyes are narrowed.

I need to get away from here and think. I stand up, my eye on the part of the entrance she isn't blocking. I make a sudden gesture to indicate one way, but actually turn the other and at the same time manage to hit the torch from her hand. In the confusion, I am able to bolt ahead. 'Kat, just go,' I shout after me.

'Don't, Paige. Just leave it. Please,' I hear Kat saying behind me, our voices overlapping.

It's raining harder now, falling into my eyes, blurring my view. I run as fast as I possibly can, sliding every now and then on the muddy grass. I don't know where I am, exactly. Unsure if the next step will land me on firm ground or plunge me into the furious river. I can't hear anything except the water and my own breathing. I stop and sneak a look back. Kat is running with me but there's no sign of Paige. I have to stop to breathe. My chest is painful and I am gulping in solid air. Kat comes up alongside me.

'Don't stop. Don't stop now. You can't wait here. We have to get away.'

'She's not following us. Just give me a minute. I'm twice your age, remember?' I look back and there's still no sign of Paige. But it feels that she could appear out of the blackness any second.

'It's not just Paige – we seriously have to get away from here right now. Paige is hard but they'll kill you. Seriously.'

'Who? What are you talking about?'

She's already running on ahead of me now. So I start again, losing my footing on the mud, something twanging painfully in my thigh. I reach the path where the football field is again. Kat is nowhere to be seen. I look back and Paige is gaining on me. I need to get back to the caravan or to the police station, call Detective Fisher on the way. One last push. My legs feel jelly-like and numb underneath me, and I am out into the road again, taking large strides.

But suddenly I am disorientated by white light – headlights from a car. It's blinding me, I can't see around it. A door slams and I hear shouting as a hand reaches from behind, covers my mouth.

Something explodes against my temple.

CHAPTER THIRTY-SIX

Thursday, 19 November

When my eyes open, I am going up a narrow stairway, backwards. Someone is pulling me by my arms, fingers digging into my armpits, my feet dragging underneath me. The walls are peeling woodchip; I hear a TV blaring somewhere. I think of Mum's place. But we are not there. My legs are limp, lifeless, scraping up the steps. There's an acrid smell too. Everything is swimming again; going black.

When I wake next, I am sinking into what feels like a springless armchair, a soft velour covering. I am aware of chatter and shapes around me. A number of people in the room. I keep my eyes closed and try to make sense of the echoey voices, praying it's a bad dream. That I am back at the caravan… that the dream began much earlier, before I saw Kat's face in the window. The pain in my head now tells me that isn't the case.

'So what are we going to do with her then? I don't know what the fuck you brought her here for.'

'Keep your voice down, will you.'

It hurts when I swallow and I am trying to restrain myself from gagging – there's a bitter, metallic taste in my mouth. So much so that I think they must be able to hear the gulp each time. Men's voices. I realise they are ones I have heard before. Daz and Ashy.

'I just don't understand why you've brought her here?'

'Paige here called me, didn't you, babe? She's loyal, she tells me what I need to know. You want to get yourself a drink, darlin'? Pass me one too.'

There's the sound of a can being caught and the hiss of the ring pull.

My eyes want to open, take everything in, but I will them to stay closed. I can learn more if they think I am still passed out.

'Oi, you, Twinkle Toes. I hear you've been shooting your mouth off. What have you been saying?'

'Nothing! I ain't said nothin'. She was asking me questions and stuff. But I didn't tell her anything. She don't know nothing.' It's Kat.

'Paige? Darlin', that isn't what you said about your little friend on the phone. Now you wouldn't lie to me, would you?' Ashy says.

'Ow, that hurts. Please don't.' It's Paige's voice.

'You rang me. Why did you ring me and tell me Kat had been shooting her mouth off?'

Paige is whimpering. 'I'm sorry, Kat. I heard you talking. I panicked.'

'Oi!' It's Ashy. 'You talk to me when I am talking to you, not her, right?'

'Ow! My hair, you bastard.'

'So what did she say? What did you hear little miss goody two shoes here say?'

'I didn't hear her say nothing about you. I swear.'

Kat tries to cut in.

Ashy's head whips round. 'Shut it, you! Paige is talking.'

'I went up to get Kat, like you said. She weren't answering her phone and I knew where she'd be so I went to see her, like you told me, to talk to her. I heard her crying and saying she was sorry. It was her fault.'

'I didn't say anything about you, Ashy, I wouldn't.' Kat's voice is pleading. A sharp crack sound. Someone has been slapped. Kat. She sucks the air in between her teeth.

'Don't say my name, you stupid bitch! Well, there's nothing to say about me, is there? It was you that pushed Kayleigh in. I weren't even there, was I?'

'We didn't push her!'

'Whatever, love. I told Paige to have a word with her, get her in line. She was getting sloppy, tearful. She didn't want to do it no more.'

He mimicks a girl crying.

'I told Paigey that Kayleigh was after lover boy over here and she went off like clockwork. I said to give her a scare; I didn't tell you to fucking kill her.'

The men in the room laugh. How many are there?

'I thought we were just going to see her, see if she was OK. It wasn't supposed to go like that.' Kat sniffles.

'Like I told you... Good luck convincing the police of that. Heh! You came round here for help and I gave it to you. And this is what I get? This bitch has been sniffing around for weeks because of you two.'

The atmosphere in the room has changed.

'Now listen. Your little friend Kayleigh thought she was too good to keep coming round here. So I told Paige to get her in line. And Paige was jealous because she thought her boyfriend fancied Kayleigh, so she pushed her in. What do you think is going to happen to you? Little Paigey don't muck about.'

'Fuck off,' says Paige.

'Do you really think he wants to go out with you, Paige? That you're the only one he's seeing? You don't get it, do you, you lot? You're replaceable. All of you. He's keeping you sweet because you're working for me. It's the only reason he was seeing you in the first place – I needed someone the police wouldn't twig onto to shift some gear for me. And all the pervy old junkies love buying off little Paige, don't they? Well, not so little, eh, chunk?'

Paige snivels.

'And you, the Little Mermaid. You think you're too good for us, don't you? So you better remember the fate of your little pal. She took an early bath, didn't she?'

'I fucking hate you,' Kat hisses.

'You won't be saying that later on, lovey. You'll be screaming my name if you're not careful.'

More sniggering.

'I helped you out and I told you not to make any trouble for me, didn't I? I've been nothing but good to you. Given you drinks and money, somewhere to hang out. And your ungrateful little friend, Kayleigh. I've protected you. But you couldn't keep your mouth shut.'

'I'm not surprised she didn't want to come round here anymore.' Kat sounds like her teeth are clenched when she's speaking. 'You're disgusting. She didn't want to be involved with you and neither do I. Maybe she is better off where she is, rather than having you lording it over her.'

Another crack. Kat screams again before whimpering.

'Don't forget I know where both you girls live. And I've told you before, I will pay your families a friendly visit if you step out of line. Kat and her lovely little sister. Your old mum, Paigey.'

'Ashy, man, what are we going to do with *her*? We can sort these two out later.'

I think it's Daz.

'Fuckssake! Maybe she should go the same way as little Kayleigh. Nobody will think anything of it. She thought her husband did bad things to innocent little Kayleigh, and she couldn't handle it, so she decided to join her in the water. Boo hoo.'

'Ashy, I don't know man – that's pretty... I mean this is getting out of hand.'

'What do you suggest then, genius?'

'I don't know. I guess we have to. I...'

'Harris, you need to bring the car round the back. Me and Daz will stay here with these three.'

'What about...?'

'We'll worry about these two little slags later. Right?'

I have to open my eyes now. And think of a way out, fast. The room blurs in and out of focus. My breathing is quick and shallow.

'Oh, hello there. Glad you could join us.' Ashy waves his hand in front of my eyes.

'Look, I won't say anything, I promise.' I know it's pointless. 'Kat told me it was an accident. They didn't mean to do it. I won't say anything.'

I try to meet Kat's eye; give her an encouraging look. Calm her down. Her crying is making Ashy more angry.

'Nice try, love, but I don't believe you. I don't believe any of you. *She* told me she hadn't said anything at all. *You* tell me you won't pass it on. You're all lying bitches, all of you.'

Ashy gets his phone out and brings something up, wafting it under my nose. It takes a few seconds for my eyes to focus. It's the pictures of me outside the pool, the ones that Paige took. He zooms in, removing my head. Rubs his fingers on the screen where my breasts are, between my legs.

'Might stick these online. Probably a market for them when you're gone, given what people are saying about your husband. There's some sick fuckers out there.'

His grin reveals wet, yellow teeth.

Paige is guzzling a tall can of cheap lager down in one. He looks at her for a while, his lip curling up.

'Daz, why don't you pay Paige's mammy a visit. Paige here has a little part-time job she's not told Mammy and Daddy about. Don't you, babe?'

'I'll tell them the drugs are yours. The police would know you made me do it.'

'Made you do it?' Ashy lets out a laugh. 'Paige, babe – who do people buy the gear off? Who do they give their money to, all these little druggies. It ain't me. What would your mum think?'

I look to Kat and Paige. Kat is sobbing. Paige hovers at the back, refusing to look up, her shoulders hunched up. Behind her on a kitchen counter, dirty crockery is stacked up, empty milk bottles, takeaway cartons.

'You want shit, don't you – phones and watches. Shitty trinkets.' Ashy goes over to Paige and grabs her, yanking up her sleeve to show the pink watch, the crystals sparkling. 'You have to earn it like everybody else.'

He drops Paige's arm and she rubs at her wrist.

'Mikey, go round to the garage and get some rope,' Ashy says, looking at me. 'Something we can wrap her in, yeah? Harris, you go with him, bring your car round.'

'Why have we gotta use *my* car?' Harris says under his breath.

'Because I fucking said so, right?'

They both go past me, trying to avoid eye contact.

Paige tries to stop one of them at the door, but he pushes her aside and she staggers, almost falling over. It's the younger lad who was working in the takeaway on Jeannie's night out.

'God, you're pathetic,' Ashy says to her. 'Do you really think he is bothered about you? Have you listened to a word I said? I don't know how he even pretends.' He shakes his head, laughing to himself. 'Eurgh. You sit round here shovelling chips into your gob. You're a means to an end.'

I look around the room. It's strewn with pizza boxes, cans, half-rolled cigarettes. There's a smell of strong marijuana.

I am scanning the room for something, a way to get out. I re-adjust myself in my seat, feeling my pocket for my phone, but it isn't there. I must have dropped my bag when we were running, or when they grabbed me. Someone might find it in the street, hand it in at the police station. They'd surely realise something had happened, look for me.

'You want a drink, love? You could probably do with one.'

'No.'

'Paige, get her a drink. Something strong.'

'I don't want anything.'

Paige picks up a tall, dirty glass and fills it quarter way with cheap vodka and the rest of the way with coke. It's a light, clear brown colour. She takes a sip of it and twists her face. She brings it over to me and I make eye contact with her, trying to plead with her to do something. But what could she do? Her face doesn't change but she holds my gaze for a second.

'Drink it. Paige here has gone to the trouble of making it for you.'

'I don't want anything.'

'Paige, make her drink it. You'll be glad of it, love. I'm trying to be nice.'

'Ashy. Come on. Let's have a drink, eh?'

It's Paige. She is forcing her voice to sound soothing.

'Leave it, Paige. Not now babe, yeah?'

Kat and I both jolt when he grabs Paige. He has her by the hair and her neck is locked, head to the side to try and stop the pain from the pulling. The violence of his action is all the more jarring because he's speaking so calmly.

'We could go through to the other room for a bit,' Paige says.

My stomach rolls over.

'Sloppy seconds from my nephew? Piss off – I'm not that desperate. I've got proper women, thanks.'

He releases Paige, and she stumbles back.

I pretend to take a drink from the glass but I just let it wet my upper lip.

I try to catch Kat's attention but she won't look up. Her fingers are folded into her lap, shoulders bunched up, head turned in. She is fidgeting with her hands, scratching at the back of them. There are red lines criss-crossed up her forearms. Some are faded. Others look like fresh, angry welts. She notices me looking and pulls her sleeves back over her fists.

Then I see it; my bag is on the table behind her. No one found it; no one is coming.

I try to placate him, buy some time. 'Look, Ashy, you need to calm down. Please just calm down. I honestly won't say anything. I don't want to get Kat and Paige into trouble. I know they didn't mean to hurt anyone. Not me or Kayleigh.'

He's coming towards me now. I try to get out of the chair but it's too low; I can't pull myself up. His face swims in front of me. He grabs me by the chin. I flinch but he tightens his grip.

'They ain't as sweet and innocent as you think, love. Paige sells drugs to anyone who'll have them. She doesn't care and she doesn't mind taking her share of the cut. Little Kat here won't sell them yet, but she keeps them at her house. She knows what will happen if she doesn't. And they both don't mind coming round here, drinking every night, getting stuff for free.'

'She only does it because you make her and threaten us.' Kat bunches straight up again as soon as she has spoken.

Ashy doesn't say anything for a while. Dread is coursing through me, waiting for what he'll do next. But then he just laughs.

'You don't get a free lunch, love. You've had all sorts from me. I sorted you out; helped you cover it up when you mad bitches murdered your mate. What's in it for me? You fucking owe me. Don't they, Daz?'

'Yeah, mate.' Daz has slumped into the chair next to me now. He's drinking too.

'We didn't murder her,' Kat mumbles, but she doesn't look up this time.

'Whatever. You fucking owe me.'

Daz tips his head at me. 'So we seriously gonna do this with her?' His eyes tilt up at Ashy.

'Got any better ideas?' Ashy looks to me. 'You probably don't mind, do you? You've probably had enough of all this anyway. We'd be doing you a favour, what with your husband fucking off and everything.' He laughs to himself, like he's made a great joke.

'Actually, come to think of it, you can take these two with you, Daz, in your car. I'm sick of them thinking everyone else is going to do everything for them. Take them with you, get them to do it – they've had practice – then they definitely won't say anything. Will you, girlies?'

'Get us another drink, Paige,' Ashy says without turning round.

I listen for the click and fizz but there's nothing.

'Oi! I'm talking to you.' His expression changes.

I follow his gaze. She isn't there; Paige isn't there.

'Where the fuck is that little bitch?'

The door to the stairway is still open. Daz runs over to it. 'She ain't there, mate.'

'How long has she been gone?'

Daz shakes his head. He throws open the other doors in the room. A bedroom, no bed clothes on the double bed, just a mattress; clothes and CDs strewn around the floor. A tiny bathroom with a sink and toilet, lino curling up, stopping the door opening properly. Daz loses his temper with the door, kicking it hard.

He shakes his head at Ashy. 'She ain't here.'

'Did you see your mate go? Oi you!' Ashy kicks at Kat's foot with his.

'Didn't see nothing,' she says, without looking up.

Ashy runs his hands over the sides of his head. 'Right, think. We've got to move. Get her downstairs now.'

Daz stands over me, thinking about how to drag me out of the chair. It's my last chance. I bunch my fists. I read somewhere you should try scraping your shoe down someone's shin, or aim to hit the bridge of their nose with your head if they grab you from behind. Plunge your thumb into their eye; I am flexed.

I try to send a mental signal to Kat; that we need to work together. We have to get away. But when I look over at her, she's looking at the window. Blue lights are popping across the glass, and I become aware of the sound of sirens.

Daz goes for the door but there are already sounds of feet coming up the stairs. Kat is shaking, her head buried in her hands.

CHAPTER THIRTY-SEVEN

The rain on my hair and clothes is uncomfortable as soon as I go into the overheated home to see Mum. I feel sticky and irritable. It reminds me of mornings in London going to work on the Tube.

Mum's sitting in her chair today in a coffee-coloured, cable-knit cardigan, Doodlebug on her lap, his body curled around. Simon told me before I came in that she's having a 'good day'.

I don't know where they get these clothes from. They're not Mum's clothes. Probably from a charity shop or people who've lived here before. Died here, maybe. When I ask him, Simon says it's because she's been gaining weight. She eats more than she needs, if they don't watch her. She forgets what she's had, doesn't know when to stop.

She's watching *Countdown*, seemingly enthralled. The conundrum clock is ticking down in the background. Time is running out. She looks up when I say 'Hi', and gives me a big smile. I pull up the chair next to her and we hold hands. Her hands are soft and warm.

'I've got something for you, Mum.'

She struggles to get out of the chair, standing up without warning so that Doodlebug falls straight down, just springing his legs out in time to land. Sheepish, he heads for the door, mewling to be let out. I go over and open the door a crack and he scampers through.

'You don't need to stand up, Mum. Sit down.' I take the box out slowly. I don't want her to be more shocked and confused than she needs to be. It's an old-fashioned ring box; a hinge at the back and a red velvet cushion inside, the ring held in a slit in the fabric.

'I found your ring, Mum. Here, hold out your hand.'

She claps her hand to her mouth, so I take it in mine and put the ring in her palm. It won't go on her finger; it will have to go back into the jewellery box later.

I went to the pawnbrokers in town to get it. They keep the items for six months before selling them on, the man said. It was a traditional place. He had a shirt and tie on, a brown tabard.

'It's not that often people come back, love, I'll tell you. But this is a nice one. And to be honest, there's not all that much call for this style these days. I think it's a bobby dazzler, though, don't you? Such an unusual colour. I'm glad it's going back to its rightful owner.'

I asked him, 'Do you remember the man who brought this in?'

He pushed his glasses onto the top of his head and chewed on his pen. 'I don't, to be honest, pet. I get a lot of people through here every day. Between me and you, some people set off my spidey senses and I'm suspicious about the stuff so I have a closer look. I have to protect myself. I don't want stolen goods, you know. But this, this doesn't ring any bells. Probably a good sign that I don't remember him.' He gave me a warm smile but started to close his book to signal the conversation was over, that he had to get on.

Mum is looking at me, searching my face.

'I'm sorry, Mum; I'm sorry for not listening to you properly. Your ring was lost, like you said. And Chris did take it. You were right. I'm sorry.'

Mum looks up at this, but then she goes back to admiring the ring between her fingers, tilting it from side to side to admire the sparkle.

I fix my eyes on the TV screen, concentrating on the maths problem presented on *Countdown*, but the numbers jumble around in my head. I feel so tired, even though I have done nothing but rest: rest and think, since the night with Kat and Paige. Mum doesn't look away from the screen either, but she gives my hand a gentle squeeze. Hot tears soundlessly pour from my eyes. Mum looks panicked for a second. But I look at her intently to tell her I'm OK. She strokes my hand.

'I know he's sorry, Mum.'

I can't get my head around the fact he was so unhappy or in such a bad situation that he couldn't talk to me. That I didn't realise. I don't know if he just hid it all or I wasn't paying attention. My view is so warped from looking back at our life through the lens of Kayleigh's disappearance, that I can't put things back in place now.

But I know we were happy, we had been happy. That much is true. I have that.

Mum puts her hand on my back. I don't know if she can process what I have told her.

When I come round, the room is on its side. It takes me a moment to realise where I am, here in Mum's room. The strains of *Coronation Street* play in the background. How long did I sleep for? I must have fallen asleep on Mum's bed somehow. There's a purple crocheted blanket over me. Mum or Simon? I take a drink from the water by Mum's bed. It tastes stale: warm and dusty.

I lie for a few more seconds, not wanting to get up. Mum's still watching TV. When I go over to her, she is looking glazed at the TV, twisting the ring between her fingers.

She turns to face me. 'Is Chris coming today? Can I see your dad?'

CHAPTER THIRTY-EIGHT

Monday, 23 November

Outside on the seafront, the Christmas lights have been switched on. We don't bring in celebrities here to cut ribbons or sing in daft festive jumpers. The council just quietly turns the lights on one evening. The coloured bulbs must sit there, grey and unlit, for days or even weeks before they're switched on.

I wander back towards the caravan, feeling dazed from the sleep and the heat. The sudden temperature change is making my eyes swell. I know that it's happening today. And I know that I shouldn't go. But something is drawing me, too. I am gravitating towards the park.

The park is full of people – over 200, it looks like. I stand at a safe distance. Not long after Kayleigh's vigil was supposed to happen in this same place, they're holding a memorial service for her. They're holding white paper lanterns, ready to release them, flaming into the air. Standing on the edges behind a tree, I stay hidden but close enough to watch.

There's coloured balloons too: blue, pink and yellow. Drifting across the town.

Flowers and teddy bears have been piled carefully around a tree; heads bent weeping, girls and women huddling together in twos and threes. Adam from the phone shop is there and I recognise some of the boys from the park and the school. No sign of Kat or Paige. I wonder how they are, if they'll be OK. Where do they go from here?

Kids from the local schools are carrying candles, wearing their uniforms and singing hymns. 'Colours of Day'. A stab of pain reminds me that we had that at our wedding. It was one of my grandma's favourites.

Seeing Janice, Kayleigh's mum, twists my guts. Her face is etched with pain.

There's a ghetto blaster on the floor and one of the teenagers fiddles with it, then walks away. I strain to place the song at first, although I know I have heard it before. On the radio, I think.

It's a woman's voice. Young. It's poppy, an ethereal sweep to it. Maybe Kayleigh liked the song.

Janice falls to the floor, to her knees, choking on her sobs. People gather round her, rubbing her back uselessly, like anything could be of comfort to her. Eventually, she is helped back to her feet, distraught and uneasy, unable to manage her own balance. She looks over in my direction, seemingly distracted, holding my gaze for longer. It feels as though she is looking right at me, but I can't be sure. And for those moments she is calmer. After a while she turns towards one of the women with her, hiding her face in their shoulder. The music is still playing, floating across the park, as I turn to leave.

The sky is darkening, a thick fog hovering above the water. The colours from the amusement arcades cut through it, twinkling in the winter light.

When I get back to the caravan, Detective Fisher is sitting on the caravan steps blowing into her hands. I give her a wave. I feel awkward walking towards her, conscious of the time it's taking me to reach her, and she keeps looking away.

'You'll get piles sitting there like that in this weather,' I say as she starts to get up.

'I've had worse.'

I open the caravan door and she follows me in.

'Tea?' I ask.

'Nah, I'm OK, thanks. I've been drinking it all day. How are you?'

'I've been better. But I suppose I've been worse as well, in a way.'

She tilts her head to the side a little, seemingly unsure of what to say.

'Do you need more information about… about the other night at Star Pizza?' I ask her.

'Not right now. I mean, I am sure I will, but thanks for your cooperation there. One of my colleagues will follow up with the next steps.'

'Oh, so has something else happened?'

'No. Actually, I was just passing so I thought I would drop in.'

We sit in silence for a while. Until I break it.

'He isn't coming back, is he?'

Detective Fisher doesn't flinch. It isn't really fair of me, I know that. But I think she was expecting this. She reflects before she answers me. Her legs are slightly apart and she rubs her hands on her thighs.

'Well, I have to be honest. People who are… well, people who are missing for this long, usually if they are going to be found, if they *want* to be found… it's… well, it's earlier. Usually within forty-eight hours.'

'I think he was depressed.'

'Well, the gambling, the work problems. It could be the case. We see it,' Detective Fisher says.

'The work computer. Was it just gambling?' I hate myself for asking.

She nods.

'Do you think he's dead?'

She looks up at the ceiling. 'I can't answer that. You know that.'

'Did you ever think he did it then? Kayleigh?'

'Rebecca, we were doing our job. We had to investigate all the possibilities. It didn't add up, but the fact they disappeared on the same day – you can understand why we couldn't let it go. He wasn't the sole focus of the investigation.'

'Yeah, you were "exploring all lines of enquiry"… You said.' I realise what I sound like, check myself. 'Sorry, I don't mean to be such a cow.'

She smiles at me. 'Don't worry. I get it. I have a question for you.'

'OK, go on.'

'I still don't understand why you didn't call us sooner. When he was missing. I've never really got that.'

The film of that morning starts playing in my mind. I was asleep when he got in the night before, my head woolly with the virus. I didn't hear him come in. When I woke the next morning, he was about to leave. He was almost creeping out. He would usually wake me up to say goodbye.

'Did you get me some cold and flu stuff?' I asked him.

'Oh shit, I forgot,' he said. He looked sorry.

My temper snapped. 'You're useless, do you know that?' came out of my mouth. I spat it. He grabbed his bag and went. It's the last thing I ever said to him in person.

When he didn't come back, I assumed he was upset, cooling off, that we'd sort it out. I hadn't reacted like that before. It was just illness, tiredness, a bad patch – the combination of everything. That's why I didn't call straight away. I thought he'd gone home to Peterborough or back to London for the weekend. But I didn't tell Detective Fisher or anyone else about that. Because I didn't want that to be the way we are cast. I won't now either, because it isn't who we were.

'There are two ways to be fooled. One is to believe what isn't true; the other is to refuse to believe what is true.' I read that somewhere once, a version of it anyway. Now, it keeps washing up into my mind.

Maybe I chose to ignore some of the signs with Chris, maybe they were never there. Everything is distorted through the prism of Kayleigh's disappearance. It's like reading a book backwards.

But now I have to decide how to think of us from here, which memories to keep and the ones to push aside.

The text he sent me later that day, saying he loved me. That's who we are. That's how I choose to remember us.

'Rebecca?' Detective Fisher prompts me. 'So, why was it?'

'I've already told you,' I say. 'My answer hasn't changed.'

'Suit yourself. What about you? Did you ever think he'd done it?'

'Gut feeling was always no, of course,' I tell her. 'But I let myself be swayed. By coincidences. By being exhausted and desperate. By I don't know what. But I don't know if I can forgive myself for that.'

'Well, you should forgive yourself. You have to. No one would know how to react in your circumstances.'

I look out onto the caravan park.

'And for what it's worth,' Fisher says, 'my gut feeling was that he didn't do it. But, well, I can't do my job on gut feeling alone.'

'I thought I saw him again the other day. Chris. Someone on the beach. Just for a moment and then he was gone. You think you're making progress, you know, you have to find a way to deal with it and then in that second, it just brings it all back again.'

'So what's the plan, then? Will you go back to the house? Or back down to London?'

'Nah, I'm just going to stay here for now. I kind of like it.'

'What, even in the winter? It's brass monkeys!'

'Yeah, but I'll have to think about what I'm going to do in the summer. I think the place will lose its charm when it's full of screeching kids.'

'I'd say so.'

'The house is on the market. The agent said it's a good time to sell because they're building a school on the estate. But I'll still be in Shawmouth, rent for a while, see what happens. I need to stay close to Mum anyway and I've made some good friends here. Jeannie's always been there for me, and Simon and Julie have both done loads to help me out through all this.'

'Well, you need them after everything, that's for sure.' Her voice is warm.

'How are Kat and Paige?'

A flicker of something I can't read goes across her face at this, and she tightens. 'They're doing as well as they can be. They are being supported.'

'Will anything happen to them? I mean about Kayleigh and the drugs and everything?'

I keep thinking about whether they'll be charged with manslaughter or perverting the course of justice or something. There's that word again, 'pervert'. I'm still getting the mental flashes now. Less often, though. I don't like to put my head underwater at the pool anymore. My chest seizes up thinking about Kayleigh panicking in the water, what it must have been like.

'The investigation is ongoing. We are supporting them as best we can and they are getting professional help. They have both had a traumatic experience and… this is going to take time. I don't have easy answers for you, I'm afraid.'

'They're so young. They can't be blamed for Kayleigh; for what they did. They were so scared of Ashy and Daz. They'd been threatened.'

'As I said, Rebecca, I can't say any more at the moment. But Kat and Paige are not our targets here. This is part of a much bigger investigation. We're talking about a significant drugs operation.'

The story broke in the paper yesterday that a fourteen- and a fifteen-year-old girl are 'helping the police with their enquiries' about Kayleigh's death. Those anonymous sources again. Three men have been arrested 'in connection with a related enquiry'.

It said the girls couldn't be named for legal reasons, but when I looked on Twitter, I saw Paige's and Kat's names, photos too. And the names of other girls who have been wrongly connected with what happened to Kayleigh. The rumours whirring again.

The article in the paper says that Chris has been 'eliminated' from the investigation. But online there are still comments about him, fewer than before, but a steady trickle. Garish memes, his face photoshopped onto a picture of the Child Catcher.

'And Chris?' I ask Detective Fisher. 'What now?'

'The investigation has been scaled back, Rebecca. I'm sorry. Given the circumstances and how long he has been missing. But it will remain open... should there be any new evidence, of course, we will... I'm sorry, I know this is hard for you.'

'So that's it then.'

'For now.' She gets up to leave. 'Before I go, Rebecca, there is one more thing.'

CHAPTER THIRTY-NINE

Tuesday, 24 November

I'm nervous approaching the bungalow, double-checking the scrawl on the envelope that I have the right one.

The lane where the Archibalds live is on a slope, and their garden is on a vertical slope too, creating a curiously skewed balance. It's filled with gnomes, over twenty – fishing, sleeping, golfing. Some just standing, all grinning. There are windmills too, the colourful paper ones that you used to get as a child. A small, home-made pond edged with seashells sits in the middle.

Detective Fisher had passed me their number as she left the caravan.

'I probably shouldn't even be giving you this,' she said. 'But, just give him a ring. And if anyone asks, you didn't get it from me.'

It was his wife – Margaret, she told me to call her – who answered the phone. She introduced herself when I told her who I was. Called me dear. 'Brian, it's her,' I heard her whisper, loudly, even though I could tell she had her hand over the mouthpiece of the phone.

Brian took a while to get to the phone. I imagined him sighing, putting his paper down, struggling to get out of his chair.

'Hello, love,' he said. He sounded more amiable than I expected. I was so nervous about calling. 'I thought you might ring sooner or later. You better come over, love. It will be better in person, I think. Do you mind, love? I can come to you, if you prefer.'

When I knock, Margaret answers. She's wearing a pink velour tracksuit, cosy-looking – and fur-lined slippers. Her dyed blonde hair is perfectly tonged into place away from her face, and her make-up is old-fashioned but precise – turquoise eye shadow and a metallic pink lipstick.

'Come on in, pet,' she says, touching my upper arm to pull me inside.

The bungalow is cluttered but tidy and immaculately clean – the cream carpet looks barely walked on, so I remove my shoes.

When we go into the front room, Brian is fiddling with the reclining armchair he is sitting in, putting it upright again. Horse-racing is on the TV.

'Eeeeh, turn that off, Brian,' Margaret says, already pressing the 'off' switch. It's an old TV – the picture shrinks to a tiny square in the centre before disappearing.

'Fancy a cup of tea, love?' Margaret asks. 'I'll make some tea,' she adds, without waiting for an answer.

Her eyes lock with Brian's. I can see they've discussed how this will go before I arrived. He's awkward, nervous. He doesn't know how to handle the situation.

Behind, there's a dark brown cabinet, a half-drunk bottle of brandy, egg-yellow advocaat and a dusty bottle of ouzo. They have crystal-style glasses like Mum used to have at the house. Lots of ornaments: a china Labrador, a wicker swan full of dried flowers.

There are family pictures. Brian and Margaret next to a woman in a wedding dress with big, puffy, 1980s sleeves. Their wedding photo is there too, black and white.

I'll start.

'So, I understand you saw my husband, Chris, by the river.'

'I did, love, that's right. Listen… I'm really sorry for everything that you've been through. I… I feel bad about the whole thing now. When I rang the police – I didn't know what we know now – you know, about the young lassy. Terrible business,' he says, shaking his head. 'But Miss Fisher rang me, she's very nice. She told me what had happened. She said would I talk to you about when I saw him… Chris.'

'Thanks for agreeing to see me,' I say, trying to spur him on.

Margaret appears with the tea – china cups and a teapot with a tea cosy on a tray, a plate of biscuits. A fluffy white dog scampers at her feet.

'I… I… I just don't know if I should be saying anything. I don't know if it feels right,' Brian says.

Margaret shoots him another look. 'Just talk to her. She's his wife, Brian,' she says, firmly but kindly.

Brain nods, resigned. 'I saw him up by the river, back in the summer when all this happened. That day,' he says. 'He wasn't right.'

I can see it's paining him.

'I was walking her, wasn't I?' He points at the dog, scrunching her fur. 'He was upset. Your husband.'

'Where was he? I don't understand why he was there,' I say. 'Was he going to jump?'

I see Margaret put her hand up to her mouth.

'It wasn't that, love. He was just sitting on one of the benches there. It were a sunny day. Do you remember that week, in July? Well, 'course you do. Sorry, love, I weren't thinking. 'Course you bloody remember it. Anyway, he were reading. It was this one that went over to him.' He gestures at the dog. 'She's always wanting attention, aren't you?'

The dog looks up, its tongue hanging out.

My chest feels bruised to think of him out there alone, trying to pass the days when he should have been at work. *Why couldn't he tell me?*

'But when I went over after her, I could see he was upset. He were sitting there in a shirt and trousers. Work gear. Summat were off, you know? So I asked the lad if he were OK. Actually, silly old fool I am, I asked him if he were reading a sad book.'

A fresh pain blooms in me, at the idea of Chris upset.

'I didn't expect him to answer, really, but he did. He looked sort of a bit dazed, you know. He told me he lost his job.'

'Yeah, I didn't know about that at the time. But I found out, of course. After… after everything.'

Margaret tuts and shakes her head.

Brian shifts in his chair. 'I didn't push it but I thought as much. He said he had been sitting there pretending to go to work. Just reading and sitting there every day.'

He pauses and looks at Margaret. She doesn't nod this time but she doesn't take her eyes off him either.

'As I say, he was upset. It feels like a betrayal repeating this.'

'I need to know,' I say without emotion.

'Brian,' is all Margaret says. She is pouring the tea.

'He said he'd got himself in a mess. And that he'd done something he couldn't change.'

My throat throbs.

He takes a deep breath in through his nose. 'He said he'd gone too far. Betrayed someone in a way he never thought he would and he didn't know if he could ever make it right again. Yeah, them were his words. I don't want to embroider it.'

'Did he say what he'd done?'

'No, love. As I say, I didn't feel like I should push him. He didn't know me at all. I felt like he just needed to talk to someone, so I listened. That's it.' He shakes his head.

A betrayal. Something he could never make right again. I think of the emptied bank account, of Mum's ring. Her twisting her hand under the light to admire the stone.

'So you didn't say anything?'

'Well, I just said there's not usually anything you can't make right again. Especially with people you love. I'm old enough and ugly enough to know that – eh, Margaret? But that was the end of it.'

'Are you OK, lovey? You look a bit peaky.' Margaret is thrusting a box of tissues at me.

'I'm fine, thanks.' I take one to be polite, and remove my scarf.

'I mean, listen, love, I feel awful.' Brian leans forward. 'It were just when I saw him on the news and that, when they were appealing for information. And when I thought about what he'd said, I felt I had to go forward and tell 'em what I'd seen. Even if it were nowt. She were such a wee lassie, you know?'

'It's fine, I understand. You're right – you did what you had to.'

'But Margaret will tell you, and I told the police – I couldn't marry the idea of him doing anything that awful. He seemed like a nice lad.'

'He is,' I say, feeling a rush of warmth, pain.

'I mean I don't know what the police made of it, I don't – but I feel bad if it built a case against him, especially when we know now he wasn't involved with that poor lassie. Rest her soul. I'm sorry, love, I'm sorry,' he says. I can hear the anguish in his voice. 'Don't get upset.'

Margaret reaches over and takes his hand between both of hers, kissing his fingers.

'I shouldn't have left him, I knew at the time I shouldn't. I felt it. I'm sorry. I don't like to see a young lad upset like that and I don't like to upset you.' He shakes his head again and strokes the puppy with his free hand.

'Do you think he jumped?' I blurt it out. There's no other way.

Margaret releases his hand, giving a little start, and sips her tea sharply.

'I can't answer that, pet. Maybe he went away somewhere. Maybe he will come back. Maybe no news really is good news.'

It hangs in the air.

Margaret sits on the arm of the chair and puts her arm around me. Usually I would shrug someone off, shirk them away, but I let her. I even reach up and pat her arm in thanks, feeling the softness of the velour.

She says, 'Only you can know, love, what's best for you. It's OK to have hope, but you've got to look ahead to the future for yourself as well.'

We sit for a while, until the silence becomes heavy in the air.

'I should go.' I stand up. 'Brian, thank you for talking to me, for allowing me to come here. I know you didn't have to. I know it was hard.'

'Hey, don't thank me, love. This is… I mean this whole thing. Who knows what to do? You look after yourself, love. Really. You take care.' He touches my cheek. His hand is cold and rough, although the room is hot.

Margaret says she'll see me out. I can see Brian sitting back in his chair, massaging his temples.

As I am about to leave, Margaret puts her hands on my shoulders, looking me straight in the eyes. Darker green lines across her eyelids where the eye shadow has sunk in. Her tone is almost as if she is giving me a telling off. 'You don't be hard on yourself now, love, you hear me? You can't second-guess other people and you sure as hell don't know what's around the corner. Believe me, we oldies know that.'

I wonder what she is referring to, what pain she's suffered.

'And, hey now. If ever you need something, you want to talk to Brian or whatever, you come back here. Or give us a call. Any time, you hear me?'

I tell her I will. It's a nice idea. I like the idea of drinking tea with Margaret and Brian. Perhaps watching a film or playing cards. This bungalow, it's a nice place to be. But we both know I won't come back.

It's getting dark outside, some of the street lights starting to stutter on, and the wind is picking up, the paper windmills flipping round at speed.

CHAPTER FORTY

Friday, 25 December

'It is true that the world has had to confront moments of darkness,' says the queen gravely. She seems to be finding it hard to think of many positive things to say about this year. I know how she feels. I dunk a fifth chocolate biscuit into cooling tea – my attempt to get into the Christmas spirit. I can at least keep some traditions, get on board with the gluttonous part of it, the staying in pyjamas all day.

I know I shouldn't, but I flip through my phone, back through weeks and months of thoughtless snaps. Last Christmas. It is unfathomable to me how much has changed. Chris in a green party hat, proudly offering up the turkey. The first we cooked together and far too much for just two people. This time last year, we had our first Christmas in the new house. We drank fizzy wine in our pyjamas, not opening our presents until after midday. I thought it would be the new Christmas tradition.

The sky is a cold, stark grey. It will be dark soon.

I have a few cards up on the table. One from Jeannie, Dan, Ellen and Sam; another from Sandra and Geoff, promising to visit in the New Year. Jeannie bought me a new swimming costume to use at the site pool. Ellen gave me a cup with pictures of caravans on the side when I went round for tea last night.

A knock at the door makes me jump. I ignore it; it's probably Julie trying to get me to go down to Barnacles – she said she didn't like the idea of me spending Christmas alone. 'Especially not this year.'

Another sharp rap.

'Who is it?'

'It's me, Simon.'

'Give me a minute! I pull jeans and a jumper on over my pyjamas. There's a bobble in the jeans pocket and I twist my hair into a bun.

'Let us in, will you? It's freezing out here.'

'Has something happened to Mum? Is she OK?' I shout, fiddling with the lock to get the door open.

'She's fine. See for yourself,' he says, stepping back.

'Oh my God. What are you doing? Are you mad?'

Mum is in her wheelchair, looking down, and Simon stands there shivering.

'We thought you might like some company?'

'Erm, I don't know if I'm a good person to be around at the moment.'

'Don't be daft. Just ten minutes, let your mum get warmed up? She wanted to see you... It's Christmas. And I did too,' he adds, mumbling.

I sigh and help him carry Mum's wheelchair in. It barely fits through the door.

Mum looks around the caravan, wide-eyed.

'Does it remind you of holidays, Mum? When I was a kid?' She's never been to the caravan before. 'I'm not even going to start explaining,' I say aside to Simon.

'That's fine,' he answers. 'No need today anyway, eh? Christmas dinner?' He is holding up the half-pack of chocolate biscuits that remains.

'You could say that.'

'You should have stuck around this morning. I saw "Santa" had been with some presents and a card for your mum but there was no sign of you.'

'I was in and out very early. Sorry.'

'It's fine. We've had a busy old day – Chrimbo dinner. We had a music group in this morning – playing ukuleles and singing carols. It was well good. Anyway, we've come to see you now. And we've brought some goodies! Haven't we, Averil?'

He begins to unpack the bag. Tupperware, a bottle wrapped in paper.

'You taking your coat off, Averil?'

I help her out of the camel-coloured woollen coat.

'That jumper's a cracker.'

Mum's wearing the jumper I took her for Christmas – it's more her style. Neat-fitting: navy, white and red stripes.

'Looks good, Mum.'

She runs her hands up and down the sleeves.

Simon unwraps the bottle. Port. 'Averil's favourite, I hear?' He gestures at Mum.

'Yeah, she always used to drink port and lemon when were younger.'

'Voila,' he says, producing a small plastic bottle of Sprite.

From the Tupperware, he unpacks three cheeses, some crackers and a jar of chutney. 'Made it myself,' he says, tapping the jar.

'You must have plenty of time on your hands.'

'Says she!' Simon nudges me.

I get some glasses and uncork the port. It makes a pleasing popping sound. It's getting warmer in the caravan – Simon removes his scarf and hat, his face getting pink.

He rubs his hands. 'Hey, it's alright in here, isn't it? Pretty cosy.'

The port is thick, rich and warming. 'Just a drop for Mum,' I say when I see Simon pouring her a drink. 'She isn't used to it.'

He shoots me a knowing look. I shouldn't interfere. He pours Mum a glass of lemonade with a drizzle of port – the pink is barely perceptible.

'So, how are you holding up?' he asks. I notice he lowers his voice slightly.

'I'm OK. You know. I've never been all that bothered about Christmas anyway.' A lie. I used to love it.

'I brought some music if you fancy it?' he asks, reaching into his bag again.

'No Christmas music, please.'

'I'm not that much of a twat... oops sorry, Averil!' But Mum hasn't noticed. 'I do know this is hard for you, you know. I'm not trying to be really insensitive and throw a Christmas party. Well, not a proper one anyway. I just thought you might want to mark the day in some way. Do something, have a bit of company. I don't want to intrude either...'

'Don't worry about it. I'm glad you came over.'

'Picky tea?' he says, gesturing at the cheese. I can't think of anything I fancy less after all those chocolate biscuits, but I take a piece anyway, grateful for the gesture.

'I declare this spread officially open! Get stuck in.'

I feel a pang as I think back to family Christmases with Mum. I go over and give her a hug in her chair. Her cheek is warm and soft against mine, and I stroke it as I pull away.

Mum points at the cheese.

'Pickle?'

She nods.

I eat some too. It's dense and pungent, heartburn fizzing in my chest as soon as I swallow it.

Simon holds up one of his CDs. 'Or we could just be quiet. Or watch telly. I don't mind.'

'Erm, OK, go ahead. The player is crap, though.' It's a cheap one, which has a built-in radio, tape player and CD player on top, which usually skips at the slightest movement. I haven't used it in a while. I pop the top and take the CD from him without looking at what it is, being careful to hold it in the centre.

'Oh God, what are you doing now?'

Simon pulls a length of sparkly red tinsel from the bag and a string of knotted lights. 'May I?' he asks.

'Oh, I don't know… It's a bit… I'm not really…'

'I'll take them away with me again, I promise. Let's just do half an hour, forget all the other stuff for a bit, yeah? Go on…!'

I tut and shake my head, smiling, and he starts arranging the lights around the condensation-soaked window. He puts the tinsel around the edge of the table. 'I even brought my own tape.' He beams, a piece of Sellotape between his teeth.

'Are you warm enough, Mum?'

She nods, mouth full of cheese.

It feels strange to have music filling the caravan. In such a small space, the song consumes the environment. It feels like something solid in the air that you could grab.

'Rose Garden' plays out, decisive strings.

'Mum used to play this one when I was little.'

'Yeah, she likes the old stuff when we play it back at our place. Got myself a pretty good DJ gig back there. Sea View is rocking on a Sunday afternoon.' Simon is reaching for the CD player. 'Sorry if it's a bad choice of song. Am I being insensitive?' he says.

Mum is tapping her feet to the music.

'Don't worry about it. You can leave it on.'

I recognise the opening strains of the next one, but I can't put my finger on it. Mum is bobbing her head completely out of time.

Then 'I Started a Joke', a hard lump in my throat from the start.

We all listen to the song in silence.

'Can I ask you something, Simon?'

'You can.'

'How did you really end up in Shawmouth? Did you really move for the job?'

Simon runs his hands through the front of his hair. 'In a roundabout way, but not exactly.'

'Forget I asked. I shouldn't be nosey.'

'No, it's fine. I… well, a few years ago, I got divorced. We were living in Penrith, near the Lakes, and I needed to make a new start.' He rubs the thumb of his left hand across his empty wedding finger.

'But why *here*?'

'Must have been having some kind of mid-life crisis. I decided I wanted to learn how to surf.'

'Surf? In Shawmouth?'

'The surfing is brilliant here, you know.'

'Is it? Not exactly *Baywatch*, but if you say so.'

'I found a course here one weekend, booked it and I just liked it here. Helped me clear my head. So I just thought, sod it. Jacked my job in, moved here the next week and got a job in a pub – until I got taken on at Sea View. And that was it. Here I am.'

'Christ, you are allowed to leave, you know. You don't have to stay forever.'

'Ha, I know. But I still like it here. Got this job in the end, made friends, and what can I say? I am still surfing at the weekends or when I'm off.'

'Well, whatever floats your boat. Or should I say surfboard.'

'Not really a city slicker type, me.'

I feel a pang for London. The noise and the traffic and the nights out. Not that I want to be there now, but for the life we had there.

'Sorry to hear about your marriage.'

Simon shrugs but doesn't look at me. 'Happens, doesn't it?'

We sit again for a while, listening to the CD. Don McLean is singing about a starry, starry night. I go to the window and pull the curtains back slightly. 'Hey! It's snowing! It's a white Christmas!'

Simon leaps forward out of his seat, his face animated with excitement. 'Is it? Oh my God. Did you hear that, Averil, a white Christmas?'

I feel a bit guilty then. 'Is it bollocks! You're so gullible – you'll believe anything.'

He gives me a playful push and we both laugh. I can see Mum smiling too. She seems relaxed.

Boston, then Barry Manilow plays in the background.

'You coming round to see your mum tomorrow?' Simon asks. 'We're doing carols and mince pies in the morning.'

'Yeah, I'll come over in the morning. I'm… I'm working in the afternoon.'

'Working?'

'I'm doing a shift at Barnacles – Julie's putting a Christmas do on. Karaoke and that. I said I'd help out a few nights, see how it goes.'

Simon nods. 'Sounds… erm, interesting! I might pop in for a pint when I finish.'

'You should – you can get up and do a turn.'

'Maybe I will!' He starts to get up. 'I think your mum's had enough. We best get back.'

Mum's head is lolled forward in the chair and her chest is rising and falling.

'Sorry if some of them upset you.' He gestures at the CDs as he packs them away again.

'Honestly I would blub at the "Birdie Song". I appreciate you coming round – even if you are a bit too into the 1970s.'

'Well, I made you this one anyway. In case you fancy listening to it later.'

He hands me a CD. *Happy Christmas, Rebecca, Simon x* is written in thick black marker pen.

We finally get Mum's chair out of the door and I wave them off in a taxi. He hasn't taken the decorations with him.

I turn the light off but leave the Christmas lights on; it gives the caravan a twinkling grotto effect.

I put the CD in the player, snap the lid shut and press 'play'.

A LETTER FROM SARAH

Thank you for choosing to read *Reported Missing*. I am interested in the ripple effects that events can have and central characters who might not usually be the focus of attention. I hope you enjoyed Rebecca's story. If so, I'd be grateful if you could recommend it to others and leave a review. I'd love to hear what you think.

You can also let me know on Twitter and Facebook, or via my website.

This is my first book but I hope there will be many more to follow. If you'd like to keep up-to- date with my latest releases, just sign up at the website link below.

www.bookouture.com/sarah-wray

Thank you for reading!
Sarah Wray

www.sarahwraywrites.co.uk

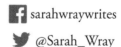 sarahwraywrites

@Sarah_Wray

ACKNOWLEDGEMENTS

I am grateful to everyone who saw the early potential in this book and helped to make it happen.

To New Writing North and Arvon for the Northern Writers' Award and residential trip which spurred me on to keep going.

To Laura Longrigg at MBA Literary Agents for all your support, enthusiasm and honest feedback. And to Keshini Naidoo at Bookouture for pushing me to make the book the best it can be.

To Helen M and Helen P for the caravan research trips. And to the North East Noir writing group for all the cups of tea and book chat.

Thank you especially to Leon.

66302906R00191

Four months ago, Rebecca Pendle's
husband disappeared.
So did 14-year-old Kayleigh Jackson.

Just a coincidence? Rebecca wants to believe so...
But as the police start to draw parallels between
Chris and Kayleigh, it's getting harder for her to
trust his innocence.

Faced with an angry town that believes Chris
has abducted the teenager, Rebecca tries to
discover the truth.

But what she finds shocks her more than she
ever thought. How well does she really know the
man she loves?

A completely gripping, suspenseful thriller,
with a shocking twist. Fans of Louise Jensen,
K.L. Slater and and *The Girl on the Train* will
be hooked until the very last page.

𝔟 www.bookouture.com

ISBN 9781786811974

90000 >

9 781786 811974